LETHAL ODDS

Their arc was nearly complete, and it was obvious that Dia's report was correct: The landing platform was solidly in place, and the Hawk-bats' sensors now showed shielding protecting the facility.

Then TIE fighters and interceptors came up out of the trees, easily a score of them, from points all around the Hawk-bats and the landing platform.

More than a score. The second flight of TIEs emerged. Wedge checked the sensor board. Thirty-six unfriendlies, three full squadrons.

Shalla spoke next, her voice subdued even in its distorted form: "We are *so* dead."

Don't miss these other
exciting *Star Wars*® books:

X-WING
by Michael A. Stackpole
#1: ROGUE SQUADRON
#2: WEDGE'S GAMBLE
#3: THE KRYTOS TRAP
#4: THE BACTA WAR
by Aaron Allston
#5: WRAITH SQUADRON

THE BLACK FLEET CRISIS
by Michael P. Kube-McDowell
#1: BEFORE THE STORM
#2: SHIELD OF LIES
#3: TYRANT'S TEST

THE CRYSTAL STAR
by Vonda N. McIntyre

TALES FROM THE MOS EISLEY CANTINA
edited by Kevin J. Anderson

TALES FROM JABBA'S PALACE
edited by Kevin J. Anderson

TALES OF THE BOUNTY HUNTERS
edited by Kevin J. Anderson

THE BOUNTY HUNTER WARS
by K. W. Jeter
#1: THE MANDALORIAN ARMOR

CHILDREN OF THE JEDI
by Barbara Hambly

DARKSABER
by Kevin J. Anderson

THE ILLUSTRATED *STAR WARS* UNIVERSE
by Ralph McQuarrie
and Kevin J. Anderson

SHADOWS OF THE EMPIRE
by Steve Perry

THE NEW REBELLION
by Kristine Kathryn Rusch
and in hardcover

I, JEDI
by Michael A. Stackpole.

STAR WARS®

X - WING

BOOK SIX

IRON FIST

Aaron Allston

BANTAM BOOKS
New York Toronto London Sydney Auckland

STAR WARS: IRON FIST

A Bantam Spectra Book / July 1998

SPECTRA and the portrayal of a boxed "s" are trademarks
of Bantam Books, a division of Bantam Doubleday Dell
Publishing Group, Inc.

ISBN-0-553-57897-9

Published simultaneously in the United States and Canada

Bantam Books are published by Bantam Books, a division of Bantam
Doubleday Dell Publishing Group, Inc. Its trademark, consisting of the
words "Bantam Books" and the portrayal of a rooster, is Registered in
U.S. Patent and Trademark Office and in other countries. Marca Reg-
istrada. Bantam Books, 1540 Broadway, New York, New York 10036.

PRINTED IN THE UNITED STATES OF AMERICA

OPM   10   9   8   7   6   5   4   3   2   1

ACKNOWLEDGMENTS

Thanks go to:

Steven S. Long, Beth Loubet, Bob Quinlan, Luray Richmond, and Sean Summers, my "Eagle-Eyes," who valiantly hurl themselves between me and the incoming artillery of my errors;

All the *Star Wars* fiction authors from whose work I have been able to draw details, most especially Michael A. Stackpole and Timothy Zahn;

Drew Campbell, Shane Johnson, Paul Murphy, Peter Schweighofer, Bill Slavicsek, Bill Smith, Curtis Smith, and Dan Wallace, for the invaluable resources they have written;

Sue Rostoni and Lucy Wilson of Lucas Licensing, for their help; and

Denis Loubet, Mark and Luray Richmond, my roommates, for keeping me in realspace whenever my brain threatened to make the jump to hyperspace.

DRAMATIS PERSONAE

The Wraiths

Commander Wedge Antilles (Leader, One) (human male from Corellia)

Lieutenant Wes Janson (Three) (human male from Taanab)

Lieutenant Myn Donos (Nine) (human male from Corellia)

Lieutenant Garik "Face" Loran (Eight) (human male from Pantolomin)

Lieutenant Kell Tainer (Five) (human male from Sluis Van)

Hohass "Runt" Ekwesh (Six) (Thakwaash male from Thakwaa)

Ton Phanan (Seven) (human male from Rudrig)

Voort "Piggy" saBinring (Twelve) (Gamorrean male from Gamorr)

Tyria Sarkin (Eleven) (human female from Toprawa)

Castin Donn (Two) (human male from Coruscant)

Shalla Nelprin (Ten) (human female from Ingo)

Dia Passik (Four) (Twi'lek female from Ryloth)

Lara Notsil (Thirteen) (human female from Aldivy)

Rogue Squadron Support Personnel

Cubber Daine (human male from Corellia, squad mechanic)

Chunky (Tyria's R5 unit)

Gate (Wedge's R5 unit)

Squeaky (3PO unit, squadron quartermaster)
Tonin (Lara's R2 unit)
Vape (Face's R2 unit)

New Republic Military

Colonel Atton Repness (human male from Commenor)
Captain Onoma (Mon Calamari male from Mon Calamari)
Captain Valton (human male from Tatooine)

Zsinj's Forces

Warlord Zsinj (human male from Fondor)
General Melvar (human male from Kuat)
Captain Todrin Rossik (human male from Coruscant)
Captain Vellar (human male)
Captain Netbers (human male)
Captain Raslan (human male)
Lieutenant Bradan (human female)

The Hawk-bats

General Kargin (human male)
Captain Seku (Twi'lek female from Ryloth)
Lieutenant Dissek (human male from Alderaan)
Lieutenant Kettch (Ewok male from Endor)
Qatya Nassin (human female)
Morrt (human male)

1

He made no pretense at being fully human. He had probably
been born human, but now mechanical limbs—obvious prosthetics with no skinlike cover concealing their artificial nature—
replaced his right arm and both legs, and the upper-right portion
of his bald head was a shiny metal surface with a standard computer interface.

He made no pretense at being friendly, either. He approached the members of Wraith Squadron as they sat, crammed
into their booth, and with neither threat nor comment he
snatched a wine bottle from the next table over and brought it
down on Runt Ekwesh's head.

The bottle didn't break. It offered a musical *toonk* sound
and coughed up a little wine from its open neck, and Runt, the
furred alien with the long, big-toothed face, slumped in his
seat, his eyes rolling up in his head.

Most of the members of Wraith Squadron were pinned in
place—with nine pilots crammed into a circular booth built for
five, they had little room to move. But Kell Tainer, seated at the
opposite end of the ring from Runt, scrambled to his feet.

Instead of diving toward his wingmate's attacker, instead
of charging with a fist cocked back to punch the man, he slid
sideways toward his target, then came up in a side kick that

caught the cyborg under his chin and lifted him clean off the floor, slamming him to the bar's floor.

Most of the members of the squadron slid out of the booth in Kell's wake. Other patrons of the bar, human and otherwise, also rose, their expressions suggesting they were unclear on whether to join in this traditional form of bar entertainment.

Commander Wedge Antilles, the squadron's leader, stayed put. He turned toward the squadron medic, Ton Phanan—the man with the mocking manner, well-trimmed beard and mustache, and prosthetic plate over the left side of his head. "How is he?"

Phanan shook his head as he delicately moved his fingers across Runt's skull. "I don't think anything's cracked. He's probably just concussed. You knew he had a hard head."

The cyborg was up now. He and Kell were an odd contrast. The cyborg looked like a fatal skimmer-and-pedestrian accident whose remaining parts had been cobbled together by an insane mechanic, while Kell, with his classic blue eyes and sculpted features, his formidable height and obvious conditioning, looked like a holoposter for military recruitment. But their smiles were identical: humorless, cold, threatening.

The cyborg reached into the next booth, past bar patrons who shrieked and ducked away, and yanked free the table bolted to the floor. He hauled it backward, then swung it faster than any human could manage, but Kell ducked forward, rolled under the table, came up on his feet a mere hand span in front of the cyborg, and planted one-two-three blows in his attacker's gut. The cyborg staggered backward and Kell lashed out with a foot, kicking the table from his fingers with an ease that made the move look casual.

The other bar patrons seemed to settle on a consensus: They held back and began putting down bets. Wedge nodded over the wisdom of that choice. Though the Wraiths were in civilian clothes, it was obvious they were in good condition, and for all the patrons knew, Kell might be only typical of their fighting skill rather than one of their best hand-to-hand fighters.

Piggy, the Gamorrean pilot, leaned back against the Wraiths' table to watch the proceedings—to the extent that the semipermanent smoky haze hovering at chest level and above permitted easy viewing. He glanced over his shoulder at Runt. "Is he hurt?" His voice emerged both as incomprehensible grunts and as electronic words, the latter being emitted by a nearly invisible speaker implanted in his throat.

"Everybody asks that," Phanan complained. Through with his examination of Runt's skull, he now shone a small light into Runt's eyes one by one. "Nobody ever says, 'What a mess! I hope the doctor is not emotionally harmed by having to deal with it.' He's coming around. He'll probably be dizzy for a few days. I need to look up information on how his species deals with concussions."

The cyborg's next punch, the second part of a skillful one-two combination, connected with Kell's midsection. The big man spun as he was hit, diminishing the punch's power, and used that spin to add force to his reply, a snap kick. The cyborg took it in the sternum and staggered back, looking outraged. Kell bent over, holding his stomach where hit, and then straightened, obviously in pain.

Then the bar was filled with uniforms—a stream of men and women pouring in the main entrance, dressed in the distinctive outfit of New Republic Military Police.

Wedge sighed. "As deep as we are, they arrived pretty quickly."

Phanan held a small rose-colored vial full of liquid under Runt's broad, flat nose. The nonhuman's nostrils flared and he jerked, reflexively trying to get away from the smell. "Easy, Runt," he said. "We're about to go somewhere you can relax for a few hours. In the company of some charming people, too, I'll bet."

Wedge grinned.

The military police led them out of the smoke-filled bar into the only slightly less oppressive atmosphere of street-level Coruscant. It was raining, a steady spray of liquid that felt like three-quarters rainwater and one-quarter vehicle lubricant. Wedge looked up, trying to spot some distant speck of color representing Coruscant's sky, but all he could see were clifflike building sides rising to infinity. Awnings, high roads, bridges between skyscrapers, and other obstacles blocked out any glimpse of clouds far above, yet still the rain came down, much of it probably runoff from rain gutters, vents, and flues far above.

Tyria Sarkin, the slender woman with the blond ponytail, grimaced. "It would be nice to be posted to a clean world next," she said. Then she saw the military policemen gesturing toward the waiting skimmer, a slab-sided model without viewports, used to transport prisoners, and she obligingly followed the other Wraiths in that direction. Phanan, supporting the still-dizzy Runt, fell in behind her, and Wedge and the cyborg who had caused all the trouble brought up the rear.

Toward the front, Face Loran, the once-handsome actor whose face was now creased by a livid scar from his left cheek to his right forehead, noted the nameplate on the nearest MP. "Thioro," he said. "That's a Corellian name, isn't it?"

The officer nodded. "I'm from Corellia. Born and bred."

Face turned back toward Wedge and smiled. "Ah. Just like our reception committee back on M2398, eh, Commander?"

Wedge managed not to stiffen. The "reception committee" on the moon of System M2398's third planet had not been made up of Corellians. It had, in fact, been a trap, an invitation to land that turned out to be a fatal ambush. Wedge nodded. "Just like it, Face. And just like then, I'm your wing."

Wedge saw casual little glances exchanged between the Wraiths and knew they had all just become alert and ready—except, perhaps, the dazed Runt. Face hadn't been Wedge's wingman at the time. Face now knew Wedge was waiting for his move.

Face walked a little faster within the crowd of Wraiths, until he was at the front of the double line of prisoners, immediately behind the first pair of military policemen. He reached the rear of the prisoner skimmer, nodded at their gesture to board—and struck, slamming his fist into the throat of one MP, jumping on the other.

Wedge saw Kell strike out almost instantly, his side kick connecting with the side of his guard's knee—and saw that joint bend sideways, a direction it was never meant to take. That guard screamed and fell.

No time to watch things unfold—Wedge heard blaster pistols clearing leather behind him. He grabbed the cyborg and swung around, hauling the startled assailant into position between him and the guards.

The guards fired, their blasters converging on the cyborg's chest, charring it black. Steam and the smell of scorched flesh rose from the wound. Wedge shoved the fatally wounded cyborg into the guards, continued pushing, bowled them over—and saw one guard's blaster go skidding across the duracrete of the sidewalk. He dove after it.

Noises he knew well: the *whuff* Piggy the Gamorrean made whenever he struck at someone in practice, followed by the impossibly loud, meaty noise his fist always made when it hit. Two blaster shots in quick succession. A howl from Runt. The man with the broken leg still screaming. Shrieks from passersby and the clatter of their feet as they retreated from the danger zone.

Wedge got his hand on the blaster, swung around, snapped off a quick shot that took his other guardsman, now rising, in the throat and threw him back to the grimy duracrete. That gave Wedge a clear view of the impromptu battlefield, Wraiths struggling with military policemen.

"Nobody move!" That was Ton Phanan, miraculously unharmed, holding the blaster rifle previously owned by one of their captors—that man, Wedge saw, was staggering away, his eyes glassy, his hands clutching his own throat, trying futilely to arrest the tide of blood seeping between and around his fingers.

The MPs paused, saw the gun aimed at them . . . and, one by one, relaxed to drop their arms or ceased struggling with the Wraiths.

Face Loran, his voice in a reasonable tone Wedge knew to be forced, answered, "He didn't walk like a Corellian."

They were now in a debriefing room in Starfighter Command Headquarters, a room as spotlessly white and clean as the bar and street had been filthy. A colonel Wedge didn't know was conducting the interview, but Admiral Ackbar, commander-in-chief of New Republic military operations, was also seated at the interrogators' table. Though Ackbar was a Mon Calamari, a species with huge, rubbery features that seemed more fishlike than humanlike, he was a friendly presence in Wedge's estimation.

"That's not enough justification to attack someone with proper credentials," the colonel said.

Face stiffened. "Respectfully, sir, it is when I'm correct."

"Don't be preposterous. You can't classify a man's homeworld just by looking at him."

"Yes, I can, sir."

The colonel, a middle-aged man with a face creased by too many years of waging war against the Empire, looked dubious. But without speaking, he stood, walked backward from the table, and then walked back and forth a half-dozen paces.

"Hard to say," Face said. "If you had any distinctive walking mannerism from your homeworld, you erased it with military training. At Vogel Seven, if I'm not mistaken. I'd say that you were injured at some time in the past and had to learn to walk again—or maybe it was a disfigurement at birth, corrected by surgery? I can't really tell."

The colonel resumed his seat. Surprise was evident on his face. "Correct on both counts. How do you do that?"

"Well, I was an actor. On top of that, I'm trained to recognize, analyze, and assume physical mannerisms—just as I am with vocal mannerisms and a dozen other things. More importantly, I lived several years on Lorrd, where my family is originally from. The Lorrdians practically invented the art of conscious communication through body language."

Ackbar finally spoke up, his voice a not-quite-human rumble. "You admit, Colonel, that Lieutenant Loran is capable of recognizing when someone's physical mannerisms do not match his professed planet of origin?"

The colonel considered. "Well, it's low for a statistical sampling, but I'd say he demonstrates considerable skill in that regard."

"Between that," Face said, "and the speed with which the MPs reached the bar—which, I remind you, is close to bedrock level, and not a place sensible New Republic military personnel are usually near—I concluded that it was a deception. The cyborg was trotted out to start the trouble and make an MP arrest look legitimate; many pilots have been run into jail while on leave exactly this way."

The colonel ignored the statement and turned to Phanan. "You defused the situation by putting down one of the ersatz military policemen and seizing his weapon."

Wedge saw Phanan struggling with a reply—probably something to the effect of the colonel being able to recognize simple facts when they played out under his nose—but restraining himself. Phanan merely said, "Yes, sir."

"That man died. Trachea cut, carotid artery cut. Yet the commander here says the MPs disarmed you before leading you out of the bar. What did you use?"

"A holdout, sir. A laser scalpel. Hard to distinguish from a writing tool without close inspection . . . and up close, I'm pretty effective with it."

"I'd say so. Did you surrender this weapon to *our* guards before coming before me?"

"What weapon, sir?"

"The laser scalpel."

"Not a weapon, sir. It's a tool of medicine. I wasn't asked to turn over my bandages, bacta treatments, disinfectant sprays, or tranquilizers either, but I can kill a man with any of them, under the right circumstances."

The colonel glanced at Wedge, a beleaguered look Wedge knew well from his own mirror—it asked, *What sort of unit have you assembled here?* Wedge merely shrugged.

The colonel closed down his datapad. "All right. Pending the results of further investigation into this matter, I'm going to release your squadron."

Wedge said, "Thank you, sir."

"How are your injured squad members? Ekwesh, wasn't it, and Janson?"

"Both in sick bay," Wedge said. "Runt Ekwesh has a mild concussion, and is thoroughly embarrassed that Phanan knocked him down to keep him out of the fight. Lieutenant Janson got a blaster crease across the ribs; he's got a bacta patch on it and will be fit for duty in a day or two."

The colonel rose; Wedge and his subordinates followed

suit. The colonel said, "I wish them every luck in getting back to duty as soon as possible." He left unstated the obvious fact that he far preferred them facing Imperial stormtroopers and warlord forces than the civilians of the planet Coruscant. An exchange of salutes later, he departed.

Admiral Ackbar came forward. "Before you go: What are your thoughts on this matter?"

Wedge said, "I'd prefer to see what General Cracken's people get out of the survivors, but my guess is Zsinj. We hurt him pretty badly when we destroyed the *Implacable*." That ship, an Imperial Star Destroyer, belonged to Admiral Apwar Trigit, a subordinate of the warlord Zsinj, who was now the chief enemy and target of the New Republic. "He's shown a vengeful streak in the past, and has enough intelligence and contacts to mount a plausible-looking trap like that. I'd say that he's figured out who Wraith Squadron is and has decided to make us pay."

Ackbar nodded. "My own conclusion as well. I will leave the matter of protection of your subordinates to you, Commander Antilles—I am sure you are fit to decide whether to complete your leave or return to duty and the safer confines of Starfighter Command's barracks and facilities. But I do have orders for you." He tapped the bulge of the datapad in his pocket. "I have transmitted them to your datapad. I think you will find them to your liking; they play to the, how should I put it, improvisational strengths of your new squadron."

Wedge smiled. "Those improvisational strengths are beginning to give me gray hairs, Admiral. But thank you in spite of that." He let the smile fade. "I hope I'm not being presumptuous, sir, but I was wondering if you'd heard anything about Fel."

Ackbar pulled out his datapad and tapped at it. Wedge wondered if the admiral really was accessing data, or whether this was a delaying tactic, a moment to give him time to prepare an answer.

Baron Soontir Fel had been the Empire's greatest starfighter pilot in the years after Vader's death. Leader of the elite 181st Imperial Fighter Group, he had bedeviled Rogue Squadron on occasion, and had been a lethal weapon used against the

New Republic on many missions. Later, he had changed his alliance to the New Republic and had even been a part of Rogue Squadron.

What wasn't as widely known was that Wedge's sister Syal was Fel's wife. Or that both Fel and Syal had disappeared, years ago. The 181st was theoretically now under the command of another Imperial officer, serving the coalition of Moffs and military officers that now acted as the unofficial heir to the rule of what was left of the Empire. And this made Fel's sudden recent reappearance, commanding portions of the 181st as part of the complement of starfighters aboard Star Destroyer *Implacable,* particularly unsettling. Fel and many of his pilots had escaped *Implacable*'s fate and their location was now unknown to the New Republic . . . but Wedge had a suspicion that Fel would be found serving Warlord Zsinj.

Ackbar met Wedge's gaze again and shook his head. "We have no news on any official cooperation between the remains of the Empire and Zsinj. No idea why the Empire would loan the One Eighty-first to the warlord. No news of Fel, the details of his return . . . or his family. I am sorry. I will let you know if his name crosses my desk."

"Thank you, sir. I appreciate it."

In the hangar temporarily assigned to the vehicles of Wraith Squadron—seven battered X-wing snubfighters, two battle-scarred captured TIE fighters, and a comparatively pristine-looking *Lambda*-class shuttle—they explained the colonel's decision to the Wraiths who had not been called in for the second stage of interrogation. "I hate to say it," Wedge said, "but leave is effectively canceled. I want volunteers to act as guards for Runt and Wes until they're discharged. I want someone on duty here with our vehicles until we lift for our next assignment, and I want everyone walking around with eyes behind as well as in front. Understood?"

The Wraiths nodded. "I'll work out a duty roster," Face said.

"Why you?" Kell asked.

Face smiled at the big man. "Because Janson's not here to

do it. Because I was promoted two minutes ahead of you, so I outrank you. Check back with me in a few minutes and I'll have assignments ready to transmit."

As the Wraiths moved their separate ways, Phanan threw his arm over Kell's shoulder. He looked at Tyria. "Tyria, if you'd excuse us for a moment, I have a few words to say in private to your toyfriend—"

She gave him an arch look. "My what?"

Kell straightened, causing the shorter man's arm to slide off, and glared. "Her what?"

"What did I say?" Phanan shrugged. "A few moments."

She shrugged and moved to her X-wing.

"Did you catch the name of the colonel?" Phanan asked.

Kell's scowl turned from irritation to confusion. "I don't think Commander Antilles mentioned it."

"Repness."

Kell glanced over at Tyria, but she had one of her snub-fighter's engine ports open and was intent on the machinery within. "That's the name of the trainer who tried to get her to steal an X-wing. Before she joined the Wraiths."

"The same. I checked on him as we were marching back from the interrogation. He's still training pilots, now here on Coruscant, though he's about to be assigned to the training frigate *Tedevium*. He has other duties as well, mostly high-profile volunteer stuff—not unusual for an ambitious officer. He was officer of the day today for the subbase the military police belong to, which is why he debriefed us on the incident."

Kell took a deep breath. Atton Repness was an instructor for New Republic pilot trainees who were on the verge of washing out of the training program. He had a reputation as being good at salvaging pilots thought unsalvageable. But Kell and Phanan knew that he had secretly altered Tyria's failing grades to make them passable, then tried to enlist her in an effort to steal an X-wing, and had used the revelation of the grade forgery to blackmail her into silence. "You wouldn't have mentioned him if you didn't already have a plan," Kell said. His voice was hard.

Phanan smiled. "That's what I like to hear. Acknowledgment of my superior intellect along with a desire to hurt somebody else very badly. It's a good day for me.

"Yes, I have a plan. We know of one and only one tactic he has used. He approached a struggling pilot candidate, female, attractive—we don't know whether those characteristics are important to his thinking, but let's put a skifter in the deck and make sure—and helped her two ways. Extra training, for legitimate gains in her scores, and doctoring of her grades, to ensure she passed . . . and to ensure that she was in debt to him, or could at least be blackmailed into silence. If we wave some bait around in front of him, maybe he'll snap at it."

"Bait." Kell scowled and leaned against the strike foil of the nearest X-wing. "Phanan, I don't know about you, but I haven't had enough time to make enough friends and acquaintances that I can just snap my fingers and find someone with the qualities you're talking about."

"Ah, but you don't have my superior intellect, do you?"

"One more mention of your superior intellect and I'll make it necessary for you to install a brain that's all mechanical."

Phanan leaned close, unfazed by or oblivious to the threat. "When I was in the hospital on Borleias, the patient in the next room was a woman. A beautiful woman. A survivor off the *Implacable*."

"So she's a military prisoner now? Ton, we can't break her out of jail for your plan—"

"Not a prisoner *now*. She was a prisoner aboard the *Implacable*. Admiral Trigit's mistress—unwilling mistress. She was snatched off a planet colony Trigit bombarded into sand, she was kept drugged . . . you can guess the rest."

Kell grimaced.

"She had a whole lot to tell New Republic Intelligence about Trigit and his methods. A very observant, intelligent young woman. Not to mention a beauty."

"You've already mentioned that she was a beauty."

"Yes, but I'm still not over her. I heard she was being transferred to Coruscant for further debriefing. If we can find her and convince her to help . . ."

"We could sponsor her to pilot training and catch Colonel

Repness in his same pathetic tactic." Kell glanced again at Tyria. "I'm in."

"Good. I'll see if I can track her down—Lara Notsil is her name—and then see if Face will keep us off the duty roster long enough to talk to her."

"And if he won't?"

"I'll bring him in on the plan." Anticipating Kell's objections, Phanan hastily continued, "I won't mention Tyria by name. I can keep her out of the story."

"Well . . . all right. Let's keep her out of this end of it, too."

"Done."

A day later, they reassembled in the same hangar, all the Wraiths and more personnel besides.

Face looked over the newcomers with interest. Tallest among them was a human male, on his head an untidy mess of straw-colored hair. Next was a dark-skinned woman with large, alert eyes, a red bead tied to one lock of hair on her forehead, and a broad smile that suggested that every minute of every day she was thrilled to be alive. The last, and shortest, was a Twi'lek woman, her features startlingly beautiful by human standards but her red-eyed stare forbidding, her brain tails hanging loose behind her instead of being draped over her shoulders in the fashion of a Twi'lek among friends and allies. All three wore the standard orange-and-white New Republic pilot's suit.

"Lots of news today," Wes Janson said, looking over his datapad. He was, Face saw, back to his usual self, his eternally youthful features merry, no sign on them of discomfort from the injury to his side. "Most of it good, some bad.

"Bad news: I'm back. Bad for me, because I was enjoying my rest, and bad for you, because if some of you had been a little quicker, I wouldn't have been shot. Keep it in mind as I make up assignments over the next few weeks."

He smiled at the chorus of groans that resulted. "Runt, also, is fit for duty, which is probably both good and bad, because some of his personalities enjoy working and some don't." The greatest mental peculiarity of Runt's Thakwaash species, now well known to the Wraiths, was that most had multiple personalities—not caused, as they were among humans, by great emotional trauma, but occurring as a natural part of their mental development. Each of Runt's personalities was adept at a different task, and new personalities tended to emerge as he learned.

"We have new pilots to fill our roster." One of the Wraiths had died at the battle on the moon of System M2398; two more had perished in the fight that destroyed the *Implacable*. "I present to you Flight Officer Castin Donn, our new computer specialist." The blond-haired man nodded cheerfully. Janson continued, "Castin is a native of Coruscant, so the next time we decide to walk into a trap here, we'll take him along to make sure it's a better grade of trap.

"Flight Officer Dia Passik is a native of Ryloth." The Twi'lek woman nodded, looking among the Wraiths as if to guess which one would attack her first. Janson said, "She has experience with a broad variety of New Republic and Imperial vehicles, especially larger space vessels, and knows quite a bit about criminal organization—she's a new resource for us where things like smuggling, the slave trade, and mercenary operations are concerned.

"Our third pilot is Flight Officer Shalla Nelprin—"

"Oh, no," Kell said. He banged his head against the fuselage of Face's X-wing.

Janson looked vaguely amused. "You have something to say, Lieutenant Tainer?"

Kell stopped hammering the snubfighter for a moment. "You're related to Vula Nelprin?"

The new Wraith's smile broadened, causing dimples to appear. "She's my older sister."

"And your father trained you, too?"

"Yes . . . though I think I'm a little better than Vula."

Kell sighed. "I think I've told you all about my hand-to-hand instructor in the commandos, the one who could throw me around as though I were a dust rag without even letting me see her sweat—this is her sister."

Janson said, "This should come as no surprise to you, then: Nelprin is going to be our new trainer in unarmed combat. You make her the best pilot she can be, and she gets to reward you by beating the life out of you. But she's also well versed in Imperial Intelligence doctrine and tactics, which is helpful to us, since Zsinj seems to be fond of employing Intelligence personnel. Wedge?"

Wedge said, "Make the new pilots welcome, Wraiths. We're going to put them, and you, immediately to work on our new mission." He drew his datapad from a pocket and punched in a command on its keys. "I've just transmitted to your datapads the details of our assignment . . . one which, unfortunately, won't take us off Coruscant yet." He waved down the chorus of groans that resulted. "Sorry. But our results on this task may determine where we're assigned next, so pay attention.

"Our efforts in tracking Admiral Trigit and insinuating ourselves into his confidence have gone over very well with High Command. We've demonstrated that we have both skill and luck on our side. But now we have to prove it beyond a doubt.

"We're going to divide ourselves into three groups. Each group is to ask the following questions: What is Zsinj up to? What are his specific plans and strategies? Once you've arrived at a set of theories, we'll put them to the test: We'll go out into the field and look for evidence to corroborate the best of the theories.

"I'm choosing three of you to head these groups based on your ability with tactical thinking and skill in getting into your enemies' heads." Wedge nodded toward three pilots in turn. "Runt, you're Zsinj-One. Piggy, you're Zsinj-Two. Face, you're Zsinj-Three. Choose your teams and confine yourselves, as much as possible, to research resources available here at headquarters. Questions?"

Janson's hand went up. "Are we going to be working with Rogue Squadron on this?"

Wedge nodded. "Once we're off-planet, yes, but not in the theoretical phase. The Rogues are being assigned to General Solo on the *Mon Remonda* to look for Zsinj; once we get out into the field, we'll work with them as circumstances demand."

Tyria was next. "Have they found out whether it was Zsinj who arranged the ambush on us?"

Wedge managed a sour smile. "The survivors of that little operation have been free with their information. But none of them knew who they were working for except the organizer, who assembled them as a team, trained them for this operation, and led the mission. He was the one whose throat Phanan cut."

Phanan didn't look abashed. "Oops."

"General Cracken's field investigators are trying to backtrack their expenditures and movements; maybe that will turn up some leads for them. Not our problem. Anything else? No? Dismissed."

In the organizational chaos that followed, Runt chose Kell and Tyria as his partners; Face took Phanan and Janson; and Piggy chose Myn, and rounded out his group by adding Squeaky, the unit's 3PO quartermaster, to his roster. By silent agreement, each of the three virtual Zsinjes took one of the new squadron members: Runt took Shalla, Piggy chose Castin, and Face took the Twi'lek Dia.

"And may the best Zsinj win," Face said. "Until he runs into Wraith Squadron, that is."

2

Gara Petothel rechecked the code for the last time, her attention skipping back and forth across screens of data, then sent the command to compile the ungainly-looking mess into what she hoped would be the final version of her program.

A work of art, it was. It would transfer a number of packets of encrypted data from her terminal deep in the low-rent warrens of the city-planet of Coruscant to public computer repositories, disguising the data as ancient archives of accounting data. Then, once the trail back to Gara's terminal was cold, it would transmit the data out across the New Republic Holo-Net, to HoloNet addresses Gara had committed to memory weeks before . . . addresses that would lead eventually to the communications station of the warlord Zsinj.

If he's a smart man, she thought, *and by all accounts he is, within a few weeks I'll have gainful employment again. Away from this cesspool and away from the Rebel police and Intelligence agents—*

A heavy knock fell on the door. She jumped. *Sign of a guilty conscience,* she thought, and tried to school her features back into an expression of innocent curiosity. She switched off power to her terminal's screen.

As she rose to answer the door, she looked into the mirror

to make sure she looked the part she was supposed to be playing. Her downy white-blond hair, cut very close, still seemed odd to her, as was the absence of a mole she'd carried on her cheek since childhood—a mole she had secretly had removed when preparing this identity. No, this identity shared only a certain delicacy of features with Gara Petothel, and hair and makeup were sufficiently different that no one should recognize her in the time it would take her to leave.

She opened the door.

Two Rebel pilots stood outside, both in pilot's jumpsuits topped with transparent slickers more suited to Coruscant's frequent thunderstorms. One had saturnine features and a prosthetic faceplate over the upper left half of his face, a red glow where his left eye would have been. The other would have been startlingly handsome, with luxuriant dark hair framing intelligent, active eyes and features suited to raising heart rates, but his face was marred by a puckered scar—a blaster graze, she guessed—running from his left cheek to his right forehead.

She knew the one with the faceplate, and it was he who spoke first. "Lara Notsil." It was a statement, not a question.

"Yes." She looked beyond them, to the pedestrian traffic in the tenement hallway. Though her tiny quarters were on the fortieth floor of a building, this hallway was part of a tube access allowing people to walk across kilometers of Coruscant at this altitude, and traffic was always heavy. Her hallway was a place of thefts and assaults, but also a way for her to lose herself quickly in a crowd, which is why she'd chosen it.

She returned her attention to her visitors. "It's Lieutenant Phanan, isn't it? From the hospital on Borleias? Please, come in before someone sticks a vibroblade in you." She backed away and allowed them to enter, then shut the door against the ceaseless stream of humanity outside.

"Actually, it's just Flight Officer Phanan," her visitor said. "The smart one here is the lieutenant, Garik Loran."

She froze in mid-handshake and gave the other pilot a closer look. It *was* him, and it embarrassed her, the way she suddenly felt light-headed. "The Face? You're still alive?"

Face gave her a smile. She knew it was an actor's smile, carefully rehearsed to suggest amusement, comradeship, and attraction, but despite the fact it did not fool her, she was still half washed away by the emotions it caused. She felt as though she'd just been invited into his intimate acquaintance. Her light-headedness worse than ever, she sat heavily at her terminal chair.

"That's me," Face said. "I get that a lot. No, the story of my death was a sort of propaganda thing cooked up by the Empire to make people think the Rebel Alliance was full of evil people who'd kill a child actor. I'm a pilot these days."

"Obviously." She struggled to bring herself under control. *Remember*, she thought. *You're Lara Notsil now. Farm girl from Aldivy. Former prisoner of Admiral Trigit. That's what they're here for, more debriefing on Trigit. Phanan had been there, one of the Rebels shooting at* Implacable—*shooting at me.* "Please, sit down. I'm sorry about the mess—it's hard to keep anything clean here. How did you find me?"

Phanan sat on the edge of the bed. Face took the only other chair. Phanan said, "Anyplace you can walk or sit without sticking to everything is very hygienic by low-level Coruscant standards. Believe me, we know. As for finding you—we asked around New Republic Intelligence. They said you'd been discharged and had declined transportation back to your homeworld. We ran a search on the worldnet looking for your name and recent employment application. You're working as an information processor for a shipping concern?"

"Yes. It pays"—she gestured at the tidy squalor around her—"for all this."

Face said, "How would you like a better job and the chance to live in better conditions?"

"I'd like that. What would I have to do?"

"Go through New Republic pilot training. The full academy course."

No, thanks. How would you like to get me a ticket to Warlord Zsinj's fleet instead? But she had to play her role. "That would be . . . nice. But it can't happen."

Face gave her another smile, this one full of confidence. "Why not?"

Gara injected a note of wistfulness into her voice. "When I was back on the farm on Aldivy, that's something I thought about every day. Learning to fly. I got to be pretty good on the farm's skimmers. I studied things like voice and Basic to sound less like a farm girl."

"It shows," Face said. "Your Aldivian accent is almost gone."

If you knew that I was born and reared less than a hundred klicks from here, you'd appreciate how much work it takes to speak with the barest trace of that accent, Gara thought. "But then, when the *Implacable* came, destroyed New Oldtown, and took me away, I sort of lost interest. All I wanted to do was see the *Implacable* destroyed. And then when Admiral Trigit chose me for his"—she broke eye contact, put an extra rasp into her voice, let a tear fall—"mistress, all I wanted was for him to die.

"You did that. You killed him. Your squadron and the other ones. Thank you." She modulated her voice to sound as though she were feigning nonchalance and concealing pain. "But I guess I don't have anything left. Any ambitions."

"I'm sorry to hear that."

"Besides, since I've been . . . associated with Admiral Trigit, the New Republic wouldn't trust me." She shrugged fatalistically.

"They cleared you. You were never charged with any crime."

She nodded. And what work it had been, all those weeks ago, to generate the Lara Notsil identity, careful planning ahead just in case her employment with Trigit didn't work out. Hooking her new identity to a real event, Trigit's punitive bombardment of a farm community that had refused to provision him. Finding and modifying the pitiful few records concerning a farm girl whose body was now a carbonized mass of powder in a charred Aldivian grainfield, replacing key bits of data with Gara's picture, Gara's fingerprints, Gara's cellular coding. Spinning a tale of secret chambers on the *Implacable*— so secret other *Implacable* survivors could plausibly not have known about her—where Trigit imprisoned his "unwilling mistress" and maintained her on a diet of glitterstim and other drugs.

They'd accepted it, the whole package, especially eager for

the scandalous details of her captivity and Trigit's evil . . . lies she'd been happy to offer out of her anger at the man. Trigit had been willing to sacrifice his crew to death when he didn't have to, a crew that had been efficient and loyal.

But this whole Lara Notsil identity had only one purpose, to get her out of New Republic hands and back to Imperial service—or service that would someday be acknowledged as Imperial.

She shook her head. "I don't think I can help you." Then she frowned. "Wait. You said 'trade favors.' What would I do for you?"

Phanan leaned forward. "Ah. That's the tricky bit. We'd want you to struggle a bit with your pilot training. Skirt along at the bottom of your class, sometimes dipping just under acceptable skill, sometimes skimming along just above. Sort of terrain-following flying, if you get my drift."

"Why? Why not do the best I can?"

Phanan said, "Because we think someone will come to you and offer to help train you, improve your scores . . . and then want to use your pilot's skills in a deal. Some sort of illegal operation."

"You're setting this person up. I would be bait."

Face nodded. "He's the sort of man who uses people, Lara. Uses them like Admiral Trigit. We thought, maybe, you'd be able to take out on him the vengeance you'd been saving for Trigit."

She shook her head. "It wouldn't be the same, and I wouldn't—"

And then the idea hit her, detonating in her mind like a proton torpedo. A plan, a simple one, one that would increase her worth in the eyes of Warlord Zsinj or any Imperial officer to whom she wanted to sell her services. The idea made her as dizzy as her long-faded teenage longing for an actor named Garik Loran had.

"Lara?" Face asked. "Are you all right?"

She began to cry. A useful talent, that, being able to cry on cue; her teachers at Imperial Intelligence had been delighted by it. "I can't do it," she said. "I'll lose everything."

Phanan leaned forward and took her hands. "What will you lose? What *could* you lose?"

"Everyone at home is dead. All I have left are people I've met since I was rescued. I was hoping for a career in the military, some civilian post. If I do what you say, if I go through pilot's training, I won't be able to help myself—it'll wake up that old wish and the only thing I'll want is to be a pilot. And then if I set this man up and ruin him, everyone everywhere will say, 'That's Lara Notsil. The traitor.' No one will want me. Everyone will distrust me."

"That's not true," Phanan said. But Gara saw Face lean back, considering her words, and she knew he recognized the truth of them.

"It *is* true," she said. "What commander would take me on as a pilot? Everyone will think I'm spying on them, and friends of this person you want me to burn down will do what it takes to ruin me. I'll have terrible scores from doing exactly what you wanted me to do, so the civilian piloting services won't have anything to do with me." She stared between them, defiant, allowing tears to continue streaming down her face. "You know it's true. And you can't speak for any squadron except your own, and you know Wedge Antilles would never take me on after I'd done what you asked."

Face still looked troubled. "We don't know that."

"But you can't speak for him."

"No, we can't."

"So you two want me to trade my entire future for a little piloting training. Thanks for the offer. There's the door."

"Wait." There was no artifice in Face's voice or manner now. "What if we could guarantee you a piloting station? Somewhere you'd be accepted for your skills, where the consequences of this operation play in your favor instead of against you?"

"Where?"

"I don't know yet."

She shook her head. "I can't trust that the commander will be as fair as you think. I just don't believe it."

"What if it were Wedge Antilles?"

She caught her breath. Then: "You just said you can't speak for him."

"Not yet. I haven't put any details of this in front of him. But I will. And if he says yes?"

She paused. She already knew her answer, but they had to think she was considering it. Finally, she said, "If it were Wedge Antilles's command, either Rogue Squadron or that new one, Wraith Squadron, yes, I'd do it."

"I'll talk to him today." Face rose and Phanan followed suit. "I'll let you know as soon as I have an answer from him."

She gave him a brave little nod.

And when they'd gone, she clamped both hands over her mouth, the better to hold in the whoops of victory that threatened to escape her.

When they were a few steps from Lara Notsil's door, Phanan said, "Commander Antilles is going to take you to pieces."

"I know." Face shouldered his way through the thick stream of pedestrians.

"You'll be pulling punishment detail until you're forty."

"Probably."

"When you put this idea in front of him, flames are going to come out of his mouth and burn you from head to foot."

"That's true. But one thing makes it easier for me to take."

"What's that?"

"You're going to be there burning with me."

Phanan grimaced. "You're such a good friend."

Flight Officer Shalla Nelprin dove toward the ground—as far as the narrowing gaps between Coruscant's endless sea of buildings would allow her to descend. She could see blurs in the viewports, blurs that had to be startled faces.

The pair of TIE fighters on her tail pursued her with agility, matching her maneuver with little effort, still firing their linked lasers at her tail. She leveled off, juking left and right as much as the narrow confines would let her, and green laser blasts slammed into buildings on either side of her and into her reinforced rear shields.

"I can't shake them, Control," she said. "They're good."

The voice of Runt Ekwesh came back. "Shalla, why do you think Warlord Zsinj employs so many former Intelligence officers? *Implacable, Night Caller,* and more ships and officers we're learning of—"

Shalla's snubfighter shuddered as another laser blast slammed into her stern shields and penetrated to reach her hull. She glanced at her diagnostics board. Minimal damage to hull, no indication of other problems. Yet. "Control, do you mind? I'm flying for my life here."

"It is only a simulator run. Your scores are not being recorded."

"Treat every simulator run like the real thing and stay alive longer. That's what my daddy says." She dropped down another ten meters to fly under, rather than through, a walkway connecting two skyscrapers. One TIE fighter mimicked her, the other rose and flew over the obstruction. "All right. First, they were available. Ysanne Isard, head of Intelligence, is killed a few months ago by Rogue Squadron. This gives every one of her subordinates a choice. Work for this council now running what's left of the Empire, work for one of the warlords, go pirate, or go hide. Wait a second."

Below and ahead was another enclosed crosswalk; beyond it, immediately below the crosswalk's level, two buildings widened so that there was scarcely any room between them. Shalla dove again, came up immediately beneath the walkway, and rotated ninety degrees, her wings now pointing skyward and groundward, to fit in the narrowing gap between buildings.

As before, one TIE fighter went high and the other followed her closely. But the TIE-fighter profile was not as variable as that of an X-wing; because of its solar array wings, no matter how it was turned, the TIE fighter needed more than six meters of clearance in any direction.

In this narrow gap, her pursuer didn't have them. It hit the four-meter opening between buildings and the buildings sheared both wings off, top and bottom. The TIE fighter dropped, its ball-shaped cockpit bouncing between buildings on its way down until it detonated.

A new voice—Shalla thought it was Kell Tainer's—came across next. "Good flying, Nelprin. One to go."

"Thank you." The gap between buildings widened. She rotated until she was horizontal again. "So, all of a sudden there are lots of Intelligence operatives and ships available. That's the supply.

"Demand is trickier. Zsinj's records say he's sort of a compulsive liar. So why hire people who are trained to see through those lies? My guess is that he doesn't mind. He doesn't lie to fool people—except his enemies, of course. He does it to entertain. To impress people with his brilliance."

The remaining TIE fighter resumed firing on her; lasers flashed past her strike foils to blow through building walls below, and her stern shields took more hits.

Ahead and above was a crowd of high-altitude skimmers— aerial traffic following one of the posted routes. But these skimmers were all decorated with the colors of Coruscant police.

"Hey, fair game." Shalla rose into the cloud of skimmers, flashing just below most of them, using them as a screen.

Her pursuer's lasers hit skimmers all around her. Several detonated, raining shrapnel upon her.

When a skimmer ahead of her blew up, she decelerated as hard as she could and was vibrated by her snubfighter's shudder. Half on main engines and half on repulsorlift landing engines, she rose through the cloud of flame and debris—

And as she cleared it she saw the other TIE fighter racing along ahead, not having anticipated her sudden deceleration. It was slowing now, preparing for one of the impossibly tight turns TIE fighters could manage.

She bracketed the TIE fighter with her heads-up display. The brackets went almost instantly from yellow to red and she fired, sending a proton torpedo straight into the Imperial vehicle's cockpit. It detonated, a brilliant flash of light and debris.

Then Shalla's view spun as she was hurled out of control. She saw a building side rushing toward her, frightened faces in the viewports—and then everything went black.

The canopy opened over her, admitting light. Runt, Kell,

and Tyria stood nearby, all of them wearing headsets. "What happened?" Shalla asked, complaint in her voice.

Kell smiled. "You were hit by a skimmer. It was flying blind through that first explosion and slammed into you from the side."

Shalla hissed in vexation and climbed out. "They say the city is a dangerous place."

"Otherwise an excellent run," Kell continued.

"So," Runt said, "the Intelligence operatives are available, and Zsinj doesn't mind that they can see through some of his deceptions. What else?"

Shalla gave the others a look. "Runt is pretty single-minded, isn't he?"

They laughed. Kell said, "No, more like multiple-minded. But any one of his minds might get very focused."

"I see." She didn't, but she figured she would eventually. She turned back to Runt. "Maybe it's more than that Zsinj just doesn't mind. Maybe he likes having an appreciative audience. Someone knowledgeable enough to understand what he's doing and be impressed by it. He has to have a tremendous ego."

Runt frowned. It wasn't a proper human frown, but his very mobile eyebrows came down over his large, expressive eyes to suggest concentration. "He likes to be appreciated."

"I think so."

"He would enjoy playing the hero. Hero of the Empire."

"Certainly. Why else make all these very public assaults on New Republic colonies and outposts? It's not all for their strategic value. They're not all valuable, and he could do more damage by being sneaky. It's to show somebody that he's a warrior. His audience, whoever that is." She bent over, pressing her head to her knees, then straightened, arms high in the air, and began repeating the motion.

Tyria sighed. "She's exercising. We have a compulsive exerciser."

Shalla didn't look up. "Just stretching. I get leg cramps when I'm in the cockpit too long."

Kell said, "Her sister is like that, too. Always in motion. Want to drive her completely insane? Tie her to a chair for an hour."

Shalla straightened and gave him her most wicked smile. "Try it, Lieutenant."

"No, thanks."

Wedge stood so fast that his chair slammed back into his office wall. "You promised her what?"

Phanan and Face were already standing. Face said, "We promised her nothing—except that we'd look into it."

"Gentlemen, this is a matter for New Republic Intelligence. Hand it off to General Cracken's people."

Face looked uneasy. "With all due respect, sir, Cracken's people haven't noticed this man yet. That means he might have a friend, a fellow officer, in Intelligence, covering for him. If he's stolen spacecraft before, and we have no reason to suspect he hasn't—"

"Or any knowledge that he *has*."

"True. But if he's stolen spacecraft before, having a friend in Cracken's group would account for the failure of any investigation to turn up evidence against him. If we turn this over to Intelligence, we may just be giving him advance warning so he can cover his tracks, play the good little officer for a couple of years . . . and then go back to stealing things and luring young, struggling officer candidates into his employ."

Wedge considered that. "If you carry out this little operation, Cracken's people may decide they don't care for us very much. For intruding on their territory."

Phanan nodded. "That's a possibility. But another possibility is that we can do this without even alerting anyone it is an 'operation.' Let's say Lara Notsil gets into flight school on the recommendation of a dashing, preposterously attractive pilot she met in the hospital on Borleias—"

"One of Blue Squadron's pilots, I assume."

"Thank you for that vote of confidence, sir. Anyway, she goes through training, Repness starts his shenanigans. Lara calls in her old friend from the hospital, they expose Repness immediately. That's the story, and it'll hold up to most scrutiny."

"To casual scrutiny, maybe." Scowling, Wedge finally resumed his seat. Phanan and Face looked a little more relieved and sat as well.

Wedge continued, "But the likelihood is that we'll be on assignment elsewhere when her troubles with Repness begin. Are you planning on resigning from Wraith Squadron to stay here near her?"

"No. But Face here is going to deposit some credits in an account for her to use for HoloNet access. Whenever it happens, she can get in touch with us almost immediately—"

"Assuming we're not undercover."

"Assuming that, yes. I'll leave instructions for her for what to do if she can't reach us. But if she can, we'll find out who's on Coruscant, someone we trust that she can depend on. There's bound to be somebody. There's always somebody." Phanan gave his commander a diffident little shrug. "You might even be able to call on Princess Leia Organa—"

"Absolutely not. She's a busy, busy woman. Besides, she's gone on some diplomatic mission nobody will talk about."

"Just a thought. Anyway, if we're not here to help Lara through the endgame, we'll put her in the hands of a friend who is. And that will be the end of it."

"Except for her career."

Both of the other pilots nodded.

Wedge leaned back, away from them. "All right, you two. I'll give you this. If she carries out this operation, I'll consider her for transfer to one of my squadrons. And I'll base my acceptance or refusal of her completely on my own evaluation of her skills and her character. Not on her academy records, not on her participation in your operation. She has to be fit to fly as a Rogue or a Wraith . . . but if she is, the next time I have a slot available I'll take her. That's the best I can do."

They took that as a signal and rose. "That's the best we could hope for," Phanan said. "Thank you, sir."

"Dismissed."

When they'd gone, Wedge said to the empty air, "Wes, they're doing it to me again."

3

"I think it's all wrapped up in the symbolism of the _Iron Fist_," Face said.

The Wraiths were in the officers' lounge of Sivantlie Base, their temporary station on Coruscant. Once a hotel catering to mid-level Imperial bureaucrats from offworld, it now housed units of the armed forces that were in transition: soldiers awaiting transport to their assignments, squadrons in rotation between bases, new units being assembled. Two stories down, where the base's tower just began to extend above the surrounding buildings, there were hangar accesses large enough for small cargo vessels. The lounge itself had vast viewports that gave the Wraiths and other officers present a clear view of the limitless sea of Coruscant's building tops, as well as storm clouds concentrating only a few kilometers away. Tiny dots like insects, actually shuttles and other craft, buzzed above the cityscape and beneath the clouds.

Face was at the viewports, staring down into the dark depths of Coruscant's streets, trying to shift his tastes around, trying to become the sort of man who would look upon this world as a thing of beauty. Trying to become a loyal Imperial officer, if only temporarily, to understand how they thought, reacted.

"You're saying the *Iron Fist* is his hammer, symbolically as well as effectively?" That was Janson, stretched out on one of the lounge sofas, a tumbler of brandy on the table at his head.

Face nodded absently. "He uses it for strikes against high-profile targets. Not targets that are easier than the others, nor harder, just more visible. Such as the assault on Noquivzor, designed to destroy Rogue Squadron—what a coup that would have been. He named *Iron Fist* after his first command, an elderly wreck of a *Victory*-class Star Destroyer. It's a symbol to him, of his rise from obscurity to power. It's the key to him, I think." He glanced over at Runt, who leaned lazily against a support pillar on the other side of the main viewport. "What do you think?"

The brown-furred nonhuman turned toward him. Face felt his own spine stiffen. This wasn't Runt's usual body language, and the long-faced pilot's eyes drooped almost closed. Runt said, "Did I give you leave to speak?" His voice was rich and deep, without his usual melodious tones and odd inflections.

"Your pardon," Face said. He felt oddly formal. "*Iron Fist*? Zsinj's primary and most important act of symbolism?"

Runt shook his head, sending his long, glossy ponytail swaying. His smile showed his large teeth but did not seem in the least friendly. "You don't understand Zsinj," he said. "To Zsinj, symbols are for others. Zsinj uses them as simple controls. Knobs and buttons by which he can cause his lessers to do their duty. Dials and gauges by which he can measure their fear. No, Zsinj's tool is that fear itself, fear and respect. Zsinj smashes with one hand and feeds with the other. One act impresses the unaligned governors who used to support the Empire. The other hand beckons them. As more and more feed from that hand, still more will be forced to." Runt finally looked fully at Face. "It is the governors. It must be. Zsinj will do whatever it takes to draw them into his camp, one by one or ten by ten. Smash them, entice them, seduce them, terrify them."

Face glanced back at Janson. The squadron's second-in-command grinned at him, obviously amused by Runt's performance, then cocked his head to one side and froze—near-universal pantomime of a droid whose power has just been shut off, pilot's shorthand for someone whose brain is receiving no power.

One of the lounge's simulators hissed as its canopy opened. The new Twi'lek pilot, Dia Passik, bounded out as though she were partially made of springs. She had a smile on her face, nearly a smirk, and she headed straight for the bar. Face watched her closely; there was something odd about the way she moved. . . .

That was it. Hers was the strut of a Corellian pilot. A *male* Corellian pilot, to the extent that her build would allow her such motion. She, too, knew something about body language and simulated manners.

The adjoining simulator opened and Phanan climbed out more sedately. He came over to Face. "Well, she dropped the heavy end of the hammer on me," he said.

"Vaped you?"

"Three times out of three. I don't think she's up to Kell's level, and certainly not up to the commander's, but she's deadly." Phanan added, a hopeful note in his voice, "Perhaps she'd show me some mercy on account of my physical appeal and personal charm."

"I'm sure she would if you had any."

They joined Dia at the bar, flanking her, and ordered a nonalcoholic fruit fizz to match hers. Squeaky, the 3PO unit with mismatched gold and silver components, drew their drinks, uttered a sigh, and murmured something about the scarcity of fresh fruit in the Coruscant market.

"Ton says you're a pretty hot shooter," Face said.

"It won't work," she said.

"Eh?" Face glanced across her at Phanan, who returned his confused expression. "What won't work?"

"You wouldn't have said that to a male pilot unless it had been a real run. Which means you only said it to ingratiate yourself with me. You want to provoke an emotional response, gratitude, that a lowly flight officer might find worth under the eyes of the famous Garik Loran. At some point I'm supposed to swoon into your arms, aren't I?"

Face blinked. "That actually hadn't occurred to me."

"I didn't see your holos, Face. When you were acting your heart out as a child star, I was a slave dancer in training, not permitted choice rewards like seeing entertainment holos. You don't occupy a place in the adolescent quadrant of my heart the way you do with most females my age. I am immune to your alleged charms."

Face glanced at Phanan again. The other pilot was turning red with the effort not to laugh. Face modulated his voice to low, resonant, romantic tones. "I am so glad I met you," he said. "I've been looking for you all my life."

"You have?" Her expression turned to confusion. "Why?"

"The one woman in all the galaxy immune to my charms? Do you know how often I've said, 'Where is she, does she truly exist?' "

Phanan got himself under control. "It's true. I raised Face from the time he was a cub, and since almost the day he could talk, he's been saying, 'Find me the one woman who can withstand me. Who can loathe me for who I really am.' He's had a long, lonely life until today. Now *you* can abuse him and give me a rest."

Face nodded sagely.

Dia's face twitched into a smile, which she quickly suppressed. "Now you're making fun of me."

Face let his expression and voice return to normal. "Oh, we've barely gotten started. Anyway, after a casual remark about your skills to open up the conversation, my plan actually was to ask you how you fouled up."

"Fouled up." She looked between the two men. "I don't recall fouling up."

"Then what brings you to Wraith Squadron?"

"I volunteered. After the story broke on your destruction of the *Implacable,* I wanted to join a unit as savage as that. Why? Are you supposed to be screwups?"

Phanan whistled. "She doesn't even know. We didn't even have time for our true reputation to circulate before another reputation swam up and swallowed it."

Face gave Dia a stern look. "I'm sorry, you appear to have

been transferred here under false pretenses. We're a hard-luck squadron. If you're not a real screwup, we're just going to have to make you an honorary screwup. Keep that in mind."

"I will," she said, her voice solemn.

"She'll do," Phanan said.

"Even if she doesn't swoon."

"How did you get into Starfighter Command?" Face asked.

She looked between them as if evaluating them, then shrugged. "My . . . owner . . . was a very rich man of Coruscant, founder of a firm that made communications equipment. Very reliable HoloNet receivers, for example. He and his preferred advisers lived on an enormous yacht called the *Violet Hem*—a reference to the Emperor's robes. Anyway, over the years I was able to persuade several of his personal pilots to teach me how to control their vehicles. Few things make a male feel as grand as the opportunity to teach a young, fascinated female." She opened her eyes wide in an expression of innocence.

Face snorted. "So you stole a vehicle?"

"My owner was visited by a pilot with an armed shuttle. I stole it and turned it over to the New Republic."

"And the *Violet Hem*?"

This time her smile was not that of an innocent. "Before I left, I locked her shields down so they could not be brought up. My first combat action of any sort was to blow *Violet Hem* out of space."

Face suppressed a shudder and decided to change the subject. "I wonder if the other new pilots are just as unaware of our true nature. Hey, Castin!"

The blond pilot, seated in a stuffed chair nearby, looked up guiltily from the datapad in his lap. "I wasn't doing anything."

Face grinned. "I'm not monitoring you. I just wanted to know what you did to end up with the Wraiths."

"I volunteered."

"Why?"

Castin looked thoughtful. "I wanted to be where things happened. And things always happen around Commander Antilles. I want to go after enemies like Zsinj and eliminate them.

Erase them. Overwrite them to the point that no one in the galaxy even remembers them."

"Well, that's admirable . . . but again, why?"

"People like Zsinj, they have to be squashed as hard and as fast as you can. Because the next thing they do is going to be something awful. They never do anything that isn't awful, and ordinary people get killed." Castin's tone was bitter, and other Wraiths perked up to listen.

"You're speaking from personal experience."

"Oh, yes." Castin looked around blankly, staring not at his fellow Wraiths but at some point in the past. "The day the Emperor died—what were you doing?"

Face didn't have to think back. Most people recalled exactly what they were doing the moment they heard that Palpatine had been killed at Endor. "I was in civilian flight school on Lorrd. In class studying astronautics. Why?"

"I was in one of Coruscant's plazas. A little one, couldn't have held more than a couple of hundred thousand people, way up high where only a half-dozen buildings cast shadows down on it. The word spread like fire through an old building. The New Republic HoloNet broadcast was being rebroadcast on a wide band so that every personal comlink would pick it up. All holoprojectors were showing the second Death Star exploding.

"The crowd went crazy. Loyalists were turning white. Some of them fainting dead away. Rebels and people with Rebel leanings were going berserk. Before very long, they were actually tearing a statue of Palpatine down. A big one. It took cables and skimmers to knock it over." Castin shrugged. "And then stormtroopers came."

"To restore order."

"If you want to call it that. They opened up on the crowd pulling down the statue. And their blasters weren't set on stun. You could smell the burning-meat odor all over the plaza. I was right next to a young mother who took it right in the head. I grabbed her baby on the way down so he wouldn't be trampled in the stampede." He shook his head, his expression bleak, and fell silent.

Face said, "The Imperial HoloNet wouldn't have transmitted the news of the Emperor's death over normal channels like that. Not before they'd had time to sweeten up the story and turn it into some sort of Imperial victory."

Castin shook his head, not meeting Face's eye.

"So someone else, someone technically proficient, had to have intercepted it and rebroadcast it like that. You?"

Castin nodded. "My group was one of them, yes."

"So Zsinj is another Imperial killer, and if you don't stop him personally, it's the plaza all over again. Is that it?"

"Maybe."

"Well, that's as good a reason as any." But that was an answer for Face. Castin might have volunteered for this duty without a blemish on his record, but there was still a possibility of volatility there. Now he had to wonder if Dia and Shalla were also carrying around emotional demolition charges just waiting to go off.

"Pirates," Piggy said, interrupting. The Gamorrean settled into a stuffed chair situated between Janson's sofa and the bar, near Donos and Castin.

"Pirates to you, too," Phanan said. "Is that a new greeting? Something Gamorrean? 'Scabrous pirates to you this morning.'"

" 'And bleeding pirates to you.' " Face gave his wingman a formal bow.

"Zsinj was negotiating with the pirates on M2398, trying to enlist their services," Piggy continued. In spite of the mechanical simplicity of Piggy's voice translator, Face thought he could detect a contemplative quality in the Gamorrean's tones. "It's a tactic we haven't seen with him before. Is he in such dire need that he must rely on pirates? I don't think so. He's assembling a second navy, perhaps a disposable one."

Runt shook his head again. "Zsinj needs such scum only to hear what their prattling mouths have to say. To obtain news, intelligence, that he cannot derive from some more legitimate source. The pirates are nothing."

Piggy grunted a laugh. "You'll need plenty of cleanser for that scum when it assembles and comes at you. At all of us."

·   ·   ·

"A minute of your time, sir?" Castin Donn stood at the door to Wedge's interim office. Rather, he leaned against it, his body language suggesting a man who'd prefer to be elsewhere— definitely anywhere but a military base. He was unshaven, his eyes tired.

Wedge would have accepted this pose and manner from one of the established Wraiths, but not from a newcomer. He merely cleared his throat and looked expectant, as though the pilot hadn't spoken.

Castin apparently got the hint. He straightened, slowly enough to demonstrate reluctance, and threw a salute. "Flight Officer Castin Donn reporting, sir. I was wondering if I might have a moment of your time."

Wedge took a moment before responding with his own salute. "Certainly, Donn. Have a seat."

Donn's posture, once he was seated, reverted to that of a career code-slicer; he slumped into his chair as though he'd left his spine in his locker. "I was wondering if I could get assigned to different quarters."

Wedge brought out his datapad and tapped up the infor- mation on living assignments. It showed that Donn had been put in the same bunkroom as Runt Ekwesh. Runt's former roommate had been Kell Tainer, but that pilot had been as- signed solo quarters ever since his promotion to lieutenant. "Is something wrong with your current assignment?"

"Yes, sir. I'm not getting any sleep."

"I don't understand. Does Runt snore?" Kell had never made any such complaint.

"No, sir. It's just not working out."

"Personality conflict."

"No, sir."

"Request denied, Donn. Unless you can come up with something a little more substantial than 'it's just not working out.' "

Castin squirmed in his chair. Wedge thought it an unusu- ally childlike mannerism from a grown man who'd been through pilot training and scored high enough to be fit for Wraith Squadron. "Sir, he, uh . . . he smells."

"I take it you mean he smells bad."

"Yes, sir. It's keeping me up at night."

Wedge kept his face impassive and thought about it. Runt Ekwesh was a member of the Thakwaash species, humanoids who averaged over three meters in height and were covered with fur; Runt came by his nickname because he was, in fact, very short for his species, the only reason he could fit in standard New Republic cockpits. And his odor was indeed different from that of humans, though it was very faint, usually undetectable except when he was wet or had been in the cockpit for several hours.

Wedge kept the pilot waiting, still squirming restlessly, while he brought up Castin's full record. The man, a native of Coruscant, had been a code-slicer since he entered his teens, and had belonged to a rebel group not associated with the Alliance. Shortly after the Emperor's death, nearly four years ago, he had forged himself a false identity, arranged passage offworld, and had ended up in New Republic–controlled space, where his technical skills had served him and the New Republic well. After two years as a coder for the fleet, he'd transferred to Starfighter Command and entered pilot training.

The synopsis said very little about him as a man. Wedge switched to the record of his citations and reprimands. He'd seen all this data before, while reviewing the new pilot candidates for approval, but he'd been looking only for specific types of information then.

There were citations for courage and ingenuity under fire, but also many punishments for failure to perform routine duties in a reliable fashion. That hadn't bothered Wedge; he knew Castin would either shape up in that regard or be kicked out of Starfighter Command altogether, a motivation that should keep him in line. But in the record was also a chronicle of personality conflicts with fleet bridge crew members, mostly Mon Calamari. Transfer from the fleet accepted after a fistfight . . . with a Sullustian navigator. Hmm.

"I could put you in with Piggy. Voort saBinring," Wedge said.

Castin's squirming became more acute, and Wedge suspected he had the answer.

"I'm not sure that would work either," Castin said.

"Same reason?"

"Yes, sir."

"Donn, this independent revolutionary faction you belonged to—were there any nonhumans in it?"

"No, sir."

That was interesting. Most such factions on Coruscant had high proportions of nonhuman members. The factions that didn't include nonhumans tended to be just as anti-Imperial . . . but had still supported Coruscant culture's legendary suspicion and dislike of nonhumans.

"So you've had very little protracted contact with nonhumans."

"Well . . . that would be correct, sir."

"I'm sorry, Donn, but I'm afraid this is something you're just going to have to get used to. Whenever it bothers you, you need to ask yourself, 'I wonder what I smell like to *them*?' "

Castin's voice dropped and came close to but did not quite cross into the realm of surliness. "I don't smell at all, sir. I keep myself very clean."

"But their senses aren't like yours. If you ever get up the nerve, ask them sometime if they can smell you and what it's like. You might be surprised by the answer."

Castin's expression became one of distress. "But, sir, we have plenty of room here at base—"

"But not everywhere we're going. I'll modify room assignments when there's a genuine reason to do so. Not before."

"Sir—"

"That's all, Donn."

It looked just like the bridge of the *Iron Fist*. It had its own command walkway facing the forward viewports, the ones that stared out into depthless space. It had its crew pit below, with its numerous crew stations.

But it was actually a portion of Warlord Zsinj's private quarters, a replica of the true bridge, and it had no crew. The viewports were actually screens receiving holocam views from the real viewports. The viewscreens at the crew stations showed the data or visual feeds the crewmen on duty would be accessing if they were here; commands flickered across the screens and were executed as though the station operators were in place. But sounds from the console speakers—beeps, dialogue, noises indicating errors or computer achievements—were the only ones to be heard. No one spoke.

Warlord Zsinj moved among the ghost stations, peering over the shoulders of imaginary crewmen as if to evaluate their performance. A small man whose waist outperformed his chest in dimension and magnificence, he looked like a holo comedian pretending to be an officer: His spotless white uniform was that of an Imperial grand admiral, while his bald head, luxuriant mustache, florid complexion, and too-cheerful manner suggested a backwater bandit.

He bent over the back of a chair; the screen before him showed a fleeing Y-wing attack craft as if seen through the viewport of a pursuing TIE interceptor. The background was a busy battlefield; Zsinj recognized the chaos of the battle above Endor's sanctuary moon, just under four years ago.

He leaned closer to see the name of the crewman logged onto the computer. "Ah, Ensign Sprettyn," he said. "Running attack simulators again while on duty. Shirking your responsibilities again."

"Perhaps he wants to become a pilot."

The voice, smooth and reassuring, came from behind Zsinj. The warlord straightened and turned. "General Melvar. What have I told you about creeping up behind me?"

The general, a tall man with features that were elegant when he was paying attention but impossibly bland and unmemorable when he lost concentration, smiled. "Not to."

"And what did you just do?"

"I stomped up to you with all the silent grace of a gut-shot rancor. You were so intent on your observation of poor Ensign Sprettyn's activities you failed to notice me."

"It's the sign of pure concentration. The ability to shut out all other concerns."

"Of course."

"What do you want?"

The general handed him a datapad. Lines of data were already up on its screen. "A private communication for you. Through Admiral Trigit's old routing system."

Zsinj gave him a look that was all raised eyebrows and curiosity, then scanned the text. "Hmm. Lieutenant Gara Petothel. Expects to be a member of one of Antilles's squadrons within a few weeks. 'Would you be interested . . . ?' I see she has a fine sense of irony. What do you have on her?"

"I've put her file in there with the communiqué. In short, she's an Imperial Intelligence prodigy who was orphaned—she was in deep cover as a Rebel mission coordinator when Ysanne Isard was killed. Her controller was a member of Isard's support staff and also died. Petothel managed to get in touch with Apwar Trigit, offered her continued services to him, and fed him information that led Trigit to some important temporary provisioning centers and allowed him to annihilate an entire Rebel X-wing squadron. She joined his crew and was presumed dead when the *Implacable* was destroyed."

"Oh, she's that one. So she eluded capture. Or perhaps not. Perhaps she was captured, then turned, and is being used to flush us." Zsinj shrugged. "Where's her holo?"

"We found that holos of her in both Imperial and Rebel records show the wrong woman. She has covered her tracks well. I'm having a simulation assembled from people who were in her Rebel academy class . . . which will take some time and caution."

"Very well." Zsinj handed the datapad back. "Pursue this. Have an agent or a cell on Coruscant try to do independent verification of what she's saying. Find out what identity she's currently wearing. Once that's determined, we must find out where her loyalties lie before we commit any real resources to her."

"Done. And Ensign Sprettyn?"

"Do you want to handle that? It's a task for his executive officer."

"I'd be happy to."

"Very well. Sprettyn is under direct orders not to waste time with the simulators, but he just wants to fly too much. So spirit him off into the night. Tell the rest of the crew he's been executed for disobeying orders. But tell him that he's being taken aside for pilot evaluation. Put him through the simulators."

"And if he turns out to be a good pilot trainee?"

"Weren't you listening?" Zsinj looked regretful. "I deplore the waste of good crewmen, I really do. But we can't have pilots who disobey orders. Evaluate his piloting performance, chastise or compliment him as appropriate, then execute him."

"The evaluations of the three Zsinj theories have come back from Admiral Ackbar's office," Wedge said.

They were in the briefing room temporarily assigned to Wraith Squadron. This was an office far enough down in the building that there were no viewports; viewports would only have shown a depressingly bleak vista of dark, grimy duracrete corridor between the lower reaches of skyscrapers. Instead, the orange walls were decorated with large holoscreens that transited between views shot from planetary orbits, vistas of distant and beautiful worlds, and promotional images of hotel resorts belonging to the same chain that had once owned this facility. The Wraiths were all seated near Wedge's lectern, except for Shalla Nelprin, who paced at the back of the hall—until Wedge caught her eye. She quickly sat in the seat nearest to her.

"Before I get to the admiral's conclusions," Wedge continued, "I think we ought to let the writers of the three reports synopsize their conclusions; not everyone has heard these. Runt?"

The long-faced alien stood up. His body language changed; his posture became that of a human carrying a fair amount of extra weight and he folded his hands over his belly in the fashion of a well-fed senator. "In our considered opinion," he said, once again taking on the mellow voice of the ersatz Zsinj, "the warlord's overt and covert tactics suggest that he will continue to add resources, industrial and planetary, with as much cost-effectiveness as possible. This means continuing the expansion of the secret financial empire whose edges we detected . . . and a more direct appeal to the unaligned governors that previously belonged to the Empire and now belong to the Empire's successors. I think this means using *Iron Fist* in actions of direct interdiction that benefit these governors more than Zsinj himself, an effort to bind the governors to him in debts of gratitude."

"And your recommendations for ways to counter this?"

"Examine the resources of unaligned governors, find out which one it would best serve Zsinj to court, and cause that governor problems only Zsinj can solve . . . luring him to that system and confronting him directly."

"You're very erudite in this mind, Runt."

Runt's body language changed back to normal; he once again seemed lanky, overall, a little awkward. "But it makes our ego puff up like a gas giant." He sat.

"Piggy?"

The Gamorrean stood. He cleared his throat. Once upon a time, that would have blasted the Wraiths with a burst of static, but his throat translator had since been reprogrammed to squelch a wider variety of irrelevant sounds. "In the last few weeks, as we were nibbling at the edges of Zsinj's organization, we found three anomalies. One was the network of manufacturing corporations owned within unaligned and even Alliance-controlled space by Zsinj under false identities. One was his attempt to hire a pirate nest made up of outlaws somewhat under his usual standards. And the third was the presence, at one of his companies, of prison-cell components identical to the cell where I was raised after Imperial scientists altered my biochemistry." The scientists' alterations were what gave Piggy his unusually temperate personality—for a Gamorrean—and his inhuman mathematical acumen, both traits that allowed him to become a proficient New Republic pilot.

Piggy waved, his gesture taking in Myn Donos, the 3PO unit Squeaky, and Castin Donn. "My group feels that the industrial connection is something better suited for New Republic Intelligence to pursue, so we eliminated it from our recommendations. Of the two that remain, the site where I was scientifically modified and reared is of great interest to me personally, but we all feel that we would have a greater chance of discovering Zsinj by disguising ourselves as a pirate band and trying to impress Zsinj enough for him to employ us. This would keep us in close association with starfighters and play to the strengths that I think we demonstrated in the pursuit of Admiral Trigit and the *Implacable*."

"Well put, Piggy. Face?"

The onetime actor stood. "Well, first I have to admit to a certain dissension in my own group. Lieutenant Janson and Ton Phanan here think that Runt's idea is best. Dia Passik and I both favor Piggy's pirate scheme. But since I was obliged to come up with a tactic, I have.

"Intensive analysis of Zsinj's history suggests that he draws much of his inspiration from the performances of small theatrical companies. I suggest that we pose as a traveling troupe of players performing the sorts of works he seems to have the most affection for."

Confused, Wedge scanned his records of the proposals the group leaders had generated. Face's was on top, but its contents did not match what he was saying.

"I've discovered that Kell has a pleasant tenor singing voice, and Runt is actually an accomplished mime, a skill that few know is widespread on his homeworld of Thakwaa. By integrating modern holographic technology with traditional song-and-dance routines, we could capture the warlord's attention—"

By now the other Wraiths were snickering. Wedge caught Face's eye and glowered. "Perhaps you could give us the set of conclusions you turned in to *me*, Loran?"

Face had the gall to look surprised. "Oh, those. Sorry." He sobered. "I think the *Iron Fist* is of tremendous importance to Warlord Zsinj, not just as a powerful weapons platform but also as a symbol, both of his career and his power. If Warlord Zsinj were more like us than he were like himself, I think he'd launch an expedition deep into the territory governed by Ysanne Isard's successors, make a strike on the Kuat Drive Yards building facilities, and steal the next Super Star Destroyer in production."

Wedge gave him a look of amusement. "That presupposes that Kuat is working on another Super Star Destroyer. They're horribly expensive. And even though they can do an incredible amount of damage, they can be destroyed by a much less expensive enemy force . . . though usually at a tremendous cost of life."

Face nodded. "Correct. But Zsinj doesn't admit anyone is his equal in military intelligence, so he thinks he can keep it intact. And I keep remembering that he, Zsinj, hinted that he was promoting Admiral Trigit to a better position. We all thought maybe he meant captain of the *Iron Fist,* but what if he meant another Super Star Destroyer?"

Phanan spoke up. "Don't forget your goofy ideas that never made it into your final proposal."

Face waved him away, but Wedge asked, "What goofy ideas?"

Face looked unhappy. "Just an idea. Ysanne Isard is alive."

"What?" Wedge looked as stunned as if someone had picked up a chair and broken it over his head.

Ysanne Isard had been the head of Imperial Intelligence when Emperor Palpatine died years ago. She survived Palpatine's successors, a consortium of Palpatine's advisers, and gradually assumed control of the Empire herself—though not in name. Months ago, she had died, killed fleeing the planet Thyferra in a battle-equipped shuttle, shot down by Rogue Squadron's Captain Tycho Celchu.

"Follow me on this," Face said. "Months ago, Ysanne Isard is chased off the world of Coruscant. Actually, she abandons it voluntarily to let the Krytos Plague infect the nonhuman population and lock up all of the New Republic's resources when we occupy Coruscant. But she actually stays on Coruscant for quite some time after she pretended to flee. Eventually she really does leave, goes to Thyferra, takes over there, and is finally wiped out by the Rogues.

"Except—she was never seen climbing into the shuttle she was supposed to be using for escape. Except—it was not particularly intelligent for her to run off in a vehicle slower than the X-wings she had to have suspected would follow her. Except—she'd already shown a tendency to hide out with her head down when she was supposed to have fled. It raises the question: What if she actually wasn't on that shuttle, and was communicating with the Rogues 'chasing' her through a remote-control link?"

Wedge said, "You've got to be wrong. There was no lag time in her transmissions, nothing to suggest she wasn't there."

"A shuttle she'd personally fitted as an Emperor's escape vehicle might have a miniaturized hypercomm system. With instantaneous transmission and reception, there wouldn't *be* any lag time."

"Face, do you believe she's alive?"

Face shook his head. "Sometimes I hope she is. I'd still like to kill her myself. But I believe Captain Celchu actually killed her. Still . . ." He shrugged and resumed his seat.

Wedge gave him an exasperated stare. "Well, here's your punishment for nearly giving me a heart attack. Write this theory up and I'll route it on to the new Thyferran government and to General Cracken at Intelligence. Between them, they should be able to sniff out any other evidence for Iceheart's survival . . . if there is any."

His expression cleared. "All right. As I said, Admiral Ackbar has evaluated these theories and made a decision. He's asking Intelligence to step up any operations involving Kuat Drive Yards to find out if, in fact, they are building a new Super Star Destroyer. But that's low priority and not our concern. For us, he wants to combine both Runt's and Piggy's ideas. We'll be founding our own pirate band, Wraiths, and then assaulting a planetary system that Zsinj is courting—or should be, if he isn't. Officially, we'll be assigned to the *Mon Remonda* with Rogue Squadron; funny, though, the other pilots will never see us in the ship's corridors.

"We have a little reorganization to do to accommodate our new pilots. Flight Officer Donn, you're now Wraith Two, and my wingman."

The pilot with the unruly blond hair smiled. He couldn't have known that the position of Wraith Two, by Wedge's policy, usually went to a raw pilot, one in need of additional instruction or protection.

"Wes, you're now Wraith Three, with Dia Passik, Wraith

Four, your wing." Janson waved at the Twi'lek female, who gave him a grave nod.

"Kell, Runt, you're still Five and Six. Runt, incidentally, is in training to be our new communications specialist. Phanan, Face, still Seven and Eight. I'd hate to break up the best comedy team this side of the janitor's closet."

"I love an understanding commander," Phanan said. "Know where I can get one?"

"Myn Donos, still Nine. Flight Officer Nelprin—can you still hear me back there?— you're his wing, Wraith Ten. Piggy, you're still Wraith Twelve, and Tyria, you're now on his wing as Wraith Eleven. I lead Group One, Face leads Group Two, and Donos leads Group Three. Questions?"

Wedge waited for the inevitable reaction from Kell. Previously, Kell had led Group Two and had been very twitchy whenever Face received recognition that might affect his own—Kell's—position, and now Face had replaced him as group leader.

But Kell looked easy with the new arrangement, which surprised Wedge considerably.

It meant—Wedge wasn't sure. Either Kell was content to let Face have a go at command, or Kell's goals had changed and command was not so high on the list.

Wedge would wait. The truth would come out eventually. "Intelligence gives us a good candidate for our new piratical occupation. The world is called Halmad. It's an Outer Rim world not far from the loose border to what we consider Zsinj-controlled space. It's also a trade center at the hub of several well-traveled trade routes. A century or so back, their mining industry—ground, lunar, and asteroid belt—failed, leaving a number of facilities abandoned there. New Republic Intelligence has a team already in-system to check them out for us; if they haven't found us a base by the time we arrive, they will at least have found us a place from which to stage."

Kell asked, "Do we get the *Night Caller* back? Since we'll be pirating in TIE fighters, I assume we'll have to have something to haul us around when we hit sites out of our home system."

Wedge shook his head. "Not the *Night Caller*. Think about it. Admiral Trigit is destroyed by a covert fighter squadron supported by a Corellian corvette, and then a pirate squadron pops up supported by a Corellian corvette? That would probably set off at least one alarm bell in Zsinj's mind." He gave Kell a grim smile. "No, we'll receive hyperspace transport from an old *Xiytiar*-class transport. Unarmed. Slow. Creaky. Leaky. And instead of having a cargo bay full of your sophisticated metal brackets to hold our fighter craft, we'll be using a few crossbeams and *netting*—so we can quickly switch out X-wings for TIE fighters without having to reconfigure our brackets every time."

Kell sat back, his expression suggesting he'd just swallowed a mouthful of hydraulic fluid.

Phanan's hand shot up. "Do we get new snubfighters?"

Wedge shook his head. "No. No new X-wings for the foreseeable future. We got lucky when we were putting the squadron together; when Rogue Squadron captured Ysanne Isard's facilities on Thyferra, we also seized a number of X-wings she'd been accumulating for various Intelligence missions. That's where four of our snubfighters came from. But the New Republic hasn't had another windfall like that, and Incom is producing new X-wings as slowly and meticulously as ever. So we're stuck with what we have . . . and what we can seize. Dia Passik was transferred with her snubfighter, but we're still four short to make up a full squadron. However, the two TIE fighters we have remaining from the *Implacable* attack, the ones Wes and Piggy were flying, are assigned to us. And part of our assignment involves acquiring new fighter craft for our pirate identities . . . and that means stealing whatever we can get our hands on. From the Imps and from the warlords, that is. Do any of you new pilots have TIE-fighter experience? Simulated or real?"

Both the women raised their hands. Castin Donn looked unhappy that he couldn't follow suit.

"Excellent. Castin, Kell, Phanan, since you three lack X-wings and TIE experience, I recommend you spend time in the TIE-fighter simulators and checking out our small complement of TIE fighters. Once we're at our new station, that is.

For now, you have only a little while to pack and settle your affairs; the transport *Borleias* takes off for Halmad in three hours." He ignored the chorus of groans and cheers. "Dismissed. Phanan, Face, can I see you for a minute?"

As the others trickled out, he asked, "What is the news from what's-her-name, Notsil?"

The two pilots exchanged glances. "Well," said Face, "Lara seemed reassured by what you offered. We helped her put together her application for fighter-pilot training, and both of us and Kell wrote recommendations for her. Face set up an account for her so she could afford some limited HoloNet access to us; we'll leave a router so she can reach us through Sivantlie Base. Things are in motion."

"This had better work . . . or had better produce absolutely no results," Wedge said. "Because if there are any foul-ups, General Cracken will personally feed you, and me, into a food reprocessor."

4

He made no pretense at being fully human. He had probably been born human, but now mechanical limbs—obvious prosthetics, shiny stainless metal arms and legs with crude-looking joints—replaced his original flesh, and his entire upper face was a shiny metal surface with a standard computer interface inset in the center of his forehead.

He made no pretense at being friendly, either. He approached the booth where the big, good-looking businessman drank alone, and with neither threat nor comment he swung the wine bottle he held in his hands and brought it down on the businessman's head.

The bottle shattered, spraying glass and red liquid all over the businessman. The man blinked, stood—demonstrating both a resilience and a physique others in the bar found admirable—and struck the cyborg, a blow that rocked the mostly mechanical man's head and staggered him back into the booth filled with carousing Imperial pilots.

The pilots seated at the aisle shoved the cyborg forward, straight into the businessman's professional-looking right cross. The blow caught the cyborg across the jaw, spinning him around. The cyborg staggered back to fall across the laps of two of the pilots in the booth. His flailing arm caught their glasses and bottles, throwing wine and liquor across everyone.

The pilots shoved him off to the floor and rose.

"Don't do that," the bartender said. But his voice was a plea and he wasn't aiming a weapon. No one paid attention.

Suddenly hard-faced, a formidable group of six, the pilots glowered at the businessman and the cyborg. Their leader, the shortest of them, a dark-haired man with a face craggy enough for tiny snubfighters to fly their famous Trench Run Defense across, said, "You two owe us for a round and two bottles of local press, and we'll take your booth and a hundred extra credits for our trouble."

The businessman gave him a frosty smile. "With a hundred credits I could buy a pilot of your qualifications to lick my boots clean."

"I'm calling the military police," the bartender said.

The pilots surged toward the businessman. The first of them caught a knuckle punch in the solar plexus and dropped like a sackful of tubers. The second one was tripped up as the cyborg grabbed his knee and squeezed; the pilot's shriek was shrill enough to resonate on empty glasses throughout the bar. The other four slammed into the businessman and bore him to the floor.

The bartender punched his emergency code into the comlink and began wailing to the distant listener.

Two minutes later, it was all but over. Two tables had been smashed, their entertained patrons now occupying booths on the other side of the bar. Five pilots and one cyborg lay at intervals across the floor, stretched out in various poses of very uncomfortable rest, often lying among broken glasses and platters of unhygienic appetizers. The businessman and the pilot leader were still standing, the latter glassy-eyed, barely responding to outside stimuli, while the former still occasionally swung ineffectual blows against his stomach. Both were drenched with sweat and booze, staggering with every slight move they made.

Then a half-dozen stormtroopers in the uniforms of military police poured into the bar. Some patrons—those who still had bets going on which of the fighters would win—groaned, but the bartender breathed a sigh of relief.

With calm efficiency, the stormtroopers manacled the eight malefactors' hands behind their backs; the two men still standing put up no fight. Three of the downed pilots could not be brought back to consciousness, but one of the stormtroopers picked up two of them, slinging them with considerable ease over his shoulders, and a second picked up the last stubbornly unconscious pilot. The stormtroopers began to move out.

"Wait," the bartender said. "Where do I sign?"

Two of the stormtroopers exchanged a glance. "Why would you want to sign?" asked one, the ranking officer.

"So I can put in a claim for damages!"

The cyborg sighed. "Oh, just tally up the bill. I'll pay for the damages."

The bartender rocked back, mollified. "Well, all right, then. Come back soon. We appreciate your patronage."

As they swept out through the door, onto a rainy street of Halmad's capital city of Hullis, the ranking officer among the pilots, the one who'd taken so much abuse at the businessman's hands, gave the cyborg a dizzy but appreciative look. "Hey, you're not all bad."

"I just like a good scrap now and then." The cyborg shrugged. Unfortunately for him, the motion put extra pressure on his shackles. They opened and dropped to the muddy ground behind him.

The pilot leader stared. "Hey, what the—"

"Fire," said the stormtrooper leader.

Three of the stormtroopers obliged him. Stun beams hit the pilots' torsos. The pilots dropped into the mud.

The stormtrooper leader looked around. There was no one to see, not much skimmer traffic this rainy evening, no one entering or coming out of the bar. He pulled off his helmet, revealing the features of Wedge Antilles, and took an unencumbered view around. No sign of witnesses. "Let's hustle, people."

The other troopers grabbed the three fallen pilots. They dragged and carried their prisoners around the corner of the building, then around behind, where their skimmer awaited in the darkness of a fallow field. It was no military skimmer, just a medium cargo carrier with a deep bed.

While the others dumped the pilots into the rear and draped blankets and netting across them, Wedge stripped off his stormtrooper armor and threw it in after them. "Good work, Tainer, Phanan. Either of you hurt?"

Kell shook his head and flexed, popping his unsealed manacles loose. "This suit's probably a loss."

Phanan waggled his head. "Kell didn't do me any harm, but the bottle one of them hit my head with wasn't fake glass like mine was. It didn't even break. I hear ringing."

"Sounds like a mild concussion. See our doctor about it."

"Oh, I'm too important a doctor to see anyone as lowly as myself."

Wedge waved at one of the ersatz stormtroopers. "Face, grab these pilots' wallets, money pouches, whatever they're carrying. I want every credit they have, hard currency only. How much damage did you two jokers do?"

Kell and Phanan looked at one another.

"Maybe a hundred," Kell said. "Counting everything."

"All right," Wedge said. "If these pilots' personal fortunes don't add up to a hundred and fifty, we'll make up the difference ourselves. Face, run the credits in to the bartender. Tell him the cyborg paid off, instant compensation for the damage, so sorry, he's a miserable old drunk whose only entertainment is causing trouble at bars."

"Hey," said Phanan. "I resent the use of the word *miserable*."

"Then get back here fast. We take off in three minutes."

Wedge and Janson, still in stormtrooper armor but with their helmets off, lay atop a hill overlooking the nearby Imperial base. The optics Wedge held before his face made greenish daylight of the night. "Same as last night and the night before. I make four TIE fighters at the ready scramble-pad, under the watchful eye of half a stormtrooper squadron."

"Not that we care," Janson said.

"Not that we want *those* starfighters," Wedge corrected him. "But we may have to deal with them on the way out. Anything coming up the road?"

Janson cast a negligent eye the other way. Down at the

base of the hill to his left, the other Wraiths, their prisoners, and their cargo skimmer waited. Down to the right was the main road into the base. "A distant set of lights," he said. "Oncoming. Probably just another staff skimmer carrying an officer home after a night on the town."

"Castin Donn laid enough money down at enough cantinas, we're bound to get what we want."

"You may be right. That thing's not maneuvering like a staff skimmer. It's big and sluggish."

Wedge twisted to look at the oncoming vehicle through his optics. "Imperial Military Police. Signal Runt."

Janson waved a handheld light down at the other Wraiths, flicking its beam three times across them. This close to an Imperial base, Wedge preferred they not use comlinks, whose transmissions, even if coded or extremely short, might be noticed. At the base of the hill, Runt would now be using a portable scanner on the distant vehicle. . . .

From the Wraiths' position came an answering blink of light, a single pulse.

"Runt signals yes. It's loaded with personnel," Janson said. "Move out."

Wedge and Janson scrambled down the side of the hill, not directly toward the other Wraiths, but angling toward the right, an intercept course. By the time they reached the base of the hill—with Janson's armor now somewhat battered by a fall he'd taken during his descent—the other Wraiths were almost to the road.

Wedge and Janson caught up to them and put their helmets back on.

"Snap it up," Wedge said, "march formation. Left foot, right foot."

And the Wraiths managed something like a proper formation in spite of the loads they carried.

Runt carried one of the unconscious pilots over his shoulder, moving without difficulty. The Gamorrean Piggy could also have carried one of the pilots with fair ease, but could never have worn one of the sets of stormtrooper armor; he remained with the skimmer. Kell, now suited up as a stormtrooper, and Dia dragged an unconscious pilot between them;

they held the pilot's arms over their shoulders so the man remained upright. Phanan, also in a set of stormtrooper armor, and Face also dragged one of the pilots, as did Castin and Shalla, with Donos and Tyria dragging the fifth. The sixth pilot, the ranking officer among them, remained with Piggy.

It was several hundred meters to the gate into the base, but if Wedge calculated correctly, they wouldn't have to walk the entire distance.

They heard the humming of the heavy skimmer behind them and Wedge turned to look. It was a large model, nearly identical to the one that had been part of the trap on Coruscant: It had an enclosure over the bed, and only the pilot and the guard assigned to his protection were exposed to the elements. On the side was painted the stooping bird-of-prey insignia of Victory Base; over that design were the crossed batons of the base's military police.

The skimmer pulled alongside Wedge's troop of ersatz stormtroopers and prisoners. Its pilot called, "What happened to you?"

"Skimmer broke down," Wedge said. "Repulsorlift failure in the energy transference array."

"Care for a lift?"

"I'd put you up for a Hero of the Empire medal."

The pilot tapped a button and a door in the rear enclosure opened; its hinge was at the bottom, allowing it to open down into a ramp. Wedge peered inside. The spacious enclosure held four stormtroopers and another pair of prisoners in the uniforms of Imperial maintenance personnel. Both prisoners were awake, though apparently anesthetized by alcohol.

Wedge's people hauled their unconscious prisoners up the ramp and settled them down on the padded benches against the enclosure walls. Wedge, at the rear of the line, stayed tense. The stormtrooper armor the Wraiths wore—seized from prisoners during some of the countless clashes the Alliance had had with the Empire and brought as part of the squadron's gear—was authentic enough, but the military-police insignia the Wraiths had meticulously painted on the armor might not pass close inspection. Also, the officer in charge of these real military police should, if he kept strictly to procedure, demand to see Wedge's papers, and the forgeries Castin had put together . . . well, Wedge just didn't know the new pilot well enough to rely unquestioningly on the man's work as he'd come to do with Grinder, the squadron's former computer expert.

But the Wraiths all shuffled into the enclosed bed of the skimmer, Wedge followed, the door closed behind him, and the vehicle lurched into motion, all without an unwelcome demand for papers. Wedge smiled. If security was lax here, it might be just as lax within the base.

"Hey, that's Lieutenant Cothron," one of the real stormtroopers said.

Face nodded. "He's a pretty belligerent drunk."

"Nice guy the rest of the time, though."

"Oh, yeah."

"Ever play sabacc with him?"

"Sure, he took me for a week's pay once."

"You're joking. He's the worst player I ever saw."

There was the slightest of delays in Face's response as he adjusted his story in light of new information. "No, I think *I'm* the worst."

"Really? You up for a game tonight?"

"No, I've learned my lesson."

The stormtrooper settled back, his posture one of disappointment.

Moments later, the skimmer slowed. Wedge heard a verbal exchange between the pilot and what must have been the gate guards, but he couldn't make out the words. Then they were in motion again.

It was a long minute before they slowed once more. Then the skimmer's repulsorlift depowered and the vehicle settled to a hard surface.

The door beside Wedge opened. They appeared to be in a vehicle hangar, and a few steps away was a table where a uniformed officer and another pair of stormtroopers waited. The officer, a man with graying hair and hard lines to his face, looked bored and irritable. "Move them out. It's time for instant justice."

Wedge waved the real stormtroopers and their prisoners to proceed while his people got their unconscious prisoners up.

Then the Wraiths moved out. Wedge was the last one out of the vehicle.

"Papers," said the officer in charge. Wedge tensed. But the stormtrooper he addressed handed him standard identity cards bearing the likenesses of the prisoners in his charge. Wedge glanced at Face, who discreetly held up the handful of identity cards taken from their own prisoners. Wedge turned away again.

The officer looked over the identity cards. "Facts?"

The stormtrooper in charge said, "Drunk and disorderly at Ola's."

The officer grimaced. "You two idiots ought to find a better class of drinking establishment. Charges?"

The stormtrooper in charge shook his head, the motion exaggerated by his helmet. "None."

"Well, that's not too bad." The officer glanced up at the two prisoners. "You two are confined to base for six days."

The prisoners looked relieved.

"That's three days starting now," the officer continued, "and three days starting next payday." He ignored their expressions of dismay and gestured for them to be on their way. "Next."

Wedge stepped up. He reached over without looking. Face put the identity cards in his hand and he presented them to the officer. "Drunk and disorderly at Rojio's. Brawling with civilians."

The officer gave him an I-don't-want-to-believe-you look. "They're all unconscious. They lost to civilians?"

"Yes, sir."

"How many?"

"Two."

The officer looked pained. "Five of them against two civilians, and they're too drunk to make a good accounting of themselves. They'll pay for letting the unit down." He frowned. "Five. Say, these are Captain Wanatte's drinking buddies. Where's the captain?"

Face spoke up: "Before he passed out the last time, Lieutenant Cothron said the captain had found some companionship for the evening."

"Ah. Well, then. Let's see the damages."

Wedge said, "One of the civilians paid for the damages before we dropped them off with the city authorities."

"Commendable. All right. I think these five will be improved by doing a few days of cleanup and breakdown work for the next morale event. Get 'em to their quarters."

Wedge saluted smartly and headed off in the direction the other stormtroopers had taken to leave the hangar. He heard the Wraiths fall in step behind him and the dragging noise of their prisoners' boots scraping against the duracrete. Then he heard the skimmer's engines start up again.

He breathed a sigh of relief. The pilot of the skimmer hadn't noticed that eleven footsore stormtroopers had boarded the skimmer, but only ten had emerged. Janson had taken Shalla's place and was working with Castin to carry a pilot. Now, if this base followed standard Imperial procedure, that pilot would take this skimmer back to the military police motor pool.

Then it would be up to Shalla. She was still in the skimmer's enclosure, and her job was to prevent the pilot and his guard from talking to anybody.

Her *first* job. She had other things to do as well. Wedge was reluctant to assign so much responsibility in a commando mission to a newcomer to the squadron, but Kell had spoken in such glowing terms of the Nelprin family's formidable skills that he'd decided to go ahead with this approach.

Outside the hangar, he took a moment to get his bearings, and silently cursed the restricted field of vision afforded by stormtrooper helmets; lacking peripheral vision, he had to turn in a slow, complete circle to acquire a mental picture of his surroundings. He had a fair idea of the base layout from the reconnaissance they'd done on the hilltop, but not an idea of where in the base they now were. When he had his bearings, he headed straight toward the group of dome-topped buildings he'd earlier decided were officers' quarters.

They'd never make it there, of course. They'd dump the unconscious pilots in the first dark alley or trench they found and go about their mission.

Lara Notsil, originally Gara Petothel, flinched as pair after pair of TIE fighters broke formation and dove, their engines screaming, toward her and her wingmates. *A good mannerism, flinching,* she decided. *If they're observing me, they'll log it.*

Her wing leader's voice came over the comm unit: "Gold One to Gold Squadron. Break by pairs and engage."

Lara keyed her own comm unit. "Gold Seven?"

"I'm your wing, Eight."

She rolled to starboard, getting clear of the main formation of X-wings, and saw other paired fighters also breaking off.

Then the first blasts of green Imperial laser fire fell among them. Lara's X-wing was rocked by a stern hit; her aft shields were knocked partway down and she reinforced them with energy from her forward shields. The pair of TIE fighters raining laser fire down on both her and Gold Seven slid neatly into killing position behind them.

"Dive for cover, Seven," Lara said, and nosed the stick forward. The terrain below, a sprawling city in ruins, grew larger. She and Gold Seven dropped into a debris-littered street, flying lower than the tops of the surrounding buildings, but their pursuers never lost sight of them and stayed tucked behind. Lara's snubfighter was hit by another pair of laser blasts and its aft section slewed slightly to port; she corrected with a deft application of etheric rudder.

Up ahead, the road forked left and right. She knew from seeing the area from above that the two forks turned toward one another farther on, rejoining after only a couple of kilometers. That should have been her tactic: send Gold Seven to starboard while she went to port, then fire upon Seven's pursuer while Seven fired upon hers once the roads rejoined.

But that would probably have worked. And that wasn't what she was here for.

"Seven, at the big blue building, hard to port."

"I read you." Seven's voice sounded a bit worried.

Lara suited action to words. As the X-wings came alongside what had once been a warehouse of tremendous size, painted an eye-hurting cyan, but was now a hollowed, burned wreck of a building with scorch marks surrounding blast holes in the walls, she executed a smart portward turn down a street that ran at right angles to the one over which they'd been flying. She rotated ninety degrees leftward, so the street was to her left and one row of buildings was beneath her keel.

The sharpness of the angle was more than the X-wing's inertial compensator could bear; she felt weight again, settling into her seat, as the snubfighter turned through the tightest portion of her maneuver.

There was a sharp metal shriek as her keel scraped along one of the building facades; her X-wing lurched. The snubfighter's shields were no protection against such a graze. She glanced at her diagnostics board, looking for the telltale red glows of system failures.

Behind her, the sky lit up. The sound and shock wave of an explosion rocked her X-wing. And the blue dot representing Gold Seven disappeared from her sensor board.

Lara grimaced. Gold Seven didn't have the skill to manage a turn like that. Lara had known this, had counted on it, but it wouldn't do for her observers to see a smile of satisfaction cross her face. Knowing she would get no answer, she keyed her comm unit. "Seven? Gold Seven, come in."

Behind her, the two TIE fighters, having no trouble with the sharp turn into this side street, came screaming through the smoke cloud that was what was left of Gold Seven. As soon as they cleared the smoke, they opened fire again.

Lara felt her aft section shudder. It slewed again. Lara deliberately overcorrected and let an expression of shock cross her face as she veered into the side of a building. She had just enough time to read the words WELCOME TO MOFFICE'S GROCERS before impact—

Or lack of impact. There was no sharp blow, no deceleration, just the abrupt dimming of all cockpit lights to nothingness. Then the canopy opened above her.

Captain Sormic—short, bald, human, usually apoplectic, with a face like pink clay molded into a fair approximation of human features—stood outside the simulator, glaring at her. "Candidate Notsil. Would you explain, for the benefit of the class, just what you were trying to accomplish with that last maneuver?"

Lara let a note of uncertainty creep into her voice. "I was trying to regain control—"

"Not that. The suicide turn down the side street."

"Oh. Uh, I was trying to shake the TIE-fighter pursuit—"

"Right. You presumed that a pair of novice pilots could outmaneuver more experienced pilots in more agile spacecraft in clear air. Correct?"

"Well, uh—"

"Say, 'Correct, Captain.' "

"Correct, Captain." Lara kept an expression of distress on her face.

"And you got yourself and your wingmate killed."

"Correct, Captain."

"Candidate Lussatte, is that the tactic you would have chosen?"

Lara glanced at her wingmate, who was still in the next simulator over. The Sullustan female gave Lara a look of apology. "No, Captain."

"What would you have done?"

"I would have fired a proton torpedo—"

"The Imperial fliers were already behind you, Lussatte."

Lara saw Lussatte take a deep breath. "Yes, Captain. Let me explain. I figure I can't outfly the Imps. I figure that if I make a rapid deceleration, they'll make an even more rapid one, because they're better fliers in more maneuverable craft. But if I drop a torp about a city block up, that gives me a smoke cloud to fly through and a few moments where they can't see me. If I have the impact site visualized well enough, I can risk a turn down a side street, throw them off, maybe get turned around so I can get them under my guns before they're on me again."

Captain Sormic paused, then gave her a brief nod. "Pay attention to what she just said, class. It would give her a one-in-four, maybe one-in-two chance of surviving the next ten seconds and perhaps bagging one of the TIE fighters. Which is a much better chance than she had following Deadstick Notsil here. Dismissed."

Pilot candidates rose from the classroom seats; others climbed from the simulators. Lara didn't rise; Captain Sormic still stood outside her simulator, blocking her exit.

He turned back to face her, and his expression was suddenly sympathetic. He dropped his voice nearly to a whisper. "Candidate Notsil, you earn great scores in astronautics and communications. Just say the word and I'll transfer you over to officer training in one of those divisions. You have a tremendous career ahead of you as a technical specialist on a capital ship's bridge."

"No, sir. I'm going to be a pilot."

"It's not as though you'll be washing out. It's just a transfer. And you'll be a real asset to the Alliance there."

"No, sir. *I'm going to be a pilot.*"

His face hardened. "Then I have one piece of advice for you."

"Yes, sir?"

"You think about Candidate Lussatte and anyone else you might have made friends with. You think about how you're going to feel if you get them killed for real. Trust me, the kind of pilot you're shaping into, it's going to happen. And that's not the worst thing that could happen to you. The worst thing would be for you to *survive* a bad decision that kills everybody you care about." He turned away and followed the last departing pilot candidates from the room.

Lara sagged into the simulator seat. Only part of her dejection was simulated. It felt bad to be considered such a screwup when she was capable of doing so much better.

She shouldn't even care what these Rebels thought; they were her enemies. But her fellow candidates had such naive enthusiasm, such a light of life within them, that it was growing increasingly hard not to like them.

She felt a little tickle at the back of her neck. She turned to look through the simulator's rear viewport.

At the back of the classroom, a man in an Alliance uniform was turning away, heading toward the room's rear exit. From his height and build, she recognized him as Colonel Repness.

When had he come into the classroom? Had he been watching her in the moments after her exchange with Captain Sormic? She watched until he was gone, until she was alone in the room.

She checked her chrono. There were no classes scheduled

in this room for an hour. She pulled up the instrument panel before her and did a little bit of deft rewiring, a bit of electronic trickery at which she was becoming quite adept. Then she clicked the panel back into place and manually pulled the canopy back down.

When she hit the button that, on a real X-wing, would initiate an emergency restart, the simulator came back online. But now it would not transmit its results and recordings to the training facility's central computers. Whatever she accomplished here would remain her secret.

The world with the ruined city came into view again, and once more she was surrounded by a squadron of X-wings.

5

Shalla tried to interpret every sway, every course change taken by the skimmer in whose enclosed bed she rode. Eventually the vehicle *had* to return to a motor pool or other vehicle hangar. Eventually she'd be able to begin her portion of the mission . . . a portion she had to accomplish alone.

The vehicle went through a protracted right turn, then slowed and settled to the ground with an unmusical metallic clang. Shalla raised her blaster rifle to cover the door. Some stormtroopers were thorough and efficient enough to police their vehicles; others weren't.

Hers apparently fell in the latter category. The door remained resolutely closed. Then the lights went out.

She heard, from outside the skimmer, a man's laughter. She tensed. But the laughter was the type that came in response to a joke, not malicious laughter directed at a trapped enemy. When she heard the heavy footsteps of stormtrooper composite armor falling on duracrete, she relaxed.

She gave it another minute. She wanted the stormtroopers to be well away from the skimmer, but couldn't afford them too much time to realize that something was wrong. Then she rose, used her glow rod to find the door switch, and pressed the switch.

Nothing, not even a beep. It had been deactivated with the rest of the power to the skimmer's enclosure. She swore to herself, but it was only a minor inconvenience.

She switched off her helmet comlink. She took off her stormtrooper helmet and spent a couple of minutes carefully extracting the comm gear inside it, then detached the miniature power pack from the gear. It took another couple of minutes to remove the door-switch cover and wire the power pack into it. Then she put the now comm-free helmet on again and took up her rifle.

This time, the door opened smartly. Outside was the slab-like side of an identical skimmer just barely far enough away to let this skimmer's door descend as a ramp. When Shalla peered out, to the right she saw another row of skimmers of various types, some small and sporty, and the motor-pool wall beyond; to her left was open duracrete and then closed hangar-style doors of the motor-pool building. Voices reached her; she couldn't make out the words, but they were male, two or three at least, raised in laughter and amused comment. They came from the rear of the motor-pool building. She thought she also heard a man's voice, in conspicuous speech, from the front.

So far, so good. She stepped out, alert to trouble, and hit the button to close the door again. But the ramp raised only halfway up, then made a whining noise and stopped. It slowly began to sag back toward the duracrete floor.

She got under it and lifted. The power pack from her helmet was obviously not up to powering door machinery. By sheer strength she got the door lifted back into place. Though it did not lock, it fit snugly and would look normal to casual inspection.

Now, three problems to solve: two groups of Imperial workers or stormtroopers, plus whatever security was installed within the motor-pool building. She looked around for the places, often at corners and on the metal beams supporting the curved ceiling, where sensors tended to be set up.

Nothing. She breathed a sigh of relief. Skimmers weren't valuable enough to this base to require constant surveillance. One problem down. She walked forward, toward the source of the droning speech, and wished she had Tyria's aptitude for near-silent movement.

.   .   .

The Wraiths kept themselves flat against the exterior wall of the hangar, deep in the darkest shadow cast by the building.

Wedge, one man back from the building's front corner, suppressed a snort. The glossy white stormtrooper armor they were wearing practically glowed in the dark. Even in deep shadow they would be impossible to miss if a passerby glanced in their direction. Still, old habits of stealth died hard, and Wedge didn't want them to die at all.

Janson, ahead of him, helmet off, turned back and held up two fingers, then shook his head. Two guards on the front of the building, and they weren't going to be easy pickings. Wedge traded places with him and took off his own helmet, luxuriated for a moment in the sensation of air moving once again on his face, and hazarded a peek.

The front of the hangar was well lit by two overhead sources of light, both attached to the building's front wall. The center of the wall was dominated by a large sliding door in two sections; one section would slide right, the other left. The duracrete leading up to the door was decorated with many thin scorch marks, sign of numberless too-hasty departures by TIE fighters shooting out of the hangar and angling immediately for the sky. That suggested the pilots on-base considered themselves hotshots and had a commander who encouraged such behavior, also not a good thing for the Wraiths.

On either side of the door, perhaps twenty meters apart, were guards in stormtrooper armor. Their stances were angled in toward the door, and each had the other plus most of the front of the building in sight. They might have been chatting over a private channel on their helmet comlinks, but otherwise they were very much on duty.

Wedge dismissed the simplest of tactics for such situations, the make-a-noise-and-one-of-them-will-come gambit. Guards like these, professionally on duty even when out of sight of their officers and fellows, would certainly investigate, but first they'd call in the anomaly. If the investigating guard didn't report back continuously to his fellow, the other one would call that fact in, too. Within moments the place would be swarming with stormtroopers. Wedge and the Wraiths needed some considerable uninterrupted time with the vehicles inside— perhaps as much as half an hour.

There was another door on the building front, immediately left of the leftmost guard, but it was securely shut and looked like an armored door—quite defensible if someone inside wanted to make a stand of it.

Wedge switched places with Janson again and let the man act as guard. In a whisper, he explained the situation to the others and asked, "Ideas?"

Castin said, "I might be able to slice into the base's main computer and have them relieved of duty; we just march two of us in and dismiss them or blast them."

Wedge considered it. "That could work, but you'd have to maintain the computer breach or execute another one just a few minutes later when we sort out our escape vector."

"True."

Dia said, "I vote we wait until we can be sure there's no cross traffic nearby and no one observing them—"

"Which means waiting until we also know they're not in communication with someone else over their headsets," Kell said.

"—and just step out and shoot them. Two shooters, no waiting. Run out, grab them and haul them back beside the building, substitute a couple of us for them. Then take as long as we need to get their access keys and codes and go in."

Wedge shook his head. "Sounds too simple." Then he reconsidered. "On the other hand, that's probably a virtue. All right, we'll do it that way. But first, Runt, can you find out whether those two are broadcasting? Search nonstandard frequencies in the Imperial ranges and look for low-powered signals; if they're just chatting, they're not going to be on the usual bands."

Runt nodded and, from a belt pouch, brought out the field dispatcher's comlink that was among the latest toys the New Republic had given him when he volunteered to be the squadron's new communications specialist. The item looked like a slightly bulkier datapad. It had nowhere near the range of features of the field communications unit their former comm specialist,

Jasmin Ackbar, used to carry, but it was the biggest comm unit they could carry inconspicuously while in stormtrooper armor.

Runt tapped through a series of functions, grew impatient with the device, and traded places with Wes. There, he could set the device on the ground and protrude its nose just beyond the building corner. Finally he nodded. "We have it," he whispered back at the others. "Their signal sounds like dispatch information, but it is confusing. Set your comlinks to oh-three-oh-seven-four if you want to hear."

Wedge did so, and immediately picked up the two guards' traffic.

One of them, his voice a mellow bass, said, "Light assault vehicle twelve to block alpha two."

The other, whose hoarse voice probably started in the baritone range, replied, "TIE four to block delta sixteen."

"That's outside your range."

"It is not."

"So you're crossing through the plasma wall and exploding? Nice of you to concede a piece that way."

"Uh . . . make that TIE four to block delta twelve."

"Heavy emplacement one fires on TIE four. Scratch TIE four."

"Damn. Target-paint heavy emplacement one."

Wedge switched off the channel and looked at the others. "Anyone recognize that traffic?"

Dia nodded. Wedge imagined that she had to be quite uncomfortable with her brain tails stuffed up in her stormtrooper helmet, but she hadn't made a noise of complaint. She said, "It's called Quadrant. It's a game out of the Imperial Academy. An old game, but it has recently become all the rage."

Wedge asked, "Runt, is there a data transmission accompanying that vocal signal?"

Runt shook his head.

Wedge snorted. "They're playing just by visualization. Wonderful. We get the hangar guarded by intellectuals. All right, here's how we play *our* game. Wes, Donos, you're our shooters. Wes, march around to the far front corner and situate yourself. We're not going to use a comlink signal—it might be picked up. We'll time it. You two set your blasters to stun. Sync your chronos and fire at three minutes from sync . . . unless you hear or see anything anomalous, in which case you duck under cover and try again at six minutes. If no opportunity presents itself by six minutes, scrub the mission and get back here. Tainer, you go with Wes to haul off the other guard; Phanan, you take the place of the other guard. Runt, at this end you'll haul off the unconscious guard; Face, you'll take his place."

It was a long three minutes. Halfway through it, a flatbed skimmer hauling two stormtroopers and some sort of laser artillery piece cruised by the hangar. Wedge and the others flattened themselves against the building wall, but the skimmer's occupants didn't even glance in their direction.

Wedge saw Donos keeping a close eye on his chrono. At twenty seconds of three minutes, Donos pulled his helmet off. At fifteen seconds, he checked his blaster rifle to make sure it was switched to stun and ready to fire. At ten seconds, he peeked around the corner, and did so again at five seconds. Then, precisely on cue, he stepped around the corner.

The sound of the stun blast was impossibly loud; Wedge was sure it could be heard off in the city of Hullis. Wedge stayed flat against the wall while Runt and Face ran past him. Only then did he peek around the corner, his own blaster ready in case his squadmates needed cover.

Runt almost tripped as he skidded to a halt over the unconscious form of his target; he picked the man up with inhuman ease, slung him over his shoulder, and came charging back toward Wedge. Beyond him, Kell arrived from the far corner, repeated his action with less speed and less pure strength, but was still swift. He arrived mere seconds behind Runt, his unconscious cargo bouncing painfully across his shoulder.

Now there were just two guards in front of the hangar, angled toward one another, at attention. Wedge checked his chrono. Fifteen seconds had passed, and the world was, cosmetically at least, the same as it had been at the start of those brief seconds.

"Castin," he said.

"I'm way ahead of you," his computer and security expert informed him. "Helmets off, no traffic from their control, I'm checking now for their orders and passcards. No passcards. That means a transmitted or spoken password. Let's hope it's transmitted. Hmm . . ."

Shalla stayed in a crouch behind a self-powered tool cart. Not four steps away was the doorway into the motor-pool office. Two stormtroopers—she suspected they were the ones who'd been in charge of the vehicle she'd ridden in—were within, one seated, both with helmets off. One, tall and fair-skinned, stood by the door, holding a glass with blue liquid on the inside and condensation on the outside. The other, apparently of average height and with skin as dark as Shalla's, was seated at the main terminal, dictating in a bored tone. Shalla could catch most of his words. It sounded like a routine report, which made him the ranking officer. ". . . without struggle. No charges expended. Net expenditure: skimmer fuel, total of seventy-eight klicks."

The other said something Shalla didn't catch. The seated man nodded, then continued, "On return, about half a klick from base, stopped to offer aid to patrol of Sergeant—what was his name?"

The other one shrugged.

"I'll put a placeholder there for now. Sergeant Placeholder, whose skimmer had broken down; gave him, his squadron, and his prisoners, including Lieutenant Cothron, transportation to base. Additional expenditure: fuel of hauling mass of five extra prisoners and ten additional stormtroopers—"

"Eleven," said the other man.

"Ten." The seated man thought about it. "Well, you were paying attention and I wasn't. Eleven additional stormtroopers, distance of two kilometers." He frowned, then shook his head. "End of report. Let me go through and edit out redundancies and program that placeholder to fetch the name of that squad leader, and we're done for the night." But he didn't reach for the keyboard yet. "You're sure about the eleven thing."

"I'm sure."

Shalla stood and walked, as confidently as though she were the base commander, to the door. She shouldered aside the man standing there and tapped the door switch. The office door dropped into place with the disconcerting suddenness of Imperial engineering.

Both men looked at her. The man she'd shoved aside said, "You know, it's been a long time since I taught a nerf-herder like you some manners."

"It's going to be a while longer," she said, and swung the butt of her blaster into his jaw. The man dropped, splashing his glass of blue ale across the floor.

The ranking officer was halfway out of his seat before she shot him. The blaster shot took him in the chest, burning through the armor and dropping him to the floor.

She froze. She thought she had set the weapon to stun.

Then she was hit from the side as her first target slammed into her, barely slowed by the blow she'd dealt him. His rush propelled her and bent her sideways over a desk. If not for her armor, she'd have been impaled on the collection of trays, spikes, and knickknacks littering its surface; instead, the force with which she hit the top of the desk smashed them flat.

Instead of struggling to get free, instead of wrestling with him for control of her blaster, which his big hand now gripped, she braced herself with a free hand on one edge of the desk, extended one leg as far as she could, and then swept with it with all her strength. Her kick caught her assailant behind his knees and knocked his legs out from under him. He crashed to the floor, dragging her on top of him.

With his free hand, he reached for her throat. She abandoned her grip on her blaster, swept aside his hand, and, her striking hand formed into the flattest, tightest fist she could manage, struck at his throat.

Her blow was hard and true. She felt his windpipe give way under it. Her opponent's eyes grew wide in sudden shock and he, too, released her blaster, clutching at his throat with both hands.

She grabbed her weapon and stood away from him to watch him die. He made strangling noises as he tried to draw breath through a channel no longer capable of conveying it. He cast an imploring look her way, but she shook her head; this injury was beyond anything she could repair.

A sudden wave of trembling swept her. She knew it wasn't all the aftereffects of adrenaline. Two men dead because she'd fouled up. Killing didn't bother her unduly; it was the act required of a warrior in wartime. But killing because of a lapse in judgment . . . well, her father would not be proud of her.

She shook her head, willing away the unwanted vision of the old man's stern features, and tried to force the trembling to stop. She stepped around the dying stormtrooper and hit the light switch on the wall. Now the other hangar residents, if they looked over, would see a dark and presumably unoccupied office.

She made a quick checklist of things to do, and found that it had lengthened considerably because of her mistake. Move the two bodies into the bed of the skimmer she'd come in on. Clean up this office so the next person in didn't wonder about the spilled fluid and ravaged desk. File that stormtrooper's report. Repair her helmet comm system with components from one of these troopers' helmets. Choose a skimmer, perhaps the one she came in on, mark it out of service if possible, disconnect its comm system so that it couldn't be used to trace the skimmer or override its controls. And then stand by. All within hearing of the men working, or playing cards, or doing whatever they were doing at the back of the motor-pool building . . . unless she chose to assault them, too.

She sighed. It was going to be a long several hours' work . . . packed neatly into half an hour or less of available time.

It took Castin another agonizing five-minute wait before he cracked the guards' code. One of the two guards had thirty-two classic Quadrant games recorded on his datapad—every move the games' master-level players had made, plus commentary by analysts who were far too serious about the game. Thirty-two was also, Castin pointed out, the number of days in the local monthly calendar. He transmitted the name of the match whose number corresponded to the day of the month, and the front personnel door opened right up.

Wraith Squadron marched into the hangar in formation . . . a formation they lost as soon as they saw the hangar's contents. "Boss," Tainer said, "we have hit the jackpot."

Wedge was, for once, grateful for the stormtrooper helmet. It concealed his openmouthed surprise.

In the hangar was not a complement of TIE fighters, but eight far more formidable, far faster TIE interceptors.

Wedge took a moment to find his voice. "Even better. It's the pirate's life for us, and these are better pirate vehicles. Come on, people, Phase Three, snap it up."

Castin found the hangar's main computer terminal at the back of the building. He brought up the main menu and began looking at what was available to him. The others, once they were sure that the roof-mounted holocams observing the hangar were positioned to view only the vehicles, clustered around him.

Castin leaned back from his keyboard. "Good news and bad news, Commander."

"Let's hear it."

"I can get into this pretty easily, do everything I'm supposed to do from here."

"But?"

"But, security seems to be based on flag counting. For every anomaly in routine the computer registers a marker, or flag, that it keeps track of. When flags grow too numerous at any one site, the computer raises an alarm. It might send a routine query, in which case an incorrect response would raise more flags; it might just send investigators out. If this system works like other, similar Imperial systems, flags have greater or lesser 'weight' depending on just how anomalous they are. For example, a storage-room door being unlocked at the wrong time will raise a little flag, while the door into a hangar full of valuable interceptors being unlocked at the wrong time will raise a big one."

Wedge nodded. "Have we dropped any flags yet?"

"Probably not. We did open a door, but the guards outside

have to have regular access to the refresher, so I doubt that's a flag."

"Very well." Wedge considered. They had to ready six of the interceptors for departure, disconnect any tracer comm units functioning within them, sabotage the other two vehicles and perhaps the hangar, exit the hangar, and cover the separate escapes of the interceptor hijackers and the Wraiths who would be departing on foot. "I assume, then, that a change in maintenance schedules would raise a smaller flag than the holocams observing a bunch of anomalous pirates moving around their hangar."

"That's a fair assumption."

"Then get into the base scheduler. Forge a request for immediate maintenance of this hangar's interceptors. Timestamp it an hour or so ago. Assign it to a fictitious work crew, or, if you can get into the personnel listings, a crew that's off-duty. Follow this up with an acknowledgment of the arrival of the work crew a few minutes ago. Then do the same thing with a request for servicing of the hangar's holocam system. Timestamp that one earlier today, lower priority, also with an acknowledgement of arrival in the last few minutes."

Castin managed the task within a few minutes, then switched off the hangar holocams. The Wraiths got to work.

Castin stayed at the computer terminal and began working on their escape distraction.

Wedge, Janson, Kell, Runt, and Dia checked out the eight interceptors. All but Runt had some experience flying TIE fighters; Runt, as communications specialist, used what gear he had to find and disable slave circuitry that might enable the base commanders to seize control of the interceptors remotely, then disabled automatic tracer systems built into the comm units.

Tyria and Donos had what the others enviously referred to as "vandalism duty." With the hangar mechanics' own industrial cutters, metal-shearing tools utilizing a tight, focused form of the same destructive energy that made blasters formidable weapons, they burned messages across the interior walls of the hangar: HAWK-BATS NEEDED THESE MORE THAN YOU! KNEEL TO THE HAWK-BATS, WORMS. GET OUT OR BE SORRY; THIS PLANET IS

NOW OUR PROPERTY. Then there were some choice epithets, and Donos's fairly artistic rendering of a hawk-bat, one of the tenacious flying predators of the duracrete canyons of Coruscant. Tyria added some creative misspellings to her efforts.

When they were done, they looked over their handiwork. Donos nodded. "Pretty close to the work of ego-ridden, semi-literate pirates," he decided.

Tyria smiled. "As a former counterinsurgent, are you offended?"

He managed a wry grin. But he was saved from answering by a sound—a warning pop across the comm channel the Wraiths were using.

All the Wraiths stopped what they were doing and either donned their helmets again or held pocket comms up to listen.

Face's voice came across in a whisper. "Skimmer full of stormtroopers approaching. Not a hostile attitude, but they're coming right here."

Wedge replied, "Stay loose. Keep us informed." He looked among the Wraiths. "Tyria, Donos, get on the door. Be prepared to support Face and Phanan. The rest of you, what's our status?"

Kell answered, "Five interceptors prepped, Runt and I are on the last, no work yet on the two we were going to sabotage."

"Don't worry about the sabotage. If we're pressed for time, we'll just blast them on our way—"

Phanan's voice came in over the comm: "It's shift change. They're supposed to drop off two and take us away. Face is talking to them. He's been listening to those Quadrant recordings and knows the guy's voice. But—it's not going well—"

The next sound was the scream of blasters from outside. Blasters, shouts, armored bodies hitting the duracrete.

6

Face had tried to be reasonable. "We're ready to go, Lieutenant. But our packs are inside. Permission to go inside and retrieve our packs."

The stormtrooper seated next to the skimmer pilot sounded contemptuous. "What idiot let you bring unauthorized gear out on a normal sentry watch?"

Tactic: When asked for information you don't have, try to present the asker with a variable he can define himself. Face said, "The new one, sir. What's-his-name."

"Balawan?"

"That's him, sir."

"Well, he's an idiot. But sharing some kitchen duty with you two might smarten you all up. All right, you can get your unauthorized gear. First, let's finish this." The officer turned to look at the bed of his skimmer; he nodded. Two stormtroopers stepped out. They stood before Face and Phanan in the same stance of attention. Face said, "I relieve you of this post."

Face swore to himself. That was a nonstandard phrase. *Tactic: When obliged to participate in a ritual you know nothing about, provide a reason and grab all the sympathy you can.* Face said, "I—" And then he coughed, a deep, racking cough that shook him. The coughs continued and bent him nearly double. Still, he half straightened several times, saluting all the while, the very picture of a man fighting to do his duty in the face of overwhelming opposition.

If anything, the officer's contempt increased. "What is this man doing on duty? He should be in his deathbed."

Face heard Phanan say, "Dedicated."

"Oh, very well. Just give me the damned password."

Phanan said, "Amelkin versus Tovath." That was the name of the classic Quadrant game that had given them access to the hangar.

"What? The shift password, you idiot."

Tactic: When no other options present themselves, shoot everything in sight. Face straightened, grabbed the top edge of the chest armor of the stormtrooper before him to hold him in place, and shot the man in the stomach. Phanan shoved his own stormtrooper back and fired, catching the man in the helmet.

Face dragged his dead or dying target to him, holding him up as a human shield, and, one-handed, swept fire across the occupants of the skimmer. He saw at least two men, including the lieutenant, hit, but there would still be only a split second before the stormtroopers brought their own weapons into line and fired—

To Face's and Phanan's blasts were added lethal cross fire from the door into the hangar. Face hazarded a glance. Two Wraiths stood there in stormtrooper armor—he couldn't tell who—and then advanced, firing as they came.

A bad tactic, Face thought, *abandoning the shelter of the doorway,* but he understood when their place at the door was taken by more Wraiths.

The pilot of the skimmer banked up and away from the firing Wraiths, a maneuver sharp enough to shake the surviving stormtroopers in back but skillful enough to place the skimmer's bottom between them and the Wraiths for a few long moments. The skimmer's maneuver carried it across the wide lane between buildings. It had to level out or smash into the face of one of the buildings, but when it did so it was far enough away, and moving fast enough, that the Wraiths' concentrated fire was not so lethal. With all the blasts they poured into the moving target, Face saw only one more strike a stormtrooper, and assumed that the anonymous Wraith who fired it was Donos, their sniper. The skimmer made a corner and was gone.

The stormtrooper at the door was Wedge; his shout was distinctive. "Two, get the hangar doors open and lock them that way; we can't afford for the central computer to lock them closed. Do you have a distraction ready?"

"My number two distraction is ready. My best one will take a couple of minutes more."

"Go with the number two. Then join Six, Eight, Nine, and Eleven, get out of here on foot—"

Castin's voice rose in something like a whine. "But I was going to fly one of the interceptors!"

"Pipe down. We only have five. Move out in any direction but the one those stormtroopers took, running in Imperial formation, and get in contact with Ten for whatever transport she can provide. The rest of you, to your interceptors."

"They have the hangar door open," reported the skimmer pilot, now standing at the corner of a building not far away. "I can hear ion engines inside firing off. I've got my men scattering to firing positions. I—"

His next words were lost in the wail that rose all around him. It was the anguished cry of some long-forgotten god, a moan that rattled his bones despite his armor; he saw transparisteel viewports on the buildings around him vibrate under the fury of that sound.

It was, in fact, the base's air-raid siren system, an antiquated measure to inform every person on base and anyone within several klicks that enemies were coming by air. In the days when this base was first built, those enemies were the Empire; after the Empire took over, the base operators maintained the system. Just in case.

And now the impossible had happened, someone was attacking the base from the sky. The stormtrooper saw columns of light crisscross the sky in search of targets, then heard and saw the base's huge automated turbocannons begin firing at targets high up in the air. He couldn't see the targets . . . but if the big guns were firing, they were up there.

Distracted by the aerial show, the stormtrooper did not see the first of the interceptors emerge from the hangar.

Face broke formation to draw abreast of Castin as they trotted. He had to shout to be heard over the siren wail. "Two, what did you do?"

Two's body language momentarily suggested an aw-shucks embarrassment. "I found some of their old wargame projections about Imperial raids. They weren't under much security; they were just archives. But I was able to patch the data into their sensor net, as though it were data being received now, and it triggered an automated response. Any second now—"

In the distance, two squadrons of TIE fighters lifted, racing toward the sky and the presumed enemies waiting there. Instead of continuing his thought, Castin just pointed.

Face said, "Six, do we have anything from Ten?"

"We have. She is coming. We have given her our vector."

"Coded, I hope."

"Coded." The Wraiths' code for this mission included a very simple method for transmitting locations, in case their scramblers were decoded: Locations were given in standard Imperial grid format, but with the values reversed, south for north, east for west. It might take only one visual check by stormtroopers to confirm that the locations were incorrect, but the time tolerances for this mission were so tight that this might be all the help the Wraiths needed.

Kell and Phanan, the pilots least experienced with TIE fighters—and experienced not at all with TIE interceptors, even in simulators—were the first to emerge from the hangar. Running close to the ground on repulsorlifts, they crept out tentatively from the hangar's interior. Even with their caution, Phanan failed to decelerate correctly and slowly glided into the building across the lane, stopping with a bump.

Wedge, Janson, and Dia, more sure of their control over

the vehicles, emerged next. On Wedge's cue, they turned, ori-
enting back toward the open hangar door, and fired, destroying the three interceptors remaining within. Then they turned
up the lane and cut in their twin ion engines, accelerating far
faster than their X-wings. Phanan and Kell fell into position
behind them.

"Stay next to the ground," Wedge ordered. "Keep repulsorlifts running at full until I give the word." He glanced over
his sensors. They showed his small squad of five interceptors
running at just above ground level, plus another thirty-six TIE
fighters, three squadrons' worth, rapidly ascending toward
presumed enemies.

One switch gave him access to the sensor data being
broadcast by the base. It showed a sky crowded with enemies.
Initial telemetry identified them as somewhat antiquated TIE
fighters and some other Imperial-style support vehicles. Though
they were Imperial vehicles, their sudden appearance, their
aggressive pattern of approach, and their lack of response to
normal hails had caused the base computer to flag them as
probable unfriendlies. The three squadrons of base TIE fighters looked decidedly overmatched in numbers, but as Wedge
watched, another two squadrons rose to join them.

As buildings flicked by right and left, Wedge locked down
the broadcast sensor signal and transmitted its source to the
others. "All right, Wraiths. We're doing one pass, then we're
going home." He pulled back on the stick, popped up over the
rooftops, and angled toward the source of that signal. The others fell into formation behind him.

They came within firing range almost instantly. Wedge
linked his four lasers for quad fire. The interceptor's weapons
screen initially had a little difficulty identifying the base's command center, a huge, rounded bunker, as the intended target,
but once it locked the target in, it managed to define the building, its bristling gun emplacements, and its numerous sensor
emplacements as discrete targets. Wedge tagged the nearest set
of sensors as his first target and said, "Fire."

The interceptors roared toward the bunker, their twenty
lasers acting as five channels of destruction, laying waste to the

surface of the bunker, tearing through the sensor arrays and gun emplacements as though the metal were so much paper. Wraith Squadron screamed across the bunker, mere meters above its now nearly molten surface, and then banked off toward freedom.

There was now traffic on all the base's lanes—skimmers carrying stormtroopers to ready areas, civilian workers running on foot, some of them only partially dressed, to their duty stations. But no one seemed inclined to question a well-disciplined group of five stormtroopers running with purpose.

Up ahead, two squads of stormtroopers, more than twenty, turned onto the Wraiths' lane and headed toward them. "Stay alert," Face said. "If they address us, respond on the run. If they challenge us, open fire and run harder."

But a skimmer with an enclosed bed turned onto the same lane behind the dual squadron and accelerated into them, flattening some of the stormtroopers, knocking others hard out of the way. The skimmer accelerated toward the Wraiths. Runt said, "We think our ride has arrived."

The skimmer pulled up and swerved as it settled, placing its port and rear sides between the Wraiths and the nest of angry stormtroopers. The door was already half down when the skimmer touched the ground.

"Good work, Ten," Face said. "I'll take gunner position. Everyone else in back." Face slid into the seat beside Shalla; the rest trotted into the bed.

Face heard one of them, Donos from his voice, trip, fall, and swear. He glanced at Shalla. She shrugged. "I had to leave a couple of casualties back there," she half explained. A moment later, the first of the blaster shots from the pursuing stormtroopers hit the vehicle's rear and side armor, and Donos came over the comm: "Go go go!"

They exited via the same gate by which they'd entered. This time, though, they didn't stop to get authorization or for the guards to open the gates. As they approached at full speed, Face raked the guardhouse with blaster fire, forcing the officer on duty to duck, preventing him from activating the magnetic locks, magnetic containment fields, repulsor-activated land mines, or other traps the Imperials routinely had laid out for vehicles approaching or departing a base in an unfriendly fashion.

They hit the spare metal gates, slamming them open and off their hinges, and roared up the road out of the base.

But a mere half klick away, around the first of the bends in the road and sheltered from sight by the very hill Wedge had earlier used for reconnaissance, Shalla set the skimmer down again. The Wraiths scrambled out. Shalla keyed a code into the keypad on the control panel and the skimmer rose once more, winging off into the night toward the distant lights of the city.

"What course is it taking?" Face asked.

Shalla shook her head. "I wrecked most of its higher processes when I destroyed the comm system. All I was able to do was give it a ballistic course toward the city."

"That should be enough. Let's get out of sight."

The Wraiths were in a ditch, helmets off, only the eyes and the tops of their heads showing, when the three pursuit skimmers flew by, following the skimmer's course.

A minute later, they were with Piggy at the site of the civilian skimmer that had brought them here. Captain Wanatte, still unconscious, was trussed up in back.

The Wraiths peeled out of their stormtrooper armor, leaving them in sweat-drenched street clothing appropriate to the world of Halmad. They quickly loaded all the armor components into a plastic crate in the back of the skimmer. Then they boarded. "Back to the spaceport," Face said. "Slowly. Sedately. As befits a bunch of tourists who've been off drinking and recreating all evening and are now too tired to twitch."

Shalla nodded. "Pretty close to an accurate description."

Hawk-bat Base was situated on a large spherical rock deep in the asteroid belt of the Halmad system.

Years before, it had been the Tonheld Mining Corporation's Site A3, tasked with bringing high-quality metals up from the depths of a large asteroid formed during the long-ago destruction of one of the Halmad system's outer planets. The asteroid had a thick outer shell of stone and a center made up mostly of cooled nickel and iron. Tonheld Mining Corporation, all too efficient, had removed the majority of the useful metals, leaving only those that were trapped in veins and pockets within the stone shell. Then the company had dismantled its machinery and housing modules and departed, leaving the site deserted and cold for forty years.

Now, when approached by spacecraft, it still seemed the same. Its thick stone sheath, still intact, was sufficient to block sensors from detecting the life-forms and vehicle emissions now within it.

Halfway down the main shaft, a side tunnel, once a staging area for the mining corporation, turned off at a ninety-degree angle, running parallel to the asteroid's surface. This was now sealed off by a duracrete plug perforated only by large motor-driven doors at either end.

Beyond, inside, where the side shaft was broadest and tallest, was the hangar area where the Hawk-bats' vehicles rested. There were two TIE fighters and five TIE interceptors, and the biggest vessel on site, a *Xiytiar*-class freighter named *Sungrass*.

Among the least elegant of all cargo vessels serving in the galaxy, the *Xiytiar*-class freighter consisted of a long blocky bow that was mostly cargo space, an equally long connective spar in the middle, and a short blocky component that was mostly engines at the stern. *Sungrass* didn't improve the vehicle line's reputation for stylishness; scarcely a centimeter of its once-gleaming surface was unmarked by scrapes, sloppy paintwork, ion scoring from too-close passes alongside other vessels, or old blaster burns.

But its hull was solid, its engines were recently rebuilt and in fine tune.

Once it had belonged to an Imperial shipping corporation. It had been in dry dock in a repair hangar when the entire site was destroyed by elements of New Republic Intelligence. Its bow cracked, its superstructure buried under the wreckage of the hangar, it had been reported as destroyed by reconnaissance units of the Empire. Now, after a couple of seasons of repair, it flew again, its name changed, its history fabricated, its mission to support Wraith Squadron.

On its bridge, Wedge Antilles snorted. He supposed that was symbolic of the New Republic as a whole. Making use of the Empire's castoffs, getting a few extra years of functionality out of them, almost always making do with scraps and crumbs in a way that confounded the remnants of the Empire. Yet it was a far cry from the pretty vision of an Empire-free future that the New Republic still doggedly pursued. He wondered if that image, where everything was new and gleaming and free of any memories of the Empire, would ever come to pass.

He glanced over at the man in the captain's chair. Captain Valton seemed ideally suited to command of this ship. He, too, looked weathered and battered but still fit for many years of useful service. His long, tanned face was unmemorable, though his eyes were sharp, possessed of intelligence. Wedge thought that if they put him in a janitor's uniform he'd blend right in with the service personnel of any New Republic or Imperial station, and wondered if the Wraiths might someday make use of that fact.

And, mercifully, he didn't apparently have a need to hear himself talk. He saw Wedge's side glance, looked over in case Wedge were trying to get his attention, and when he saw that was not the case, returned to the datapad on which he was calculating fuel-mass ratios, all without saying a word.

Wedge turned his attention to his Wraiths, visible through *Sungrass*'s forward viewports, hard at work painting the stolen interceptors. The one Tyria and Kell worked on was now decorated with a red spiderweb pattern, a design that was at once rakishly dangerous-looking and a little unsettling. Phanan and Face left the basic paint job of their interceptor unchanged but had added a ludicrous number of kill silhouettes to the hull—including a number of X-wing silhouettes to rival the genuine kills of Baron Fel, the Empire's greatest ace after Darth Vader. Shalla and Donos were painting theirs with fake blaster scorings and had even painted the engine to look as though it were slightly askew, as if knocked out of alignment by enemy fire. Wedge wondered about the advisability of that; it would probably convince some enemies the interceptor was damaged, perhaps persuading some opportunistic pilots to finish it off when otherwise they might treat it with more caution.

He decided not to interfere. It was an experiment. They'd see how the enemies responded to their "damaged" interceptor.

His personal comlink crackled into life. "Commander."

"Yes, Runt."

"*Narra* returning. ETA fifteen minutes."

"Thank you. Please set up the conference module. Out."

He exited *Sungrass* through its docking tube and passed through the hangar, where the sharp smell of the paints scratched at his sinuses and the chatter of his pilots was so much more immediate. Good men and women in a brief respite from making war. He wished such respites were the norm.

Then, passing their interceptor, he saw Tyria finish another line of red spiderwebs, set her brush down atop her paint can, and wrap her arms around Kell to kiss him.

Wedge stopped short, a rebuke on his lips, a reminder that public displays of affection were not appropriate . . . and then he turned away and kept walking.

Such a warning might have been appropriate for other units, but not elite squadrons under his command. There were no restrictions against relationships between pilots, even when there was some disparity between their ranks, as was the case with Tyria and Kell. There were no regulations against demonstrations of affection in off-duty and most light-duty situations, such as this little painting exercise. They were doing no wrong.

Then why was he so annoyed? Why had he been ready to drop kitchen duty on either of them, had his warning been protested?

He passed through the third set of motorized doors, leading deeper into the shaft, into what Wraith Squadron called the Trench.

It had been a squarish tunnel bored out of solid stone, a straight shaft notable only for its featurelessness. Now its two walls were lined with medium-sized locking cargo modules stacked three high and stretching for some distance down the shaft. Some had been outfitted as living quarters, some as refreshers, others as conference chambers or communications offices or storage lockers. Roll-away staircases gave pilots easy access to the upper tiers of modules.

Face had been the first to note that if you flew a toy X-wing down between the rows of modules, the shaft would look a little like one of the deadly surface trenches of the original Death Star. Then, a few days later, when returning from a scouting mission to the surface of Halmad, Wedge had discovered that some joker had painted the shaft's ceiling black, except for the lights, and had strung strings of miniature twinkling lights here and there, creating an illusion of star-filled sky.

Wedge had let the decoration stand. It was a bad idea to interfere with things his pilots did to make a gloomy place like this more inhabitable, or, so long as it didn't interfere with morale or efficiency, with things they did to make their lives happier.

Yet he'd been ready to do just that a few moments ago, and he grew increasingly annoyed with himself because he couldn't figure out *why*.

The main conference module was on the second tier of the left-hand bank of modules. He took the stairs up and found Runt still there, still sweeping bottles and wrappers from someone's impromptu meal into a bag. The long-faced alien gave him a salute before finishing up.

Wedge settled into a seat beside the main table. "Runt."

Runt straightened. His ponytail swayed. "Sir."

"Do your minds ever confuse one another?"

The alien grinned. At least, that was how Wedge and the others had learned to interpret it when Runt pulled his lips back over his enormous teeth in an expression that looked more like a prelude to a biting attack. "Yes, Commander. Often. If they were meant to be the same, and therefore easily comprehensible to one another, none of us would have more than one."

"Right . . . What do you do when one acts in a confusing manner and its answers don't really explain why?"

Runt sobered and thought about it for a moment, taking

the opportunity to pick up one last piece of wrapping. "We have to remember that there are many paths to every answer. The thought path. The emotion path. The memory path. The biology path—we cannot rule out hormones and natural cycles. And every problem might be made up of combinations of those four things."

"Good point." Wedge gave him a nod, his leave to depart.

And Runt might be right. He couldn't think of a logical reason to protest Tyria's show of affection. Nor had witnessing a kiss ever caused him emotional turmoil in the past. He ruled out biology; he was not irritable with fever, had experienced nothing to unsettle him.

That left emotion, and he already knew what emotion he'd felt.

Or did he? He'd recognized irritation. Had it masked something else? He thought back over the incident, Tyria's unthinking affection. . . .

Jealousy.

He shook his head, trying to dismiss the thought. Nonsense. There was nothing for him to be jealous of.

He'd never entertained any notions about Tyria. She was, to be sure, physically attractive, but she was a very junior officer under his command, and he preferred to steer clear of the extra complications a relationship like that might bring. Too, she was just not the type of woman he was drawn to; she was a little too unsure, too self-critical.

Nor had he felt any jealousy when it became obvious that Kell and Tyria had fallen in love. If any time were the time to be jealous, that would have been it. So it wasn't jealousy.

Except that *was* what he was feeling. A hard little knot of envy.

Maybe it was just the fact that he had no one of his own.

Every so often, he would indulge himself and wonder about the man he would have been had his parents not died in the mishap that had destroyed their refueling station. Who he'd be had he not turned first to smuggling, then to piloting fighter craft for the Alliance and discovered a tremendous aptitude for it. Had he not dedicated himself to a cause that must inevitably kill him. This other Wedge Antilles was probably safe in the Corellian system, owner of a chain of refueling stations, with personal wealth and a waistband measurement that expanded in relationship with one another, with a wife and who knows how many children. A happy man. That was the person Wedge was envious of.

Not that the real Wedge was unhappy. He was content . . . but alone. Probably best if he kept it that way. He'd beaten the odds for so many years, years in which literally hundreds of pilots he'd known had died in battle around him, as though they were living shields for his X-wing. Someday his luck would run out and the deadly statistics would catch up to him.

Yet marriage and family and some sort of normalcy could be his. All he had to do was accept Admiral Ackbar's offer of a generalship and a staff position.

Angrily he pushed the idea away. That was a selfish thought. His life meant more as a pilot and squadron commander than it would as a deskbound planner. More citizens of the New Republic were alive and more Imperial enemies were dead because he was the master of a pilot's yoke instead of a datapad. So long as that remained the case, he didn't have the right to accommodate himself or pursue his own wishes.

"Wraith Three to Wraith One."

Wedge jolted out of his reverie and stared up into the face of Wes Janson. Behind Janson, Dia Passik stood at attention. Wes was grinning, and even Dia's stone face suggested amusement.

There were drinks, still in the bottle, on the table, with condensation collecting on their surfaces. Wedge hadn't even noticed whether it was Janson or Runt who had brought them in.

Wedge cleared his throat to cover his momentary discomfiture, then asked, "What's the word from Coruscant?"

"Well, they're cracking down hard on officers caught napping on the job." Wes handed over a sealed case. "Orders."

Wedge popped the seal. From within the case he drew a datapad.

Dia asked, "Should I leave, sir?"

"No. Have a seat. You can be the pilots' official spy for the moment. If there's anything sensitive here, I'll discuss it with Lieutenant Janson later."

Janson and Dia made themselves comfortable as Wedge scanned the text on the datapad. "Congratulations on the raid on the base at Halmad. They seem to think that five interceptors is a better haul than projections called for. Authorization to fund our continued operations from our pirate activities."

Janson said, "Whoa. You don't see that very often."

Dia's brow furrowed. "If I may ask, why is that so unusual?"

"It's the place where a lot of long-term secret operations go off course," Wedge said. "The mission commander sets up a private means of income and funds his operations with it. Then he begins reporting less income than he's actually taking in. He stashes the surplus away somewhere or uses it for missions not authorized by his control. Soon enough, he has some of his subordinates working with these unauthorized activities, and they're coming up with more effective means of generating money—such as spice smuggling—that will never get reported. Left long enough, an operation like this can become a full-fledged criminal syndicate within a few years. That's why the New Republic, particularly Intelligence, doesn't like doing that. They're putting a lot of faith in us."

Janson glanced at Dia. "In *us*, he says. He actually deludes himself that anyone's reputation but Wedge Antilles's figured into that equation."

She managed another cool little smile.

Wedge returned his attention to the orders. "Authorization to conceive and execute missions against the Imperial and governmental forces in the Halmad system and other systems. In addition, we have a couple of missions here to perform as Wraith Squadron, strikes in collaboration with Rogue Squadron and the *Mon Remonda*. And no word on replacement X-wings." He shut down the datapad. "Pretty much as expected. Passik, questions?"

"No, sir. Thank you for letting me stay, sir."

"I know all about the relative value of fresh news. Dismissed."

When she was gone, Janson said, "I've got some of the mad painters unloading the *Narra*. We came back with some entertainment holos, some luxury holos, some more ID sets squeezed out of Intelligence, an interceptor simulator module for the TIE-fighter simulator, and that passive sensor set you wanted to monitor the Imperial base."

"Good."

"Is everything all right?"

Wedge nodded. "Just feeling my years. Speaking of which, I think I'll get in some simulator practice and beat up on the youngsters."

"That'll make you feel better. It always does me."

Wedge punched his personal code into the keypad located on the hatch of the TIE-fighter simulator. Instead of being located atop the ball-shaped cockpit, where the standard hatch was on real interceptors, the simulator hatch was at the cockpit's stern, where the twin ion engines would normally be mounted.

The hatch swung open. Beyond, a shadowy figure pointed a blaster at Wedge. Wedge dropped out of reflex, rolled to the side, came up on his knees with his own blaster in hand.

But no enemy emerged to fire upon him. He kept his own aim on the hatch and reached for his comlink.

"Is there a problem, Commander?" That was Face, leaning unconcerned against the X-wing simulator only a few meters away.

"Get down, there's a hostile in there—"

Face half ducked behind the corner of his simulator, then took another look. "I don't think so, sir." His mouth twitched, a partially successful effort to hide a smile.

Wedge rose and came forward, leaned out far enough for a quick peek into the simulator cockpit, then leaned in again for a longer look.

His intruder was an Ewok.

Not even a living Ewok. It was a stuffed toy the size and girth of a real Ewok, and designed to look just like one, but just a toy.

It was dressed in a scaled-down version of a New Republic fighter pilot's uniform, down to the authentic-looking suit system control panel on his chest, helmet on his head, and blaster in his paw.

In his other paw was a datapad. Wedge retrieved it and looked at the message. It read:

> *Lieutenant Kettch reporting for duty, sir.*
> *Yub, yub, Commander!*

Wedge shook his head sorrowfully. "Sometimes I miss my sanity." He retrieved the toy and handed it to Face. "Deal with that."

Face, who was working so hard to repress a laugh that he couldn't speak, simply threw a salute and escaped with the Ewok pilot.

"Transferred to Colonel Repness's group?" Lara glanced again over her orders and feigned ignorance. "I don't understand. I haven't completed my basic training set in X-wings. I'm going to get advanced training now?"

The student leader of her own group, a redheaded man, barely out of boyhood, whom she could outfly on the worst day of her life if she weren't shackled by the demands of the role she was playing, gave her a superior smile. "You *don't* understand. Repness handles the remedials. Including you. Notsil, you've washed out. All Repness is, he's a temporary reprieve for you. This time next week, you're going to be an empty bunk."

"Lowan, you're a stain."

"I'll forget you said that. You'll be tossed out of here fast enough without my putting you on report."

Lara stared after him as he departed, and pictured a target painted on his back, a blaster in her own hand, and a sudden improvement in the average merit of this class of candidates.

But, no, that wouldn't be appropriate. Better still to make her way to Zsinj's company, return as a TIE-interceptor pilot, and flame Lowan in a dogfight.

Then again, what if she came up against Lussatte, who was also not her equal as a pilot but was not the blemish Lowan was? A simple matter to vape her . . . but Lara had the uneasy feeling that such an action would cause her a lingering regret.

She shook off the feeling. Transfer to another group meant transferring to another dormitory. It was time to pack.

7

If this is a reward, Face thought, *I need to stop earning them.*

He sat in weightlessness, strapped securely into the control seat of one of the captured interceptors, staring at stars and a tiny, distant sun through the starfighter's viewport. The image hadn't changed in an hour, and the music he was playing on the fighter's internal speakers was, on its eighth repetition, getting on his nerves. He resolved to carry more entertainments on missions, especially those where keeping comm silence was a priority.

In a bar in Hullis, Face had been the one to spot the freighter navigator whose hand trembled with more than eagerness when the man reached for his first drink of the night. He'd been the one to get the man so drunk that discretion wasn't an option, and to listen to the fellow's rambling praise of his captain's intelligence.

The ship the alcoholic navigator served on was the *Barderia,* and it hauled cargo on three-way runs out of Halmad with an admirable record for avoiding pirates. With enough liquor in him, the navigator told Face their secret for success. "Leave each system from a random point, enter each system at a random point. Your courses can't be plotted."

"That makes for pretty complicated courses," Face had said.

"Not really. On arrival in each system, you first drop out of hyperspace just outside the outer planet's orbit to sample the comm frequencies and get any pirate reports available, then make a course correction and jump in where you want to arrive."

"Ah. And this first arrival, before you make your course correction, is to the same spot every time?"

"That's what keeps things simple."

Face was nice enough to make sure the man made it back to his ship when all the night's drinking was done and the navigator was too far gone to recognize surroundings, friends, or his own features. But first Face played a hunch and assumed that a man sloppy enough to reveal a crucial detail to a stranger might be sloppy in other ways. He copied the encrypted contents of the fellow's datapad to his own, and when back at Hawk-bat Base from this intelligence-gathering run, he handed that data over to Castin Donn. Castin cracked the code and the files yielded up no information about freighter routes . . . but did have a file of specific locations just outside a large number of planetary systems. It was a simple matter to find out to which planets *Barderia*'s next cargo run would take her.

The skin around Face's mouth itched, but he could not scratch it, even if he took his Imperial pilot helmet off. His whole face was crisscrossed with horrible puckering scars—artificial ones, created by painting a makeup chemical across his skin and letting it dry. His own genuine scar was not missing; it was just incorporated into the design of false scar tissue.

That real scar made things a little difficult. Every disguise he wore had to conceal it or incorporate it. A simple, if somewhat pricey, cosmetic skin abrasion and bacta treatment would eliminate it. But it was part of him now, a constant reminder of the debt he would never be able to pay off. As a child star of holodramas, he had unknowingly helped boost Imperial morale, promote Imperial projects, even improve Imperial military recruitment. Crimes he'd never be able to erase. The scar was the living sign of those crimes. *Look at me. I know what I did.*

Regardless, all the extra scars, the false ones, made a good disguise, but they itched. And itched. While the same music played over and over again.

His sensor board lit up as an eighth blip suddenly joined the seven waiting there in space. *Barderia* had arrived, within range of his guns, of Wedge's.

His comm crackled as he reached for his yoke. "This is One, targeting engines. Shields still down. Firing!"

As Face brought his interceptor around, he saw the bulk of *Barderia,* a boxy Corellian freighter about a hundred meters long, below him and to his starboard. Green laser fire from a point in space nearly two klicks away was dancing across its stern. Face marveled at the speed of Wedge's response; the commander hadn't been any closer to or oriented any better toward the freighter's arrival.

Face got his guns lined up on the freighter, saw a turreted turbolaser swinging around to aim in on Wedge. He gritted his teeth, but that was not the ship's most dangerous remaining system. He ignored the gun and targeted the ship's communications array. He fired, his first shot scoring the ship's hull, the second turning the comm gear into molten metal and escaping gas in a minor explosion. Then, as he accelerated toward the vessel, he belatedly linked his lasers to quad fire and opened up on the turbolaser.

This blast was larger and much more satisfying, eliminating the turret completely. His interceptor and Wedge's crossed one another in flyovers of the crippled vessel as they visually surveiled the damage.

"This is One. Engines out. No sign of atmosphere venting. Hull integrity seems to be fine."

"This is Eight. Comm antenna down. Main weapon down. I'd call this definitely a strong negotiating position. I'm opening communications." He switched his comm frequency to a wide band including the range normally used by personal comlinks and jumped his power setting up so personal systems would be likely to receive him. He cleared his throat in a deep growl that was his mnemonic for this character's vocal mannerism, then said, his voice a gravelly rumble, "*Barderia,* this is General Kargin of the Hawk-bat Independent Space Force. We are seizing your vessel. We are businessmen and will do no harm to surrendering crew members, to whom I guarantee safe passage into the hands of this system's rescue forces. But we are rather short-tempered businessmen and any crewmen offering resistance will be brought back to our base for a debriefing session they will never forget . . . much less survive. Surrender your vessel and prepare your docking ports for boarding . . . or prepare to breathe vacuum."

His response was not long in coming. A man's voice, raspy and dismayed, replied, "This is Captain Rhanken of the independent cargo vessel *Barderia*. I surrender my vessel. Port and starboard docking ports standing by."

It seemed like such a small boarding party. Face, Castin, and Phanan, wearing only gray versions of the standard TIE-fighter pilot's uniform, arrayed against whatever forces occupied the cargo ship. But five sets of starfighter guns in the hands of the other Wraiths kept *Barderia* in their sights, and the freighter, lacking engines to power its shields, stardrive, and weapons, would be easy prey to any one of them.

The Wraiths, led by a visibly trembling navigation and communications officer, the very man who had inadvertently given Face the information he'd needed for this act of piracy, entered the freighter's spotless bridge. Waiting there were other members of the bridge crew: the captain, a middle-aged, graying man with the look of a former Imperial officer about him, and a younger chief pilot whose hard look and demeanor suggested that he was also the ship's master at arms and would like nothing more than to eradicate the pirates.

Face took off his helmet, revealing his gloriously horrible makeup job, and was rewarded with sudden intakes of breath from the two younger officers. "I am," he said, "the glorious General Kargin, founder and leader of the Hawk-bats." He kept his voice low, gravelly. "Captain?"

The freighter's master did not salute, but he straightened with pained formality. "Captain Rhanken of the *Barderia*."

"Captain?" Face injected a note of menace into his voice.

"And I am obliged to surrender this ship to you."

Face extended a hand. "Cargo manifest?"

The communications officer, jolted into action by the demand, searched his uniform pockets increasingly frantically until he found the object he was searching for—a datapad, which he handed to Face.

Face handed it in turn to Castin. "Two, slice into their master computer and find the cargo manifest there. If it does not agree one hundred percent with this list, we execute them all." Face turned his gaze back to the captain. "Though I can be forgiving. If you anticipate any errors in your list, you can tell me about them now and avoid unpleasantness."

Captain Rhanken met his eyes unflinchingly. "I anticipate no problems. If my crew has done its customary good work." He glanced at the communications officer. "Will there be a problem, Lieutenant?"

The communications officer, no master of concealing his emotions, went pale. "I d-d-don't recall whether I called up the final inventory-match manifest or used last week's projected manifest, sir."

"Get the final manifest and give it to him. Just to be sure."

"Yessir." The officer bent to his task.

Interesting. Face had to work to keep both amusement and contempt from his expression. The captain wanted to play the unerring officer and was willing to let his subordinates assume responsibility for a tactic that had to be the captain's own decision. Depending on the pirates involved, that could have led to the lesser officer's death.

Long minutes passed while the officer brought up the correct manifest and Castin verified it by cutting through the computer's defenses and slicing his way down to the original file. They matched and Face and Castin looked through their winnings while Phanan kept the bridge officers under guard.

"Look at this," Face whispered. "Halmad Prime, shipped by the ton. Halmad's best and most expensive grain alcohol. You can't get it on-planet except through the black market; they ship it to other Imperial worlds as one of their major exports. Various medicines. Duracrete sprayers. Prefabricated shelters. We'll take all the Halmad Prime and a cross section of the medicines; that's about all we can load on *Sungrass*. See anything else we need?"

"TIE fighter and interceptor parts."

"What? Where?"

Castin turned his datapad so Face could see the screen. It showed a different inventory list. "I pulled this off their computer when I was verifying the current manifest. It's an estimated inventory from the second leg of their voyage. We could really use some spare parts and maintenance gear."

"True, but our little raid here is bound to change their schedule for the rest of their mission."

"But if we can figure out what they'll change it *to* . . ."

"Good point." Face straightened and glared at the captain. "Rhanken, have your cargo handlers assemble lots twenty-eight through one hundred twenty-seven and two hundred at your cargo bay. Two, call *Sungrass* and have them move in to accept delivery."

"And then what?" asked Captain Rhanken.

"Then we leave."

"Leaving us to drift, without communications, without enough power to limp into the system, to die out here?"

Face gave him a tight smile. "You have escape pods sufficient to get a message to your rescuers. But we'll save you some time and call in an emergency signal. Wouldn't want you to be inconvenienced. And you can tell your fellow captains, whom I'll be meeting in the foreseeable future, that the Hawk-bats don't kill. Unless we're annoyed. Or become bored. They can take that under advisement."

Colonel Atton Repness, leader of the Screaming Wookiee training squadron aboard the New Republic frigate *Tedevium,* pointed the device at Lara as though it were a miniature blaster.

She looked curiously at it. It was shaped like a standard cylindrical comlink, but that's not what it was. She was sure of this because she'd examined the device inside and out, and done far more than that, when she'd broken into Repness's quarters two days ago. "I'm sorry, sir. Should I be putting up my hands? Or making a speech?"

He smiled. "Very funny. This isn't a weapon. It just ensures that we aren't being recorded."

"Who would want to record us?"

The colonel looked around, though he and Lara were the lightly furnished conference room's only inhabitants. "You'd be surprised. I'll just keep this on."

"You're the colonel." But, inwardly, she smiled. He wasn't speaking as a colonel; his mannerisms had shifted, probably without him realizing it, to those of a friend. Or conspirator.

"You're aware that your scores have come up since transferring to the Screaming Wookiees."

"Yes, sir."

"Well, this is in part from improvement in your skills."

"Only in part?" She affected surprise.

"Only in part." Repness pulled a datapad from a pocket and slid it over to her.

The file it displayed was her training record. But the scores from after her transfer were shown in two columns, labeled "True" and "Adjusted."

She gave him a troubled look. "I don't understand, sir. The 'True' column would indicate that I'm still failing. Just barely failing. What are the adjustments from the other column?"

"Oh, I merely wanted your scores to be higher."

She let her features go slack, as if caught so far by surprise that she didn't know how to react or what to say.

"You see," he said, "I think you have the potential to become a good pilot. So I've temporarily adjusted things to keep you from being booted. But I don't think you can do this without help. It will take a team effort . . . and you haven't been a team player, have you?"

"Well, I'd . . . like to be. I just don't know how. Things are so different here."

"Excellent! We could use you on my team. Working on my team calls for some extra effort on your part . . . but it comes with rewards you can't get from any other unit."

And then he told her of a mission. It would be a milk-run training mission within the atmosphere of the nearest uninhabited planet in an A-wing. Her control boards would register a critical failure of the engines, which would overheat and threaten detonation. She'd be ordered by Repness to eject, which she would—well after the trouble-free A-wing was safely on the ground. An ion bomb detonated in the atmosphere would give investigators the evidence they needed to corroborate the fighter's utter destruction, and a rescue crew would pick her up well after Repness's crew ferried the expensive fighter away for sale in some distant black-market port.

Lara listened, bored, to the whole inevitable deal, feigning puzzlement, shock, indignation, futile resistance, and finally pained acceptance as the hopeless nature of her situation was made clear to her.

And she knew, with a growing glee that was hard to conceal, that every word she and Repness said was being sent, by the very device he thought was a transmission-detecting sweeper, to a file under a forged pilot account on the frigate's main computer.

Contact Wraith Squadron for help when matters with Repness came to a head? Why bother, when she could engineer his destruction and her own career's salvation with far more panache than those pilots could ever manage?

It was a different star system—the Halmad system, well outside the orbit of its outermost planet—but the situation was very familiar.

Captain Rhanken could not maintain an expression of imperturbability the second time the Hawk-bats boarded his freighter. His voice was one of pure despair: "How did you know where we'd be?"

"We asked the right people," Face said. "Your trade guild has a security breach in it I could pilot a Death Star through."

It was a lie, a big one. Castin Donn had downloaded a number of the cargo ship's records the last time they were aboard, and covered his tracks. The records didn't say how *Barderia*'s master would adjust his schedule to account for the act of piracy committed upon him . . . but they did show how he'd reacted in the past to such situations. And now the Hawk-bats had taken him a second time, on his return leg home.

If the analysts of the trade guild didn't believe the lie, that was all right; nothing would change. But if they did, they might institute a sweeping change in the guild's standards for secure transmissions and information flow. Eventually that would be an impediment to the Hawk-bats' piracy, but in the short term, possibly as long as the Hawk-bats were to exist as a pirate band, it would cause disruption and confusion in the guild, changes that New Republic Intelligence had a couple of agents ready to examine and take advantage of.

It was a good time to be a pirate.

Face said, "Rhanken, have your cargo handlers deposit lots forty-three through seventy-nine at your cargo door. Then we'll be on our way. Good doing business with you again."

When Lara Notsil examined the file containing the recording of Colonel Repness's offer to her, it seemed much larger than their conversation should have accounted for. *Perhaps,* she thought, *he's been using his transmission-detecting sweeper in conversations with others.*

He had. In the file were her conversation with Repness, plus the colonel's subsequent discussions with one of his "team" subordinates, an instructor captain named Teprimal; in their talk, they noted details of their plan for the hiding and subsequent sale of the A-wing.

And there was more. Lara discovered, with glee mixed with a measure of professional horror, that Repness tended to turn on his sweeper when doing his most private work at his computer terminal. His paranoia about unseen listeners was his undoing, because he tended to mumble to himself, verbalizing his passwords and secret computer account names when working this way.

Within minutes of listening to the recording, Lara could access all of the man's recordings that concerned his lucrative side business. It was a black-market business, well entrenched on Coruscant but just getting under way on the training frigate *Tedevium,* in which cargo was diverted from its intended destination—not even making it onto incoming-supplies manifests—and sold, profits making their way into the pockets of Repness and his team.

She found records of her own scores as a pilot trainee, plus those of a dozen other pilots Repness had subverted or tried to subvert this way. Some, like Wraith Squadron's Tyria Sarkin, had refused to steal for him . . . but had been blackmailed into keeping silent. Others had joined his team. The records didn't indicate whether they had been willing or reluctant. Still others, pilot trainees Lara knew, were going through the ensnaring process even now.

There was no sign that Repness had any allies in the Intelligence division of the armed forces, or in the Inspector-General's office. She wrote a letter to both General Cracken of Intelligence and to the latter military division. It read,

> i am the unseen, the unknowable, the unstoppable.
>
> no computer can stand before me. gates open for me. back doors are revealed to me. knowledge willingly spools itself out for my inspection. i am the jedi of the electronic world.
>
> i have found evil aboard tedevium. i have found corruption. like the jedi, i shall cut it down.
>
> examine these files. test them for integrity. you will find they are the truth.
>
> go where these files lead you.
>
> do what you must do, as i do what i must do.
>
> signed, white lancer

She went back in and inserted some random misspellings and some painful grammatical errors. When it was done, it was, she decided, a note typical of code-slicers who performed anonymous sabotage on computer systems. The true extent of her computer skills were not known on *Tedevium*, and those of many other crewmen and pilot candidates were; many of them would be suspected of this act, and in order to boost their reputations, some would probably allow the investigators to believe that they were, in fact, the secretive White Lancer.

To the letter, she attached Repness's recordings and all the passwords and account names she had so far uncovered.

Then there were the files demonstrating how Repness had ensnared other pilots. She paused over those.

Best to expose all those pilots, she decided. Their careers would be ruined, at tremendous training cost to the New Republic—that is, the Rebels—and this would help deplete the Empire's enemy of skilled pilots. Besides, if they became pilots, most of them would eventually die in action against Imperial pilots. They were better off having their careers torpedoed. If they knew she'd done it to them, someday they'd thank her for it.

Still her hands paused over the keyboard. As a child, she'd hoped to be a starfighter pilot. When she'd followed her parents' career path instead, going into Imperial Intelligence, she'd demonstrated skills necessary to become a pilot and had undergone basic pilot training, which her controllers had decided would be a valuable side skill . . . and there she'd discovered a genuine love for flying. But her request for permanent transfer to the pilot corps was denied. Her intelligence-related skills were better and rarer than her pilot's skills, so against her wishes she'd been obliged to stay in Intelligence. *Believe us, it's better this way,* her instructors had told her. *Someday, you'll thank us for this.*

It came before her, the face of pilot candidate Bickey, in her class under Repness. He'd been transferred to the remedial training unit just days after Lara had. If Repness kept true to form, in just a few days, Bickey would be approached on some similar scheme of theft. He was such a young, eager, boyish pilot, anxious to demonstrate his skill and bravery. He had once said he'd prefer to die young, in battle against his enemies, than old and content on a farm somewhere. No, he'd never thank her for what she was about to do.

Uneasy, Lara attached her own file of scores to the letter she was sending General Cracken, then systematically destroyed the original and backup files implicating other pilots and pilot candidates now serving. *Let them die as they choose,* she told herself. *Let them die as pilots.*

She arranged for the package of letter and files to make its way through secret routes to the offices of General Cracken. It would be at his headquarters office and under the eyes of one of his subordinates by day's end.

Which left her one thing to do today.

. . .

She looked at the sweeper in Repness's hand and let an expression of contempt cross her face. "Careful as always, aren't we, Atton?"

The colonel looked around, concealing nervousness, though the classroom was empty of other personnel. "You'll address me as Colonel Repness and show respect."

"I'll address you as Colonel Bantha Sweat and show you whatever I want."

He looked at her, mouth open, but didn't respond immediately. Lara pressed on: "I've decided not to join your team, Repness. I'm not going to steal an A-wing for you. In fact, I'm going to tell your superiors about what you're up to."

He managed to laugh. "That won't do you much good. There's no proof. And that's the end of your flying career. You'll never sit in a cockpit again. Think about what the rest of your life will be like."

"I don't care. I can live without flying. I *can't* live without honor." For a moment, she was troubled as the unwelcome possibility flashed through her mind that the words she'd just spoken had come from her true self, not the role she was playing. She suppressed the thought, shoving it aside. "That's the end of *your* career."

"I don't think so. When they look over your psychological profile—a new one I'll be working up over the next few days—and see what a compulsive liar you are, they wouldn't believe you if you told them that hard vacuum is bad for the lungs."

She gave him a mocking smile. "And you think I'll give you those few days to falsify my records?"

"Certainly. You'll be sleeping." His blow was so fast that she saw it only as a blur. His fist struck her high on the cheek. She felt her skin part under the force of the blow.

Everything went white, her vision gone, sudden shock depriving her of most of her senses. She drifted a moment, aware that she may have overplayed this hand, and dimly felt her back and head hit the floor. It should have hurt, but it didn't.

Her vision cleared a little, momentarily, and all she saw was Repness standing over her, his leg drawn back.

Then his booted foot swung forward to connect with her temple and that was the last she knew.

The X-wings of Wraith Squadron—the eight snubfighters remaining in the unit—made one pass before the bridge of the Mon Calamari cruiser, waggling S-foils as a show of respect, then curved around smartly and lined up, by pairs, for their approach to the vessel's portside landing bay.

Wedge and his temporary wingman, Face, were first through the magcon field separating pressurized hangar from depressurized space, first to see the reception party that awaited them in the one clear area tucked in among a sea of X-wings and shuttles. Wedge cut in his repulsors and reduced power to his main engines, settling into a slow glide forward, and was pleased to see Face mimicking his maneuver precisely. They settled onto the first pair of landing zones, facing the crowd that had gathered there, and brought their canopies up in unison.

Rogue Squadron stood before them, arrayed as precisely as a firing squad. In front of the line of pilots was General Han Solo, uncomfortable-looking in his New Republic uniform, his expression a cocked smile that had to be from relief at seeing Wedge.

Wedge climbed down from his cockpit and removed his helmet. He could feel as well as hear the repulsorlift whine of the other Wraiths' arriving, plus the distant metallic chatter of powered tools being used on repairs. That, and the smell of fuel and lubricants, of ozone coming off the magcon shield, made this hangar more comfortable and homey than any set of quarters Wedge had occupied.

He approached Solo and threw a precise salute. "Commander Wedge Antilles and Wraith Squadron reporting for duty, sir."

Solo's return salute was far less military. "Welcome aboard *Mon Remonda*. Let's get the rest of your pilots in . . . so I can get out of this torture suit."

Wedge affected surprise. "But, sir, I was just going to say how smart you looked in your uniform. I think we ought to stay here, in uniform, a couple of hours so the holographers can capture the image. You know, for the historians."

Solo's grin didn't waver, but his expression was suddenly somehow different. Something like an animal backed into a corner. He kept his tone cheery. "Wedge, I think I'm going to have you killed."

"Yes, sir. I trust you'll wear your *dress* uniform for an event like that."

Han slumped in mock surrender. "You know, with my history, I'd be the laughingstock of the New Republic if I ever brought one of *my* officers up on charges of insubordination."

"Yes, sir, I was sort of counting on that."

Once the other pilots had landed and their X-wings were shut down, it was handshakes all around. Wedge introduced Rogues to Wraiths, and met Captain Onoma, Mon Calamari master of the *Mon Remonda*.

On the walk down from the hangar to the officers' quarters, through hallways that seemed more organic than constructed with their smooth curves and eye-pleasing rather than industrial colors, Solo filled Wedge in on some pertinent facts. "*Mon Remonda* officially has four fighter squadrons assigned to her. The fighter squadrons are: Rogue; Wraith; Polearm; an A-wing unit; and Nova, a B-wing squadron. Of course, you Wraiths are usually out on long patrols. In practice, of course, Rogue, Nova, and Polearm have been doing all the work while you Wraiths play pirate."

"Is that irritation or envy in your voice?"

"Envy. Want to trade?"

"No."

"You could boss this whole anti-Zsinj task force. I could arrange for a generalship for you."

"No."

Solo sighed tolerantly. "Anyway, we've been cruising at the theoretical borders of so-called Zsinj-controlled space. When our scouting missions or Intelligence auxiliaries report a good target, we go in and blow it up. We also assemble data on probable movements of *Iron Fist*, hoping to determine her home port or predict her next destination. So far we're not having much luck on that front, though we're pursuing data and leads as aggressively as we can."

"You might actually want to pursue leads a little *less* aggressively than that, if you get my drift."

Solo led the parade of pilots into a large personnel turbolift, which carried them downward into the vessel's interior. "What do you mean?"

"Zsinj uses a lot of intelligence-oriented techniques. If he's planting any of the leads you're following, he may be building up a profile of how *Mon Remonda* responds to leaked information. Once he has a reliable profile in place, he can drop the exact type and quantity of information to lead you into the kind of trap not even a cruiser like this comes out of."

Solo whistled. "Good point. The data we've been getting has been so fragmentary, so difficult to piece together, that we haven't had any reason to believe any of it was fabricated. But if we assume that Zsinj demands a pretty high level of performance even of enemy analysts—"

"He does. If you'd like, I can have my intelligence specialist—Shalla Nelprin, you met her in the hangar—"

"Yes."

"I can have her analyze the data you've been getting and your responses to it to see if you're exhibiting any sort of pattern."

"I'll have it sent to the terminal in her quarters." Solo now no longer looked uncomfortable. He looked serious and intent, and finally seemed the officer his uniform said he was.

Face came out of the turbolift behind Dia and one of the Rogues, a Twi'lek who had been introduced as Nawara Ven, and overheard the Rogue try to start up a conversation. Face didn't understand the words, assumed they were in Twi'leki, the language of Ryloth, homeworld of the Twi'leks.

But Dia's response was not in the same tongue. Her voice was emotionless. "Speak Basic, please."

Nawara Ven took a second to compose himself. "I'm sorry. I said, we must get together sometime at your convenience to talk."

"About what?"

"About home. About our experiences as Twi'leks in the armed forces."

"Ryloth was where I was born, but then it spat me out, made me property of an Imperial crime-syndicate leader. Ryloth is not my home. I don't have a home. And I doubt our experiences have been similar. Unless you've been a slave."

"Well, no, but—"

"Then we've probably exhausted available topics of conversation." She picked up the pace and moved up away from the Rogue.

Nawara turned to the other Rogue Twi'lek pilot, a larger man with the upright, aggressive posture of a warrior. Face remembered that he had been introduced as Tal'dira.

Tal'dira shrugged and gave Nawara a little smile. "I think you lost that case, Counselor."

"I don't think I was ever even in the courtroom."

Face was just getting settled into the quarters he'd be sharing with Myn Donos when his comlink blipped. It was Wedge's voice: "Lieutenant Loran, report to Commander Antilles."

"Yes, sir."

When he arrived in Wedge's quarters, his commander was seated behind a fold-down desk and scowling over a datapad. Face saluted. Wedge returned it absently and gestured for him to sit, all without looking up.

Wedge said, "The Lara Notsil situation seems to be . . . resolved."

Face felt a little coldness settle in his stomach. "That sounds pretty ominous, sir."

Wedge finally met his eyes. "Well, not as ominous as all that. She appears to have dropped the heavy end of the hammer on Colonel Repness . . . without involving you or Phanan. Or indicating in any way that this was a setup."

"Sir?"

"I've just received her record, because she has put in applications for transfer to Rogue Squadron or Wraith Squadron. According to this document, Repness attempted to recruit her to his unit of black-market thieves, she refused, he assaulted her and had her drugged out of commission, a prisoner in the infirmary . . . but a mystery code-slicer aboard *Tedevium* caught Repness's activities in recordings and forwarded them to Intelligence. They moved in and seized Repness before any further harm could come to her."

Face thought that over. "But if she otherwise kept to the plan, then her scores would probably not let her graduate."

"Right. According to this, when she was recuperating from Repness's attack on her, she told *Tedevium*'s commanding officer that deciding to oppose Repness had settled some problems she'd had, some issues remaining from the destruction of the colony where she'd grown up. She insisted on a chance to demonstrate those changes, and the training officers decided to give it to her. She went through an accelerated training regimen and vaped it. Even averaging those results with her earlier scores let her graduate—and her efficiency profile puts her within the range suitable for inclusion in my units."

"I'm glad to hear it."

"Both Rogue Squadron and Wraith Squadron are at full pilot strength, so neither unit needs her. However, she has been assigned—and this is fitting—Colonel Repness's personal X-wing."

Face snorted. "An act of revenge on the part of *Tedevium*'s commander?"

"Probably. *Tedevium*'s new commander is General Crespin, from Folor Base, and that sounds just like his sense of humor. It's also possible that Repness's snubfighter was considered bad luck—you know how superstitious some pilots are. So, anyway, I'll be bringing her into Wraith Squadron to help boost our complement of snubfighters."

"That's great news, sir."

Wedge gave him a challenging look. "Your job, and Phanan's, is to make sure that it *stays* great news, Face."

"Yes, sir."

"You're awfully subdued, Face. Your sarcasm generator not getting any power?"

"Something like that, sir."

"Relieved that this whole Lara Notsil situation hasn't shot your career into a black hole or made an enemy of General Cracken?"

"Yes, sir."

"Well, I'll inform the smartmouths in the Wraiths that you're temporarily easy pickings for them. Dismissed."

8

"She has just been assigned to Wraith Squadron, which is aboard *Mon Remonda*," said General Melvar.

He and the warlord were alone in *Iron Fist*'s officers' lounge. Yet the lounge was full of the noise of leisure and pleasure—pilots chatting, glasses clinking, drinks pouring—all part of an ambient-noise recording Zsinj usually played at such times.

The warlord froze with his drink halfway to his mouth. Melvar could smell the drink; it was a good Coruscant brandy. But Melvar knew that this had to be a synthesized substitute, alcohol-free; despite appearances, Zsinj never drank while in command of a ship. Yet he would knock down shot after shot of the synthesized stuff and allow his subordinates to believe that he was getting drunk, and his body language and speech would confirm that analysis.

Zsinj said, "But that's perfect. Arrange for her to give us *Mon Remonda*'s course and schedule. We'll destroy it, and General Solo, and those most annoying X-wing units. For a prize like that, I'll set Gara Petothel up for life and give her whatever position on *Iron Fist* she wants."

"Other than mine, I hope."

"Including yours." Zsinj smiled. "I'll find something even better for you."

"The problem is, we're not yet in contact with her. It took us some time to put together a visual image of her, and more time to compare it against and disqualify all current female pilots in Antilles's squadrons, and even more time to trace it to Lara Notsil, a pilot candidate in training. She'd extensively changed her appearance."

"Wise of her."

"And then she was on a training frigate at an unknown location, and then in custody there, and then in an advanced training program there under intense scrutiny. We've been able to follow her . . . but never approach her."

Zsinj merely blinked at him. His expression said, *How nice that you have a problem. Now solve it.*

"So we've found one of her relatives. The relative will make contact for us."

"A relative of Gara Petothel?"

"No, of Lara Notsil, the woman whose identity she took. The community where she grew up, New Oldtown—"

Zsinj shuddered. "Surely you're joking about that name."

"On Aldivy. It was blasted out of existence by Admiral Trigit when it refused to offer him supplies."

"You're sure he didn't destroy it because of that name."

"Since he's dead, I'll have trouble asking him. Anyway, one of the real Lara Notsil's siblings, from New Oldtown—"

"Don't ever say that name again. It annoys me."

"—returned home after spending months at a naval job under an assumed name. He was supposed to be serving time in a jail in his hometown-whose-name-is-nevermore-to-be-said."

"So you recruited him."

"I have an agent with him, teaching him to eat with implements, wear shoes, and pretend that Gara Petothel is his sister. He'll be transmitting a message saying, 'I'm alive, understand you are the same.' With enough subtext that she'll have no problem figuring out what's going on."

"Good. Be speedy with this, Melvar. I want *Mon Remonda* off my trail as soon as possible. Its crew and pilots are too lucky and too efficient by far. Their continued existence threatens to be very expensive to me."

. . .

The world shown on the briefing room's holoprojector was not a promising one. A medium-sized chunk of reddish-brown rock with a few dark seas thrown in for contrast, it circled around a yellow star notable only for its averageness.

Wedge, on the dais, gestured to a tiny bright spot on the world's surface. "This is the world Lavisar, and this point is its chief port city, Syward. According to Lavisar's central library, the planet was once part of a much larger very-high-gravity world, one that was destroyed in a series of asteroid collisions; Lavisar was ejected. It's a world where heavy metals are abundant, with mining and refining industries to match, plus a strong economic base in shipbuilding."

"Just the sort of world Zsinj loves," said Face. At a questioning look from Rogue Squadron pilot Corran Horn, he explained, "We stumbled across the edges of a financial empire belonging to Zsinj, one no one knew about previously. He likes fairly innocuous worlds that have strong economies, and he usually owns at least one business there under an assumed name—a different name with each world. It might be that he wants to have a fallback position in case these worlds decide to side with the New Republic—his business would still be able to help fund his military activities."

Wedge continued, "And recent data supports the idea that Lavisar is one of these worlds. Although the world is just outside what we think of as Zsinj-occupied space, a recently captured transmission, which our Intelligence people have decrypted, indicates that there is a Raptor unit in Syward, set up in the main construction plant of Skyrung Manufacturing, a licensee builder of *Lambda*-class shuttles."

The Raptors were Zsinj's elite enforcement units. Better trained and better equipped than Imperial stormtroopers, they were the most commonly seen and recognized symbol of Zsinj's power, much as the ubiquitous TIE fighter was the universal symbol of Imperial domination.

"So what is the plan?" asked Tal'dira, one of Rogue Squadron's Twi'lek pilots. "Aerial strike, commando strike, or a combination of the two?"

"Maybe neither. Shalla, let's have your report."

Shalla stood, apparently a little nervous under the scrutiny of the Rogues. "I did an analysis of the way *Mon Remonda* and her task force have been responding to various outside stimuli—captured transmissions, confessions of captured Zsinj personnel, that sort of thing—*not* including official orders from the New Republic. This was against the possibility that Zsinj has been leaking information to gauge our responses. And although there is some variation in response time, this task force shows a pretty consistent set of responses. Each stimulus is graded as high priority, medium, low, and of possible interest—those are my terms, not those of the task force's officer corps—and a response is assigned according to grade. High priority, for example a response to a distress call from a New Republic ship that is nearby and under attack, will yield, without variation, an assault force of a size calculated to be marginally superior to the enemy force, sent in a straight-line path from *Mon Remonda*'s current location to the site of the trouble. A stimulus like this one, the Lavisar signal, will inevitably call for a ground team to confirm the signal source is a target, followed by an aerial strike." She shrugged as if in apology. "These responses have been predictable." She sat down and began fidgeting.

"And predictability," said Corran Horn, "gets you killed."

"Then what should we do?" That was Gavin Darklighter, the Rogues' pilot from Tatooine, a brown-haired young man whose innocent features and country-boy demeanor belied his combat experience. "Instead of an aerial strike, send flowers and sweets?"

"It's better than going in as usual," Shalla said. "It would confuse them."

Asyr, the Bothan flier, who sat beside Gavin with her arm upon his, shook her head, rippling her fur. "But at the first point we don't respond predictably, we tip Zsinj off that we're onto him."

Wedge smiled at her, and it was a hard-edged smile. "Welcome to the dilemmas of command. You're right. Now, let's make the situation even worse. After I received Shalla's—wait a moment." He took his comlink from its clip and spoke into it. "Yes?"

The Rogues and Wraiths heard a murmur from the comlink's speaker but could not make out the words. Wedge said, "Yes, by all means. A good time for it." He returned the device to its clip. "After Shalla made her preliminary report on this matter to me this morning, General Solo, Captain Celchu, and I went over the data of *Mon Remonda*'s mission so far. Intelligence reports are very sketchy, but indicate that in at least five of the sites this task force has attacked in recent sorties, Raptor movements have drastically increased and been quite public immediately after the sorties. Anyone want to hazard a guess?"

There was no immediate response. Then the Rogues' executive officer, Nawara Ven, raised a hand.

"Go ahead."

"If Zsinj wants to lead us around and gauge our responses, he has to do so by giving up targets for us to attack. Until a moment ago, I was assuming he was giving up targets he owned or occupied, places that weren't very important to him. But that wouldn't necessarily result in more public Raptor activity after the raids." He frowned in concentration. "But if he were planting evidence that sites that *didn't* belong to him actually *did* . . ."

Tyria said, "Then we'd be assaulting sites he wouldn't particularly mind being hit."

Nawara gave her a close look. "Even worse. If they were planets and facilities he'd been trying to add to his empire by diplomacy, but failing, our attacks would have knocked down their defenses drastically. Leaving them open to easier conquest by Zsinj . . . or at least further negotiation with him, and not from a position of strength."

Face put his hand on his head to quell a sudden threatening headache. "You're saying that the task force has been doing his work for him. All in the name of running down every lead."

Wedge nodded. "Very possibly. Further examination of

available data on Lavisar's central library computer indicates that the population has a strong independent streak, which accounts, more than anything else, for its continued lack of interest in joining the New Republic or Zsinj, or rejoining the Empire, which lost control of the planet after the Emperor's death.

"So our task is to respond predictably to this 'stimulus,' as Shalla puts it, without doing Zsinj's work for him, and without setting ourselves up for Zsinj's inevitable trap. Hobbie, this was your idea."

The mournful-faced second-in-command of the Rogues stood uneasily. "Zsinj has every confidence that we can penetrate standard planetary defenses and get our snubfighters and support crews to the surface. We generally do. So my idea was to send down a ground crew, plant a bomb on the side of their main sensor station, and set it off . . . and it doesn't destroy the emplacement. They keep full sensors."

Gavin Darklighter frowned. "Wait a minute, wait a minute. So we go blasting down toward the planet and they're completely aware of our approach?"

Hobbie nodded. "And they send up their forces and we turn tail, having been repelled by the mighty defenders of Lavisar."

That got laughter from most of the pilots.

"Rogue Squadron doesn't run," said Corran Horn, deadpan. "Unless we really, really have to." That got more laughter.

"No," said Wedge, "this will be Wraith Squadron's mission."

"We don't mind running," Face said. "Even *when* we don't have to."

"More importantly," Wedge continued, "we need to establish that Wraith Squadron is indeed on *Mon Remonda*. Every chance we get, we have to support the deception that we're here all the time. So—hold on, here's someone I want you to meet."

The door at the back of the briefing chamber finished hissing up and open. In walked a woman in standard New Republic pilot's uniform, still carrying her helmet and bag of possessions. Face recognized Lara, despite the bandage she wore on her left cheek. He waved her over and she headed his way.

Wedge continued, "Rogues, Wraiths, I'd like to introduce you to Lara Notsil, newest pilot in Wraith Squadron. She hasn't seen any action yet, but she's already brought down a black-market ring operating on a New Republic training frigate. That's a pretty good start."

Over the other pilots' applause, Lara settled in beside Face. He decided that she looked weary, probably from her long flight in, but alert. "Thank you," she said. "But before anyone feels that his *own* sideline business is threatened, let me just say that I am susceptible to bribes."

That got a chuckle, and Wes Janson drew a hand over his brow as if relieved.

Wedge waved to return everyone's attention to him. "Back to Lavisar, the subject at hand . . . we will be sending down an Intelligence team, to plant our dud of a bomb . . . and to stay there after our task force leaves the area. We're going to take Shalla's analyses and present them to the planetary governor. Try to persuade him that Zsinj was setting him up and that we, in our pragmatic mercifulness, let him go. Maybe he'll be grateful. Maybe he'll side with the New Republic. Second best would be him remaining with the Empire . . . but as a confirmed enemy of Zsinj."

Face said, "That's pretty dangerous for our agents on the ground, isn't it?"

Wedge nodded. "Only one member of the team will make contact with the governor. It'll be a volunteer from our Intelligence pool. If he or she doesn't return . . . the rest of the team will transmit the bad news and decide whether to stage a rescue operation or just try to get offworld."

"He likes sunfruit liqueur," Lara said.

Wedge stared at her. "Come again?"

"Governor Carmal of Lavisar. He likes sunfruit liqueur. I mean, just having some as a present for him might help a little bit."

"How do you know this?"

She shifted, a little uncertain under the directness of

Wedge's stare. "When I was making my living on Coruscant, I worked for a shipping company, processing data for them. Lavisar was in their records as 'lost by separation,' a term meaning the company had trade relations with them before Coruscant fell to the New Republic but not afterward. There was a lot of data on worlds and companies 'lost by separation,' including information that the New Republic doesn't have because it's trade-specific, so the company representatives might have a slightly easier time resuming relations once contact was made again."

"Good to know. Do you have some sort of perfect memory?"

"Well, a trick memory. Miscellaneous facts, trivia, statistical information, they all get pulled into my head and stay there forever. I'm not so good with faces, but I can tell you all the official holidays of more than fifty worlds, and some holidays from another five hundred or so."

"Interesting." Wedge turned to Squeaky, the 3PO unit with mismatched gold and silver body parts, who lurked, as was his custom, at the back of the briefing hall. "We—"

"You don't need to say it," the droid said, his tone admonishing. "We need sunfruit liqueur. And, doubtless, some of the good stuff from a tropical world that knows how to turn it out, not one of the Coruscant synthetics. I'll get to work on it with my customary efficiency."

"Well, in that case, let's wrap things up with *our* customary efficiency. The squadrons' senior staff will be putting together the mission profile, but anyone who wants to earn some extra points can work up his own version of this approach-balk-and-run mission, and we'll take the best parts of what we get. Questions? No? That's all."

"A moment of your time, sir?" Tyria Sarkin stood in the doorway to Wedge's quarters. She looked distinctly unhappy.

"Of course. Come in."

She declined to sit, instead standing at ease—though her tense pose suggested that relaxation was impossible for her.

"Sir, there are lots of rumors about Flight Officer Notsil and that black-market ring."

"Yes?"

"And I think you ought to know . . ." An expression of dismay struggled across her face, but she managed to banish it. "No, you should have known some time ago, and I'm sorry I didn't tell you. But you need to know that you might lose me as a pilot."

"Why?"

"Because Notsil wasn't the first pilot candidate Major Rep—*Colonel* Repness came to with this starfighter-stealing scheme."

Wedge regarded her steadily. A number of puzzle pieces suddenly clicked into place. Face's and Phanan's personal involvement in this Repness matter. Phanan had talked of a former trainee who'd spilled the story of Repness's black-market activities to him . . . but had hinted that this trainee had washed out and had met Phanan on Coruscant.

He wondered if Tyria had been part of Phanan and Face's plan all along. No; she was unskilled at deception, an honest spirit who took no satisfaction in lying. A refreshing change from most of the other Wraiths.

"You didn't—"

"No, sir. I didn't steal anything for him. But I did something just as bad. I let him blackmail me into keeping quiet. I could have turned him in, opposed him the way Notsil did . . . but I didn't." Her shame was evident in her expression. "Repness was an obsessive record keeper, sir. He has records of my scores. He can prove that he doctored them to let me pass. And when that happens, they're going to vape my flying career."

Wedge sighed. "In the face of evidence like that, I doubt I'll be able to offer you much protection."

"I'm not here to ask for protection, sir. There is no protection. But I thought you ought to know—so you can prepare for it—that there's a possibility that I'm going to be yanked from the squadron."

"I understand. But let's say Repness doesn't accuse you. That he gets in touch with you privately and says, 'I can torp your career, but I won't. All you have to do is send me a few creds to help pay my legal team for my defense.' "

She took that hurdle without hesitation. "If he asks for one credit, sir, he doesn't get it. Let him turn me in and be damned."

"You're sure."

"I'm positive. I'm not going to let him have even the most tenuous of leashes on me. No more. Not ever."

He was silent a long moment. A shame she hadn't come to him right away upon joining Wraith Squadron's training program. If she had done so, he could have—

Could have? No, perhaps he *had* done so. Just after joining the Wraith Squadron, Flight Officer Sarkin had come to him, not knowing who, further up along any official channels, might be part of Repness's organization. Wedge had assigned Face and Phanan to find someone to act as bait, and within weeks they'd done so, in the hospital on Borleias. It was his plan, as well as Face and Phanan's, that had sent Lara Notsil to *Tedevium* and Colonel Repness.

The one thing that made him uncomfortable about this altered history was that he would be taking credit for initiating a plan actually brought into being by two of his subordinates . . . but the results would be worth this little deception.

"Flight Officer Sarkin."

She heard the change in his voice and snapped to attention. "Sir."

"You're too good a pilot for the squadron to lose you this way."

"I'm at the bottom of the squadron rankings, sir."

"No longer true. One of the new pilots has taken over that singular honor, at least temporarily. And even if it were true, the so-called worst Wraith is one of the galaxy's most dangerous opponents by any standard, else he or she wouldn't be in the squadron."

"Um—"

"That didn't call for a response. Now, this is a direct order: If anyone comes to you with questions about your dealings with Repness, you will give no answers. Instead, tell him you are under orders, from me, not to discuss the matter—until he has come to talk to me. Do you understand?"

"I understand the order, sir, but not what it means."

"What it means is that you're going to be with the Wraiths until you die or you decide to transfer—not until someone outside the unit decides you're not one of us. Now, dismissed."

Startled, she saluted and fled.

Wedge sat back. His story would survive interrogation up until the time anyone involved was called on to testify, but his gut feeling was that it wouldn't go that far. If it did, neither he nor his subordinates would commit perjury, and so they'd be in for punishment from the investigators. . . . But they'd all endured such punishment before. And would again, to retain the skills and loyalty and comradeship of a pilot like Tyria Sarkin.

Lara Notsil paused just inside the broad opening to *Mon Remonda*'s port hangar doors. Just stepping into the hangar was entering a different world.

The high-pitched whine of repulsorlift engines being tested cut into her. It was a welcome noise now, one she'd come to appreciate. Less welcome was the cold that accompanied it. The great doors at the hangar's far end were open, the chamber's atmosphere held in only by its magnetic containment field, and magcon was not an insulator—heat fled through the field into the vacuum of space. Outside the atmosphere, fighter hangars tended to be chilly places.

The hangar was occupied by twenty-one X-wings, and they'd been settled in tight to one another. Taking off without grazing an adjacent snubfighter would be a minor challenge. But that appeared to be characteristic of Commander Wedge Antilles—never letting his pilots grow complacent, even with such a simple task as taking off for a mission.

She headed toward her X-wing. As the last squadron pilot to land, she was in the rear of the packed formation, nearest the magcon shield, so she'd be among the first to take off. She waved at various Wraith and Rogue pilots, who acknowledged her with waves of their own, shouts of encouragement, or mock disparagement.

She didn't know what to make of them or how they were reacting to this mission.

The mission itself made perfect sense. Go in, stage a failed assault, try not to kill anyone—but defend yourself with all necessary force—and then get out safely. Let Zsinj jump to the wrong conclusion, that they'd fouled up and been driven off.

What was different, what was wrong, was the lack of disappointment among the Wraiths. Admiral Trigit's TIE-fighter pilots would have accepted such a mission with just as much discipline, but they would have been relentlessly unhappy about the restrictions against unnecessary elimination of the enemy. How can you reach the rank of ace, establish a name, gain fame as a fighter pilot, without killing the enemy? And the very prospect of leaving an armed enemy alive would have been repellent.

But these Rebel pilots took the restriction in good grace, and their relaxed attitude about it seemed to be genuine.

That, more than anything, bothered her about this unit. The Rebel pilots were supposed to be barely restrained mad dogs. Sure, she'd met several at the hospital on Borleias who didn't match that profile, but those were men and women recuperating from injuries, anxious to have some rest and recreation. But these Wraiths and Rogues were gearing up for combat. Their desire to eliminate the enemy should have been strong in them.

Perhaps Imperial evaluations of Rebel pilots were simply wrong. Not even accidentally wrong—just distorted to provide the Imperial pilots with more and better motivation to fight fiercely. Imperial pilots were, in fact, kept at a honed edge of ferocity, held at a barely contained level of fury that sometimes boiled out into violence at inappropriate times—in their quarters, with their families, on leave. By comparison, these X-wing pilots seemed emotionally quite healthy.

She shook her head. That had been a treasonous thought, dangerous to a woman who would be once again working for Imperial forces in the near future. She tried to banish it.

She climbed the ladder to her snubfighter's cockpit. A *Mon Remonda* mechanic was up there on the fuselage, making sure the R2 unit tucked in behind the cockpit was securely attached. "You've got a beauty here," the man said.

The R2 unit emitted a chirpy series of musical notes, acknowledgment of the compliment.

She stepped up into the cockpit and settled into her pilot's couch. "Brand-new from the factory." It was true; Colonel Repness could requisition new gear whenever a shipment was delivered to his training squadron, and apparently did. Her R2 unit, nicknamed Tonin, "Little Atton" in the Basic dialect of Aldivy, since she'd had its memory purged, was brand-new and unscathed, its base color a pretty silver white, its trim color an arterial red. It was loaded with several bells and whistles of top-of-the-line units. Warlord Zsinj's quartermaster would doubtless feel a little flicker of gratitude when she handed it over to him.

"Best of luck, pilot."

"Thanks."

Moments later, she had her helmet on and canopy down and was going through her power-up checklist. Four engines showing green, full power—Repness had made sure his personal X-wing was in tip-top shape, too. She still needed the mechanics to move the pilot's couch forward; it was adjusted as far forward as it would go, and she had to extend herself a little uncomfortably when handling rudder pedals. Repness had been a tall man.

Her comlink crackled into life. It was Wedge's voice: "All right, Rogues, Wraiths. Call 'em out in order."

"Rogue One, ready."

"Rogue Two, four lit and in the green."

"Rogue Three, ready to dance."

Only the Wraiths would be going as far as Lavisar. The Rogues would accompany them as far as the Lavisar system's outermost planetary ring, and would wait there. If, though odds were against it, this mission was a Zsinj trap against *Mon Remonda*, the Rogues would be ready to jump in and give Zsinj's forces a surprise they might not be ready to withstand.

A sudden chill passed through her, one not even her insulated pilot's suit and cockpit heater could immediately dispel. The Wraiths were supposed to fire a few shots, even land a few hits if they thought they could do so without unnecessarily taking life, and then flee.

But anything could happen. A laser blast aimed at a solar wing array could miss and hull a starfighter's cockpit. A sudden maneuver could startle a TIE-fighter pilot into veering straight into the path of one of his fellows.

Lara didn't want to kill today, and it wasn't for the apparently altruistic reasons demonstrated by the Wraiths. If she killed an Imperial pilot, how would she be regarded when she returned to Imperial employ?

"Wraith Twelve, ready for lift." That was Piggy's mechanical voice. She'd left a note to herself, in the portions of her mind that were so usefully automatic, for his voice to cue her own response. She shook away all the thoughts distracting her and said, "Wraith Thirteen, four green and topped off."

"Exit by current formation, by proximity to the magcon field, then form up by wings and units."

That made her first.

She began to run through the checklist in her mind that covered repulsorlift backing, rotating, exiting this type of facility—but no, it was not a good idea to overintellectualize among these pilots. She took the pilot's yoke, engaged the repulsorlift, and pulled up and backward with a smooth motion, beginning her rotation before she was two meters into the air. She smoothly cruised through the magcon field, which permitted her passage without the slightest discernible resistance. And she was in space.

Not for the first time; she'd flown training missions with the Y-wings of Screaming Wookiee training squadron after Repness's arrest, had soloed in both Y-wings and Repness's X-wing, had flown her own choice of course to rendezvous with *Mon Remonda*. But this was her first action.

She continued with repulsorlifts and rose until her stern pointed into empty space well above the entrance to the hangar, then engaged her thrust engines and pulled smoothly away from the Mon Calamari cruiser. Smooth, and by the numbers—but she was still acutely aware of the eyes that were and would be upon her.

Moments later, Wedge pulled beside and slightly ahead of her, and Face Loran took up position on the other side of the commander, drawn back level with her. As the ninth pilot of a unit that normally flew by paired wingmen, Lara had been assigned as the temporary third member of an existing pair.

They'd timed their arrival so that the face of Lavisar featuring its capital city, Syward, would be dead ahead when they emerged from hyperspace. And so it was: When the dazzling light show that was the end of a hyperspace jump faded, the Wraiths were aimed squarely at the portion of Lavisar's red-brown face that featured the largest recognizable glowing dot. Off to their starboard and ahead was the planet's largest moon, black in the eclipse shadow of the planet. The moon's gravity well, whose influence extended into hyperspace, had, as they'd intended it to, plucked them back into real-space. While this close to the moon, they would not be able to reenter hyperspace, and as they got closer to the planet's surface, the situation got even trickier; Lavisar had a number of moons, all of them large enough to hinder hyperspace jumps.

"Great placement, Twelve." Wedge's voice again. "All right. We should have a five-to-ten-minute window before they can bring online any secondary sensor arrays worth worrying about. Remember, you'll be aiming for a complex three times as long as wide, featuring sky-blue buildings—"

"Leader, this is Eight." Face's voice. "Visual sensors on the Syward military base show TIE fighters scrambling. I see two full squadrons mobilizing. They're wearing planetary defense colors."

"They can't be coming after us, Eight. Their sensors—can you visually scan their main sensor station?"

"Working on it, Leader."

Lara smiled. Though their transmissions were encrypted, she had to assume the Wraiths would be using a code sequence that had been in use for a while—one whose useful lifetime was nearing an end. If the planetary defenders recorded enough of these transmissions and could crack them, the Wraiths' prescripted dialogue would sound perfectly normal for a botched mission in progress.

"Tonin, scan normal Imperial frequencies," she said. "Send anything you hear that sounds like pilot traffic to my helmet comlink. When Wraith transmissions and Imperial transmissions conflict, continue recording the Imperial transmissions but let me hear only the Wraiths."

The display unit set aside for communication with the astromech popped up with a quick reply: UNDERSTOOD.

And almost immediately she began to hear faint, fuzzy transmissions, garbled words: "—ming up. Deploy by fists—"; "—file suggests still in approach vec—"

"Leader, Eight. Visual sensors show the ground sensor complex intact. There seems to be some scoring damage on the northeast wall and civilian crews there. It looks like our ground team fouled up."

Even distorted by New Republic comm equipment, Wedge's voice was hard. "They're going to be sorry they got back to us. They'll wish they only had Lavisar authorities to deal with. Wraiths, come about in formation. Twelve, confirm and then transmit our escape vector."

"Twelve, understood."

The Wraiths began a slow sweep, bringing them around toward deep space again, taking them back out the way they had come.

"—trol indicates enemy force is flee—"; "Stay in formation, we're chasing them all the way—"; "—like banthas to the hunters. Stay tight."

Lara frowned. That last transmission had not sounded right. "Tonin, can you plot the origins of the Imperial transmissions you've received so far?"

APPROXIMATELY.

"Do so. Put them up on my sensor board."

Her sensor screen, which previously had shown only the two nearby planetary bodies and a single blue blip representing all the Wraiths, now added two fuzzy red fields—one at the planet's surface, one near the nearest moon's surface at a point not too distant from the Wraiths' escape vector. The fields wavered as the astromech continuously recalculated probable points of origin and projected them onto the screen.

"Tonin, subtract the Lavisar transmissions from the image."

DONE.

"Transmit the image to Wraith Leader's R2 and ask him to put it on his sensor screen."

DONE.

She activated her comm system. "Leader, this is Thirteen. I'm picking up indications that we have company ahead. Probably the garrison of a lunar station."

"Understood, Thirteen. Good work. Wraiths, break to starboard on my lead. Twelve, give us a new escape course."

"Twelve, understood."

Wedge rolled out to starboard, a course that would take the Wraiths past one of Lavisar's secondary moons—and keep them within troublesome gravity wells, unable to jump to hyperspace, even longer, but now the shortest course away from the planet and new enemies. Lara followed, her maneuver as smooth as that of the commander's other wingman.

New activity on the sensor board: a single red blip distancing itself from the primary moon, heading toward the Wraiths on an intercept course. As Lara watched, the blip became two, one ahead, one lagging behind. She adjusted the display to zoom in on the image and saw that the forward blip was registering as a full squad of TIE fighters, moving at maximum speed, while the rear blip was four units "unknown type" with a 75 percent probability that they were *Lambda*-class shuttles.

That made sense. A manufacturer making *Lambda*-type vehicles probably had a production combat model, one with heavier armor and equipped with heavy guns, to supplement its space forces.

"Wraiths, this is Leader. My astromech calculates that the lunar unit will be on us before we clear the gravity well of that second moon. Once they encounter us—assuming we engage them—we'll have about three minutes before the planetary units catch up to us. Mission Order One is rescinded. Engage and eliminate the lunar force with all dispatch. Then form up and get back to our escape course. Twelve?"

"I have a flexible escape course plotted, lacking only the

crucial variable—the exact point we join up and prepare to exit."

"Good. Get ready."

9

When the incoming TIE fighters were only a handful of kilometers away, Wedge announced, "S-foils to attack position. Break by pairs, choose your targets, make it fast." He suited action to words by rolling out, a smooth maneuver that carried him directly toward the enemy force.

Lara followed suit, with Face Loran a split second late but equally sure-handed. The sound of someone's breathing, harsh and ragged, filled her ears, then she realized she was listening to herself. She forced her breathing to slow, forced herself to concentrate.

The first part would be a head-on confrontation between TIEs and X-wings, the two forces approaching at maximum speed, firing as they came. Once the lines crossed, the more maneuverable TIE fighters would whip around to try to get on the slower X-wings' tails—simple strategy. And the X-wing pilots would be doing everything they could, using all their combined experience, to shake this deadly pursuit.

She put all shield power to her bow shields for the head-to-head approach. Wedge and Face had to have done the same by now.

That was an interesting thought. Wedge Antilles, flying

mere meters ahead of her with no power to his stern shields. She could put a quad-linked laser blast into his engines and erase his name, so hated by Imperial pilots, from the roster of New Republic warriors.

Rebel warriors, that is. Then—what? Take out Face Loran with an identical shot, transmit a surrender to the Lavisar forces, get an escort down to the planet's surface . . . and live the rest of her life in the fame that belonged to the pilot who shot down Wedge Antilles.

Such an odd feeling. Wedge Antilles was under her guns, yet he trusted her with his life.

He had no reason not to, of course. But he *did*. No one had in—how long? Forever.

She could eliminate him with a twitch of the finger.

It should have been tempting. Yet, somehow, it wasn't.

Such an attack would be treacherous.

She laughed. *Listen to yourself. There's no such thing as treachery. Only efficiency.* That was one of the basic tenets of Imperial Intelligence, and she had lived by those words.

But at a certain point she had decided that Admiral Apwar Trigit was treacherous. He'd chosen to sacrifice a shipload of dedicated servicemen so their vessel would not fall into the hands of the New Republic, and she had engineered his destruction because of that decision. She had taken revenge on him for a concept as simple, and as out of place for an Intelligence officer, as personal honor.

Tonin beeped a warning. The range meter dropped to two kilometers, the distance at which New Republic targeting systems could begin to place shots in an almost accurate fashion. The numbers continued to drop, and Wedge and Face both fired, their red laser blasts, quad-linked beams of pure destruction, lashing out toward Lavisar's defenders.

Her breath became ragged again as something, a fog that thoughts couldn't quite penetrate, closed down over her brain. *Defend your wingman. Can't kill Imperial pilots. The price on Wedge Antilles's head means years of security. Zsinj is the same as Trigit.*

She switched her lasers to single fire, fast cycle, which would allow her to fire an almost continuous stream of low-powered blasts, and brought up her targeting computer. Immediately the system's yellow brackets settled in a jittery fashion around one of the oncoming TIE fighters and turned green, indicating a lock. The cockpit audio system howled in confirmation.

Reflexively, she fired. Her red laser streaked past the oncoming TIE fighter, but she held the stick down and the system cycled, blast after blast emerging. She shook the yoke in her hand, spraying fire around as though using a nozzle to water a patch of grass, and saw one of the beams strike home, charring a hole in the starfighter's port solar array wing.

It was so close—she tried to keep her spray of fire concentrated on it, and then there was a tremendous bang and her X-wing shook from bow to stern. The module holding the S-foil configuration switch popped out of its housing and dropped before her eyes, swaying there, held to the upper bank of controls by wires.

She swatted it out of the way, tried to look out the viewports, at the diagnostic display, at the sensor display all at the same time. The viewport showed Wedge rolling out up and to port. She gave up on the viewscreens and followed. "Tonin, give me a loud beep if we're badly hit."

No beep.

"Good job, Thirteen." That was Three, she thought. "That's a confirmed kill."

"Thanks, Three." His words hovered outside the shield of stray thoughts that seemed to be insulating her brain.

Behind—the enemy would be coming up behind. She looked back, saw only the top of Tonin's dome head, and checked the sensors again. Yes, two TIE fighters were coming around fast, trying to take up positions behind her. But they were making a broad loop to do it, perhaps intimidated by the firepower they'd just come through. She could try to cut hard to starboard and might be in position for another head-to-head by the time they got their guns fixed on her—

No. Her job was to follow her wingman. Protect him.

Wedge cut hard to starboard. She followed, her turn not quite as precise. The maneuver was too much for the X-wing's inertial compensator and the metal box holding the S-foil configuration switch swung on its wires, slamming into the side of her helmet. She ignored it, tried to stay with her leader, and held to his port rear quarter, though space opened up between them. A glance out her own port viewport showed Face there, struggling to maintain formation.

A green laser blast appeared, blindingly bright, between her and Face. Wedge finished his maneuver, firing already at the two oncoming TIE fighters. Lara tried to place her targeting brackets on one of the two, couldn't manage it—the starfighter was too maneuverable, jittering out of the way. She fired anyway, her spray of single-shot lasers slicing through vacuum near the TIE fighter's starboard wing.

The TIE pilot jerked away from the bombardment of red fire, drifted to port . . . straight into Wedge Antilles's quadlinked blast. The quartet of lasers sliced cleanly through the fighter's spherical cockpit. The TIE fighter disappeared in a glorious explosion of red, orange, and yellow, and Lara heard clanks and pings as her X-wing sliced through the cloud.

There were also the echoes of a scream. Lara shook her head. She couldn't have heard the pilot.

Unless he was transmitting. "Tonin, cut my reception of Imperial comm traffic at once."

DONE.

"Two for Leader, one for Thirteen." That was Two again. Lara swatted at his intrusive voice as though it were that damned configuration switch. She tried to find the other TIE fighter on her sensors, but the closest enemy was outbound, head toward the cloud of red blips representing the two full squadrons from Lavisar's surface.

In fact, all the remaining TIE fighters—five of them—were outbound.

"Wraiths, Leader. Form up. Twelve, make your calculations and get us out of here. I make it less than a minute before they overtake us. Give me status reports by number."

"This is Three. No kills. Minor damage to port topside fuzial engine. I'm shutting it down."

"Four. Two kills. No damage."

It was there, battering at her head as insistently as the switch housing swinging into her helmet, a thought that wouldn't let her go. *Zsinj is the same as Trigit.* Why had she thought that?

Because it was true. Raptor forces had not risen against the Wraiths. Had this been a Zsinj-controlled planet, Raptors would have been the first forces up—they had to maintain their reputation for brutality and efficiency. So this world *was* independent and the intercepted Raptor transmission a false lead, as the Wraiths had said.

And since the forces of Lavisar weren't set up for the Wraiths—else there would have been a lot more of them—this was just what Commander Antilles had said: a plan by Zsinj to have New Republic—

Rebel.

—Rebel forces hurt the planet's defenses, maybe knock them down. So Zsinj could move in, either as a conqueror or a defending hero. Those two choices were the same: Zsinj in control.

She wanted to admire the plan, especially as it extended to the other worlds *Mon Remonda* had been assaulting. It was clever, efficient.

But those pilots, who'd just been sacrificed, who'd died to satisfy Zsinj's sense of efficiency. It was like Admiral Trigit. And it wasn't—

"Thirteen."

—honorable. There was no honor in it.

And the last fifteen years of Gara Petothel's life closed in around Lara Notsil like a coffin. Her parents' work for Imperial Intelligence. Their arrest and execution for unspecified treason. How Gara had hated them, missed them. How she'd learned, so eagerly, and demonstrated such loyalty, so that nothing like that would ever happen to her.

"Thirteen."

All her life, she'd known not to believe the Rebels and their simplistically optimistic propaganda. Now she could no longer put her faith in the forces that had taken her, trained her, shaped her. There was nothing for her.

Tonin's irritable beeping finally caught her attention. LEADER WANTS TO KNOW IF YOU'RE HURT.

"Oh. Uh . . ." She keyed her comlink. "Sorry, Leader. Thirteen reporting—" She finally scanned her diagnostic board. "Forward shields down to forty-seven percent but climbing. I

think I took a hit in that first head-to-head. Some gauges out."
She grabbed the S-foil switch where it hung and switched it.
Her S-foils did not close up into cruise configuration. "S-foil
actuator seems to be out. And I think I hit my head."

"Drop your shield, you don't need it. Don't worry about
your S-foils. Just acknowledge receipt of the new course and
prepare to enter it on my mark."

"Understood, Leader. Um, I've received the course and it
checks out."

"Three, I want you to engage hyperdrive five seconds after
the rest of the squad launches, in case battle damage has
knocked out anyone's drive."

"Got it, One."

"On my mark, three, two, one . . . Jump."

They returned to *Mon Remonda*'s port hangar much as they'd
left it, a little more battered, with Piggy's fuselage scored by a
laser graze, with Lara's S-foils unable to assume cruise position, but otherwise unhurt.

Lara climbed out into a chaotic sea of backslaps and embraces, handshakes and congratulations.

Everyone seemed to move in slow motion. Words were
slowed, almost incomprehensible, and sounds were muted.
Tyria's blond ponytail swayed with the sinuous motion of a
snake. Piggy's reserved arm motions, as he described some
complicated maneuver or another, seemed to be those of a
Gamorrean in low gravity.

Yet the one thing Lara understood was the expressions
turned on her. They were the eyes of a group to whom she
belonged.

Not since her parents' loss had she seen that expression.

And the Wraiths and Rogues weren't saying it, weren't deliberately expressing the thought, "You are one of us." No, it
was implicit, a backdrop to whatever else they were saying.
*Good job noticing that backup squad. Nice shot; how'd you
manage it with your lasers on single fire? Your first kill silhou-
ette, congratulations and condolences.*

One of us.

She worked her way out from the midst of the crowd and walked, still somehow insulated from the words and physical sensations of the world around her, to the pilots' quarters she now shared with Tyria.

Maybe she could do it. Maybe she could just *be* Lara Notsil, forever, with Lieutenant Gara Petothel, that poor, unhappy creature, truly among the dead of the Star Destroyer *Implacable*.

One of us.

She slept, and in her dreams Gara and Lara argued with one another, speaking words she could barely hear and couldn't understand, exchanging thoughts that would make no sense when she awoke, and she did not know which of the two wore her face.

When the Wraiths returned to Hawk-bat Station, with their new member in tow, they found that the other members of the squadron had not been idle. On his own initiative, Kell Tainer had plotted and led two missions, all because of Runt.

"We determined that they, the people of Halmad, had made a mistake," the long-faced alien said, pride in his voice. He stood at the head of the cargo module that served as the Wraiths' conference room; the pilots were packed in around its narrow oval table. "They had installed a new set of sensor stations on the west coast of Hullis's continent and decommissioned the older sensor stations out in the western islands. But when we examined the specifications of those new sensors, we discovered that their effective range was a couple of hundred kilometers short of the area they were supposed to cover. Meaning that we now possessed a narrow corridor of airspace we could drop into without any real likelihood of detection. After that, with terrain-following flying to make other sensor tracking difficult, we were able to stage raids on ground emplacements."

"Raid number one," Kell said, "was on a port warehouse district in the city of Fellon. Not much booty there, I'm afraid. We picked up a large stock of recreational holos being produced by the Imperials, propaganda dramas to make Face blush—"

"That'd take some doing," Face said. "I'm shameless."

"True. But also, in taking off, we strafed the marina where the recreational water vessels of the city's wealthy—and other people, including the wealthy of the city of Hullis and the officers of Victory Base there—were docked. Did a few dozen million credits' worth of damage to some very pretty vessels.

"In our second mission, we struck at Hullis herself. We put Castin on the ground the day before to do what he could with security systems, and then Phanan and I flew in, blew a hole in the side of a building, and flew out with as much cargo as we could load without sacrificing the flying speed of our TIE fighters."

"What cargo?" Wedge asked.

"Imperial credit notes, coin, gems. We hit one of the official money-exchange sites used by the Imperial base."

Wedge gaped. "You robbed a bank."

"We did. It was fun, too. Getting clear was a little tricky— that close in, it's impossible to elude their sensors—but we just took off straight for space, suffered their antiaerial-invasion gun barrage, and outflew the TIEs they sent in pursuit. End result, a few dings and pits in Phanan's starfighter."

"To match," Phanan said, "the few dings and pits in its pilot."

"Tell them what I did," Castin said.

"Oh, that's right. In the day or so he had before his extraction, Castin managed to forge us a high-level account on their global information service. We're now being bounced visual and sensor data from their planetary defense satellite network. It's not being beamed straight at us, don't worry—we've set up a relay near one of the existing satellite-belt mining colonies. If it's detected, we can detonate the retransmitter before they're likely to get it open. Anyway, we've picked up signs that they're constructing a couple of small starfighter bases, possibly as a counter against our ground missions. One of them is near Fellon, the other way out east of Hullis in a region that doesn't seem to need the extra protection, so now we have to wonder what *is* out there." Kell smiled, his expression reflecting a simple pride in the Wraiths' accomplishments while most of the officers were gone. "Castin has also modified the comm systems in all our TIEs so they distort our voices more effectively—the new computer-controlled distortion actually modifies accents and changes genders, making it even harder for listeners to identify our voices."

"That's good work," Wedge said. "But on this pirate activity, I just wish you all didn't look as though you'd enjoyed yourselves so much."

Phanan snorted. "A happy worker is a productive worker."

Wedge nodded. "But a happy pirate is a career pirate. You do remember that the Hawk-bats are a front, a sham?"

Kell and Phanan exchanged looks suggesting that this was news to them.

"That's what I thought. Anything else?"

Runt said, "Yes. We have also identified the regular schedule and course of a refueling tanker that leaves Halmad, takes a tour of government mining operations in the asteroid belt, and returns to the city of Hullis. It is now escorted by a couple of TIE fighters, but I think that with the proper surprise we could take them before a distress signal is sent. If we capture the tanker but fly it along its regular course, that gives us one opportunity to drop our entire squadron and perhaps *Sungrass* as well down on Hullis, should we ever need to mount a larger-scale mission there . . . or just capture a refueling tanker should we ever need one."

"Good to know. All right, Wraiths—"

"Hawk-bats," corrected Kell, absently.

Wedge gave him a stern look. "Wraiths, make sure your pirates' take is logged to the last credit for your report to Coruscant. Now, with the good work you did while we were gone, you've added quite a lot to the sting the government of Halmad has to be feeling." He began counting items off on his fingers. "We've hurt them militarily with the theft of the interceptors and then of the replacement parts. We've put civilian pressure on them with that water-vehicle raid. We've hurt them economically with the money changers' strike, and that will also result in more civilian pressure. And we've demonstrated that we can enter their airspace and leave at will, no casualties, no apparent effort that they can discern, and that's the *most* important thing. They've lived at a relative level of peace for too long and don't know how to cope with a unit like the Wraiths. With any luck, that will put them in the camp of Zsinj and his protection—"

"So Zsinj can come and squash us," said Face.

Wedge smiled. "If you're as tough to squash as you are to predict, he'll be in for an unpleasant surprise.

"All right. Let's keep the pressure up on them. I want those two starfighter bases eliminated—a clear message to the Imperial forces on Halmad that anything they can construct, the Hawk-bats can knock down. And I think, to demonstrate our superiority and their helplessness, we ought to stage those two eliminations simultaneously. So let's settle in and do some planning."

One of the base's inhabitable cargo modules had been equipped to serve as the squadron's cafeteria, with an adjoining module serving as the galley. While most of the Wraiths had been away on *Mon Remonda*, Kell and mechanic Cubber Daine had used laser cutters to open a large portion of the wall facing the Trench, giving it the aspect of a large viewport minus transparisteel, and had improvised additional chairs and tables out there. Now the Wraiths had a dining choice of "inside" or "outside on the patio." Face had seen Wedge shaking his head over these minute decorative differences, but the squadron commander had never stepped in to regiment the Wraiths on such matters.

Tonight, after the last long planning session before Operation Groundquake—as Tyria had nicknamed the plan to knock down two Imperial bases—Face ate at a table "on the patio." Usually he shared a table with Phanan, a platform from which the two of them could harangue the other diners, but tonight his wingman was at an inside table with Lara Notsil. Face couldn't fault Phanan his choice of companions; Lara was attractive, quick-witted, good company. He saw her laugh at one of Phanan's jokes.

There was a little tension in her body language. She probably still didn't feel that she fit in with the Wraiths. It was likely that she wouldn't for a while.

Lara spoke a few words to Phanan, good cheer still evident in her expression, then policed her tray and left. Phanan remained behind.

And Face saw his partner do something uncharacteristic. Phanan slowly settled into an attitude of stillness so profound that it would have been difficult for an observer to tell whether he was alive or dead, had he not been breathing. Other than the slow rise and fall of his chest, nothing moved; his one human eye was closed, and his posture gradually slumped into an attitude of profound resignation, of complete defeat.

Face rose and approached him, stepping over the low lip of the new opening. "Ton?"

Phanan jerked upright, and his expression was suddenly merry. "Face! Just the man. Polish my boots, would you, son? I have a mission tomorrow."

Face gestured at his own lieutenant's insignia.

"Oh, that's right. In spite of my superior intellect, you figured out who to bribe first. My loss." Phanan rose and quickly cleaned off his tray, stowing it in the rack set aside for that purpose.

"Are you all right?"

Phanan looked at him, evidently confused. "Of course. Oh, the boots thing is a disappointment, of course. Maybe I can get Wedge to clean them."

Face snorted. "You're angling to get in some laser targeting practice, aren't you? As the target."

"No, I've been there. No desire to repeat the experience." Phanan stretched and yawned. "I'd better hit my bunk. Mission tomorrow."

"That's right."

Phanan breezed past him with a final smile and headed up the Trench toward the flight officers' quarters. Face let him go, but felt unsettled, as though he'd seen some sort of simulacrum of Phanan walk by, with the real Phanan missing and unaccounted for.

. . .

An hour later, after doing a last simulation run against Fellon Base, Face stopped by the quarters Phanan shared with Piggy. His initial rap at the door elicited no answer, so he knocked again.

"Go away. Or, if you're at lieutenant rank or higher, go away, *sir*."

"I need to speak to you, Ton."

"Tomorrow."

"Right now."

"I'm with somebody."

"I know. Piggy said you'd asked him to bunk out for the evening. This will only take a moment."

The door into the modified cargo module opened with a hiss. It wasn't a mechanical hiss; the modules didn't have hydraulic doors. The noise was a sound of exasperation, and Phanan made it. The cybernetically enhanced pilot wore a loose robe of scarlet silk and an irritated expression. "What?"

Face squeezed past him into the module's first chamber. These modules were divided into three chambers, the largest for socializing, the next largest containing two bunks, the smallest acting as a refresher. Face saw that the terminal here in the main chamber was alive but with nothing on it. "There's no one here."

"Keep your voice down. She's back in the bunkroom."

"There's no one there, either."

"Are you calling me a liar?" There was no anger in Phanan's tone, just curiosity.

"You don't drink when you're entertaining. And I can smell the booze in the air."

Phanan shrugged negligently and pulled a bottle from his robe pocket. The label identified it as Halmad Prime, doubtless a diverted part of the shipment the "Hawk-bats" had seized off *Barderia*. Phanan held it out. "Care for some?"

"No. What's the matter, Ton?"

Phanan shut the module door and sat—slouched, rather—on the chamber's inflatable sofa. "I get drunk faster these days."

"A sign of age?"

"No." Phanan shook his head. "There's less of me for the alcohol to pollute. Every year, less meat, more machine. So the alcohol goes to work faster."

Face pulled the terminal chair around and sat wrongways in it so he could lean forward against its back. "I'm not sure I understand."

"She wasn't interested, Face. In me."

"Lara?"

"Yes, Lara. Well, actually, at various times, Falynn, Tyria, various ladies on Folor, Borleias, and Coruscant, then Shalla, Dia, and most recently Lara." He tipped the bottle up and took a long pull from it.

Face snorted. "Maybe you need to work on your technique. What sort of invitation did you make her?"

"Ah, that's just it. I didn't make *any* sort of invitation. I just sat with her, and talked with her, and read her eyes. She thought my jokes were funny. She was interested in my stories about the campaign we waged with Admiral Trigit. She liked me, I think she did. But . . . other than that . . . nothing. I held no other appeal for her. And that's the way it's been for quite some time."

"Look, Ton, being at war kind of limits all our social lives. I'm sure you'll find someone—"

"Finish that idiotic gesture of reassurance and I'll be obliged to put your face through this wall," Phanan said. His tone was mild, but there was no mistaking the seriousness in his words. He wasn't even looking at Face, he hadn't moved or tensed, yet something in his tone made his threat very real. "You don't understand."

"Make me understand."

Phanan looked up at the low ceiling of the cargo module as if seeing through it, as if staring at a starry sky in the hope that it could provide inspiration. "A long time ago, back at the Battle of Endor, the frigate I was working on as a doctor was hit by an Imperial barrage. Blew out whole sections of the hull, sucked crewmen out into hard vacuum. I was hit by a falling beam superheated by laser fire. One minute I'm helping a pilot with a concussion, the next minute that pilot's been dead for two weeks and I'm just waking up with a mechanical half a face and a mechanical leg.

"Ever since then, no woman has looked at me with any sort of serious interest."

"It's not the leg or the face, Ton."

"I know that, you moronic nerf." Phanan glared at him, the glowing optic that served him as a left eye making the expression malevolent. "But something died when I was hit in that medical ward, and I think it was my future. I think people, maybe only women, can just look at me and say, 'There's no future in him.' "

"That's ridiculous."

"There's no mechanical replacement for a future, Face. And every time I take a hit, and they have to cut away another part of me and replace it with machinery because I'm allergic to bacta, every time that happens I seem to be a little further away from the young doctor who had a future. He can't come back, Face. Not all of him is here anymore."

"Ton . . ."

"Don't give me some line about my not knowing what I'm talking about because I'm drunk and morose. I know I'm drunk and morose. But the truth of what I'm telling you is around me all the time, even when I'm not drunk. Even when I'm enjoying everything about my life. No future, and no one in my future."

"You have your friends, Ton."

Phanan nodded. "Yes, I do. And I'm grateful for them. But my friends are my present. And when I try to look from where they are to where my future is, there's just no one there. No future."

"I don't know what to tell you. I wish you didn't feel this way."

"Me either."

"Give me the bottle."

"I know. Mission tomorrow." Phanan handed over the bottle, two-thirds of its contents gone.

"If you're not right for the mission tomorrow morning, I want you to tell me."

"Yes, Lieutenant."

Face wanted to say more, but the sudden formality of Phanan's last reply had somehow propelled him out of the conversation. He just shook his head and left.

10

Tyria entered the bunkroom module she now shared with Lara and waved the datacard she held. "Mail from home."

Lara gave her an uncertain smile. "Should I leave so you can watch it in private? That's not a problem."

"It's not for me. Most of my family is gone, and what's left is on Toprawa—and no mail comes off Toprawa." This was true; the world, where Rebel Alliance forces had staged delivery of information that had been vital to the destruction of the first Death Star, had been punished by the Empire as an act of warning. Its cities had been destroyed, its people reduced to barbarism. "And this is addressed to you. I'd be happy to leave if *you* want privacy."

Lara took the card, curious, and slid it into the appropriate slot on her terminal. Her name came up at the top of the screen, and a prompt to enter her password. File information showed that the message was much too large for a mere text transmission, so it was bound to be voice and image. "No, that's all right. I have no secrets." She entered her password and brought up the mail message.

A man's face, good-looking and somewhat roguish, surrounded by black hair cut close and a trim mustache; behind was a plain beige wall, a table with some holos on it, an open viewport showing a landscape of blasted, black ground. "Hello, Lara," the man said. "I don't imagine you ever thought you'd hear from me again."

Lara frowned. Who was this man? Then she recognized his face, a face she'd only seen a couple of times in files she'd hastily memorized some time ago, and she felt her jaw drop. "It's—it's—Tavin Notsil. My brother."

"I thought he was supposed to be—"

"I know you must have thought I was dead," the recording continued. "Just as I thought you were. It seems that fate has spared us both. I'd made some unusual arrangements with the town constable and was earning an honest living on the Sea of Aldiv under an assumed name when New Oldtown was hit. I came home and everything I knew was gone. But now I find out that you've survived. I can't tell you how happy I am."

Lara felt Tyria squeeze her and heard her whisper "Congratulations." But Lara's mind was racing down pathways far from human contact.

She'd have to reply to this boob. Somehow break off all family contact forever, and without letting him see a holo of her—of Gara Petothel.

Then her attention fell on the holos on the table behind Tavin. They showed family scenes. The real Lara Notsil's mother and father sharing a swing tied to a tree behind their farmhouse. A much younger Tavin Notsil swimming in the family pond. And, seated atop a repulsor thresher, her expression cheerful, Lara Notsil—

Not the real Lara Notsil. Her, Gara Petothel, in farm clothes, with fine blond hair, wearing a sunburn she'd never suffered in life. She froze the picture, looked at it, willing it and its wrongness away.

The world spun and Lara's knees went weak. She slumped back in her chair and felt Tyria support her. Heard her murmur, "Whoa, there. Obviously this is a big shock for you. I'll get Dr. Phanan."

Lara clung to Tyria's hand, not letting her leave. "No doctor. I'm all right." Her words were faint in her own ears, but she knew she didn't want anyone else seeing her. Not until she had this sorted out.

She'd never been on the world of Aldivy. She'd never been seated on that thresher. Before a few weeks ago, she'd never been Lara Notsil. Or was that a lie? Was she really Lara, and her memories of Gara Petothel some bizarre dream? The walls still seemed to spin as she tried to force her way through the sense of unreality that possessed her. She unfroze the message.

Her brother was now looking at a datapad. "Listen, you'll probably find this ironic. Do you remember putting in for a transfer to move to Greenton and transmitting an application to Lachany Foods there? I have your original letter here. 'If I can effect this transfer, would you be interested in employing a technician with my skills and special knowledge? It is my hope that you would.' "

Lara shut her eyes and resisted the temptation to cover her ears against the barrage of confusing half memories. She knew those words. She'd written those words. And if those were Lara Notsil's words, then she was Lara, not Gara.

"Well, Lachany Foods wrote back. They apparently didn't cross-index the destruction of New Oldtown with the season's applications before they did that—in other words, they don't know you're dead. I mean, that you're supposed to be dead. Anyway, they're offering you the job you wanted, at the salary you were hoping for. They're really interested in what you have to offer them." Tavin's expression became earnest. "Listen, Lara, I understand you have some sort of job on Coruscant processing data. And if you're happy there, that's fine. But I doubt you are. All those tall buildings—if you want this job, send me the word. I'll let them know. I can even arrange passage for you back to Aldivy. You just let me know."

Tavin's eyes flickered to something offscreen, then back. "It looks like I'm almost out of time, if I'm going to keep this message affordable. Whether you want this job or not, let me hear from you. Good-bye for now." He half smiled and the picture froze.

Words popped up on the screen, superimposed over his face in white. They were the chronicle of the path the message took to reach her—from Aldivy to her former quarters on Coruscant, then to the main New Republic message authority on Coruscant, then—with the secrecy flag activated—to *Tedevium* and *Mon Remonda*. Finally it had come here, though there was no chronicle of that final bounce; the Wraiths' presence in the Halmad system was still top secret.

Lara just sat and tried to breathe, tried to sort out what was happening to her.

Then it came to her. Those *had* been her words. But she'd written them on Coruscant in a letter to Warlord Zsinj. She, Gara, had written them, not she, Lara, the false identity.

She felt her breathing relax, as though a belt tied across her rib cage had been suddenly loosened. She knew who she was again.

Why was Tavin Notsil quoting her a letter she'd written to Warlord Zsinj? Obviously, this was an indirect message from Zsinj. Tavin Notsil was in on it. That made sense. He was supposed to be a crook, a confidence man.

She felt wobbly again. That meant Zsinj had penetrated her Lara Notsil identity. It was no longer a haven for her. She felt tears welling up, and for once she could not contain them—her legendary ability to start and stop crying at will abandoned her. She buried her face in her hands and cried.

"It's all right," Tyria said. "Even good news can be a big shock. Are you sure you don't want to see the doctor?"

"No doctor." What was she going to do? Just days ago, she had abandoned her plan, her desire to serve Zsinj. She had decided to stay here, to belong here. And now Zsinj had denied her the future she'd stumbled upon.

She rose, the motion made difficult by her suddenly shaky legs, and turned an uncertain smile on Tyria. "I think I just need to walk for a while."

"I understand. Later, if you need to talk—"

"Thank you."

Outside her habitation module, she turned right on the Trench, heading deeper into the mine shaft that served the Wraiths as home. Deeper tended to mean away from people.

.   .   .

Face, again at his favorite "patio" table, making some final notes on tomorrow's mission, saw Lara exit her bunk module and walk away. He returned his attention to his work, then looked at her again. There was something odd about her movement . . .

She was angry, no question of it. But that wasn't all. All of a sudden, her carriage was appropriate for Coruscant—shorter steps, hunched shoulders, the posture of a woman who lived within the imposing and paranoia-inducing canyons of the Imperial throneworld for many years.

Or, perhaps, Admiral Trigit had taught her to walk this way when she'd been his drugged captive. That made more sense; a man like that might be offended at the long, rangy stride of an Aldivian farm girl and have modifications to her physical mannerisms on the list of things to change when he broke her spirit.

Face sighed. He suspected that the mind of Lara Notsil was a deeper mess than anyone had realized before now. With luck, she'd turn to her fellow Wraiths when she realized she was in trouble. Until that happened, all he could do was watch and be ready.

A little troubled, he returned his attention to his planning.

One "block" from her module—a block being one uninterrupted series of cargo modules—Lara ran into Kell Tainer. The big lieutenant was working out against a combat dummy, a human-shaped object made of materials tough and malleable enough to withstand the fist, foot, elbow, and knee blows Kell was raining upon it. When he saw her watching, he stopped.

"Is that how you get rid of tension?" she asked.

"That's right."

"What do you do when you just want to scream?"

He pointed farther down the shaft. "Two blocks down, there's a powered door to the left. It leads to a cross tunnel. It has lights and gravity until you get to the boundaries marked in yellow, about a hundred meters. Don't go beyond those boundaries."

"Thank you."

He was right. Once the door to that cross tunnel shut behind her, she could feel that she was cut off from the Wraiths, from all contact with people. She was surrounded by the reassuring solidity of stone walls and metal doors.

She screamed, an expulsion of anger and confusion that stripped her throat raw. Her cry echoed down the half-lit corridor and was lost in the distance. She did it again and again, until she had almost no voice left. Almost no bewilderment left. Just tiredness. Then she put her back against the rough stone wall and slid down to sit, her face in her hands.

Her little vacation was over. It was time to think analytically again.

First, Zsinj was about to consume the future that she'd just decided she wanted. What could she do about that?

Second, she'd just had a crisis of identity she should never have suffered. She never should have felt any confusion about who she'd been. Where she'd come from. Much as she wanted to be Lara Notsil, there should never have been any doubt that she'd originally been Gara Petothel. What was that all about?

All right. First problem.

Possible solution: Return to original plan and join Zsinj. She shook her head over that. At Lavisar, she'd decided, once and forever, that Zsinj was unworthy. Not just unworthy of her, unworthy of any aid, of any success. He was dishonorable. She would never join him.

Possible solution: Confess all to her commanding officer. No, that would solve only some of her problems. Wedge Antilles might accept her aid in the continued campaign against Zsinj, but he would never trust her again. No one would. That trust, she'd found, was more addictive than spice was supposed to be. She could not live without experiencing it again and wondered how she'd lived so long without it. And on a more pragmatic note, Lieutenant Myn Donos was a member of Wraith Squadron. Before he'd been a Wraith, he was the commander of Talon Squadron. And during the time when Gara had been a deep-cover operative working for Admiral Trigit, she'd blithely obeyed orders and spliced some false information about the security designation of a specific world into the

New Republic database; Talon Squadron, later relying on that information, had been annihilated. All but Donos. If he knew what she'd done, he might kill her.

Possible solution: Put Zsinj off, delay him, perhaps feed him false information, and ride out this campaign against him. Once he was destroyed, he could no longer expose her. That was possible. With delicate handling, that might work. She decided on that approach for the time being.

Now, her emotional crisis of a few minutes ago.

You must become your role.

The voice was male, silky. Its tones caressed. A casual listener might think that the speaker cared about the person he was talking to. Lara knew better; he was simulating affection.

But whose voice was it? She couldn't remember. She supposed it was one of her teachers when she was training to become an Imperial Intelligence agent. Context made that clear.

Plant your triggers deep in your mind. When they are activated, come back to yourself. Achieve your objectives. And then bury everything beneath your role again.

She couldn't quite see the face; it was a man silhouetted by lights behind him. Peering into those lights made her eyes water.

Let Gara go. All today, you'll be Kirney.

That jolted her, brought her eyes open. She'd forgotten about Kirney Slane. Her first role, her practice role. A Coruscant student of economics, daughter of a hotelier who had never existed. Within the mind of Kirney Slane, Lara had walked among the middle society of Coruscant, fluent in the small talk of officers' spouses. She'd flirted, promoted herself like so many whose goal began and ended with marrying a promising officer.

Lara shook her head to clear the memories. Kirney was distant, Kirney was dead. Once her usefulness as a training tool had ended, she'd been forbidden to assume that name, that manner, that mentality again.

If it has practical application, retain it. If it has only sentimental attraction for you, abandon it. He, her mystery teacher, was not just talking about details of false identities. He meant emotional attachments. Even memories. She was supposed to scrape away everything that did not pertain to her profession, to her current mission.

She missed being Kirney. So carefree.

Before her service with Admiral Trigit under her true name, she'd spent some time as Chyan Mezzine, a communications officer for the New Republic frigate *Mother Sea*. Lara remembered, almost word for word, the secret communiqués she'd passed on from the frigate to her Imperial controller, then to Admiral Trigit. Yet she couldn't remember her life as Chyan Mezzine. What had she done? Who had she known? Had she had friends?

There was something very wrong in her head, something her teachers had done to her starting when she was just a child. She wanted that wrongness out. But she had no idea where to begin to look for it.

She belatedly realized she was looking at a pair of booted feet. She looked up into the face of Myn Donos. The lieutenant was in a pilot's suit and had a rifle case slung over his back.

"Are you all right?" Donos extended a folded handkerchief to her.

She took it and looked at it stupidly.

"For your eyes."

"Oh. Thank you." She dabbed away tears she hadn't remembered crying.

"I heard you had some happy news. But you don't look happy." He shrugged. "Not my business. But if you want to talk . . ."

She did. It was wrong, she knew. Her trainers would never approve. But she had to talk. "I heard from my brother. He was supposed to have been killed when my town was destroyed by *Implacable*. But he survived."

Donos set his case down and sat against the wall opposite from Lara. "And that's not good news?"

"Not really. I . . . really don't care for my brother," she said. "He was a criminal. He should have been in jail when New Oldtown was destroyed, but he'd managed to sneak off under an assumed name. That's the sort of man he is. So, I suppose I'm glad he's alive, but if you knew him the way I did, you'd know that his letter to me . . . well, it dripped with sarcasm and irony that no one but me could have seen. He wants to drag me back into his habits of deceit, into his confidence games. He has no other reason to get in contact with me. He wants something."

Donos rubbed his chin while he mulled over that. Finally he said, "Could Zsinj have gotten hold of him?"

"*What?*"

"No, bear with me. We know that Zsinj has a considerable level of interest in Commander Antilles and Wraith Squadron. Let's say he finds your name on the unit roster and checks into your background, then finds this scofflaw of a brother of yours alive when the man should be dead. Would your brother turn you over to a man like Zsinj for money?"

Lara's mind whirled. Try as hard as she might to keep her fictitious background separate from her current life, they continued to threaten collision. "In a Coruscant second," she said.

"So maybe this is just him wanting to graft some credits from you . . . and maybe he's angling to lead you into a Zsinj trap. Possible?"

"Possible," she admitted.

"I think we need to find out. I mean, that's intruding into your family business . . . but if Zsinj is taking a run at you through your family, he might do the same with the rest of us. We need to know."

"You're right. But I have to do this myself. He wouldn't trust anyone but me."

"Not *all* by yourself, no. What if it's a trap? As in, the instant you walk into his house, he hits you with a stun rifle and a bunch of Zsinj's Raptors take you up to *Iron Fist* for some of his delicate interrogation?"

She answered with a shudder. She was surprised to find that her dread was real. "You're right."

"If you like, I'll put together a mission proposal and run it past Commander Antilles. Just you and a small team going to Aldivy to clear this up."

"Would you? I'd appreciate that." The way her head was filling up with whirling emotions and irrelevant remnants of roles and personalities she'd abandoned, she didn't think she could think clearly enough to plan a shopping-trip.

"I'll do that." He rose and took up his rifle case.

"What's that for?"

"Down about two hundred meters, this tunnel takes a turn to the right and opens up into a long, wide gallery, straight as a laser beam, about a kilometer long. I have targets set up at the far end for practice."

"That's past the artificial gravity, isn't it?"

He nodded. "Doing it in zero gravity adds a little to the difficulty, but this is one of the skills Antilles brought me in for. I'm supposed to stay sharp. And it really does focus and clear the mind."

"Maybe I should take it up. I could stand some focusing and clearing."

He smiled. "Try getting some rest. We're going to need you alert and ready."

"I know. Mission tomorrow."

He gave her a little wave good-bye and left her alone with her thoughts.

She should never have agreed for him to plan and propose this Aldivy mission. She had to be in charge of it, every part of it, or something would come up to ruin her, expose her.

But she was oddly unworried. It was because she, she . . .

Trusted Myn Donos.

Trusted him.

Trusted *someone*.

She shook her head. That was wrong, she couldn't trust. It went against all mission parameters.

But she did, and once again she found herself crying without entirely understanding why.

Wedge ascended the ladder to the interceptor and peered down into the cockpit to make sure Lieutenant Kettch, Ewok pilot, was not waiting for him once more. But his cockpit was clear. He glanced up and saw Face, lowering himself into the cockpit of his own interceptor, smirking at him, obviously having figured out what he was looking for. Wedge gave him a mock glower and clambered down.

A moment later, he heard Face's exclamation of "Son of

the Sith!" and Lieutenant Kettch came flying up out of the open hatch of Face's interceptor. Phanan, walking toward his TIE fighter, neatly fielded the stuffed toy and handed him off to Squeaky.

Wedge shook his head. At least morale was high. He began his power up and systems check.

Kell, Runt, Donos, Tyria, Piggy, and Castin were already off in the *Narra*. Their mission was to conclude at about the same time as that of the other Hawk-bats, but required more time in its initial stages. In some ways it was even more dangerous, and Wedge wondered briefly about the advisability of putting Kell Tainer in charge. But the man had not demonstrated any recurrence of the problem that had plagued him during his first few weeks with Wraith Squadron.

Wedge suspected, though he had never voiced his thought to Janson or any other member of his command, that Kell's problem had not been cowardice. Kell's father had died—at Janson's hands, in fact—when fleeing from a fight in the early days of the Rebel Alliance, but Kell's own problem with freezing up in the face of adversity had always seemed more like a very strong case of performance anxiety. But he'd gotten past it during the final battle with the *Implacable*. Wedge and Janson would keep a close, if surreptitious eye on him, but for now all seemed well.

All systems were go, and diagnostics showed the interceptor performing at something like 98 percent overall efficiency. Not bad for a crew of mechanics whose training with Imperial starfighters had begun so recently.

"Hawk-bat Leader to squadron, give me your status." Face's voice was now low, growling. Wedge wondered whether Face was performing already, or whether Castin's modifications to the individual starfighters' comm systems were already in place.

"Hawk-bat Seven, two in the green, all systems charged, and I'll have a mint liqueur with a lomin-ale chaser." Phanan's voice was a bass rumble, which he couldn't have managed in person.

"Hawk-bat Ten, all ready." And Shalla's voice was distinctly that of a male.

Wedge cleared his throat. "Hawk-bat One, ready to launch."

Laughter erupted from his comm set, several voices' worth. Frustratingly, he couldn't even recognize the voices now. He said, "Is there a problem?"

Face's growl answered, "No problem, sir. We're receiving you at full power." But Wedge could hear poorly restrained laughter in his voice.

As the count continued, Wedge switched his comm unit over to a private frequency, one he shared with his X-wing and his astromech. "Gate, are you receiving?"

His R5 unit responded with a cheerful mechanical tweet.

"On my first mark, record my transmission. On my second mark, cease recording and transmit what you've recorded back to me. Mark. 'We, the Rebel Alliance, do therefore in the name—and by the authority—of the free beings of the galaxy, solemnly publish and declare our intentions.' Mark."

His words came back to him a moment later. But they were not in his voice. In fact, they were high-pitched and fuzzy, a type of jabber Wedge well recognized. They were exactly what an Ewok would sound like if trained to speak Basic.

He sighed. "Thank you, Gate. Out." He switched back to the Hawk-bat Squadron channel and banged his helmeted head on his pilot's yoke.

At least morale was high.

Escort duty was tedious, but it drew extra pay. That's how Lieutenant Milzin Veyn, native of the city of Hullis and starfighter pilot, looked at it. And as a husband and father of three, he could always use the extra credits.

Today he and his wingman were guarding the tanker *Bastion*. Such a warlike name for an inelegant, rusting hulk of a spaceship . . . Currently, it was in dock at Station 17, one of Halmad's few remaining asteroid-belt mining colonies, while Veyn's TIE fighter and his partner's watched protectively from a distance of about a kilometer.

Veyn's comm system hummed. "Hey, Lieutenant."

"Veyn here."

"Bad news. We have a fuel-pump failure. They're repairing it, but it's going to be a couple of hours at least."

"Maybe you should just disengage and go home."

"We should . . . but the captain says we'd just have to come out again tomorrow, and we can repair with parts on hand, so that's what we're doing."

"Wonderful."

"Listen, we can power sensors back up . . . and you and your wingmate can come in for some caf. There's a fresh pot brewing."

"Ooh. Shouldn't." But the thought of spending some of those extra hours in a heated mess with fresh caf instead of drifting in zero gravity was an appealing one.

"Well, what if I said, uhhh, that the captain wanted to consult with you on matters pertaining to the future protection of *Bastion*."

"Sounds serious. We'll be right there."

Two minutes later, in the colony's crowded main hangar, Veyn and his wingman clambered out of their cockpits, climbed down the access ladders, and turned to face into the muzzles of blasters.

Two figures wearing TIE-pilot gear—but colored gray instead of traditional Imperial black—held blaster sidearms on them. One appeared to be a tall woman, the other a very corpulent man. A third enemy, a man of slightly better-than-average height, wearing a gray pilot's suit and a cold-weather mask but lacking the extra equipment of a pilot, covered them with a blaster rifle.

Veyn and his partner raised their hands.

The man with the rifle said, "There's bad news and good news. The bad news is that we're the Hawk-bats, and we're going to take your starfighters and blow up some ground facilities with them. But the good news is that we really do have fresh caf for you in the mess." He gestured with a flick of the rifle tip toward the main exit. "Let's go."

When the rifleman and his captives had gone, Tyria activated her comlink. "Five, the pilots are on their way. We're going to need Two to get through any security on the TIE fighters."

"He's on his way, too."

"How's the wiring going?"

"*Bastion*'s ready to blow. She's going to make a big mess."

The Hawk-bats, in tight formation, dropped toward Halmad in the narrow corridor they knew to be unprotected by the planet's sensor arrays. Their own sensors told them that *Bastion* was making its own approach to the planet, via a government-approved course, theoretically on the return leg of its regular refueling mission. But they would not be communicating with *Bastion*, could not get updates on the other team's progress.

Within minutes, they were cruising at just above sea level and on a course for the port city of Fellon—or, more accurately, for a small, hidden Imperial base just south of the city. It was still before dawn in Fellon and points west, and several of Halmad's moons shone down upon the Hawk-bats.

At the head of the Hawk-bats' formation were Face and Phanan. Face, playing the role of Hawk-bat Independent Space Force founder Kargin, had to be in charge of the mission; their broadcasts were certain to be intercepted and recorded, and it would not do for Hawk-bat One to be heard issuing orders to Hawk-bat Leader. Wedge had few worries about Face, but Face's wingman, Phanan, was not as skillful a flier in either X-wings or TIE fighters.

Behind Face and Phanan were Wedge with his temporary assignment of two wingmen, Lara and Shalla. Lara, low pilot on the rank ladder, had been assigned one of the squadron's two TIE fighters, a less formidable starfighter than the interceptors, but she seemed to be handling it with uncommon grace and skill. Nor had Wedge any worries about Shalla's skill with her interceptor. In fact, between her flying skill, her ability to work with the other pilots, and her ease with planning and analysis, he had placed her high on his list of candidates for lieutenant's rank. She had yet to demonstrate leadership qualities, but Wedge was certain they lay within her.

At the rear of the formation were Janson, the unit's

second-most-experienced pilot, and Dia, who had made two kills during the escape from Lavisar, equaling Wedge's total. No, Wedge was accompanied by a skilled team. This should be an easy run for the Hawk-bats.

Not that he ever put his trust in the promise of an easy run.

11

"About to enter atmosphere, on final approach for Hullis," Runt said. He occupied *Bastion*'s pilot's seat. He looked uncomfortable in a chair built for a much shorter human. "Five minutes until the break to the east."

Kell, in the command chair, typed another diagnostics command into the oversized comlink-equipped datapad in his lap. It was the type of unit an infantry squadron used for reliable long-distance communications. "Have you got the new navigational program in place?"

"We do."

Kell activated the comlink in his glove. "Nine, how's the shuttle?"

"Ready to lift."

"Stand by to lift." Kell patted Runt on the back and rose. "Run the nav program. Then *we* run."

"Initiating."

Tyria and Piggy in the TIE-fighter escorts needed no further orders. Their task was simple: Pace *Bastion* as the ancient tanker dropped toward Hullis, then diverted east toward the second fighter base the military forces of Halmad were building. Protect the tanker from the starfighters that would inevitably rise against it, at least long enough for *Bastion* to get within a couple of kilometers of the base. And then be far, far away when Kell activated his comm unit and detonated *Bastion* and all the fuel remaining within her. At two minutes before detonation, safely away on the shuttle *Narra,* Kell would communicate with the base, recommending an evacuation. The base's destruction was their aim, not the needless murder of base personnel.

With the nav program activated, Runt rose and Kell followed suit.

Then the sensor board lit up like a fireworks display. Kell and Runt stared, disbelieving, at the flurry of activity it showed in the west, the enormous signal from the east.

Kell dropped into the communications officer's chair and activated *Bastion*'s comm unit. "Five to One, do you read?"

There was no answer, just the ominous hiss of suddenly overloaded airwaves.

"Five to One, we have a problem. Do you read?"

Forest, with occasional rivers and lakes, had replaced waves beneath the Hawk-bats. Wedge was sure, in fact, that he'd felt a treetop scrape the underside of his cockpit a moment ago. All around him, the squadron's fighters and interceptors bobbed and weaved like fighters in an arena as they adjusted to changes in the terrain below.

The range meter put them at twenty seconds from their target. Ten, five—and then Face and Phanan were firing just as the Imperial base came into Wedge's view.

It was a landing platform, one long, durable landing deck suitable for shuttles or starfighters, supported by two massive columns containing turbolifts and crew quarters. Beneath the deck was an enclosed crossover walkway providing easy passage from one column to the other, and there should have been nothing other than the support columns to the ground. But with this design, below the crossway, almost out of sight below treetop level, was an enclosed hangar deck as large as the landing deck.

Wedge noted these details without taking out time for analysis. He brought the interceptor's aiming brackets around his target of preference, the standard landing platform's tractor beam emitter up on the landing deck, and fired.

Then he was past, following Face's lead in looping around for another run.

"Good shooting, Hawk-bats." That was the gravelly voice of Face's persona.

"Leader, this is Four. We hit shields."

"Four, what did you say? There were no shields."

"Not as we were approaching, sir. They came up as we opened fire. The platform has sustained no, repeat no, damage."

Their arc was nearly complete, and it was obvious that Dia's report was correct: the landing platform was solidly in place, and the Hawk-bats' sensors now showed shielding protecting the facility.

Then TIE fighters and interceptors came up out of the trees, easily a score of them, from points all around the Hawk-bats and the landing platform.

More than a score. The second flight of TIEs emerged. Wedge checked the sensor board. Thirty-six unfriendlies, three full squadrons.

Shalla spoke next, her voice subdued even in its distorted form: "We are *so* dead."

Bastion shuddered.

Runt looked over the diagnostics board. "Are we hit?"

"No, we're tractored. By that." Kell tapped the sensor board and the huge shape on it. "Look at this. We're gaining altitude."

Donos's voice came over the intercom. "What's happening?"

"They've got us. Our mission is scrubbed, and so are we, if we can't figure out a way to get clear of them. Hold on a second. Runt, fire up the comm system and put all the power you can into our signal."

"Done."

"Five to One, do you read? Over."

His reply was a static hiss.

"Five to Eleven, do you read? Over"

"—leven, read—you. Sig—breaking up."

"Abort mission. Repeat, abort mission. Over."

"Neg—ve. Standing—your departure. Over."

"Do not stand by. This is a direct order. Abort mission. Acknowledge. Over."

There was no reply.

"We have incoming starfighters from the capital ship," Runt said.

"Of course we do. Our day wouldn't be complete without them, would it?"

Tyria's voice came back, "Ack—ed. Aborting. Over." On the sensor screen, the blips representing her TIE fighter and Piggy's veered off on an escape vector.

Kell took a deep breath. He wanted to make one final transmission. *I love you.* But he couldn't give the enemy forces any clue, any extra information to help them pry into the Hawk-bats' identities. He shut down the comm system. As he settled on his next course of action, he felt his body, his spirit, grow heavy.

Donos's voice came over the intercom again. "What's the plan, Five?"

"Runt joins you in the shuttle. At a time of my choosing, probably when we're as close as we're going to get to that capital ship without being trapped inside, you launch and get a few seconds of acceleration before another tractor beam grabs you. In that time, I set off our explosive charges."

Runt's eyes went wide. Kell saw them flicker, a sign that Runt was flipping between personalities, looking for the one with the most pertinent skills to add to the situation.

Donos's voice came back. "Uh, you need to be aboard the shuttle to do that."

"Can't do it, Nine. The transmitter I have and the one in the shuttle won't be able to cut through their jamming."

"Then use a timer."

"Then we can't count on it being precisely positioned to do the most damage to the capital ship."

"Use *Bastion*'s proximity sensors."

"*Bastion*'s proximity sensors, at anything under two klicks, are called human eyes, Nine. We're lucky this crate had refreshers."

"Wait a second, I think Castin and I can work out something." Donos paused a moment. "Yes. I can set off the explosives at a distance."

"Without a comlink?"

"Without a comlink."

"How?"

"Because I'm special and you're not. Now, I need you to set *Bastion*'s comm system to pick up tight-beam transmissions across the electromagnetic spectrum."

Kell felt the heaviness leave him as he grasped what Donos was planning. "I read you. We'll be right there."

"Break by groups." Face's voice sounded strained even under distortion. "Fire at will. And may—"

There was the slightest pause. Wedge knew Face had been about to say, *May the Force be with you.* A bad idea, a giveaway. But Face recovered so quickly Wedge doubted anyone not familiar with him would have recognized the slight lapse. "—we drink from the skulls of our enemies tonight!"

Wedge broke to port, where the ring of enemy TIEs was thinnest. Shalla and Lara smartly followed suit.

Tactics. The enemy was relying on its superior numbers and was confident. Confidence, then, was what the Hawk-bats needed to strafe first.

Of the handful of paired fighters winging in toward them, Wedge picked out the most dangerous-looking duo, two interceptors that moved with more sureness than their fellows. As they came on, visual sensors showed that their solar array wings wore the horizontal red bars of Baron Fel's 181st Imperial Fighter Group. Wedge resisted the temptation to swear. "Ten, Thirteen, take the target to port."

He began juking his interceptor around at three kilometers from his target. A small part of a second later, the closing distance crossed below two klicks and the enemy squints opened fire. Green laser beams flickered between Wedge and his wingmen.

His return fire grazed one of the oncoming interceptors, charring a portion of the hull near the upper viewport—and

then they were past, with more forest and a more distant set of
TIE fighters beyond.

Now the challenge would be to come around, trying to
maneuver behind the enemies they'd just gone head-to-head
with. But Wedge ignored conventional tactics, rolled to starboard, and dove toward a pair of fighters that were maneuvering to get a shot in on Janson and Dia. His first quad-linked
shot was a brilliant one, hulling one fighter, turning it into a
glowing cloud of orange and black, and that fighter's wingmate exploded a second later under cycling paired laser fire
from Wedge's wingman to port. Shalla? He spared a glance.
No, it was Lara's fighter, not Shalla's interceptor there.

He rolled to starboard again. The interceptors whom
they'd traded fire with initially were in pursuit, distant pursuit,
but quickly catching up. However, three TIE fighters were
ahead and above, beginning a dive toward Wedge's group.

He brought his interceptor up in a climb so rapid that it
slammed him back into his seat. As the oncoming enemies
dropped within the field of coverage of his targeting systems,
one briefly jittered within his brackets. He fired out of reflex,
was rewarded with seeing a TIE's solar array wing explode under his lasers; that starfighter half rolled and began an uncontrolled descent.

Wedge continued his loop upward, a tight maneuver that
kept him crushed to his chair even as he came upside down. In
his mind's eye, that put him and his group at the upper edge of
the engagement, with no attacks possible from above for the
moment.

Ahead and below, Wedge saw a paired interceptor and
fighter the sensors flagged as friendlies; that had to be Face and
Phanan. They were turning his way.

"Leader, Seven, this is One. I'm coming at you in a head-
to-head. Two on my tail."

"One, Leader. We have them. You can have our tail as
well." Behind Face and Phanan, two pairs of TIE fighters were
jockeying for position, firing shots that strayed for now but
must inevitably connect with the Hawk-bats' sterns.

Wedge, Shalla, and Lara roared toward Face and Phanan.
All five Hawk-bats opened fire, a deadly barrage of green

lasers, but not at one another—at the fighters and interceptors pursuing each wing. Wedge saw his concentrated fire hit a solar wing pylon and shear it off at its base, sending the fighter spinning down toward the thick forest below. He directed his stream of fire against another TIE as the two lines converged. Then one of that fighter's mates detonated and Wedge was momentarily blinded as he flew through the cloud of debris and shrapnel. He heard metal pinging from his fighter's hull and he repressed a wince; a heavy enough piece of shrapnel could take out a shieldless TIE interceptor.

Wes's voice: "Six up, six down."

"What?"

"That little head-to-head you pulled. One hundred percent effective. Six up, six down."

Wedge glanced at his sensor screen. A moment ago, the screen had showed three dozen enemies, seven friendlies. Now it showed twenty-five enemies, seven friendlies. Wedge whistled.

"Leader, Three. I just flipped my sensors over to long-range. I show a capital ship clearing the horizon and heading this way."

"A cruiser?"

"A Star Destroyer. At least."

It was a Super Star Destroyer, by name *Iron Fist*. As Kell and Runt clattered up the boarding ramp and came forward into the cockpit, its image, enhanced by the shuttle's visual sensors, dominated the forward viewscreen. It was still well above them in orbit, but it seemed terrifyingly close.

"We are so dead," Kell said.

Castin and Donos sat in the second row of seats, bent over a long weapon—Donos's laser sniper rifle. "We did not know you had brought that," Runt said.

Donos snorted. "I take it to parties, dining engagements, and the refresher. It was in the smuggling compartment. Kell, you have the detonation code?"

Kell tapped the datapad in his chest pocket.

"Give it to Castin."

Runt took the pilot's seat while Kell transmitted the code.

The image of *Iron Fist* wavered, its blue and white running lights blurring, as something passed much closer to the shuttle. Runt killed the visual enhancers.

Their shuttle was docked with *Bastion,* its viewports oriented so its occupants had a view mostly of sky, with only a little of the tanker intruding on the view. And now that sky was full of TIE fighters buzzing back and forth.

Kell forced back his rising surge of panic and counted blips on the sensors. Only six. Moving so fast, they seemed more numerous. This had to be nothing more than a show of dominance, since the enemy vessel had already tractored the tanker and was hauling it up to captivity. "Keep calm," he said. "They're not here to shoot."

"In your opinion," Donos said.

"It's all I have to offer."

Wedge plotted the engagement on the sensors and in his mind's eye. The engagement zone had spread out through a hemisphere about eight kilometers across. Now his group was at a high altitude in the southern portion. Janson and Dia were about a kilometer below them. None of them was actively engaged with an enemy. The TIE force had contracted a little, the nearest starfighters being about a kilometer to the north and not yet spinning out to engage them. Face and Phanan were in the northern quadrant, dogfighting with a pair of TIE fighters as a pair of interceptors headed toward them.

He checked the position of the sun and then rolled around to begin an approach out of the sun against Face's and Phanan's tails. But almost immediately he saw one of the pursuing TIE fighters' shots strike home, hitting the engines of one of the friendly TIEs. That starfighter rolled in a random fashion, briefly regained controlled flight, then dropped below the line of trees and was lost to sight.

On the sensor board, Hawk-bat Seven, Ton Phanan's signal, faded to blackness.

· · ·

"This isn't going to work," Castin said. He was watching *Iron Fist*'s approach. "Our docking port is relative up. We'll be taking off into their hangar bay."

"I'll take care of it." Kell rose. "Runt, take the pilot's seat, stand by to power up and launch without checklist." He charged back down the boarding ramp.

Once he was on the tanker's small flight deck, he brought up the controls for the ship's artificial gravity and repulsorlifts. It was a simple matter to scrub the identification of a large mass—*Iron Fist*—as that of a ship and instead identify it as a planetoid. Then he configured the gravity system to orient the ship so that its bottom descended toward the surface of the planetoid. Now, unless *Iron Fist* spent an unusual amount of tractor beam power and used a lot of fine control to reorient *Bastion*, its upper surface would rotate to face the planet below and not the Super Star Destroyer above.

The rotation had already begun by the time he reached *Narra* again. And *Iron Fist* was much closer. Kell took the copilot's seat and strapped himself in. "You ready?" he asked Donos.

The sniper shrugged. "If Castin here is any good, yes. Otherwise, we're doomed."

"It'll work," Castin said. "My code and patches always work."

The others turned to give him an arch expression.

Castin gave them the look of someone caught in a lie. "Well, *usually*."

Wedge felt ice slash through his gut as the most likely scenario went through his mind. The Hawk-bats would circle around the fallen pilot, trying to determine whether Phanan was dead or alive, and would protect him from the strafing runs of the enemy TIEs until they, too, fell one by one.

He keyed his comlink. "Hawk-bats, this is One. Recommend abort mission. Stormies." On some worlds, *stormies* was the panicked cry of bar patrons who'd detected a raid by stormtroopers, and it replaced Omega Signal as the evacuation command when the Wraiths were in their Hawk-bat identities.

He steeled himself against a protest from Face. And Face's voice came across immediately, but not with the words he expected: "Hawk-bats, Leader. Confirm stormies."

But Face's interceptor dropped below the tree line, pursued by two fast-moving TIE fighters.

The half squadron of TIE fighters preceded *Bastion* into the Super Star Destroyer's main landing bay. Kell waited until *Bastion* was brought into line directly below the bay. In a moment, the tanker would begin its ascent into the hands of Zsinj. He brought his comlink up. "Remember," he said into it, "we'll have a handful of seconds from the time we launch to the time they get another tractor on us. Nine, that's all the time you have."

Donos was now back in the emergency airlock, his pilot's suit on and sealed against space to give him a bare few moments of protection from the hard vacuum he would be experiencing. A last-minute change put him there instead of in the main compartment, as he'd realized that the phototropic shielding of the shuttle's viewport, designed to give the vehicle some protection from incoming laser fire, would be even more effective against the lighter beam of Donos's rifle.

Donos simply said, "Ready."

"Do it."

Runt hit the control to release the *Narra* from its dock with *Bastion*. He cut in the shuttle's thrusters at full power, blasting away from the tanker, the shuttle's thrusters burning and scarring *Bastion*'s hull in a manner that would invite retaliation from any ship's master.

Runt immediately put *Narra* into a climb, toward the surface of Halmad, then continued the loop so that the charred, antiquated black surface of *Bastion*, and the surrounding gleam of the Super Star Destroyer *Iron Fist*, came within sight.

There was a little flicker of light between *Narra* and *Bastion*.

Nothing happened.

Kell felt his stomach sink. It was too difficult a shot. Donos, as good as he was, was trying to fire a laser beam modified to carry data instead of a lethal intensity of power, and trying to hit *Bastion*'s communications array from a moving shuttle.

Donos fired again. No effect.

Narra shuddered with the characteristic trembling of a small craft in the grip of a tractor beam. Kell shook his head.

Donos fired again.

A bright orange glow appeared in the viewports and hatch seams of *Bastion*. Then the tanker vanished, replaced by a globe of yellow and orange destructive force, an expanding cloud that swelled up into the main landing bay, out across the lower surface of *Iron Fist,* and toward *Narra.*

Face dropped into the trees, one pursuer back about two hundred meters, the other—the one who'd shot down Phanan—twice that distance away. Here, Face's superior speed would not help him; it was pure pilot skill and maneuverability that would allow survival in this obstacle-rich environment. The forest's large trees were well spaced; it was possible to maintain a high rate of speed here, jinking back and forth to arc around obstructions in his path.

His purser fired, a blast that incinerated a tree bole immediately to Face's starboard. He cursed. He'd hoped that there wouldn't be any immediate firing opportunities, but his pursuer was already gaining on him.

Suddenly the trees were gone and there was water below him—he'd emerged over a lake. No cover, but it gave him an opportunity. He curved around to starboard, rotating up on his starboard wing, the ferocity of his maneuver crushing him back into his seat. Through his topside viewport, he could see as his first pursuer screamed out of the forest and immediately followed his loop.

Face couldn't see the second pursuer, but his timing sense said the pilot was mere fractions of a second from emerging from the trees—if he were following his wingman. Face opened up with his lasers.

And the second pursuer emerged right into his stream of

laser fire. Face was rewarded with the brief vision of that TIE fighter's starboard wing evaporating under the blast, its cockpit punctured and detonating.

Ahead was the tree line again. Face rolled level and shot into the trees at a ninety-degree angle to his original course. The other TIE fighter followed.

Face instinctively ducked as a half squad of TIE fighters roared by overhead, a kilometer up, obviously searching for him. They didn't turn back to pursue him—they must have missed him.

He twitched his pilot's yoke, resisting the urge to become frantic, as tree after tree appeared in his path. Then there was a brief break as he was over another lake, this one much smaller and covered in huge green leaf-shaded pads that floated atop the water, and beyond he was in trees again.

They were becoming denser. Harder to veer back and forth to find the gaps that would accommodate his starfighter. His pursuer hadn't been able to fire on him in several seconds— that was good, but sooner or later the increasingly difficult terrain would stop protecting him and would kill him.

Unless—he remembered Shalla's tactic in her Coruscant simulator runs. And the next time he had to vector to find a safe gap, he chose one so narrow that his stomach tightened up. It was too narrow, too narrow—but he rolled up on his port wing array and shot through, the slightly thinner profile of the TIE interceptor making the maneuver possible. He heard his wings shred through leaves and twigs.

His pursuer tried to stay on his tail, then realized too late that such a tactic was fatal. Face heard the explosion a mere second after he cleared the too-narrow gap.

He slowed and came around. Off in the distance to his right, a section of forest was burning, ignited by his pursuer's detonation.

All right. Sensors showed that the rest of the Hawk-bats were spacebound, most of the TIE force pursuing them, while the half squad he'd seen mere moments ago were now a couple of kilometers to the west and breaking up to search for him.

He had a window. He could make a break for space.

No, he couldn't. Not with Phanan still out there. He *might* not be dead. There had been no explosion when his TIE fighter fell into the forest.

By memory, by luck, Face found the small lake with the leaf pads in it and dropped as swiftly as he dared into the water near shore. Before the lake water was halfway up his forward viewports, his descent was arrested by the lake's muddy floor.

He goosed the repulsorlifts, driving him forward, and the lake water rose. He continued, shoving his interceptor forward, until the water rose to the height of the top of his front viewport.

He used the emergency power switch to power down, then manually cranked his access hatch open and clambered halfway out.

There was a lot of splashing going on in the lake, and he got half visions of large amphibious things entering the water. Not his problem now.

One of the huge leaf pads was within reach. He leaned over and grabbed its veined surface, then dragged it across the top of his interceptor.

Then he settled back into his cockpit to wait.

Either their sensors would pick him up, or they'd be baffled by the presence of other life-forms, by the shielding effects of the water, by the fact that his interceptor was completely powered down. Either way, he'd know soon.

The expanding cloud of fiery gas enveloped *Narra* and shook her harder than the tractor beam ever had.

Runt let out an exultant whoop. "We are free."

"Punch it. Get us out of here," Kell said. He was jarred as something heavy and metallic slammed into the shuttle's rear. "Nine, are you all right?"

No answer.

Kell grabbed at the buckle on his harness and started to pull it free, but thought better of it. As much as he wanted to get back and see how Donos was doing, this explosive turbulence would take him off his feet and perhaps pound him to death. He had to wait until they were clear of it. "Nine, acknowledge."

His comlink crackled. "Nine here. Dogging the hatch closed. I'm a little toasty."

"Great shot, Nine. Stay where you are until the ride is smooth."

"Acknowledged."

They shot out of the explosive cloud like a proton torpedo leaving an X-wing. Behind them, visual sensors showed *Iron Fist*'s keel enveloped in black-and-orange-glowing debris.

Kell kept his eye on that image even as it got smaller. "Come on, come on, give us a present—break up!"

But the eight-kilometer-long capital ship stayed sturdily in one piece.

"No tractors, no pursuit," Runt said.

"Let's hope it stays that way. Castin, plot us an escape vector and hyperspace jump, any direction."

"Already working on it, Chief."

12

Face could see the sky brighten through the leaf pad above. As time passed, his cockpit grew warm and humid, and he could hear the distant moan of TIE fighters overhead. He sweated and waited.

Then there was nothing but the sound of wildlife, musical tweets he ascribed to some sort of birdlike creatures, coughing grunts he couldn't associate with any animal he knew, splashes that seemed consistent with the human-sized amphibians he'd seen earlier.

Blaster in hand, he emerged through his hatch and dogged it closed, all the while keeping the leaf pad in place atop him, and then slid off the dome of his interceptor and into the water. The shore was a few dozen meters away, a challenging swim in his pilot's suit.

He'd marked the sensor location of Phanan's crash and compared it with his own landing position. He was certain he could find Phanan's TIE fighter. He was certain he *would* cut down anything that tried to keep him from reaching it.

They were a gloomy group, gathered in the conference module at Hawk-bat Base.

No injuries among them, except for something like a sun-burn on Donos's face. Yet they wore the expression of defeated soldiers.

Wedge said, "We're all concerned about Face and Phanan, and we have to face the possibilities that they didn't make it. But I want you all to understand this. It's very important. To-day, tactically, was a victory, a tremendous one. We cost them far more than they cost us. We also led them into this situation, and if the Hawk-bat identities remain uncompromised, we can continue with our plan. If we're going to have any perspective on what this has cost us, we have to remember that."

Tyria said, "What are we going to do about finding them?"

"We'll put a team on the ground as soon as it's feasible. First we have to get as much information as possible. About the movements of our enemies in the region where they went down." He glanced at Castin Donn. "You were going to get us information from your satellite account."

Castin nodded. "I couldn't."

"Explain."

"The account had been shut down. When I accessed it, I got nothing but a pointer to two files. One was a brief, anony-mous letter saying that the client, that's me, didn't have autho-rization for such a high-level data stream. The other was a big file, full holo, from Warlord Zsinj."

There were startled noises from the other pilots, but Wedge waved them down. "You've viewed the file?"

Castin nodded. "I didn't know it was Zsinj until I did view it. It's a letter from him to the Hawk-bats."

"Put it on."

Castin leaned forward to tap a command into the controls of the room's small holoviewer.

Above the table appeared Warlord Zsinj in all his white finery, about a meter high. Castin adjusted the image's orienta-tion so that it faced directly at Wedge.

"I presume," said the warlord, "that I'm addressing the so-called General Kargin of the Hawk-bats." His expression became merry. "As you can see, the rules around Halmad have changed. The planet belongs to my alliance now, and you will not be permitted to stay here and continue causing trouble.

"Now, what you must understand is that a lesser man would be most angry with you. I'm not. To be honest, I'm impressed. The two pincers of your movement annihilated two entire squadrons of my fighters against minimal losses of your own. That's quite admirable. Oh, certainly, you've lost, but my victory was far more costly than it should have been, testimony to your own skill and ferocity.

"So, you now have a choice to make.

"You can stay here and continue to try to prey on Halmad. In between all my other activities, I will eventually hunt you down and kill all of you. My guess is that this will be very costly to me, but it's what I've promised to do. The problem with this choice is that everybody loses, though you lose more.

"You can leave and set up operations in an area of space not yet controlled by Zsinj. This isn't a costly choice, but nobody gains anything. And I'll have lost two squadrons with nothing—well, other than alliance with this planet—to show for it.

"Your third option, however, includes potential gain for both of us.

"I'd like to meet you. Attached to this holo is a data stream that includes a hyperspace navigational course. Send a ship with a representative who can speak for you along that course. You will meet a navigational beacon that will direct you further. We will meet, and I will make it worth your while to come to terms with me.

"I will not give you my word that you will not be harmed. Not that I don't have a word to give; I simply don't think you would believe it. But this you can trust: Zsinj is a businessman, and it just makes good business sense for us to join forces. Take it under consideration.

"Zsinj out."

The corpulent warlord's image faded away.

Wedge leaned back, unaware until then that he'd leaned forward during the warlord's recitation. "Wraiths," he said, "it may have cost us dearly . . . but the Hawk-bat operation has just begun to pay off. We're going to need a contact team."

He glanced among the Wraiths present. "I can't be on the team, nor can Wes. We're just a little too well known to Imperial forces. Not even a good disguise would necessarily prevent us from being recognized." He didn't add that this was especially true with their most proficient artist of disguise, Face, being missing or dead.

"Castin, before the liberation, you were considered a criminal on Coruscant, an insurgent, so information on you is probably in Zsinj's files."

The code-slicer nodded. "I tried to wipe out my records wherever I could find them, but they just propagated too fast for me."

"Kell is a possibility, but you're pretty distinctive."

The big man smiled. "I like to think so."

"Myn, not a chance for you. You're a casualty of being well known as a decorated member of the Corellian armed forces and then a New Republic squadron commander. Runt, you're right out, at least until midget Thakwaash number more than one in the ranks of starfighter pilots across the galaxy. Piggy, however—"

The Gamorrean pilot nodded. "I can dress up as a barbarian and simply be appropriate scenery."

"Correct. Though Zsinj, as a product of the Imperial school of thought, may be unhappy with the presence of a non-human in the Hawk-bat party. We'll have to think that one over. Dia, Shalla, Tyria, Lara, all of you are distinct possibilities. I'll need a little time to work out the best mix for the greeting party."

Shalla said, "But it sounds as though it's a go."

Wedge nodded. "It is. This is what we're here for. Such a mission would have to be a volunteer operation, though, so anyone who does *not* wish to be included, send me a note. Dismissed, everybody."

Wedge noticed that they filed out with their backs a little straighter, with more energy in their steps, than they'd had when they arrived for the conference. Yes, they'd probably lost friends down on Halmad . . . but they hadn't lost their sense of purpose.

Castin Donn was the last in line to leave, but he shut the door before him and turned back to face Wedge. "Sir, I'd like to be part of this operation."

"Castin, you yourself agreed that you were probably too well known in Imperial records."

"That's right, sir. But I want to go in unknown, undetected. I have an idea."

Wedge gestured for him to sit. "Let's hear it."

Castin took a chair again. "I'm familiar with a wide variety of Imperial computer systems."

"I know."

"What if I put together a program that induced *Iron Fist*'s computer to broadcast an occasional signal saying, 'Here I am, come and get me'?"

"One that Zsinj wouldn't detect?"

"Correct, sir. This program would piggyback its message to outgoing signals so there would be no extraneous broadcasts for the ship's crew to detect. Now, given a capital ship's protocols for scans of its programs, for frequent memory flushes, and so forth, even with maximum stealth characteristics, a program like this couldn't last too long. Maybe a month, maybe a week or two less or more. But in that time, we could build up a database of the ship's movements."

"Like Admiral Trigit tried to do to us with his Morrt Project."

"Correct. We might even get a break. Find the *Iron Fist* staying in one place long enough for elements of the fleet to arrive and hit it."

"What would you need?"

"Well, I already have the programming simulators here. I'd just need a full set of stormtrooper armor for disguise, and a datapad portable terminal with a standard ship's computer interface. I'd go in *Narra*'s smuggling compartment—if it can hold Piggy in a pilot's suit, it can hold me in stormtrooper armor."

Wedge considered for a long moment. "Castin, I want you to work up this program."

"Thank you, sir!" Castin saluted and started to rise.

"Wait, now. I'm not going to authorize your mission, not this time."

"What?" Castin sank back into place, looking as angry as though he'd been slapped.

"Zsinj is no fool. We're already flying in a crew of pirates he doesn't know. They are going to be under constant scrutiny. This first encounter is not the time to try such a stunt. Later, when meetings become more routine and security gets lax, *that's* when we try your plan."

"Sir . . ." Castin's jaw trembled as he visibly tried to bring himself under control. "Sir, I'm better than any security they can offer. I don't tell you how to fly—you're the best at that. Please don't tell me what sort of security I can and can't breach."

"Now you're being impertinent. Tell me the name of Zsinj's chief security man."

"I don't know that, sir."

"Then how do you know that you're better than he is? That he doesn't have measures in place against the sort of program you're planning to introduce?"

"Because I'm better than everybody, sir."

Wedge sighed. "Flight Officer Donn, I'm giving you a direct order. Design your code. But take your time and do a very clean job on it. Because you will not be accompanying this mission to *Iron Fist*. We will use your program at some later time. Dismissed."

Castin flushed red and looked as though he wanted to argue the point, but stood, saluted with a military precision that was, for him, obviously an exercise in sarcasm, and retreated.

Phanan's TIE fighter had apparently hit the ground in a soft glade, bounced like a rock skipping across the surface of a pond, and crashed into a line of young trees. Now it rested, its port solar wing array crumpled, its cockpit canted forward, so its main viewport was half-buried in the dirt, against a trio of trees bent almost to the ground, their roots half up in the air. The twin ion engines at the vehicle's rear were now encrusted with a foamy substance—probably a fire-extinguishing foam sprayed on by those who had come later.

Now a stormtrooper stood guard on the damaged vehicle, and was engrossed in conversation with two men in the distinctive uniform of Zsinj's Raptors. Two speeder bikes in Raptor colors hovered beside the starfighter's intact wing.

Face, a few dozen meters away, in the heavy underbrush characteristic of the light forest of the area, insects crawling across his back and sides, wiped more stinging sweat from his eyes and crawled forward to hear what they were saying.

The stormtrooper's voice, amplified by the electronic speaker of his helmet, was easiest to make out. ". . . see here. Spots of blood. He was crawling here, but we didn't get any units . . . ground at this site for half an hour, so he wasn't crawling for stealth; he was hurt. We have men on speeder bikes . . . now. They say his trail goes a little less than a kilometer and just disappears on stony ground where things get hilly."

The two Raptors looked at one another. The first, the taller of the two, said, "Is there any sign of repulsorlift dust-up along the trail?"

"Ehh, no. They would have mentioned it. They're assuming he's out there hiding in the hills."

"I don't think so. They would have found more blood. Even if he'd bandaged himself, he'd be cutting his flesh to pieces on that hard ground—unless he stopped crawling and started walking. Which isn't likely. Scanning isn't doing any good?"

"There are a lot of people, humans, in the region. Professional hunters. And some large game they hunt. We're ushering them out as fast as we come across them, but they're playing havoc with our scanners."

The Raptor sighed, testimony to the stormtroopers' incompetence, and turned back toward the speeder bikes.

The other one said, "We'll find him. Then we'll tell your people how it was done." He followed his partner.

Face crawled forward as fast as he could manage while remaining fairly quiet. The stormtrooper was watching the Raptors, his body language suggesting that perhaps he'd enjoy beating the two men senseless with the stock of his blaster rifle, and did not turn in Face's direction.

The Raptors mounted their speeder bikes, talking to one another, their low, amused tones and occasional chuckles making it likely that the stormtrooper and his fellows continued to be an object of derision. They fired up the bikes' thrusters and headed out.

Face stood up from behind a bush in their path. His first blaster shot took the right-hand Raptor in the chest, sending him tumbling from the back of the vehicle. Face traversed left and fired just as the second Raptor came abreast of him. His shot took the man in the side of the head and the dead or injured man passed so close that Face could feel the wash from his repulsors and smell the char from his helmet.

Ahead, the stormtrooper was raising his blaster rifle's stock to his shoulder. Face threw himself to the ground, once again partially concealed by the bush, and squeezed off three shots. The first two went wide, with the stormtrooper's return shot charring soil less than a meter in front of Face, but the third blast took his target in the gut, where sections of white armor were connected by flexible black material. The stormtrooper let out a moan and fell forward.

There was an explosion from behind Face. He rolled over and brought his blaster up, but there were no enemies to confront—the second speeder bike had slammed into a broadbased tree and exploded. Fiery fragments rained down upon the tree and surrounding underbrush.

No time to worry about that. Face hurried to Phanan's TIE fighter, clambered up one broken wing pylon, and peered into the cockpit. No sign of Phanan, as the conversation he'd overheard had suggested, but it would be good to deny Zsinj's forces any information they might glean from analysis of the craft. He fired several blaster shots into the cockpit, and when the pilot's seat and control board were fully ablaze, he dropped again to the ground.

The first speeder bike had fetched up against a tree, but had not detonated. Still, the forward outrigger looked bent, even from this distance, and that wasn't good; it would seriously restrict the vehicle's speed and maneuvering capabilities.

Face took the stormtrooper's blaster rifle and hurried toward the bike. En route, he passed the bodies of both Raptors. Both men were dead. He took their blaster pistols, comlinks, and various cards and datacards.

As he'd feared, the outrigger of the surviving speeder bike was twisted out of alignment. A repair job was out of the question with the tools he had on hand. He swore to himself, mounted the vehicle, and set it into motion.

The thing's thruster engine rattled and coughed, and the bike showed an immediate tendency to pull down and to the right—the new bend to the forward directional vanes made that inevitable. Still, it would be faster than walking. By brute force, he kept in line with the still-distinct trail Phanan had made and set out along that route.

Distantly, he could hear the roar of other speeder bikes. He snapped on his vehicle's comlink, and that of one of the Raptors. The airwaves were active with communications: "May have some sign of passage here, looks something like crawling. But there's no blood." "Ay Dee Seven Four Two, have Ajaf and Matham reported in to you yet?" "Grid Two-Four secure. No large life-forms here except us." "Too bad we can't scan for *intelligent* life-forms, Dofey, that would let you out right away." "No personal remarks, Private."

The damaged speeder bike carried Face along Phanan's trail of crushed underbrush and scored mud. Phanan had managed to crawl a fair distance, Face decided. He traveled a quarter kilometer through this forest, then a half kilometer, and finally reached a narrow, shallow river that must have been the one mentioned by the stormtrooper.

On the other side of the river, Face could see that the forest thinned, and not much farther it graduated to rocky hills that were thick with underbrush but not much for trees. Face shook his head. It didn't make sense for Phanan to head for terrain like that, where it would be easier to spot him from above— and as he watched, a TIE fighter swooped by over the nearest ridge of hills, flying slowly enough that it had to be on recon-naissance detail. Still, Phanan's crawling trail emerged on the other side of the bank, more obvious than ever, and headed toward those hills.

Face paused, sensing some of Phanan's innate perversity at work. The stormtrooper had said the trail disappeared on stony ground, and the searchers hadn't had any luck finding Phanan. No luck finding an injured pilot who was limited to crawling.

Phanan knew as well as Face did that a downed pilot who found a river would, under most circumstances, be much better off following it downriver. Human settlements tended to be built along rivers. Rivers tended to join other rivers. Rivers usually meant fresh water.

What if—*More obvious than ever*. What if Phanan had crawled as far as the first batch of terrain that would no longer carry sign of his passage, then had crawled *back* to the river? It was a sensible strategy. It might throw off his pursuers. It *had* thrown off his pursuers.

Face turned rightward, the direction the river flowed, and began cruising slowly above its surface.

This was a much better route. Trees along the riverbanks shielded long stretches of the water from view from above. Long grasses beside the water draped the banks, sending leaves into the river itself—did they drink as roots did? Face shook his head; now was not the time to worry about botanical studies of the planet Halmad.

Then there were the river's larger inhabitants. Far ahead and sometimes far behind, Face saw large splashes and roilings in the water that suggested the human-sized amphibians he had glimpsed before. Perhaps they were keeping their distance because they were easily frightened. That was much more soothing than the possibility that they might be stalking him.

A kilometer downriver, Face felt a blinding flash of pain to the side of his head. He almost fell off the speeder bike. He came upright fast, blaster in hand, aiming at the elegant drapery of grasses to his left.

Grasses—and one pale hand sticking out beyond them, waving.

He brought the speeder bike around, hopped off into the thigh-high water, and shoved his way through.

It was Phanan, sweating, paler than usual, leaning against the bank in the shade of the leaves. His gray TIE-fighter pilot's suit lacked its breathing gear, helmet, and gloves, and was torn in the front—a tear Face suspected Phanan had inflicted to help cool himself.

"I'm glad to see you," Phanan said. His voice was weak, very hoarse.

"So glad you decided to brain me with a rock."

"I can't shout."

"Are you hurt?"

Phanan nodded.

"Badly?"

Another nod. "I'm pretty sure I'm bleeding internally. I don't think I'm going to get much farther."

"You're going to get to Hawk-bat Base. Can you ride on the back of the bike?"

Phanan was long in answering. "I think so."

"Let's get you up on it. You've thrown off pursuit pretty well. I'm going to get us out of their search area before they decide to range out this far."

Face helped Phanan up on the back of the bike. It wasn't easy. Halfway up, Phanan let out a bark of pain and curled up into a knot and stayed that way, shuddering, several long moments while Face held him up. Then, finally, Phanan could uncurl enough to take a normal rider's position on the back of the bike. Face noted that Phanan began sweating heavily as soon as he left the cooling water of the river, and the sweating did not stop.

Face climbed up in the driver's seat and goosed the thrusters.

The thruster engine let out a more vigorous cough than ever, shuddered once, and died.

"It take it you bought this used," Phanan said.

Phanan lay on his back on the bike. In his hand he held the bike's sensor unit, which Face had pulled from its post, leaving it attached only by wires.

The bike's repulsorlift was fine. So Face, finding a rope in the vehicle's small cargo compartment, had tied the rope off to the outrigger and was now a couple of meters ahead, dragging the bike by the rope while Phanan rode.

"This is pretty sweet," Phanan said. "Why don't you peel me some sunfruit while you're at it?" There was still a rasp of pain in his voice.

"Sure. You kill it, I'll peel it. What does pursuit look like?"

"Sensors don't show any vehicles within our scanning range. I disabled the transmitter on this one's comlink so they can't bounce a signal and find us."

"Good."

"Face?"

"Yes?"

"Thanks for coming back for me."

"If you got captured, I'd have to fill out forms."

"Reasonable. By the way, do you have a plan, or is walking in the river pretty much the extent of it?"

"That's the biggest part of it, sure," Face said. "Walking downriver for exercise and to broaden my awareness of the incredible diversity of human culture. But sooner or later we have to reach a community. At that point, I'll sneak in and kidnap you a doctor."

"Right," Phanan said. His eyes were closed. "As though I trusted you to find your own backside without help from a spotter satellite."

"From there, we can also rig a signal to base. We'll probably be off this rock by dawn."

"Right."

"Maybe I'll find a congenial female doctor in town and she'll be taken with you and your little ways."

"It won't happen. You know what her first words will be?"

"What?"

"She'll say, 'Garik Loran? The *Face*? Ooh, I'm feeling faint. . . .' "

Face turned around. "Look again."

Phanan craned his neck to look. "Oh, that's right, you're still in your Horrible Burn Victim facial makeup. Maybe I have a chance after all." He winced and half curled up as another wave of pain hit him.

"Oh, forget this. We've got to get you medical help immediately. And that means calling in Zsinj's forces and surrendering."

Phanan uncurled again, but rocked back and forth a little, obviously unable to hold still. "Come here."

Face splashed back to him.

When he was alongside, Phanan grabbed him by the neck of his pilot's suit. His organic eye blazed almost as much as his mechanical one. "Listen to me, Face. We do *not* surrender. Your face under the makeup and my prosthetic modifications are going to be too easy to identify. If we surrender, the whole Hawk-bat plan just evaporates, and we have to start all over where Zsinj is concerned. I'm not going to have that."

"Even at the cost of your own life."

"That's right." Exhausted by his exertions, Phanan lay back on the seat. "Starting over means more time. More time for Zsinj to bombard more colonies, to destroy more ships. Another day may mean some bright young doctor gets it the way I did and ends up what I am."

"What you are is pretty good."

Phanan shook his head. "Not as good as some kid with a superior intellect whose only aim is to make people better. I'd rather he be out there than me." He took a long breath. "If I die—"

"You're not going to die."

"Shut up and listen, Face. If I die, you can't let them find my body. They'd identify me. Do whatever it takes you to get back to the unit, but don't let them find me."

"You're not going to die."

"Promise me you'll dispose of me."

Face shuddered. "I promise. But you're not going to die."

"Well, I'll try to hold you to that promise, too." His organic eye closed. "There's no traffic, yet we're stopped. Why is that?"

Face grinned and splashed back to his towing rope. "Your fault for hiring an incompetent driver."

The sun went down and Halmad's myriad moons were brightly illuminated. Behind them was a rich carpet of stars— for all its industry, Halmad had clear skies.

At a bend in the river where the trees were thin, Phanan said, "What's that?"

Face looked back to see where Phanan was staring, then looked straight up.

Just crossing before one of the moons was a brightly illuminated triangle, tiny in the distance.

"That'll be *Iron Fist*, I expect."

"Ah. Nice to have been able to see her before she was all blown up."

Two hundred meters farther on, Face heard Phanan gasping for breath. He splashed back to him. He couldn't go as fast as he wanted. It was getting hard to move; his legs were cold and felt like lead.

Phanan was not knotted in pain, as Face had expected. He was stretched out in the pose he'd found most comfortable, but there was distress in his face. "Sorry," Phanan said. "A bit of panic." His voice was fainter than before.

"Panic."

"I was just imagining what a sad galaxy this would be without my superior intellect and general state of wonderfulness." Phanan gave a minimal shrug.

"That's not something you have to worry about."

"Either way, you're right." Phanan held out a hand; there was something in it.

Face took the datapad from him. "What's this?"

"It's called a da-ta-pad. New Republic and Imperial children learn about them from the time they're very young."

"Funny."

"Take it back with you. It has some last thoughts on it."

The coldness in Face's legs crept up to inhabit the rest of him and he shuddered again. "Not last thoughts, Ton. Don't be so fatalistic. You're just punishing yourself."

Phanan managed a hoarse chuckle. "You would know. That's your specialty, isn't it?"

"What do you mean?"

"I do what I do because I very badly want to hurt the people who hurt me. You do what you do so you can punish a little boy who once made some holodramas for the Empire."

"That's ridiculous."

"Is it? Face, just how much do you think you owe the New Republic?"

"Well . . . some."

"For your acting. For the fact that it furthered Imperial causes."

"That's right."

"It's not right. You're putting a tremendous burden on the little boy you used to be."

"Well, a debt. It's as though I incurred this tremendous debt account. Now I'm paying it off bit by bit."

"The account doesn't need balancing." There was scorn in Ton's voice. "You can't reduce sapient lives to numbers and exchange them like credits. You can't measure what a boy did in innocence against what a man has to do for the rest of his life."

"Now you're raving."

"Ah. That's good to know. Hey, we're stopped again."

A bit farther, and Phanan said, in a hoarse whisper Face could barely hear over the whine of the repulsorlift, "It's up there again."

"*Iron Fist?*" Face looked up. The Super Star Destroyer was making another orbit.

It was distant, pristine, like the giant spearhead of some supernatural being from the long-forgotten mythologies of a hundred worlds. It drifted by, not caring about the lives and deaths and victories and tragedies of the humans below. And when it descended, it would bring death. That, Face decided, was *Iron Fist*. And such a thing had no right to exist.

If it took him forever, he would see it destroyed.

He made sure his sudden revulsion did not make it to his voice. "Not too intimidating from this far away, is it?" he asked.

Phanan didn't answer.

"I said, not too intimidating from here, is it?"

Phanan still did not respond.

Face stood where he was, unwilling to turn and look, to walk back on his cold-numbed legs to confirm what he feared.

But the speeder bike slowly drifted forward until it was beside him.

Phanan's chest did not rise or fall. But his organic eye was still open, directed upward, and his expression—for once lacking pain, lacking the shields of sarcasm or manufactured self-appreciation—was that of a child wondering at the glittering beauty of the stars.

Face's vision blurred as his own eyes filled with the first tears he'd shed since he was a boy.

13

At dawn, Face rose from his makeshift camp. He took one last look at the bundle he was leaving behind—ruined speeder bike, ruined pilot, and the combination of his own datapad and a Raptor comlink he'd laboriously programmed by moonlight, all beneath the thin thermal blanket he'd retrieved from the bike's cargo—and then headed into the trees.

In spite of the pulsing aches that seemed to have replaced his muscles and bones while he slept, he would be able to travel swiftly. He had good directional sense. He did not have an injured comrade to tow through difficult, slow terrain.

Within an hour, he passed by the gutted hulk of Phanan's TIE fighter. There were no bodies here. Zsinj's investigators had come and gone, and had posted no one to guard a valueless, burned-out hull. There were no distant sounds of speeder bikes or TIE fighters. The search had moved or been called off.

When morning was still young, he swam out to where his interceptor lay partially submerged, and took a long and lonely time going through the routine power-up checklist.

But when that was done, he had to act fast. His window of opportunity would be a narrow one.

The murky water behind his interceptor boiled as he cut in his engines; he could see bubbles and foam drift around to his front viewport as his interceptor strained. Then the repulsors overcame the muck that trapped his vehicle. He rose to the water's surface and then shot into the air.

Up, southwest across a narrow band of forest, a mere few moments until he found the river. Downriver just a few more moments as terrain blurred beneath him.

When he recognized the approximate area of his camp, he sent a signal across his comlink. The distant Raptor comlink responded with the signal he'd programmed into its companion datapad and a moment later he hovered over the glade where he'd spent the night.

There it was, the black thermal blanket atop his friend.

He could not wait. Revulsion for the deed he was about to perform had been his companion last night; he did not have time for it now. He rotated so that his interceptor was pointed straight down, as though it were about to fly into the ground.

Repulsor and thrust emissions kicked leaves and plants into motion, and a moment later whipped the blanket from atop the speeder bike and Ton Phanan.

Phanan's organic eye was closed—Face had closed it last night. But his mechanical eye was still powered, still staring redly, and Face wondered what it saw.

Then Face fired.

His lasers turned the center of the glade into a burning inferno, charring speeder bike, organic body, and prosthetic parts into a melted crater of ash and bubbling metal. He fired until there was nothing recognizable there, nothing for the investigators of Zsinj or Halmad to identify as Ton Phanan.

Then he turned his bow skyward and fled to space.

At the end of Face's debriefing, Wedge asked, "You've eaten?"

Face nodded. He rubbed his chin where the General Kargin scar makeup had been removed, and seemed surprised to find stubble there. "A little."

"Good. Listen, Face, I know this isn't going to help very much, but as far as I can tell from your report and your interceptor's recordings, you did everything right. You did everything possible to preserve the integrity of this mission and the lives of your fellow pilots. I think highly of what you accomplished down there."

"But I was unable to bring Phanan back alive."

Wedge nodded. "I've been unable to bring a lot of friends back alive. And I'm not going to pretend that it's not going to eat at you. It will. It still eats at me. I just want you to understand that it's not something you alone have gone through. If you need to talk, come to me, or to Wes or to Myn. I don't think we can make you feel any better . . . but we can remind you that it's possible to survive the experience."

"Yes, sir." Face looked reflective. "I'd like to try to return that favor, if you'd like me to."

"How's that?"

"I knew Ton better than anyone in the unit. I think I should at least help write the letter of notification to his family."

"Ah. Well, that's not going to be necessary, Face. We're both off that particular hook. While you were cleaning up, I went through his records and the datapad you brought back to me. The person we're supposed to notify in the case of his death is you."

Face's eyes went wide. "Me. Why not his family?"

"No living family. He was the only child of a couple who had him comparatively late in life. They both died before he completed his education. No siblings. No family member closer than distant cousins who've never met him. You're also the beneficiary of his will."

Face didn't even manage a reply to that statement. He just gaped.

"I have to process some of these documents. Then I'll get them into your hands. It won't be for a while. In the meantime, I want you to get some sleep. At least, get some rest."

"Yes, sir."

Wedge returned the pilot's salute and watched him go. He waited a few moments before calling, "Wes."

Janson stuck his head in the doorway. His normally merry features were now schooled into somber lines. "Yes, Commander."

"Assign Lara Notsil to Face as his wingman. Also, she's

had the military first-aid course more recently than any of the rest of us, so assign her as squadron medic. Get her whatever instructional holos and equipment she'll need for the task.

"And ask her to keep an eye on him, to watch out for signs of undue distress or any sort of overreaction to Phanan's death. But she needs to keep it very surreptitious. We can't have him feeling that we're all spying on him."

"Even though we are."

"Correct."

Moments after Janson had gone, there was a rap at the door.

"Come."

Donos entered and saluted.

Wedge returned the salute and tried to keep from frowning. There was something different about the pilot. The somber expression was the same, the thick mop of black hair over brooding dark eyes was the same—though lacking the air of defeat Donos had worn when he joined Wraith Squadron.

Then Wedge caught it. Donos was in casual dress, mostly black, his jacket still bearing a patch for Talon Squadron, and Corellian Bloodstripes on his pants.

Donos had earned the decorations while serving with distinction as a sniper with the Corellian armed forces. He hadn't worn them in the first several weeks of his service with Wraith Squadron, demonstrating the lack of self-esteem that followed the destruction of his former squadron.

That injury to his spirit seemed to have healed. A good sign. But Donos still wasn't the ostentatious sort and wouldn't have worn a decoration like this, even though it was his right, with his ordinary dress. Wedge gave him a suspicious look and gestured for him to sit. "This obviously isn't about Face."

"That's right, sir. It's about Lara."

Donos told him about Lara's brother, who shouldn't have survived but did, who shouldn't have found her again but did. And he described a possible mission to Lara's homeworld of Aldivy.

Face rose after a long time. Most of it had not been spent sleeping. Nor had he been truly awake; he'd been in a restless state where conscious thought could not take hold, but neither could sleep, for his mind was fully occupied by images of the last two days.

The light on his terminal was blinking, a sign of messages or files received. He brought the terminal up.

A dispatch from the commander. Lara, Wraith Thirteen, was now his wing, and the replacement medic. No surprise there.

A copy of Ton Phanan's will. Face skipped it.

A message from Phanan. It was dated and timed less than an hour before his death. Face took a deep breath and brought it up.

It was simple text, the only means Phanan had to take notes at the time. It read,

> Face:
>   I'm not going to go into the pathology of this. Suffice to say we're talking about internal injuries, internal bleeding. Maybe a ruptured kidney; I'm having trouble sorting that one out. Either way, I don't think I'm going to last too long.
>   I flatter myself in thinking that you're going to take it kind of hard. (If I'm wrong, don't let me know.) While part of me wishes you wouldn't, another part appreciates it.
>   I also know that you're going to punish yourself for this. I wish you wouldn't. There are two people responsible for me getting injured. I'm one of them, for being not quite the superior flier I needed to be. Some unnamed Zsinj pilot is the other one, and you killed him. (Which I also appreciate, by the way, in case I didn't tell you.) There's no room for a third party to blame, so butt out.
>   I've left you some money. A fair amount, actually; I was the only son of wealthy parents, and I didn't manage to spend it all on good times and prosthetics. By the terms of my will, some of what you receive has to be used for a specific project. If you don't use it for that, the whole amount goes to an already wealthy actor you've mentioned with a certain amount of contempt, and

*you'll get to watch him become even richer despite his
lack of talent or personal worth. So there.*

*I really don't have much time here, and I'm strug-
gling to find some way to sum up what I need to say. I
guess it boils down to this:*

*Thanks for being my friend. I needed one, and you
were it.*

Ton Phanan
Pilot, Wit, and Superior Intellect
*Oh, yes—don't let my glass prowlers starve. They're
cute little insects. Cuteness should be preserved.*

Face waited for some sort of blow to hit him, but he was left
only with the dull ache that had been his companion all
through the night.

He brought up Phanan's will and read it as well.

"Some of us will, as you know, be away on missions with vary-
ing levels of consequence," Wedge said. "A couple will remain
here at Hawk-bat Base for maintenance and security purposes.
The rest—now, contain yourselves—will receive leave."

He waited through the resulting cheers. They were in the
conference-room module, packed in around its table, and the
Wraiths' expressions were a study in contrasts, ranging from
glum to suddenly cheerful. Well, partially cheerful. Phanan's
death was still fresh on their minds.

"Mission One is the meeting with Zsinj," Wedge said.
"Face commands, and he has chosen Dia and Kell to accompany him. This is all intelligence gathering, very delicate,
which is why the crew is full of deadly killers." That got a
chuckle. Wedge saw Tyria give Kell a little irritable punch in
the shoulder—doubtless she was unhappy that he'd be on a very
dangerous mission, and doubly unhappy that she wouldn't be
along to get him out of trouble. "This mission will utilize the
shuttle *Narra.*

"Mission Two is Lara's meeting with her brother. We hope
that will turn out to be nothing more than a joyful family re-
union, but there's a chance that this is a probe by Zsinj. Lieu-

tenant Donos will accompany her, and they'll be in their X-wings.

"Mission Three consists of me traveling by X-wing back to Coruscant to make a routine report and pick up orders. With our complement of X-wings, up to five more of you can accompany me back and get in a little rest and recreation. Lieutenant Janson will remain here in command of the facility—because he got to go back last time and now it's his turn."

Janson's expression turned glum. "Nobody is allowed to have any fun on Coruscant. If I find out that anyone has had any fun, he gets kitchen duty for a month."

"We all promise to be miserable, Wes." Wedge noticed one of the pilots' hand raised. "Yes, Castin."

"Sir, you remember the special mission I talked to you about? Sneaking a program into *Iron Fist*'s communications system so that it will broadcast its location occasionally?"

"I remember. I remember saying it was a good plan . . . but not for the initial contact mission."

Castin waved as if to brush away the last part of Wedge's statement. "Sir, I finished the program."

"You did?" Wedge nodded. "Excellent."

"I finished it in time for this mission, sir. It still needs an experienced code-slicer to cut it into the system in question—otherwise it'd never get through the system's defenses—but it operates flawlessly on my Imperial-computer-system simulators."

"It won't be for this mission, Castin. But we'll try to bring back an upgraded simulator from Coruscant to give you that much more of an edge."

"Dammit, sir, this is the only opportunity we're certain we're going to have. We need to take it. You're being too cautious, and that's going to cost us."

The other pilots looked between Castin and Wedge, all cheer draining from their faces.

Wedge took a deep breath, giving himself a brief moment to calm himself. "Flight Officer Donn."

"Yes, sir."

"Flight Officer Donn."

Suddenly uneasy, Castin looked around, then rose and stood at attention. "Sir."

"Your tactical sense and gut feeling tell you that now is the time to implement your plan. Mine tell me that later will be better. All else being equal, whose do you think I am going to rank higher?"

"Well, yours, sir." Castin looked very unhappy under this sudden scrutiny.

"Now, think about this. If we do it my way and I'm right, we've saved lives. If we do it my way and I'm wrong, we'll have missed an opportunity—an opportunity we'll regain if the rest of the mission goes according to plan and the Hawk-bats begin doing work for Zsinj—and I'll have both learned something and suffered a slight blow to my reputation, both of which I can survive.

"On the other hand, if we do it your way and you're right, we conceivably speed up the destruction of Zsinj. But if we do it your way and you're wrong, you get yourself and the whole team captured or killed, which you can't survive. Do you see the difference?"

"Yes, sir, but—"

"Save that thought. Now, imagine that you're a New Republic pilot and you feel a need to criticize a superior officer's performance or thinking. All else being equal, should you do so in private or in a public forum?"

Castin seemed visibly to sag. "In private, sir."

"I'll give you some time to think about that. You'll be remaining on Hawk-bat Station while your fellows return to Coruscant. Now, sit."

Castin did, flushing red, looking miserable.

Wedge looked among the other pilots. "Anything else? No? Prep for your missions, then. Dismissed."

Face caught up with Castin out in the Trench. He asked, "What was that all about?"

Castin shook his head, angry, and didn't slow his pace . . . though he was just walking up the middle of the stony shaft with no destination evident. "He's wrong, Face. He's just wrong."

"Why?"

"Because, I don't know, he's so concerned about preserving our lives that he'll flinch from a tactic that could end this whole campaign in one stroke."

"No. Castin, he hasn't hesitated to risk our lives, or his own, not in the time I've been with the Wraiths. But in spite of all the jokes about Corellians not caring about the odds, he does. And he knows more about resources and strategy than we do. So if he says your mission isn't worth the risk—"

"He's right and I'm wrong."

"Probably."

"All right."

"I want your promise that you won't try anything on your own."

"I promise." Castin stopped suddenly and looked around. He and Face were now beside the kitchen and mess. "I'm hungry." He headed in that direction.

"A good, brisk walk will do that to you," Face said. He did not follow the code-slicer—better not to put him on the defensive.

There were two gray blurs, the X-wings of Lara and Donos, shooting up past the magcon field holding in the atmosphere of the Hawk-bats' hangar. Face, seated in the cockpit of the shuttle *Narra,* watched them flash by. They were followed a moment later by a stream of five more snubfighters—Wedge, Runt, Shalla, Tyria, and Piggy, off on their routine mission to Coruscant.

He envied them. It wasn't just that they'd be getting a little rest and recreation, even just a few hours of it; the prospect of facing Warlord Zsinj was making him more than a little tense. He had no abnormal fear of the man—but ever since this mission had been described to him, he'd harbored the fear that somewhere in the middle of a conversation with the warlord, a vision of Phanan would cross before his eyes and he'd be unable to restrain himself from making an assault on Zsinj. Such an attack might hurt or kill Zsinj, but it was certain to be fatal to Face and his comrades. "Power," he said.

"Ninety-seven percent, reserves one hundred percent."

That was Dia, seated beside him, in the copilot's seat. But it wasn't the Dia he was used to. She was now in the guise of Seku, her Hawk-bats identity, and as dramatically different from her usual appearance as Face was when, as now, he wore his General Kargin scar makeup.

Her normally bare brain tails—or *lekku*, as they were known to the natives of Ryloth—were now decorated with an intricate pattern of black cuneiform marks, temporary tattoos that, in the Twi'lek language, told stories of the character and misdeeds of her fictitious identity. Instead of the gray TIE-style pilot's uniforms Face and Kell wore, she was dressed in a vest, trousers, and boots of black hide—lined, she had assured him, for comfort—all decorated with shiny metal replicas of animal teeth and claws, accoutrements she'd persuaded Cubber to lathe out during some of his infrequent off-duty hours. Face found her attractive under normal circumstances; this barbaric persona was even more visually appealing.

"Ninety-seven? Why are we not at full?"

She shrugged. "Cubber said something about the manhandling *Narra* sustained in *Iron Fist*'s tractor beams causing some system problems. Nothing he can repair until the commander returns from Coruscant with some replacement parts."

"Wonderful. What else did he say we can expect to go wrong?"

Kell stuck his head up between the two seats. There was more to his head now; he wore a false mustache, beard, and absurdly long wig of fiery red hair. "Hull seals are a little more questionable. We had to repair some slow leaks when we got back. But she's in good shape. Assuming we don't have to take on another Star Destroyer, she'll do just fine."

"Good. Remember your signature action."

Kell's eyes slitted. With a slow and deliberate motion, he drew the hair hanging down his right shoulder to fall behind his back. As he turned to look at Face, he added an insolent little shake of the head that set his hair to swaying. It was an elaboration Face hadn't taught him, but it was perfect, making his persona even more obviously a victim of arrogance and self-love.

Dia gave the two of them a hard smile. "He's loathsome."

Face said, "That's the idea. All right, strap in and prep for space. We have an appointment to keep. No, wait a minute: Kell, drag Castin out of the smuggling compartment and send him packing. We can't have any stowaways."

Grinning, Kell moved aft, behind the seats, and tapped a complicated rhythm against the starboard bulkhead. A portion of what had looked like seamless wall swung down on hinges and he reached inside. An expression of surprise crossed his face and he ducked down to look. "Hey, no Castin."

"It's empty?"

"I didn't say that." Kell retrieved something fairly large and furry from the compartment's interior and waved it at the others. It was the Ewok toy. "Say hello to Lieutenant Kettch."

Face snorted. "You ever wonder how he gets around? I'm not sure he *isn't* alive."

Kell peered inside the compartment again. "And some generous spirit has loaded this thing up with goodies. A couple of blasters, some preserved food, a couple of bottles of Halmad Prime—"

"Hey, bring that up here."

Kell replaced Kettch within the compartment and sealed it. "I don't think so."

"It's every general's right to be uproariously drunk on diplomatic missions."

Kell dropped into the seat behind Dia and began practicing his signature move. With every repetition it became more obnoxious. "I'm going to keep this up until you shut up about the Prime."

"Ooh. You win, mutineer. Prepare for space."

14

Narra emerged from hyperspace at the appointed coordinates.

This was deep space, nothing to see within a half-dozen light-years, but there *was* something awaiting them—a barrage of comm messages. They flooded the communications waves, repeating variations on the same message, overlapping one another.

"Greetings Hawk-bats this is greetings Hawk-bats Warlord Zsinj not rebroadcast I welcome this is you prepare to receive them simply Warlord Zsinj a new set of I welcome follow them coordinates do not rebroadcast you prepare them simply soon we follow them to receive soon we will be will be a new dining in comfort and set of dining in coming to terms of coordinates do great mutual comfort and profit . . ." The words continued in that way, a ceaseless stream.

Face shook his head. "That's a mess. Let's see if we can lock them down to a single transmission." His hands moved over the communications console. "All right. We have a small satellite dead ahead. One signal's stronger than the others. And that gives us . . ." He punched a button to isolate the signal.

"Greetings, Hawk-bats. This is Warlord Zsinj. I welcome you. Prepare to receive a new set of coordinates. Do not rebroadcast them. Simply follow them. Soon we will be dining in comfort and coming to terms of great mutual profit." The message began to repeat.

"We're getting a file on the same band," Dia said.

"Don't bring it up," Kell said. "It might be the kind of program Castin likes to work up. Something that will give them more information about us than we'd like."

Face nodded. "Good point. It's not a big file. I'll transmit it to my datapad and we can reenter the nav data by hand. What do you figure would happen if we did want to retransmit the file?"

Dia said, "One of two things. That satellite will have an extra system. Either it's a weapons system, designed to destroy us, or it's a hypercomm system that will warn Zsinj before we get to him."

Kell dragged his hair back over his shoulder again. "It'll be whichever system is cheaper."

"Well, in either case, we won't be doing that." Face compared the navigational data on his datapad with that which he'd just typed into *Narra*'s computer. It matched. He punched the execute button and nodded for Dia to bring the shuttle around to its new course. "All right, stage two."

The two X-wings dropped out of hyperspace at the outer periphery of the Aldivy system, well beyond the solar-gravity well that would prevent their reentering hyperspace.

Lara immediately brought up her visual sensors and trained them on the planet of Aldivy. The picture that emerged, jittery and blurry, was of a blue-and-white globe with no features she could identify.

She restrained herself from making a sour face. What she knew of Aldivy all came from Imperial surveys and publicly available data. She knew the map of the planet's surface, but from space, of course, cloud cover kept those easily recognized continental borders from sight.

Her comlink crackled. "I can't detect any traffic on Imperial channels," Donos said. "Just some routine stuff on standard planetary and commercial channels. Pretty light, actually."

"Aldivy isn't heavily settled," she said. "A couple of hundred communities. Not enough value there for the Imperials to protect it when they occupied it. At the height of Imperial occupation, we had two TIE fighters and a shuttle protecting us."

"In addition to your own planetary defense forces, I assume."

"Um, yes." She wished he'd quit asking questions. Too much of this and he'd catch her out in a wrong answer. "Our police. Not much defense against assault forces, I'm afraid."

"Is your home on the day side or night side right now?"

"I'm trying to figure that out." *Shut up. Just shut up.* "I can't tell. I'll know when we're closer."

•

The main doors to *Iron Fist*'s false bridge rose with their customary startling speed and General Melvar entered. He stopped short at the sight of the dinner table now occupying the center of the command walkway. Zsinj was seated at the head chair of the bare table, his booted feet up on it. Behind him, at the bow end of the chamber, the holoscreens had been activated and were now a perfect match for the view from the real bridge's forward viewports; they framed Zsinj, making him the central feature of the galaxy they showed.

Zsinj smiled at him. "What do you think?"

"Perhaps your most ostentatious demonstration yet," Melvar said as he approached. "Shouldn't you surround yourself with a nimbus of light to complete the effect?"

"Not a bad idea. Maybe next time. What do you want?"

"Sensors have reported a shuttle's appearance from the hyperspace course you provided to the Hawk-bats. They'll be here within minutes."

Zsinj's feet hit the walkway surface and he stood. "Assemble the cast. Notify the galley. And get into makeup. This should be entertaining."

As he watched *Iron Fist* growing in the forward viewport, Face willed his stomach to quit crawling around. "All right. Here's your last bit of advice. Remember, we're just as arrogant as they are but nowhere near as strong. So respond appropriately to bad manners—but not so appropriately that you get us killed."

Kell mimed entering data on an imaginary datapad. "No get killed," he said. "I'll try to remember."

"I'd like to say leave all the talking to me, but that's not going to work—we're here to impress them with our individual skill and readiness. Just keep all your responses in character, and refer any question about our unit strength, tactical readiness, that sort of thing, to me."

"Understood, General," Dia said. Her voice was an insinuating purr, far different from the flat, sometimes emotionless tones he was used to from her. He glanced at her, and it was a stranger's face that looked back at him: Dia's features with another woman behind them. Her eyes evaluated him with the steady regard of a half-tamed animal watching its owner for some sign of weakness. He looked away quickly, uneasily aware that he didn't know whether she was simply a natural actress or this was a layer to her that he hadn't seen before.

To his disappointment, the *Iron Fist* bridge crew instructed the Hawk-bats to land in a secondary hangar well forward of the main hangar. He would have liked to have seen the damage done to the main hangar by Kell's tanker bomb, to have seen its state of repair.

Dia brought the shuttle into the designated hangar. Within already were a pair of interceptors, another *Lambda*-class shuttle, and a larger Raptor transport shuttle—an ugly, boxy troop carrier known to be favored by Zsinj's forces.

And a reception committee—an officer and a half-dozen stormtroopers. One of the troopers hand-guided *Narra* to a landing pad marked off by red paint. Dia set the shuttle down expertly.

"Show time," Face said.

They descended the boarding ramp in proper form, Face first, Dia and Kell to either side of and behind him. Face stopped directly before the officer. Neither that man nor any of the stormtroopers reacted visibly to Face's scar makeup, the first time he could remember such a lack of response.

The officer before him was not what Face had expected. The man was tall and lean, with features that might have been bland had they not been twisted into such a predatory smile. He seemed to glow with an inner light, and Face suspected that it was a dangerous light. The man liked to win, or to kill, or to inflict pain—Face wasn't sure which, but he did know that this was a man to watch. The officer also, incongruously, had long and perfectly reflective fingernails; Face suspected they were metal and would not have been surprised to discover that they were very, very sharp.

Face cleared his throat. "I am General Kargin, founder and leader of the Hawk-bat Independent Space Force." He put on an urbane smile and lowered his voice. "I believe I have an invitation."

"Indeed you do. General Melvar. I am in charge of the warlord's assault forces, and I welcome you to *Iron Fist*." The general shook Face's hand. Firm grip, fast shake—he made no effort to conduct a contest of grip strength to demonstrate dominance. "Your associates?"

Face gestured first to Dia, then to Kell. "Captain Seku, my second-in-command. Lieutenant Dissek, my bodyguard."

"Delighted. Before we continue, though, there is a bit of bureaucratic unpleasantness to accomplish."

"Oh?"

The general looked regretful. "Zsinj is a man with many enemies. For this reason, many policies surround him, policies that I do not let him overrule, for his own safety. One of them leads me to insist that you turn over all weapons to my men for the duration of your stay."

Face shrugged. Then he drew his blaster pistol with such speed that the stormtroopers present were caught off guard, their weapons out of line; he could have shot Melvar and one or two others before they would have been able to react. But just as quickly he flipped the blaster in the air and caught it, then handed it, butt first, to the nearest stormtrooper. "I have no fear of treachery here," Face said. "Alive, I promise additional strength to Zsinj. Killed, I would cost him very dearly."

Melvar gave him a polite nod and shrug, neither agreeing to nor denying Face's assertion. Dia and Kell handed over their own blasters in a less dramatic fashion.

"The second part of this unfortunate protocol," Melvar said, "is that you must be scanned for additional weapons you might have forgotten to hand over, because of your habitual wearing of them almost as clothing rather than weapons. Please."

Obligingly, Face and the others raised their arms and let a stormtrooper specialist run a handheld scanner around them. Face came up clean, then Dia.

Then it was Kell's turn. His accoutrements also failed to trigger the weapons scanner, but the stormtrooper behind him obviously thought his arms needed to be a little higher; with the barrel of his blaster rifle, he tapped the underside of one of Kell's arms to raise it.

Kell stepped back so that the stormtrooper's barrel protruded beneath his right arm. He clamped his right arm upon it, then twisted, simultaneously yanking the blaster out of the man's hand and bringing his elbow up under the stormtrooper's helmet. A slight change to the angle of his attack and the blow would crush the man's windpipe, but Kell instead brought his elbow up into the man's chin. Everyone heard the crack of the man's jaw snapping shut.

The stormtrooper dropped to the floor, his armor clattering.

The other stormtroopers aimed at Kell. With admirable aplomb, Kell slowly reached over to switch off the blaster rifle's power, then lowered the weapon onto its fallen owner. "Is there a problem?"

General Melvar's mouth twitched into what looked like an amused smirk. "You appear to be punishing one of my men."

"Punishing?" Kell looked down at the stormtrooper as if seeing him for the first time. "Oh, I assure you, no punishment was intended. That was simply reflex. If I'd intended to punish him, he'd be begging you to kill him now."

Face turned back to Melvar. "My apologies."

The general shook his head. "No need to apologize. The trooper was not instructed to behave this way toward honored guests. I think a little experience with electricity will do him some good." He gestured for another stormtrooper to attend to the unconscious man, then for Face to fall in step beside him. "How much do you pay for this man Dissek's services?"

"I'll never tell," Face said. "If you want to try to hire him away, you'll have to offer him a bribe without knowing my own economies."

Melvar offered a little sigh of vexation.

They landed in a grove of fruit trees less than a kilometer from the charred oval of dirt that now lay where the community of New Oldtown had once stood. It was night, and only the crescent of a single moon afforded Lara and Donos any light.

Together, they approached the area of char from the east, where a rise overlooked the destroyed town. Lara assured Donos that a farmhouse had once stood there; she didn't tell him that she knew this only from publicly available information taken from the community's main computer shortly before Admiral Trigit bombarded the town out of existence. At the summit of the rise, they got down on hands and knees to crawl until the ruined area was beneath them.

What had been New Oldtown was as black as cloudy night. What she could see of the terrain suggested that the onetime community and outlying farms were now a series of charred furrows and craters—certainly, the nearest terrain was like that.

In the midst of it all, though, was a house—a prefabricated brick-shaped dwelling of an incongruous blue, cheery lights in the windows. It looked like a cheap dollhouse.

Donos sighted in on it with his sniper rifle, adjusting the range on his sight. He did not speak, but worked with confidence and precision. Lara could tell he'd done this many times in similar circumstances.

"They'll probably scan for large life-forms when I arrive," she said. "In case I brought allies. Which I have."

"We're nearly a kilometer out," Donos said. "They might have a scanner that could find me, but probably not. Have you got your comlink to broadcast continuously?"

"No. They're sure to check for that. I'm going in with it off, and I'm leaving it off."

He looked at her, one eye visible in the shadow of his face. "That's not a good idea. If you get in trouble—"

"If I hold up a fist, it means I'm in trouble. Come to the rescue. If I don't, I have the situation under control."

He sighed, obviously unhappy. "All right. But call for help the instant you feel the situation spin out of control."

"If it does." She hesitated, at a loss for what to say next. His tone suggested that he wasn't just being professionally methodical—he actually cared about what happened to her. She wasn't used to that and didn't know how to respond. No words suggested themselves, so she simply rose and headed down the hill toward the ludicrous blue house.

Castin Donn watched Zsinj's scanner team go over the interior of *Narra*. The picture on his handheld screen wasn't good—a flickery blue and white, limitations imposed by the micro-miniaturized holocam lens he had set up to observe the shuttle's cabin—but it did allow him to see which of the cockpit's control panels they popped open so as to install the machinery they'd brought with them. A tracking device, probably. They brought up the shuttle's master control program, too, but didn't spend much time with it—probably just erasing the record of their entry and exit. Not that such a tactic would work; Castin had done considerable work on *Narra*'s systems, so that now what appeared to be the standard interfaces to all shuttle programs were actually a false layer. Code-slicers could adjust those layers all they wished, but their modifications would be trapped and later presented to the shuttle's authorized operators for confirmation or deletion.

The scanning team departed and the boarding ramp rose into place. It was time to get moving.

Castin switched off the holocam and gingerly set the screen down beside him. Every move had to be precise and careful. He lay on his back in full stormtrooper armor, the helmet tucked in beside his head, and could still occupy only half of the smuggling compartment. He'd arranged to extend a holocam lead and a breathing tube out through the scanner shielding—turning them off while scanning was actually taking place—but the compartment had no other comfort conditioning, and he'd been sweating in here for hours. He stank like a bantha in mating season.

Tape held the mirror in place beside him. The mirror was a long strip of reflective material set up to adhere to the bottom and top surfaces of the smuggling compartment at a forty-five-degree angle so that anyone looking in would see the compartment's top surface instead of the back. It was carefully situated so that it covered him but led anyone looking in the compartment to believe that it was empty at the rear.

Now he went through the actions that had gotten him here, but in reverse order. He detached the tape that held the mirrored material to the compartment's ceiling and lowered it in place beside him. He carefully moved aside the supplies he'd loaded into the compartment, giving him a narrow channel for escape. He flipped the switch that popped the compartment door open, and then wriggled out into *Narra*'s main compartment—and into comparatively fresh air. He lay there on the floor for a few moments, gulping in air, then retrieved his helmet and other gear from the compartment and sealed it back up.

His plan was under way. He had to get out of the shuttle and hangar without the hangar guards noticing, find his way to a full-function computer coupler, slice his way in through ship security, and upload his program—then get back and wait. It would be tough, but he was a Wraith. He could do it.

And days from now, when *Iron Fist* was a glowing ball of superheated gas or a prize vessel in the hands of the New Republic, Commander Antilles would be forced to acknowledge that Castin had been right all along.

General Melvar and the Hawk-bats swept into a bridge that was a riot of activity.

A narrow but full-length dinner table, large enough to accommodate twenty people, was set up on the command walkway and more than half-filled with diners. Seated at the head of the table, his back to the viewports now showing the swirl of hyperspace travel, a vast area of brightness in his spotless white grand admiral's uniform, was Zsinj. His hands were clasped over his expansive belly, his mustachios drooped rakishly, and his expression was one of great contentment.

The officers assembled at his table were engaged in vigorous conversation, but as the Hawk-bats entered the chamber they could hear none of it—it was drowned out by the din from the crew pit below.

There, uniformed bridge officers stood their watches with a startling unconcern for military decorum. Some monitored their screens while leaning back with their feet up on their consoles. Others stood in groups of three or four, eyes on their screens but their attention on their fellows. Several crewmen were huddled close to their screens, absorbed in low-grade TIE-fighter simulators. At one point toward the bow, two stormtroopers were engaged in a vibroblade duel, apparently a friendly one, but their blows still caused deep scores in their white armor.

They were all talking, a jumble of noise that made the chamber sound like a conference hall rather than a ship's bridge.

General Melvar led the Hawk-bats toward the head of the table and had them sit before offering introduction. "Warlord, allow me to present you General Kargin, Captain Seku, and Lieutenant Dissek, honored representatives of the Hawk-bats. General Kargin, your host, the warlord Zsinj."

Face offered a seated half bow.

Zsinj finally turned his attention to the new guests and smiled. "Good to meet you at last. Welcome aboard *Iron Fist*."

Face said, "A formidable vessel. I trust we did not do her too much damage."

"Certainly not. Oh, several such explosions would have been most inconvenient, but our capacity for repair is unparalleled."

Face drew a hand across his brow, an exaggerated demonstration of relief. "Well, that's cause for us to celebrate. I have no qualms about preying on ground-pounders like the people of Halmad, but—and it costs me no honor to say it—I would avoid earning the prolonged enmity of Zsinj."

The warlord's smile became broader. "It was already obvious that you were an intelligent pirate—else you would not have enjoyed the success you did. But before we get to our main subject of conversation for the evening, let us dine."

"Please." Face knew he'd kept all tension from his voice and manner, but it was still there, and the meal was one more opportunity for Zsinj to visit some new difficulty upon them—such as poison. If they'd read the man correctly, there would be no such subterfuge here. But they could always have made a mistake in their evaluation.

Lara drew to a stop a dozen steps from the house. She surreptitiously touched the butt of her blaster, reassurance that it was still at hand. "Hail the camp," she called out, a standard Aldivian greeting from arriving visitors—even when arriving at a vast government building or a rich villa, tradition insisted it be called a camp. "Tavin, are you there?"

The front door slid open and he was there, the human complication from her mail message, dark and good-looking, the sort of man who knew his handsomeness was a tool and used it at every opportunity. He beamed. "Lara." He approached her, arms up for an embrace.

She put her palm against his chest and kept him at bay. "Nothing like that. I don't feel that close to you right now."

His face fell. "I'm sorry. Maybe you will later. Come inside?"

"No. I spend too much time cooped up as it is. I like the breeze out here."

He shrugged. "Well, let's have some light." He returned to his door and switched something just inside it. A floodlight mounted above the door illuminated the charred blackness before his house. "I have someone to introduce you to."

"I imagine so."

He beckoned, and a moment later was joined in the doorway by another man. This one was rail lean, dressed in a brown Aldivian farmer's garments . . . but the fineness of his blond hair, the fact that there were no calluses on his hands, the autocratic expression on his face, and—not least of all—the blaster on his belt made it clear to Lara that this was no Aldivian farmer.

"Lara, let me introduce you to Captain Rossik. He has been most anxious to speak to you."

The blond man smiled, an expression that was both beautiful and manifestly insincere, and advanced to shake Lara's hand. "I have indeed. Lieutenant Petothel, allow me to congratulate you on all you've accomplished."

She took the compliment with a frosty little smile and nod. That was why she had declined to have her comlink broadcast back to Donos; she couldn't have her fellow Wraith hear her being addressed by a different name. "I'm so happy you were at last able to reach me," she said.

"Tavin, go fetch us some chairs and drinks." Rossik returned his attention to Lara. "How long can you stay without eliciting suspicion?"

"A couple of days. I received special leave because of Tavin's sudden reappearance, but it's only for a few days."

"Well, your record demonstrates that you're a smart one. It shouldn't take you too long to learn to use the equipment we're going to give you."

"Equipment?"

"A special transmitter. It sends very small information packets via the old Imperial HoloNet. Yet it's only about thirty kilos. Costs more than a TIE interceptor. We can use it to track *Mon Remonda* and put an end to her."

"With me aboard."

"No, certainly not. You'll plant it, then on your next mission just vanish and come to us. Then, and only then, do we wipe out that ship."

Lara appeared to think about it, long enough for a surly-looking Tavin to reemerge from the house with chairs for them all. He plopped them down in a semicircle and went back in.

At Rossik's gesture of invitation, Lara sat. "I'm sorry, that won't work."

"Why?"

"Security is very high on *Mon Remonda*. When we return from any leave, anywhere, we get a thorough search of belongings. And they never let us know where we are. All mission briefings use code names. We are kept completely in the dark."

Rossik's eyebrows rose. "I wasn't aware that the Rebels

had adopted such sensible security precautions. All their talk of individual freedoms—"

Lara waved his words away. "A lie. I was never under such close scrutiny on *Implacable* as I have been on the Rebel ship."

"Well, is there any way to transmit using *Mon Remonda*'s communications systems?"

"Yes, that could be done." *I could lead you right to the assembled fleet and watch as* Iron Fist *is blown out of space.* "That's probably our best approach."

Rossik's pocket beeped at him. From it he drew out a datapad. He glanced at its display and his shoulders tightened up. "Nobody react. I'm getting a signal from the life scanner inside the house. There is someone a little less than a kilometer to our east. That would put him on the first hill that way."

Lara tried to remain nonchalant. "That's my wingman. He accompanied me here for security's sake."

Rossik gave her a cool look. "Funny you didn't mention it before now."

"It wasn't relevant, was it? He stayed behind to service the X-wings while I came to visit my dear brother."

"Well, the problem is, he's now close enough that he might have seen me. We can't have that. The Rebels have holos of me in their records. You two keep talking. I'll go back into the house, exit the rear way, and circle around to get behind him. I'll need ten or fifteen minutes if I'm to do it quietly."

"No," Lara said.

"What did you say?"

"I said, no. I can't show up on Aldivy with my wingman and then go back to the Wraiths without him. They'd be curious." She did little to sacrifice the sarcasm in her voice.

Rossik considered. "Very well. New plan. I go and kill your wingman, and then we take you and your two X-wings back to *Iron Fist*. Right now."

15

Face was actually enjoying his main course, some sort of fowl in a sunfruit marinade, and idly hoping it wasn't poisoned, when Zsinj asked a question he wasn't prepared for. "Am I mad, General Kargin, or do you have an Ewok pilot in your unit?"

Face froze. He swallowed and hastily cleared his throat. "What leads you to that conclusion, sir?"

"Intercepted transmissions. Analysis of the vocal characteristics of your pilot, Hawk-bat One, suggests that he was probably, though not definitely, an Ewok. But I don't understand how that could be possible."

Face shrugged and ran through a mental list of a dozen different possible responses. "Well, he *is* an Ewok. *Mostly* an Ewok. Lieutenant Kettch. My most ferocious pilot, actually. He can't really reach the controls, but a somewhat crooked prosthetics expert on Tatooine built him a set of hand-and-leg extensions he can wear, so his height has not limited him in the least."

"Obviously. But I thought Ewoks were far too primitive to handle complex machinery or astronautics theory and practice. Too primitive even to learn an adequate vocabulary in Basic."

"They are. But Kettch was . . . modified. We don't know where or why it happened. He was taken from the sanctuary moon of Endor as a cub, reared in a laboratory somewhere, and fed chemicals that apparently increased his ability to learn. He's a genius, especially with mathematics." That was, in fact, the true background of Piggy, and Face was suddenly very glad to have it on hand as a resource.

Zsinj and Melvar exchanged a glance and Face suddenly felt his heart race. There was something in their expressions, as brief as that glance was, that told Face this subject was of vital interest to them. What did it mean?

"Anyway," Face continued, "he has a very nasty disposition. I wouldn't care to bring him to you even if you'd asked about him in your earlier communication. He bites strangers. I'd hate to have him tear away a mouthful of Zsinj and for the rest of us to be spaced for his bad manners."

Once again jovial, Zsinj turned his smile on Face. "Very amusing. Still, I hope to see him fly sometime. Perhaps even a practice run against our best pilot."

Face looked around. "Is he here?"

"Baron Fel? No, he's on duty." The warlord shrugged. "Not the most congenial of dinner guests in any case."

"So he bites, too?"

Zsinj laughed.

Castin waited until the hallway was momentarily clear. He moved up to the closed turbolift and quickly popped open its control panel. Beneath was the usual collection of wiring and computer boards. Deftly, he stripped the insulation from two wires and twisted them together.

The turbolift doors slid open, revealing an echoing shaft beyond. Castin untwisted the wires, slapped the control panel shut, and stepped out to grab the maintenance access rungs inside. He swung his feet clear of the opening just in time; the doors slid shut again just as rapidly.

Now he had to find a level where he could have some privacy—and access to a computer interlock.

Down or up? He could see the terminus of the shaft above him, some considerable distance, but not below him. That meant there was more to explore below. He climbed down.

Moments later, he gripped the rungs as though his life depended on it while a fast-moving turbolift sailed past. The wind of its passage shook him and knocked his feet from the rail they rested on. Swearing to himself, he pulled himself back up and continued downward.

If only these Imperial twits had seen fit to label the interiors of the turbolift doors. Level 15: HANGARS, ARMORY, CAFETERIA— that would have been nice.

Still, there were clues he could interpret. The pattern of wear on the turbolift's machinery against the walls of the lift shaft, for example. There were telltale marks where the lifts came to rest, marks where the metal of the shaft had been worn away, showing which levels were the most heavily accessed. He'd have to avoid them.

Six levels down, he found a turbolift door where the shaft showed almost no wear. A good sign. He opened the maintenance panel leading to the control box . . . and nearly dropped off his rung in surprise.

This control box was not standard. In it was a sealed security module, an indication that whatever was beyond the door was very important to somebody.

He leaned away and held tight as another turbolift shot past, this time rising from below, then returned to the problem at hand. This was probably too dangerous a level to enter for his task. On the other hand, he was curious. He broke out his pouchful of tools.

The sealed security module was sophisticated, but he'd grown up slicing Imperial hardware and software, so after a few minutes it yielded to his experience and opened. Within were the standard turbolift door controls, plus a variety of security measures—sensors to register whenever the doors were opened or closed, to note whenever a turbolift was called from this level or directed here, and to send all that data to the ship's main computer. He disconnected the sensors. He couldn't disconnect the computer relay; it also handled the permissions for people to enter and leave the level, and if he disconnected it and someone with proper authorization tried to enter or leave, his modifications would be detected immediately.

He could open the door from here without effort, but once the door was closed, he wouldn't be able to leave again without that authorization. It was time for some improvisation. He patched a small comm-enabled datapad into the circuit, programming it to do two things: monitor his comlink frequency and issue the command to open this door when he broadcast a specific signal. That should do the trick.

He put away his tools and brought out his blaster rifle. Then he tripped the switch to open the door.

It slid open silently, unlike most turbolift doors, revealing a darkened passageway beyond. There was no one in sight. He hopped from his rung perch to the passageway floor and swept it around in a covering arc, but there was still no one to see.

It wasn't a passageway, precisely. It was a gallery, a long hall in which one wall was made up of large viewports. The chambers beyond the viewports were well lit. He liked that; it would be next to impossible for people within them to see him. He reached back, tripped the switch again, and then yanked his arm out of the way so the door wouldn't close on it.

There was a computer interlock here, just beside the turbolift door, but that would not be safe. He advanced along the gallery with the precise pace of an Imperial stormtrooper, looking for another.

The chambers beyond the large viewports came into view as he passed them. The first was large. Against the far wall were large cages or small cells, stacked three high, made of glass or transparisteel, each occupied by a single creature. Castin saw a number of Gamorreans, a large dark arthropod whose cell was festooned with some sort of organic webbing, and an Ewok. In one oversized cell mostly filled with water was a dianoga, a tentacular scavenger with a single eye-stalk; it watched him as he passed. There was one human male outside the cages, seated at a desk with a large, elaborate computer terminal on it, his feet up on the desk as he idly tapped away at a personal datapad; he looked as though he were playing a game. He took no note of Castin.

Up ahead, despite the dimness of the passageway, Castin could make out a darkened desk and computer terminal in the left corner. He couldn't tell whether this passageway ended there or turned to the right. That terminal was what he needed, assuming he could power it up without alerting anyone.

He passed by the next section of viewports. These displayed a smaller chamber, an operating theater. There was an operation in progress, a team of four human males, gloved and masked, working on a large, white-furred creature with two large eyes and two small. Castin recognized it as a Talz, then took a closer look.

The Talz had some sort of drip tubes implanted in its head; fluids moved slowly from the bottles set up beside the operating table. The creature was strapped in place . . . and it was awake. As Castin watched, it opened its mouth and roared, the noise not penetrating the viewports. Its clawed hands opened and closed as it strained against its bonds and its four eyes glared redly at the doctors.

These were not roars of pain, Castin decided, but of rage. An unsettling image. The Talz were supposed to be peaceful creatures.

A few steps more, and the operating theater was behind him. He seated himself at the darkened terminal and brought out his tool kit again.

"Return to *Iron Fist*? I don't think so." Lara shook her head. "I'll be far more valuable to Zsinj on *Mon Remonda*."

"Not necessarily," Rossik said. "We'd be getting a couple of X-wings—which you'd be able to fly for us in covert missions—and your analyses of the missions you've flown so far and of the thought processes of the Wraiths and Rogues. These could be as valuable as getting an accurate fix on *Mon Remonda*'s position."

"I'd still prefer to return to the Wraiths."

"Well, it's not going to happen that way. Now, assuming that he's looking at us, keep your wingman distracted with some animated conversation with the most unanimated Tavin while I get into position."

Gloom settled over Lara as she realized what she had to do . . . as she realized that she was about to take prisoners who knew her secret, that she had to reveal that secret to Wedge Antilles. "I don't think so. Put your hands in the air. You're now in the custody of the New Republic."

From underneath his tunic, Tavin brought out a small blaster and aimed it at her. Rossik glanced at Tavin, his expression openly derisive, and merely placed his own hand on the butt of his own blaster. "You don't appear to be in a position to make such demands, Petothel. Your partner is a kilometer away and may not even be watching. I know you haven't been broadcasting; my scanner would have told me."

Lara looked at the blaster in Tavin's hand and raised her arms, a gesture that was half surrender, half insolent stretch. "I'll give you two just one chance. Throw down your weapons now."

Rossik said, "Keep her covered and take her blaster. I'm doing what I told you—leaving through the rear of the house and circling around behind her partner. Just keep her here and quiet until then."

"Easily done," Tavin said.

"You should have surrendered," Lara said. She closed her hands into fists.

A brilliant lance of light from the hill took Tavin right in the stomach. The sudden explosion of superheated tissues threw the man down and back; his blaster dropped to the charred ground.

Rossik turned toward the source of the laser fire and took a step forward. Lara drew her blaster. Rossik was in the air, throwing himself to the ground, when Lara's blast took him in the side. He hit the ground and lay there unmoving.

Lara rose and kept the two men covered as Donos ran down from his sniper position. She didn't need to; it was clear to her that both men were dead. She tried to simulate rattled nerves and was surprised to discover that she had them for real. Part of her reaction, she knew, was the sudden relief that her secret was once again safe for the time being.

"Are you all right?" Donos asked.

Lara nodded. "They wanted—" Her voice broke and once again it was a genuine reaction. "They wanted me to go back to *Iron Fist* with them. They weren't going to leave me an option where I could feed them false information. I was just going to disappear." She shuddered. "I couldn't do that."

Donos prodded Rossik with a foot. The body rolled halfway over, displaying staring, vacant eyes. He reached down to take the man's blaster away. "Why did your brother draw on you?"

"I said no. I said I wouldn't go back with this man, Rossik. Apparently my brother wasn't going to get paid unless I went back with Rossik. If he wasn't going to be paid, he was going to kill me."

"Not exactly a loving brother." Donos looked over Tavin's body and took his weapon, too. Then he looked back over his shoulder at Lara. "I'm sorry. That was a callous thing to say."

"That's all right. The Tavin I loved just stopped existing when I was a little girl; he turned into this. I miss him . . . but you didn't kill him."

"We can't be sure there's not more to Rossik's team. Let's grab their papers, give the house a quick look, and then head back for the X-wings. I want to get off this world as soon as possible."

Castin had to keep a certain amount of attention on the hallway behind him as he continued to hammer away at *Iron Fist*'s computer security from the terminal. So far, none of the scientists or technicians from the rooms beyond the viewports had stepped out into the hall, but he couldn't count on his luck lasting forever.

And the computer security here was *good*. Someone nearly as skilled as he had set up the multilayered defense that so far kept him from sliding his program into place in the communications system. And while Castin was certain that he was superior to this unknown code-slicer, that individual had had weeks, months, or years to perfect his code; Castin was trying to bypass it in a matter of minutes. Even with his superior skills and the tools he'd brought, it wasn't going well.

So he was upset. Barely able to concentrate on what he was doing.

No, that didn't make sense. Tough systems were a challenge

to him, not an aggravation, and sharpened his concentration rather than diminishing it. So why *was* he upset? He leaned back, away from the screen with its unhelpful rejections of all his most reasonable requests, to think about it.

Even his stomach was upset, and that, finally, pointed him to the source of his emotion. It was what he'd seen moments ago. The creatures in the cages. The Talz on the operating table, a peaceful being maddened by chemicals until it was full of rage.

It was ridiculous. He didn't care about such things. They weren't human, they weren't particularly important, and if the scientists decided to work on them, that was fine.

But the sick feeling persisted.

That Talz's life was over. Even if it miraculously escaped its captivity, it would be forever changed by what had happened to it. Could it return home to its world, its family, knowing how it had been violated, knowing what it had been made to feel and do, and still go back to the way of life it had known before? Castin didn't think so.

He swore to himself. He didn't have time for this. And he didn't need to concern himself with the fate of a grab bag of nonhumans Zsinj decided to perform tests on.

But the images persisted, crowding out the techniques and procedures he needed to use for his current mission, filling him with an unwanted emotion.

Sympathy.

Sympathy for those hairy, smelly, and most unhuman beings crowding those cells he'd seen. They were a concentration of tragedy.

Caught up as he was in these thoughts, Castin still heard the hiss of the turbolift door far behind him. He powered down the terminal, grabbed up his datapad and helmet, and scuttled around the corner to the right before peering back the way he'd come.

A half squadron of stormtroopers, dimly visible in the passageway's gloom, advanced toward him. Their steps were unhurried. Halfway toward him along the passageway, the leader rapped smartly against the nearest transparisteel. Having apparently gained the attention of someone beyond it, he tapped the side of his head, an obvious signal for someone inside to get to a comlink to receive his transmission.

Damn it. They had to be looking for him. What had he done wrong? He was certain he'd covered his tracks when powering up the corner terminal.

No, wait. When he'd first popped the cover on the control box inside the turbolift shaft and discovered the heavy-duty security there—he hadn't known about that level of security until he'd opened the box in the first place. If there was a sensor on the box itself, a sensible precaution for a set of controls leading into a very secure area, he would have set it off without ever realizing it.

He drew away from the corner. Behind him was another viewport, this one into an office area, currently unoccupied. Beside it was an armored door with a standard set of controls beside it. He tapped the "open" button and the little screen on the control pad read ENTER AUTHORIZATION CODE.

At the stormtroopers' rate of approach, they'd be on him before he could break through that security and get into the office.

What was it to be—bluff or fight? There was no way a bluff would work; it would only serve to keep him in one place while the rest of the stormtroopers approached. He readied his blaster rifle.

The lead stormtrooper came around the corner and froze momentarily. "What's your—"

Castin fired. His shot took the stormtrooper in the gut and threw him back against the far wall.

Castin didn't wait for the next trooper to appear. He fired again, this time into the viewport, shattering it inward, and leaped, following the broken transparisteel into the office beyond.

He landed and spun, aiming back through the broken viewport. Two more stormtroopers rounded the corner, bringing their long arms to bear on the spot where he'd stood a moment before. He fired again twice, his first shot taking the nearer stormtrooper in the chest. The other trooper dove for the deck, out of sight below the rim of the viewport, and Castin's second shot missed him.

A shrill Klaxon alarm sounded and the lights in the office began flickering in time to it.

There was another door out of the office, leading in the general direction of the turbolift, and its control panel was responsive. It opened into what appeared to be a scrub room, all sinks and lockers and decontam chambers, with no viewport out into the passageway.

The next door opened just as readily—into the operating theater. The medical technicians there had ceased their ministrations to the Talz and were watching the activity on the other side of the picture viewport—the last of the stormtroopers passed by, heading toward the scene of the action Castin had just left.

A blaster bolt went over Castin's shoulder and hit one of the technicians in the back of the head. Castin saw the man, his head now a black mass of char, topple forward as slowly as if sinking into heavy oil, saw the other technicians as they turned toward him in similar slow motion.

He spun, firing before he could even see his target. A stormtrooper stood in the open doorway between office and scrub room, a perfect target, and Castin's unaimed blast took him in the knee. The man toppled with a shriek.

Castin slapped the near control panel and the door slid shut. He turned back to the technicians; they already had their hands up. One couldn't take his eyes from the smoking mass that had once been the head of his colleague.

It would take just one blast to blow out the near viewport. He could leap through and get back to the turbolift before the three stormtroopers still mobile were likely to catch up to him. That was it, then. But as he traversed to aim at the viewport, he saw the Talz looking at him. Its four eyes seemed to be holes leading to a world of pure pain.

He hesitated, then pulled his vibroblade from a belt pouch. He cut through the Talz's ankle restraints, then went to work on its wrist straps.

"Don't!" That was one of the technicians, his eyes wide. "That's not a Talz anymore, it's a killer—"

"Right." Castin finished with the last strap, then backed away.

The technician who'd spoken bolted, got to the doorway, slapped the control. The door opened . . . and the technician caught a blaster bolt just beneath his gut. He folded over, still alive, and began screaming.

The Talz rolled up off the table, tubes still gruesomely inserted into its skull. It glared with malevolence at Castin, then turned toward the remaining technicians and advanced on them. The rolling carrier holding the bottle of drip chemicals tipped over and was dragged along. The Talz spotted something through the door, probably the stormtrooper who'd last fired, and paused, obviously trying to decide what foe to attack first.

Castin fired at the viewport, blowing it out, and leaped through the hole he'd made. There was nothing between him and the turbolift door. He dropped his vibroblade and dragged out his datapad as he ran.

Then there was pain, an agony so intense he couldn't even tell where it began, and he was falling, slamming down onto the passageway floor.

Pain bent him as though he were a puppet in the hands of a malevolent child. He could see, and even barely understand, the spot on the back of his left thigh where a blaster bolt had cut through the stormtrooper armor and the flesh beneath. He could see the stormtrooper who'd shot him; the man was advancing at a walk, his rifle ready for another shot.

And then there was the turbolift door, too far away for a man reduced to crawling.

They had him. They had him, and they had his datapad, which contained everything Zsinj would need to know about him and his mission here.

Hands twitching from the pain, he held his datapad out before the barrel of his blaster rifle and squeezed the trigger.

"Now," Zsinj said over the iced pastry that was their dessert course, "to the matter which has led to our meeting."

Face sat back, assuming a false expression of contentment. "Please."

"I am about to embark on a mission. It will be a large-scale military engagement."

"You're going to attack your Rebel enemies?"

"That's correct. I anticipate starfighter and capital ship response and need all the starfighter support I can get—especially considering my recent squadron losses." He made a growl of that last statement. "But if you're as effective against my enemies as you have been against me, I will have lost effectively no strength." An aide appeared over his shoulder and whispered to him. His expression did not change, but he rose. "I must attend to business for a few moments. Melvar, please continue this briefing." He took a few steps away with the aide.

Melvar smiled, an expression that suggested he'd be happiest if pulling the wings off insects. "It's an orbital refueling and trade station. In its warehouses is a considerable quantity of material we need—critical supplies. We also need some time to load that material into our cargo vessels—not a lot of time, but enough time for the planetary defenses below to begin sending up squads of starfighters from the surface . . . and to bring in more squadrons from capital ships arrayed around the planet."

Face whistled. "You're after valuable cargo. What is it?"

Melvar shook his head. "That's a secret . . . until you're at the mission site."

"What *we* need to know," Zsinj said, returning to his seat, "is how many starfighters you can bring to bear in support of this mission."

"Six," Face said. He noted that Zsinj's merry demeanor now seemed forced.

"Only six?"

"We fight like twenty."

"You fight like *thirty*. And we'll pay you like thirty."

"Meaning . . ."

"Your commission is four hundred thousand Imperial credits, deliverable immediately upon completion of the mission."

Face tried to keep from displaying the surprise he felt. That was a fortune, enough to purchase two X-wings plus replacement supplies. "And if your mission fails, no payment at all?"

"No, you get the entire amount regardless—assuming you don't let me die in the engagement."

"I'm still impressed. If I didn't know my unit's skills, I would suspect you were overpaying us."

Zsinj dropped his false smile. "I *am* overpaying. I predict that some of yours, and some of mine, will die in this engagement. I intend to pay enough that all our pilots go into battle eager to succeed, happy to risk their lives—and comforted that if they die, their widows and children will be amply compensated."

Face considered it. "I'd be happy to earn still more. I have more Hawk-bats than I do starfighters. Many with technical proficiency. Many with other skills."

"Intrusion skills?"

Face smiled. "I was right. You're going to position a team before your fleet arrives."

Zsinj shrugged. "We obviously think alike. Yes, of course."

"I have intrusion experts. Some with experience with both Imperial and New Republic systems."

"And also," Melvar interrupted, "you have him." He extended one silvery nail toward Kell.

"And his teacher," Face said.

Melvar looked surprised. "His . . . teacher?"

Kell brushed his hair back, his signature gesture, and looked miffed.

"His teacher. Deadliest unarmed combatant I ever met. A woman, deceptively sweet of appearance, which makes it easy to insert her in most environments. Not his equal as a pilot . . . but I once saw her kill a Wookiee. Unarmed."

Zsinj and Melvar exchanged glances. Zsinj said, "Surely you're exaggerating."

"He's not," Kell said, his first words since they sat. "A Wookiee's incredibly strong by human standards, but no faster . . . and has just as many vulnerabilities. Pressure points. Joints. You can't wrestle with one—that's automatic death. And its longer reach means you constantly have to drop in and out of its range. But it can be done.

"Qatya, that's my teacher, started with a shot to the spine that compressed its spinal cord and apparently damaged a couple of its vertebrae, all of which partially paralyzed it . . . especially its legs. The next time it swung at her, she trapped its hand at a position to give her advantageous leverage, then twisted it to break its wrist. She broke two of its fingers then, too, just for fun. You know how women are. Then—"

"Dissek, please." Face made his voice admonishing, but inwardly was pleased by Kell's improvisation—it was just the sort of gruesome detail he would not have felt knowledgeable enough to provide. "Do forgive him. Combat is his only love."

"Quite all right," Zsinj said. "You will provide me with dossiers on the Hawk-bats who have technical skills so I can evaluate possible roles for them?"

"I will. Just give me a way to send them to you."

"Melvar will give you a set of HoloNet times and frequencies before you leave."

"And as much data as you can give us on this mission so we can run our own simulations?"

Melvar produced a datapad from a pocket and slid it over to him.

"Would you be averse to a small commission now?" the warlord asked.

"Not at all."

Zsinj stared back toward the security foyer, the route by which the Hawk-bats had entered the command center. Two stormtroopers there were advancing, dragging a third stormtrooper backward between them. The third man was limp in their arms and had no helmet on; his hair was golden blond.

"I must be sure of your ruthlessness," Zsinj said. "I know you are capable of killing in fair combat, but I want men—oh, yes, and women—who can kill under less adverse circumstances. So, if you'd please shoot this man for me?"

The stormtroopers dumped their human cargo by the foot of the table.

The man they had carried was Castin Donn. His eyes were closed. There was a blaster burn mark on his right leg. His chest rose and fell in regular rhythm.

Face swallowed the bile that tried to crawl up his throat and hoped that he had not gone as pale as he felt. *Castin, you idiot. You've killed us all.*

Kell glanced down at Castin and then at Face, admirably

keeping his features emotionless. His look was a question—
Jump Zsinj now? Or wait? Dia kept her gaze on Castin's face,
her own expression oddly enrapt.

"Not much of a target," Face said, stalling. There had to
be something he could do without revealing their hand, some
way to preserve all their lives without managing to jettison
their entire mission.

Nothing came to mind.

"True," Zsinj said. "Would you shoot him, please?"

"Oh, I should imagine," Face said, but did not move. "It
seems rather a costly test for you, though—having us shoot
one of your own stormtroopers."

"Not one of mine," said Zsinj. "An intruder."

"You're not going to question him?"

Zsinj shook his head. "I'm not interested in what he has to
say. Would you shoot him, please?"

Face clamped down on the panic rising within him. The
ship's officers at the table were watching him with increasing
interest. And no plan was coming to mind. "Of course," Face
said. "How much?"

Zsinj looked surprised. "What?"

"How much to shoot him? How much are you paying?"

"General Kargin, you surprise me. You're already here,
and the cost of a single pistol blast is negligible—especially as
we are providing the blaster." He nodded toward one of the officers, who produced a blaster pistol. "You can't do this as a
demonstration of goodwill?"

"Intelligent life is the most precious commodity in the
galaxy," Face said, making his voice pompous. "Consequently,
I never take it without adequate financial reward."

Dia stood, her sudden motion startling everyone at the table. She smiled at the warlord, a heart-melting expression, and
said in her husky Seku voice, "The general is just looking out
for the well-being of his officers and troops, Warlord. He can't
abandon his policies; they're written up in the Articles of the
Hawk-bats. But I can do this for you as a private commission.
The blaster, please?" She held out her hand.

Face felt a sudden surge of elation. She had a plan. He saw

Kell bring his legs up under him. The big man would probably go after Zsinj. That left General Melvar for Face, with Dia to hold the others at bay with the blaster. Assuming they gave her a functional one.

Melvar nodded; his officer handed Dia the blaster pistol. She checked the charge, moved over beside Castin—

And shot him in the throat.

A chatty junior officer, apparently cheered by the murder of the intruder, led the Hawk-bats back to their shuttle.

Once the security foyer doors closed behind them, Zsinj rose. He clapped his hands, and all the talk in the room ceased. "You've done very well," the warlord said. "Thank you for a fine performance."

The men saluted and began filing out of the ersatz crew pit. Zsinj sat. "How is—what's his name? Yorlin?"

Melvar's features relaxed and became bland and nonthreatening once more. "That man Dissek hit him hard enough to give him a concussion and damage some teeth."

"Well, he's to be commended for following orders even at the cost of considerable pain. Give him a commendation, and when he gets out of the medical ward, give him a three-day leave." He nodded at the body of the intruder; smoke still rose from what was left of its neck. "Hand that over to our technicians. I want to know who he was, where he came from, where he's been living, and how he got aboard *Iron Fist*—since he appears not to have been one of the Hawk-bats after all."

"Done. What did the intruder cost us?"

"Initial reports indicate that he shot two stormtroopers and two technicians, then our best Talz specimen killed another two technicians and another stormtrooper, and finally the remaining troopers shot the Talz. Costly." Zsinj fixed Melvar with a serious stare. "Have we lost an Ewok test subject?"

"Not from *Iron Fist*. But it could be that one of the planetbound laboratories has lost one—and covered up the loss."

"I'm going to have to execute someone for that, Melvar. Find out who lost him, then kill that idiot."

"Yes, sir."

. . .

Face made it clear, by gesture and private code, that he wanted the others to remain silent even as they accelerated away from *Iron Fist*. Only when they had entered hyperspace on their first leg out did he speak. "Report."

"He was already dead." The words burst from her like water finally breaching an old dam. "He was gone, Face." Pain tugged at her words, made them waver. There was bleakness in what he could see of her face.

"He was breathing."

"No, he wasn't. It was some sort of trick. Some sort of mechanical pump, I don't know." She took a deep, shuddering breath. "He was completely limp when they brought him in. Not unconscious limp. Dead limp. There was blaster charring on his armor's pelvic plate that should have continued up into his chestplate but didn't, so they had to have put a new chestplate on him—to replace the one that was burned through when he was killed. And the guards carrying him, their posture said they were hauling cargo, not a prisoner who might wake up someday." She closed her eyes and bowed her head. "Body language is something I know a lot about, Face. He was dead."

"Accepted." Face sighed and leaned back. "Dammit. If only he'd followed orders. Will you be all right?"

"I'll be—I'll be—" Her voice choked off. She gulped a couple of times and then just stared.

"Dia?"

She shrieked as if stabbed and was suddenly a whirlwind of motion, lashing out in all directions. Her random blows landed on Kell, on the command console, on the windscreen, on the shuttle wall beside her.

Kell leaned between her and the controls, fending off her blows. "Face, get her off me before she bumps the wrong things and sends us down a blind hyperspace path."

Face leaned forward, grabbing at Dia, received a blow to his chin from a brain tail for his trouble. "Dia! Power down!"

But her shrieks and blows redoubled, joined now by what looked like painful spasms. Face reached around the copilot's seat and got both hands on her, then bodily hauled her over the chair and into his lap. He took another pair of random blows before getting his arms around her waist, pinning her to him.

She let out one last, keening moan and collapsed. Tears ran unchecked down her cheeks and Face found himself frozen, staring at them, evidence of emotions he had never believed she possessed. "Dia?"

Her voice was a moan. "She's dead."

"She? She who?"

"Dia. Diap'assik. She is dead."

He put heat and anger into his words. "No, you are not."

"Yes! She would not have done that. She would not have shot him. She would have died first. *She is dead,* Face."

He heard a snap, heard metal slide on leather, and was prepared when her hand came up with her blaster and its barrel came in line with her chin. He released Dia with his left hand and got his thumb under the trigger, preventing her from squeezing it.

She shrieked again, a haunted noise compounded of agony and bottomless guilt. "Face, let me!"

He wrenched the blaster from her hand, held it over Kell's shoulder until he took it, and pinned her again. "No."

"Then kill me."

"No."

"Yes. I will not live this way."

"You have to. We need you."

She surrendered then to silent tears and racking sobs. He held her to him and finally had a moment to think.

Dia, who in simulator combats cut down the enemy with a cold-bloodedness that sometimes shook the other squadron members—where had she gone? Who was this doppelgänger, torn by grief, in his arms? She had to be a Dia who lived under her shield of ruthlessness, some remnant of the Dia who had been stolen as a child slave off Ryloth a dozen years before. A Dia who could know terrible guilt—self-destructive guilt.

As gently as he could, he said, "Dia, thank you."

She didn't respond.

He repeated his words, and finally she drew back and looked up at him, incomprehension and pain on her face. "What?"

"Thank you."

She shook her head. "For shooting—for shooting—"

"No. For *my life*. If you hadn't done what you did, I would be dead. I would have failed to convince Zsinj, and he would have killed us. I prefer to be alive, Dia. Thank you."

He finally could see comprehension flickering around in her eyes.

Kell turned and caught her attention. "Dia. Me, too. Thank you. Without you, I'd be dead. Or in Zsinj's tender care, worse than dead. Face and I owe our lives to you."

She stared at him in confusion for a long moment, then collapsed again into Face's arms. "No," she said, and repeated it again and again as her tears flowed unchecked.

Finally she slept.

Face let Kell handle the routine tasks of getting them back to the Halmad system. They'd have to rendezvous with Cubber and—and whoever was assigned in Castin's place—in the asteroid belt, in order to do a complete sweep of the shuttle for tracking equipment, then head on in to Hawk-bat Base.

He had just that much time to compose his report, a report in which he had to explain just why it was that two subordinates had died in his immediate vicinity in just a few days.

16

Wedge listened to Face's report, asking for clarifications here and there, letting the man—who, despite his skill as an actor, could not quite conceal the fact that he was stricken with guilt over Castin's death—pour out the entire story of the meeting with Zsinj. It was a report Face had practiced; he'd given it to Janson on the day he'd returned to Hawk-bat Base, and had to repeat it to Wedge now that the rest-and-recreation unit had returned from Coruscant. Yet in spite of the extra practice, Face's emotions were still raw and on the surface, concealed not at all by his proficiency with acting.

When it was done, Face said, "I take full responsibility for Castin's death, sir."

Wedge gave him a look of surprise. "*You* take full responsibility."

"Yes, sir."

"So Castin Donn played no part in his own death. None of the blame falls on him."

"Well—"

"I knew even better than you of his history of insubordination, of rebellion. And I'm the commanding officer of this unit. Yet I bear no responsibility? It somehow is all yours?"

"Well—"

"Face, what do you think you could have done to prevent his death?"

"I could have ordered the smuggling compartment searched, rather than just looked into."

"Why would you have, when looking into it showed that he wasn't there?"

"I could have accounted for his whereabouts before we took off."

"But you did. You accounted for his whereabouts as they pertained to your mission. He wasn't with you, so far as you could tell, so the rest of the information about his whereabouts was irrelevant. He was just one step ahead of you, ahead of all of us. Did you know he'd rigged the duty roster so he wouldn't be on duty until after your return, that he'd set up a dummy and mechanism on his bunk to make it look and sound as though he were there sleeping?"

"Not at the time, sir. Lieutenant Janson told me about that."

"Castin Donn wasn't your responsibility. And though his death was very unfortunate, and took place in association with your mission, it's not your fault. Now, you tell me who *is* your responsibility."

"Well, me, sir. And Kell and Dia."

"What have you done about them?"

"I've asked the other Wraiths and support crews, and especially her roommate, Shalla, to keep an eye on Dia. She doesn't seem suicidal anymore, but she seems . . . different. Like a shelled animal that's suddenly had the shell ripped away. Injured and frightened and a lot more vulnerable."

Wedge nodded. "Your measures seem appropriate. And Kell?"

"I don't understand. What do I need to watch out for with Kell?"

"He was the one who searched the smuggling compartment. He didn't detect Castin. How do you suppose he feels?"

Face winced. "About like I do, I suppose."

"And what are you going to do about it?"

"Talk to him, I suppose. Make him understand that it's not his fault."

Wedge waited, not speaking, just watching the young lieutenant, until Face finally looked startled. "Yes, sir," Face said. "The same way it's not my fault."

"Correct. Anything else?"

"Yes, sir. I can't stress enough that I felt there was something very significant about the look Zsinj and Melvar exchanged when I was discussing Piggy's background. In the guise of Lieutenant Kettch's background, I mean. That really spooked them. Either they're involved with a project like that, or they know of one and are very interested in it."

"I'll assume that this is very significant, then, and see what I can make of it."

"Thank you, sir."

"That'll be all for now." As Face was leaving, Wedge added, "Oh, by the way . . ."

"Sir?"

"You're a good officer, Face, but you have to know that means you'll be doing this again. This was a successful mission. It may be the key to Zsinj's undoing. If I'd known, if I'd been absolutely sure, that to accomplish it would mean the life of one of my pilots, I'd have to have set it in motion anyway. You would, too."

Face looked as though he was considering that possibility, then gave Wedge a brief nod. "Yes, sir. I suppose I would." He closed the door behind him.

Wedge sat, motionless, long enough for Face to get thirty or forty paces away from the cargo module that served as the command office. Then he slammed both hands on his desktop and swept every pointless datapad, document, and knickknack from the desk surface.

Another pilot dead, this one for no good reason. Another letter to write. Another report in which he had to explain just why it was that two subordinates had died under his command in just a few days.

He came out of his office at a fast walk and headed for the hangar area. On the other side of the Trench, Janson, sitting alone on the mess patio, rose and trotted to catch up. "How did it go?"

"As well as it could."

"So, what's with this sudden brisk exercise?"

"I'm not ready yet to begin analyzing the data Zsinj gave us."

"Ah."

"I don't want to write Castin's folks."

"Ah."

Both men returned a salute from Runt, who was headed the other way. "Unit morale is bound to take a serious hit from this."

"Ah."

"I'm leading children, and I'm getting them killed."

"That's true."

Almost at the door into the hangar, Wedge skidded to a stop. "What did you say?"

"It's true." Janson shrugged. "Wedge, you asked for misfits. You had to have known that even with the ones who made the grade, they were going to take losses that were heavier than in a normal unit. So many of them are dragging around these weights of emotional problems. It makes it tougher for them to hop in the right direction at the right time."

"Well . . . maybe."

"Even with that, as a group they're doing better than they ever had a right to. Some of them are fit to eat with real people. Even to fly with other units. That wasn't the case when you founded the Wraiths."

"I suppose you're right." Wedge suddenly felt weary, all the manic energy of a minute ago having left him. He turned back toward his office. "What's the situation with Lara?"

"She's doing pretty well for someone whose brother just tried to kill her. Donos is keeping an eye on her."

"Those of us who still have family . . ." Wedge waited as memories of his surviving relative, his sister Syal, missing for so long—as her husband, Soontir Fel, had also been missing— rose and abated. "We need to notify them. Just in case Zsinj tries to get at another of us through family connections. That would be just like him."

"It would. I'll inform the Wraiths, let them know what they need to tell their people."

"Yes, but not yet. I want you to work with me on the Zsinj data."

"Ah, thank you. The adventures of Wes Janson, Ace Statistician . . ."

Wedge and Janson spent most of the rest of the day working on the data Zsinj had provided to Face.

The planet that was their target was of average size and mass, according to the planetary radius and gravity information provided. And it was heavily guarded. Ten Imperial Star Destroyers and seven Mon Calamari cruisers were shown on-station, supported by impressive numbers of planet-based starfighter squadrons—including an unusually high number of A-wing fighters.

Janson gave him a bleak look. "This is Coruscant. He's going to hit Coruscant."

Wedge shook his head. "That's what the data tells us if you dig down from the top layer. But I don't understand some things. Zsinj's mission will take place soon—otherwise he wouldn't give us this much information about it. Yet this complement of ships isn't an exact representation of Coruscant's defenses—I was just there, and he's got the strengths wrong. So is he wrong because his intelligence is incomplete, inadequate?"

"That doesn't sound like him, does it?"

Wedge sighed. "Then there's the question of what sort of cargo Zsinj is going after. Our task is to protect Zsinj's forces while they load a cargo ship—why not wait until the goods are already loaded? What does the government of the New Republic store on Coruscant's space stations that can't be acquired on the surface, or in transit?"

Janson thought about it. "The Inner Council?"

"What? No. It would be a real coup to capture or kill them, of course. But they hold all their meetings on-planet."

"Do you know that for sure?"

"No, but I have no reason to suspect otherwise. And holding meetings on a space station would be more problematic, less secret, and less secure than doing so on the surface. I think you're speculating wildly."

"All right, then, your turn. What's on space stations that isn't better found on-planet or between worlds?"

"Well, the stations themselves. Maybe they plan to tow one out to space."

Janson snorted.

"Big cargo carriers." Wedge frowned. "You know, scuttlebutt has it that Princess Leia's big, secret mission involves bringing back additional resources for the fight against Zsinj. If he's aware of that, if he knows what those resources are, if he knows when they're coming back to Coruscant—"

"Now *you're* speculating wildly."

"True. Then there are cargo ships." Wedge frowned as a shadow of a new idea crossed his mind. He stared down at the statistics on the datapad before him. "Wait a second. I have an idea of what he's after." He found a scrap of flimsi and a writing instrument and scribbled a very brief note, then folded it several times and handed it to Janson. "Tuck that away. Take it out when we have our answer and it will make my reputation as a military wizard."

Janson pocketed the note. "You already have that reputation."

"Well, then, I'll have two. Now tell Castin to come in here."

"Uhh, Castin's, uhh . . ."

Wedge put his face in his hand. "Right. I'm tired, too. With Castin gone, who's our best code-slicer and computer handler?"

"Probably Lara Notsil."

"Get her."

She was slightly out of breath when she arrived, probably having run the distance from her quarters to Wedge's office. "Flight Officer Lara Notsil reporting, sir."

Wedge waved her a casual salute. "No need for all the formality now, Notsil. Tell me something. With what you know of our computers on hand, how good is our ability to translate statistical data of large military forces—their strengths, capabilities, that sort of thing—into the equivalent forces of other cultures? Say I had the statistics for a New Republic strike force and wanted to come up with a Corellian force with exactly the same characteristics?"

Janson looked at him, confused.

Lara considered. "I don't think our translation efforts would be very good, sir. That calls for specialized programs, and we don't—" Then she looked startled. "Depending on the forces involved, sir, I think we can do a pretty good job."

"That's quite a switch of opinion."

She smiled. "I forgot. We have X-wing and TIE simulators on base, sir, and they're already linked. And already set up to analyze ship statistical data and translate into precise strength values of enemies. I can adapt that programming to do what you want. It wouldn't be too hard."

Wedge copied the Zsinj information to a fresh datapad and handed it over. "I want all this information translated into the nearest equivalent force of vessels and vehicles that are purely Imperial in origin. Then come back here and we'll compare that with some planetary defense data. How long will that take you?"

"I'm not sure. Half an hour, twelve hours—I'll know more when I've had time to look over the simulators and this data."

"Let me know as soon as you can."

Wedge stretched his legs again while waiting for her initial estimate.

Outside, something odd was going on at the mess and patio. The thermal blanket normally used as an awning over the mess picture viewport had been lowered, indicating that it was closed, and all the patio's chairs and tables had been drawn aside. A hand-painted sign decorated the main door into the module: MESS CLOSED BY ORDER OF THE PIRATE RUNT.

Runt now stood in the middle of the newly open space, goggles over his eyes as he used one of the maintenance crew's backpack paint sprayers to put a layer of matte-green paint down on the stone floor.

Wedge wandered over and watched for a while as Runt

finished transforming a large oval of gray stone into a green surface. Then Runt removed his goggles and switched off the sprayer.

Wedge asked, "Runt, what are you doing?"

Runt looked at him levelly. "Painting, sir."

"Ah. Why?"

"For the ritual, sir."

"You're going to have a ritual."

"Yes, sir."

"Something your people do?"

Runt had to consider that one, blinking a few times before he answered. "Something *some* of our people do, sir."

"And you thought you had to close the mess to conduct this ritual?"

"Yes, sir. The food is still being prepared. That is a necessary part of the ritual."

"And who is going to be part of this ritual?"

"Well, we wanted to talk to you about that, sir. It would be a help to us if you would issue an order for all pilots to be here at eight hundred hours in full dress uniform."

Wedge resisted the urge to laugh. Runt seemed so earnest, so sincere. "It would, would it?"

"Yes. Also, all civilian crewmen not on duty should be here in formal dress."

"Why should I do this?"

"Because I ask little and will deliver much."

"Ah. Can you tell me what this is about?"

"Well, no, sir."

"I see. Carry on."

It took Lara only two hours to translate the data, and took her and Wedge less than five minutes to get a close match in their comparison of the new data with sites in Imperial space.

"You're joking," Janson said. "Kuat?"

Wedge pointed to the other man's pocket. Janson retrieved the note and unfolded it. There was a single word scrawled on it: *Kuat*. He whistled.

"It's Kuat, all right," Wedge said. "Zsinj is making a raid on a space platform at Kuat."

"How did you know?"

"Zsinj is so devious it's sometimes predictable. He gave us information intended for very limited circulation, and yet he still concealed his real purpose a level or two down. I'm sure others he's working with are very pleased with themselves that they've identified the target as Coruscant. They're going to be very surprised when they come out of hyperspace in the Core Worlds."

"So his objective isn't cargo," said Lara. "He's after a Star Destroyer."

Wedge nodded. "A Super Star Destroyer. Just as Face predicted, weeks ago."

With deliberate slowness, Janson leaned back, put his hands behind his head, and put his feet up on Wedge's desk. He smiled. "Zsinj has delivered himself into our hands."

"Not yet, he hasn't," Wedge said. "In what sense do we have him? He shows up with his fleet at Kuat and—what? We drop in out of hyperspace and attack him? It would take a large portion of the fleet of the New Republic to menace him *and* defend itself against Kuat's defenses . . . and the defenses they could bring in on short notice. We'd lose far too much."

"Maybe we just alert the government of Kuat," Lara said.

"No . . . Zsinj has spies in place already. Our intelligence says that the shipyards, especially the orbital ones, are rigged to explode in case of invasion. Zsinj has to have provided for that, and his spies will notice any sudden preparations for invasion." Wedge sighed. "I think we have to let Zsinj get away with his new toy . . . and then jump them later."

"How can we be sure where they'll be?" said Janson.

"Lara, you know about Castin's plan. About the program he was going to slice into the communications system aboard *Iron Fist*."

She nodded.

"Can you adapt that for this new Super Star Destroyer?"

"Unless Castin's slicing style is so idiosyncratic that no one can make sense of it, yes, sir."

"See to it, then." Wedge turned his attention to Wes. "I'm going to draw up a preliminary plan of operation for this mission and see if I can get Admiral Ackbar to sign off on it."

"For my part," Janson said, "I'll get some sleep."

"You'll calculate which routes Zsinj is likely to take in his escape from Kuat and suggest some fleet deployments that give us the best likelihood of being able to encounter him."

"Which is something like sleep, but much less interesting."

Wedge smiled. "As for you, Lara, good work, and thanks."

Runt's preparations of the galley area became more and more elaborate.

He pressed several of the astromechs into service as painters. The little R2s and R5s, with paintbrushes held in their clamps, meticulously added black crisscrosses and hatchwork to the green floor paint, making it look like a child's impression of grass.

He rigged an overhead spotlight that would bathe his green oval in light but extend not much beyond that.

To the same pole he attached speakers whose cables snaked all the way to the base communications center, farther down the Trench.

He occasionally entered the closed galley, and Wraiths passing by could see him, through the partially opened door, exchanging words with Squeaky. The 3PO unit, who was a more than adequate chef when he could be persuaded to cook, looked more agitated than usual.

Wedge did remember to issue his command, and shortly before eight hundred hours the Wraiths did begin to assemble.

"I can't believe you got me out here in full dress," said Janson, his tone a deliberate whine. "Just because Runt asked you to. You've known me longer. You should like me better than him."

Wedge snorted. "Let's just say I was intrigued by the mystery."

"Mystery? I'll give you a mystery. I'll spend tomorrow

with my feet and forehead painted red and never tell anyone why. Is that mysterious enough?"

"Anything to stay out of dress uniform, is that it?"

"Anything."

By ones and twos the Wraiths assembled. Several obviously felt as Janson did about dressing up, or at least took the summons with less than total seriousness. Piggy scratched unhappily. Shalla asked each person present—separately—what it was all about, then stood off by herself and fidgeted. Face had added to his dress uniform a sand-colored Tatooine scarf, giving him the look of an officer who'd been stationed too long on the desert world and had partially "gone native." Some of the mechanics were still working on their hands with cleanser-cloths, trying to remove the last stubborn patches of oil stains.

By the time Donos arrived, a handful of seconds after the appointed hour, Runt was still not in evidence. The main lights of the Trench cut out, leaving only the new spotlight and the false stars overhead blazing, and Runt, quite dashing in his dress uniform, emerged from the galley. "My friends," he said, waving his hands with unusual theatricality, "how glad we are that you have chosen to accept our invitation."

That elicited some chuckles, and Runt plowed on. "We are obliged to admit that we may have accidentally misled Commander Antilles when describing this event. We think he believes this to be a Thakwaash ritual."

Wedge crossed his arms and gave Runt a stern look. " 'Accidentally misled'?"

"Well, you will have to ask the Runt you were talking to this afternoon. We are not he at this moment."

"We are now the Runt who ducks and retreats when confronted with the errors of his ways?"

Runt grinned, his huge teeth flashing white in the gloom in front of the galley. "Kell must have given you lessons in knowing who we are at any moment. So. This is a ritual we have seen among the military officers of the New Republic. It is called a formal dance. I have painted a lawn. Come forward and dance under the stars."

The Wraiths and maintenance personnel looked at one another as though to inquire silently as to which of them would summon the military police in charge of pilot sanity. Piggy huffed and asked, "And if we decline?"

Runt's expression became serious, even menacing. "We will have hurt feelings. And this is a compulsory dance, so we will shoot you."

Kell crossed to him, grabbed him by his fur-backed ears, and shook Runt's head. "Runt! That was a joke. A human-style joke. I'm so proud of you."

Runt smiled again. "We are pleased you are pleased."

Kell moved to the center of the absurd dance floor and extended a hand. Tyria came to him, smiling, and took it. Kell glanced significantly at Runt, who in turn nodded to Chunky, Tyria's R5 unit, who stood watch at the bottom of the pole on which the spotlight rested, and suddenly music blasted out at the squadron—a formal dance of Alderaan, Wedge noted. Runt gestured at Chunky, a lowering of his hand, and the volume decreased to appropriate levels.

And Kell and Tyria danced, smiling at one another, the rest of the universe suddenly lost to them.

Janson sighed. "I'm going to have Runt shot."

Wedge gave him a tolerant smile. "Wait for results before you assign punishment."

"Now you're talking like a general again."

"Oh, that stung."

Then Shalla was out on the dance floor, beckoning Donos to join her, and Wedge saw one of the female mechanics hauling Cubber out to dance, her fingers firmly clamped on his septum as the mechanic protested inarticulately.

Janson turned to Dia. "Shall we, wingmate?"

She looked startled. "I don't know how."

"I thought you were a dancer."

"Not that kind. I have never danced *with* anyone. Only *for* them."

"Time to learn." He led her out onto the floor.

Leaving Wedge alone.

He watched others drift onto the floor, some smiling, some tentative, some resigned. He watched Runt reenter the galley and emerge, carrying one end of a long table, Squeaky carrying the other, and then the two of them began bringing out trays and bowls and glasses and cutlery—the night's dinner, transformed by some extra work and attention into a wider variety of dishes, a buffet appropriate for a dance.

When they were done and Squeaky had returned to the galley, Wedge approached. Runt was now slicing a ripe ball cheese and setting slivers of the stuff on a plate. "Good job, Runt."

Runt straightened and almost saluted. "Sorry, sir. You surprised us." He returned to cutting.

"No need to apologize. Nor is there any need for formality. This is a social event. What gave you the idea?"

"For the dance? You did, sir—uh, Command—uh, W-Wedge." The name sounded as though it was almost too strange for Runt to utter. "You and the lieutenant walked by talking of the hurt that Wraith morale had suffered. When you have a hurt, you do not wait for it to heal. You set out to heal it."

"Why, precisely, a dance?"

Runt was slow to answer. "It has been our observation that dance among the people of the New Republic, when it means anything—and it does not always mean anything—is an activity of mates. Making mates. Tending to mates. Reacquainting with mates. The Wraiths have been doing little but staring at death. But mates are life, what one lives for. What better way to turn away from death than to think of mates, present and distant?"

Wedge thought that over. "Runt, I'm afraid you've just made yourself morale officer."

Runt made a noise somewhere between a snort and a deep chest cough. "We have been told that under your command one cannot do a good thing without it becoming a duty."

"Was that another joke?"

"We hope so."

Wedge smiled. "Keep it up, Runt. And good work." He turned away.

"Will you be dancing?"

Wedge paused. Over his shoulder, he said, "I'll put in one dance for courtesy's sake and then go. The Wraiths will probably loosen up more once I'm gone."

"What of *your* morale?"

"You've already lifted it, Runt."

Face watched the couples gather on the floor and join in the sweep of the Alderaanian waltz. Then he felt hands against his back and was propelled into their midst.

He turned to face his attacker. It was Lara, advancing purposefully. He put up his hands in mock fear; she seized them and pulled him into the pattern of the dance. "That's mutiny," he said.

"Put me up on charges. Then I won't have to be part of this mission against *Iron Fist*."

"Good point. Maybe I'll mutiny, too."

"Besides, I have a special right to push you around. It was you who brought me into this unit."

"True," he said. Then what little cheer he still enjoyed evaporated. "Well, it was me and Ton."

"I'm sorry. I didn't mean to make you sad. I know you were very close to him. You almost haven't smiled or made a joke since he died."

"I only met him a few weeks ago. But by the end of the second day, we were finishing one another's sentences and being obnoxious enough to drive everyone around us crazy."

"Well, you'll have to be obnoxious enough for both of you now. Phanan would want that."

"He would." Face smiled down at her. "You dance very well."

"So do you."

"Well, I was trained to. For the holos. Where did you learn?"

"A long time ago, on Coruscant."

"A long time ago?"

She tensed, then relaxed and smiled. "Well, it seems like such a long time ago. Pilot training seems to last for years."

"I know what you mean."

"*This* dance I learned on Coruscant. But on Aldivy we danced all the time. It was an important part of social life. Dances were where youngsters met and families dickered."

Oddly, in spite of these thoughts about the life she could never return to, she did not seem sad.

"So, why did you launch me out onto the floor? Just looking after your wingman?"

"Partly that. And, partly, I'm maneuvering you."

"I hate to disappoint you, but you're far from the first woman to do that to me."

Her smile broadened. "Ah, but how many women maneuver you to abandon you?"

It was the point in the dance where conservative couples would form a circle, where more proficient ones would raise their hands together and spin in relation to one another, males to their left, females to their right, coming around to face one another on the same beat of the music. Lara signaled the more elaborate move by raising her hands.

But while they were in midspin, he felt too many fingers on his for just one moment, and when he finished the maneuver he came face-to-face with a startled-looking Dia Passik. Lara and Janson, now partners, looking very pleased with themselves, pulled away and waved.

Dia's posture and the tension in her arms suggested that she was not too comfortable with the dance, but she gave him a game smile. "I think we have been fooled."

Face adjusted his pace and the flamboyance of his maneuvers to her more tentative motions. "When did they arrange that?"

"Lara was signaling something to Lieutenant Janson before she started dancing with you. I thought she was flirting."

"Well, we both appear to have been enticed and abandoned."

"I don't think so. I think it was because of something I said."

"Which was what?"

"That I—" She paused, apparently to consider her words. "That I wanted to talk to you, but that I was afraid to."

"I didn't think I was that fearsome. Especially to someone who's never seen my holodramas."

That elicited a smile, a little one. "No. I mean I didn't

know how to phrase the words. When to speak to you. I didn't know who to be when I spoke to you."

"Who to be? Who were your choices?"

"Dia Passik and Diap'assik."

"The pilot you've become and the little Twi'lek girl kidnapped off Ryloth."

She nodded, her expression somber. "The day after we returned from *Iron Fist* I woke up and I wasn't either one of them anymore. Somewhere in between a girl I thought was long dead and a woman who was too bloodthirsty for me to particularly like. But I thought about all that had happened the day before and decided that I liked being alive. So I wanted to thank you for not letting me die." The words came out all in a rush. She tensed, staring at Face, poised as if she were waiting for him to strike her.

"You're very welcome." Why had that been so hard for her? Face tried to put himself in her place—stolen child, then slave of an Imperial master, then pilot fighting for a place for herself among people she did not know, few of whom even belonged to her species. Nor had she ever spoken a favorable word about the Twi'leks; perhaps she blamed her own kind for the way she had been stolen from their midst.

Understanding where she had come from, with his limited knowledge, was too great a task for Face, but an idea emerged from his effort. "Dia, when was the last time you relaxed?"

"I relax many days."

"When you're alone."

"Yes."

"I meant, when was the last time you were really at ease among others? The last time you felt safe in someone else's company?"

Her gaze drifted off into the distance of time. "At ease? I don't know. When I was a child, I suppose. And safe?" She looked startled and came back to herself, to the present time. She tried to remove her hands from his. "Thank you for the dance. It's time for me to go."

He did not release her. "I know I'm prying, Dia. But if you won't open up to me, will you open up to someone?"

"I don't think I can."

"You could talk to Squeaky. He could use a friend."

She looked up at him, unbelieving, then smiled and stopped trying to break away. "You're joking again. It is sometimes so hard to tell when you are serious."

"For me, too."

They danced in silence for a few moments, long enough for the music to give way to a slower, more intimate dance from Chandrila. Then she said, her voice so low that he had to strain to hear her, "The last time I felt safe was not so long ago."

"When was that?"

"It was when I was at my worst. When I had shot Castin, when I'd desecrated the corpse of a brave man and pretended to do it with glee. When I tried to kill myself and you would not let me. Just before I fell asleep, I knew that you would not let anyone hurt me. You would not even let me hurt myself. And in that moment I knew myself safe, for the first time since I was a child."

He looked down into her eyes—eyes that were too large and luminous to be Dia's, eyes that were familiar to him yet opened up into a woman he didn't know. A woman who had come into being only since the mission to *Iron Fist*.

"That's what I wanted to say to you, what I didn't know how to say before," she said. "That I know that you feel you failed Ton Phanan. But you did not fail me."

He took her head in his hands and kissed her, and was swept away by the sweetness of her kiss, by the spicy taste of her, so different from human women. He felt her arms encircle his neck. And they stood motionless beneath the twinkling stars as the dancers swirled around them.

17

"Our target," Wedge said, "is almost certainly a Kuat Drive Yards facility in the Kuat system." He nodded at the holographic display, showing a central sun orbited by numerous planets and space stations, which floated above the table in the crowded conference module. Again he wished for a full-sized briefing room.

He took a pointing stick and drew a circle through a ring of space stations, an astonishing number of them, surrounding the system outside the orbit of its most distant planet. "This, collectively, is Kuat's main shipyard facility, the famous Kuat Drive Yards. It is not, however, the only place the yards build their vessels."

He gestured at one of the planets. "This is Kuat itself. There are also secondary facilities in orbit above it. Now, the data Zsinj provided the Hawk-bats, including a gravity-well delay for hyperspace jumps more lengthy than we'd experience out in the chain of satellites, and showing speed of response of a fleet arriving at the site being attacked, makes planetary orbit the most likely prospect. However, since New Republic Intelligence hasn't been able to confirm that there even is a new Super Star Destroyer under construction there, we can't be sure of this. Another planet in the system, a station not orbiting a planet, any such thing could be our objective."

The Wraiths were following his presentation with rapt attention. They seemed different this morning—more possessed of themselves, more cocksure, some of them nearly smug. Alive and eager. Once again Wedge offered thanks to whatever turn of fortune had brought Runt Ekwesh into this unit.

"Piggy," Wedge continued, "has had some thoughts on this mission I thought he should share with you. Piggy?"

The Gamorrean pilot started to rise but thought better of it and stayed seated. The proper manner to make a presentation in a standard military briefing was on one's feet, but the crowded nature of this conference module didn't allow for it. "Once again I must turn to the subject of Zsinj and pirates," he said, his mechanical voice vibrating the tabletop and the caf cups resting on it. "This time I can do so with some evidence instead of relying merely on speculation.

"We assume Zsinj is going after a new Super Star Destroyer. We *know* that he has requested the Hawk-bats to be part of this mission. My belief is that the Hawk-bats will merely be part of a large unit of mercenaries and pirates that will act as part of the defensive screen around the new Super Star Destroyer once it begins moving."

Kell waved to get his attention. "You're getting ahead of me, here. Why part of a mercenary unit, and why once the vessel gets moving?"

"From Zsinj's perspective, optimum efficiency demands a certain set of steps," Piggy said. "He can't, for example, drop out of hyperspace in the midst of the Kuat system and do a boarding action against the new Destroyer. Every minute it takes to accomplish the takeover is a minute the forces of Kuat can be using to approach and attack. So—"

"So," Face said, interrupting, "the takeover of the new Destroyer has to be accomplished before *Iron Fist* drops into the Kuat system."

Piggy nodded. "Correct. And as soon as the new Destroyer begins moving, if not before, Kuat's forces will be alerted and will move against her, to retake her . . . or destroy her."

"So that," Wedge said, "is when we predict Zsinj will

drop in with *Iron Fist* and as large a fleet as he can manage . . . and it's that fleet that will serve as a screen for the new Destroyer. It has to be escorted until it can get far enough from the nearest gravity well to launch into hyperspace."

"If the pirates," Piggy said, "including us Hawk-bats, are the first line of engagement the Kuat defenders encounter, Zsinj profits. Fewer of his TIE forces will be destroyed. Of the pirates who survive, some will belong to destroyed bands and will want employment . . . and they're most likely to be the best pilots of the bunch."

Dia frowned. "Your pardon, Piggy . . . but isn't this all just guesswork?"

The Gamorrean nodded. "Educated guesswork."

"What if you're all wrong?"

Piggy looked between Wedge and Janson. "Between the three of us, we'd have a hard time being *that* wrong."

Dia managed a smile. "Piggy, what if you're wrong?"

"We improvise," Wedge said. "We've come up with this model for Zsinj's plan because we think it's most likely. But regardless of what Zsinj's plan is, our objectives stay the same. And our objectives are pretty simple in explanation even if they turn out not to be simple in execution.

"Before we get to that, we need to remember that this is our best shot so far at taking out *Iron Fist* and Zsinj. This means that other concerns . . . such as our personal safety and even survival . . . come second." He looked around at the suddenly somber faces of the Wraiths. "I'm not asking anyone to go on a suicide mission. But I am asking you to keep in mind the same measures and balances I'll be considering. If what I do can take out this enemy, who has caused so much pain and destruction, and who will *continue* to do so if allowed to, is my survival more important than his defeat?

"So . . . our goals. Number one, most important, is to get a transmitter on *Iron Fist* or the new destroyer or both. We have several ways to do this. One is Castin's program, which any one of us invited to join Zsinj's advance party might have an opportunity to plant. Another is a standard transmitter, which we might be able to plant on one of the ships' surfaces. It's less subtle than Castin's code, but will only broadcast when the ship's main communicators are being used, which might conceal its use. A third is to get someone aboard the two ships, as a stowaway or in supposedly permanent employ with Zsinj.

"Goal number two is to stay alive and to take out as many of the enemy as possible. And don't forget—the people of Kuat, in spite of the fact that they're Zsinj's enemy, are also *our* enemy. They're loyal to the remnants of the Empire. Any damage we do them is good for the New Republic. Any questions?"

Donos raised his hand. "What are our individual roles for this mission?"

Janson tapped on his datapad and the Wraith unit roster replaced the Kuat system as the holographic projection. "We'll be broken down into two or, we hope, three units.

"Unit One, Hawk-bats. That's Commander Antilles, Dia, Kell, Face, Tyria, and Piggy. We fly, we shoot, we kill.

"Unit Two, Infiltrators. Lara has faked up dossiers on alternate identities for herself, Shalla, and Dia and forwarded them to Zsinj—you've done that, haven't you, Lara? Good—in the hope that he'll select one or two to accompany his advance team, the one we believe will be taking over the new Destroyer.

"Unit Three, Wraith Squadron. The rest of us will be taking our X-wings to join *Mon Remonda* as part of the ambush phase of the operation. We predict that Zsinj won't want to do more than a short jump away from Kuat on untested hyperdrive engines. That means we'll be stationing elements of the New Republic fleet—all of General Solo's command and anyone else we can drag in—and staging them at points as close as we can manage to Zsinj's likely escape courses. They'll be well off the major trade and military routes—an important consideration, since we'll be in the middle of Imperial-controlled space—and standing by for any signal from any of the transmitters.

"With any luck, if there's enough time between the accomplishment of the Kuat raid and the come-get-me signal from *Iron Fist,* the Hawk-bats from the first part of the plan will be able to join the Wraiths for the third."

"And when we hear that signal," Donos said, "we jump in and drop the heavy end of the hammer on *Iron Fist* and his new Destroyer."

"That's it," Wedge said. "Make your preparations. We

suspect the word will come from Zsinj pretty soon, but we don't know when—so get as much done as you can. Face, we'll need disguises for anyone Zsinj might choose to join the advance unit. Kell, I'd like for the same folk to have some backup weapons, demolitions—we want to give them every opportunity to get back to us if things go sour. Questions, anyone? No? Then get to it."

The word from Zsinj arrived later that day. It included a rendezvous course the Wraiths suspected led to another redirection satellite, and a request that Qatya Nassin—Shalla's Hawk-bat identity—join Zsinj's advance unit in the assault to come.

Hours later, the Wraiths assembled in their hangar.

Shalla was someone new. Under Face's care her hair had been transformed into a shocking white, and her left eye was surrounded by a circle of white makeup. That, and the pads she held in her cheeks, changed the lines of her face. She was dressed in flowing street clothes; doubtless Zsinj's infiltration crew would have more appropriate garments for her.

Dia, Kell, Face, Tyria, and Piggy were in the makeup and gray TIE-fighter-pilot uniforms of the Hawk-bats, and Janson, Runt, Donos, and Lara were in the standard orange, white, and black uniform of New Republic pilots.

"The commander's late," Face said. "Is anything wrong?"

"Oh, no," Janson said. "Since he doesn't have any additional responsibilities, no last-minute details to track, no need to do one last check of the plan, he's just late so you'll be that much crankier."

"That's what I thought."

While they waited, the command crew aboard *Sungrass* completed its check and did a test firing of her repulsorlifts; the aging cargo hauler lifted a few meters into the air and set down again. The ship couldn't depart until Shalla was released to join them, and then it would wait above this asteroid for the Hawk-bats to fly their TIE interceptors and fighters into her hold.

"Attention," Janson called.

The Wraiths snapped to attention in a reasonable line as Wedge approached them. Unlike the other Hawk-bat pilots, he was dressed in a traditional black TIE fighter's uniform, with a difference it took Face a moment to recognize: All the usually glossy black surfaces, such as the helmet and breathing gear, had been painted matte black. Also, there seemed to be additional snap hooks on his chest and arms. He carried a large cylindrical cloth bag in black over his shoulder; this he set down at his feet.

"I'm not going to give you some sort of stirring, half-witted speech about why we're here," Wedge said without preamble. "They're for crowds, not for fighter pilots. But I did want to say something.

"The Wraiths have had to learn lessons fast, faster than any unit I've ever belonged to or commanded. I regret the speed of your education—because, inevitably, it's intrusive and painful—as much as I'm glad you've been able to absorb it.

"Recent events, especially Runt's dance and the behavior of several of you at that celebration, have convinced me that you've learned another lesson, as individuals and as a unit. The lesson involves watching out for one another. You're now doing it as second nature.

"You need to keep that up today, perhaps more than any other day in our recent history. Do it and more of us will come back."

He looked among them, catching each stare in turn.

The Wraiths weren't wearing a collection of steely, confident expressions. Kell, just as before most missions, looked a little jittery, and more of Tyria's attention was on him than on Wedge. Dia was more wide-eyed than usual, the mask of who she'd been before now gone, a little uncertainty in its place. Face stared back with the eyes of a stranger, already deep under his General Kargin makeup and personality. But with each of them there was a commitment to the mission, to its successful completion, regardless of the cost.

Wedge finished up: "For those of you who believe in the Force, may it be with you, and guide you. For those who don't, trust in your intent, your weapons, and your wingman." He clapped his hands. "Let's go, people."

The pilots broke rank, exchanged handshakes and embraces, headed off to their individual missions. The gray-clad Hawk-bats would wait until *Sungrass* was on-station and take their TIEs out to the cargo ship. The orange-clad Wraiths would then begin the process of shuttling all the unit's X-wings out to the *Mon Remonda,* now waiting outside the Halmad system's outermost planetary orbit, with the shuttle *Narra* bringing them back in for each flight except the last.

Wedge caught the eye of his second-in-command. "Wes, a moment of your time?" He picked up his bag and headed briskly off toward his interceptor; Janson followed at a trot.

Wedge drew to a stop beside the ladder at his interceptor. He pulled at the drawstring holding the lip of his bag closed, and from the bag's interior withdrew Lieutenant Kettch. The Ewok toy was now dressed in Hawk-bat grays, and long spars of what looked like steel but swung with the mass of plastic hung from his paws.

"You have got to be kidding," Janson said.

"No. Think about it. What if one of our erstwhile allies swings in close and sees a human inside Lieutenant Kettch's interceptor?" Wedge snapped a loop sewn to the back of Kettch's cloth helmet to the corresponding metal hook on his chest. "Help me with the arms."

Janson did so, snapping the loop on Kettch's left glove onto a hook on Wedge's left biceps. "So that's why you're in black," he said, and repeated the process with Kettch's right arm. "An invisible background."

"That's it."

"So, when you joined Starfighter Command, did you have any presentiment that someday you'd be impersonating an Ewok?"

Wedge glared. "Now the waist."

"Sure. You know, pretending to be an Ewok is a felony on some worlds."

"Wes."

"And I think it's probably against regulations to fly starfighters while performing a puppet show."

"Wes."

Janson straightened up from making the last attachment and threw a salute. "Yub, yub, Commander."

Wedge returned it. "The things I put up with for this outfit."

Sungrass dropped out of hyperspace at the leading edge of Zsinj's armada.

In the midst of the swarm of ships was *Iron Fist,* the deadly blue arrowhead. Around it were numerous other capital and support ships: one Imperial Star Destroyer, an *Interdictor*-class cruiser, four *Carrack*-class light cruisers, and a number of cargo vessels and corvettes. Some of the cargo vessels were decorated with piratical designs; others were innocuous-looking. Few TIE fighters were in evidence, but that was no surprise; the TIEs would not be launched until they were within easy flight range of their objective.

"That's the *Ill Wind,*" said Captain Valton, *Sungrass*'s commander. He was pointing to the smaller Star Destroyer. "And that one's the *Emperor's Net.*" He gestured at the Interdictor. "Haven't seen either of them in a while. Not since before the Emperor's death."

Face, in the communications officer's seat, nodded. "Either of them assigned to Zsinj at that time?"

"*Ill Wind. Emperor's Net* must have joined him later." Valton glanced down at his control board. "Signal from *Iron Fist.* You might want to pick that up."

Sungrass was directed to land in *Iron Fist*'s main bay. As they rose into the bay opening and were directed to a large open area of flooring, Face could see that repairs were well along. The only signs remaining of the explosion the Hawk-bats had caused was one area, toward the bow end of the bay, of crumpled flooring still not replaced, and black charring at places along the wall. But a full complement of TIE fighters, interceptors, and bombers was arrayed for takeoff.

Face and Shalla emerged from their ship's exit port and shook General Melvar's hand.

"This is your transport?" Melvar asked, looking the *Sungrass* over.

"She's not elegant, I admit," Face said. "But we get an awful lot of work out of her."

"You'll be able to afford better soon, General."

"General Melvar, allow me to introduce Qatya Nassin, my hand-to-hand combat specialist."

Melvar shook Shalla's hand cordially. "Delighted." He looked her up and down with a somewhat aloof, evaluating expression. "This is Coruscant civilian dress. Middle to low class. Not too far from bedrock level."

Shalla smiled at him, her dimples showing. "That's correct."

"Perfect. Why do you need a datapad?" The general frowned as he looked at the commonplace device in her left hand.

"It's a weapon, General." Shalla traced her finger across the hinged edge of the datapad. "A standard scan won't show that this edge is heavily reinforced. If I decide that someone needs some additional information in his head, I can insert it manually."

Melvar chuckled.

Face did, too, but wasn't feeling too merry. They couldn't afford for Melvar to pay too much attention to the datapad. The technically proficient Wraiths had spent hours refitting smaller, more modern datapad gear into a larger, older case, and had reinforced the hinge end as she'd mentioned, but they'd also fitted in a secret slot and a number of small explosive devices that Kell had put together. A basic scan wouldn't reveal them—they'd be masked by the technology within the case—but a more thorough one would.

"Well," Melvar said, "I am delighted to meet you. Less delighted to have to put you to the test this way." He snapped his fingers.

From the semicircle of stormtroopers and officers who'd met the *Sungrass* stepped a man in a bridge officer's uniform. He was larger than Kell and looked as though his face had been used by several graduating classes for hammer practice.

"This is Captain Netbers," Melvar said. "One of our hand-to-hand instructors. I fear he must evaluate your skills."

Netbers approached, smiling, his hand extended to shake Shalla's. She stepped forward as if to take it, then swung her datapad straight into his face, smashing his nose, staggering him back. She followed through by bringing her booted foot up into his crotch, but Face heard a decidedly unfleshlike *thump* and decided the man must have been armored there.

Shalla turned and handed her datapad back to Face with a nonchalance that belied its contents, then turned back to her foe. Netbers, despite the blood streaming from his face and the pain he had to be feeling in his groin despite the armor, had taken her momentary distraction to assume a fighting posture—left side forward, most of his weight on his back leg, hands up and ready to strike. His expression was serious, his eyes intent, but unlike many fighters he didn't offer a stream of taunts and invective.

Shalla circled around him, her pose more upright, a mocking smile on her face.

Melvar moved beside Face. "He has reach on her," he said. "She has to close if she's to affect him."

As if on cue, Shalla moved a half pace forward, her advance coming with jolting speed. Netbers reflexively retreated the same distance. But she stopped her advance, keeping that distance between them. Netbers smiled and gestured for her to come on again.

She brought her hands up, a high guard, and circled, then suddenly advanced.

Netbers brought his left foot up in a high kick. But his right foot slipped, and Face saw that it was square in the middle of a puddle of blood, his own blood. Shalla caught his left foot and calf with her hands, wrenched them upward, sending him off balance, so that instead of striking at her he could only flail, and then she lashed out with her own left foot and connected with the inside of his knee.

He let out a grunt as he hit the hangar floor. She stepped forward for a follow-through kick, but Netbers continued rolling and had his hands up to intercept or trap her leg if she followed through. She didn't; still smiling, she continued circling, forcing him to do the same. Netbers tried to stand, but his right leg wouldn't sustain his weight and he remained in a kneeling position.

"Enough," Melvar said. "This exercise wasn't intended to result in injury—just to give Netbers an opportunity to evaluate the lady's performance. Netbers, I assume you consider her proficient?"

Netbers grimaced. "I would say so, sir." He fingered his nose. "My node is brogen again."

"Do you think she could kill a Wookiee? Or was that mere hyperbole?"

"I don't think anyobe gould gill a Wookiee habd to habd, sir. But she gomes gloser than anyobe I'be seen."

Melvar turned a cool expression on Shalla. "You were a bit treacherous, though. You were supposed to shake hands before opening hostilities."

Shalla lost her smile. "Nonsense. He came at me with the intent of taking my hand and then applying leverage to it. I could see that in his stance as he approached."

"Netbers?"

"She's right, sir. Anb if she's going on this mission, it's good that she can recognize the difference."

"Well, then." Melvar returned his attention to Face. "Will you be deploying your TIEs for launch from our bay?"

"No. Kettch is agitated enough as it is, and being exposed to too many strange humans would unsettle him. I think we'd prefer to launch from *Sungrass*."

"Understood. Please switch your comm systems to our frequency and cancel your starfighters' usual encryption; we *do* want to be able to talk to one another. Launch and stand by at your convenience, and I will deliver this formidable young woman to the unit she will be working with."

There were eight of them. Three men and a woman, all large, with movements like natural fighters, were dressed in the non-descript uniforms of maintenance workers, the words KUAT DRIVE YARDS emblazoned above the left breast of the uniforms. Four others were in stormtrooper armor. Melvar introduced them and Shalla filed their names away. He also succinctly explained the difference between the mission as described earlier and the way it was now. Shalla let her eyes open in simulated surprise when she "discovered" that the target was no cargo satellite but a Super Star Destroyer.

"At this hour," Melvar continued, "on this shift, *Razor's Kiss*—that's the name of the new Super Star Destroyer, unless Zsinj chooses to rename it—is almost deserted. What's left is mostly security details and workers finalizing critical assemblies.

"We've spent two years helping a colonel in charge of the ship's landing parties build himself up a lucrative little smuggling operation. He doesn't know 'we' means Zsinj, though he'll find out when they court-martial him, if not before. Anyway, to facilitate his trading and dealing, he had to arrange for ways by which his people could bypass several layers of Kuat Drive Yards defense, and by monitoring him very closely we found out what those means were.

"This crew of specialists will be taking a standard shuttle in to the officers' landing bay under access codes he uses for his little side operation. That will get you onto *Razor's Kiss* . . . but no farther, I'm afraid.

"The crew will advance from the landing bay to the bridge and seize it, then enter programming that will allow you to operate the ship in limited capacity solely from the bridge. A false leak alert should clear everyone out of the engineering section and auxiliary bridge, at which point you'll lock them out to prevent sabotage. Finally, a hypercomm signal to us will alert the fleet that it's time to jump in and *Razor's Kiss* can move out on its escape vector. Any questions?"

The faces of the other members of the team showed clearly they were all fully briefed on the situation. Shalla said, "I take it that I'm to be some sort of lure?"

Melvar nodded. "You'll take point through much of the team's advance through the ship. It's inevitable that the team will run across crewmen we haven't accounted for. Your job is very specific: Distract them, delay them for the others to get in position, but most importantly, don't let them get off any sort of signal. Any comlink notification of the bridge can ruin the whole plan."

Shalla nodded. "Except for stormtroopers, with their comlinks built into their helmets, it shouldn't be too hard. And even with them, just striking fast and hard enough should solve the problem."

In looking over the other team members, she'd noticed

that the only other female member of the team, though rather plain in her current guise, could, with a little makeup and attention to detail, have been quite attractive. Shalla said to her, "You were originally supposed to have my job."

The woman, whose name, if Shalla remembered correctly, was Bradan, nodded. "The general thought that a smaller woman would be less suspicious, less intimidating to the security forces aboard *Razor's Kiss*."

"He's probably right." Shalla shrugged. "I'm sorry."

Bradan gave her a searching look. "You bring this mission off and we'll all be covered in glory. Do it and I'll forgive you."

"Done."

18

"The sign of a perfect mission," said Captain Raslan, "is that it's boring."

Shalla nodded. The mission had been boring so far. They'd taken a dirty, creaky wreck of a first-generation Lambda shuttle from *Iron Fist,* made the hyperspace jump into the Kuat system, made an approach vector on the planet, transmitted passcodes that were apparently accepted, and now the shuttle was finishing its first orbit so that it could continue on to the shipbuilding station from a proper approach vector.

"When it's not boring," the captain continued, "you know that you've failed."

"You're obviously unused to failure," Shalla said.

"You have that right." Raslan turned his attention back to the shuttle's controls. "We're getting the automated turn-back message. I'm transmitting our passcode."

Bradan leaned forward to speak in Shalla's ear. "If this works, we won't even get a voice acknowledgment. Just several minutes of silence as we approach."

"Thus," Shalla said, "more boring, thus even better."

"That's right." Bradan leaned back.

Shalla had to consider that. It was so contrary to Face's

analysis of *Iron Fist*'s officer corps, with their rough, piratical behavior on the bridge during the dinner with Zsinj. It was, in fact, more logical, more in line with the kind of success Zsinj enjoyed. But, of course, not all the officers would necessarily share Zsinj's flamboyance.

And despite their words, the approach to *Razor's Kiss*, made in near silence, wasn't boring. As they approached the enormous arrowhead-shaped vessel, now wrapped up in the spars and projections of the shipbuilding satellite, which looked like a monstrous insect stinging the destroyer into submission, she felt her pulse and breathing increase, her temperature rise.

One mistake and she'd die aboard that ship. Even, perhaps, if she didn't make a mistake. The innocuous-looking datapad in her pocket could mean the difference between life and death for thousands in the New Republic.

Her father would be proud.

And that thought, recollections of the irascible man, already old when he'd falsified records of his death, resettled on the world of Ingo, and begun fathering children, the man who'd taught his daughters to look out for evil and watch out for good, calmed her. If he were here now, he'd be whispering in her ear: *Now you're Qatya. Keep your mercenary face on. Be nice to these people because they might hire you again in the future. Watch out for the backstab in case they decide to save themselves your fee. It won't happen before you take the bridge; right now they're anxious for you to succeed. It might not happen at all; Melvar was impressed with you, and they noticed.* With the sound of his soothing voice in her ear, she finally relaxed. She gave Raslan a confident smile. "Don't get too bored," she said. "You'll be asleep by the time we land."

Razor's Kiss grew before them until it blotted out the entire universe. Raslan guided them toward a tiny white dot that gradually grew into a standard rectangular bay opening. He brought the shuttle into a bay that was half-filled with other shuttles and with a pair of interceptors.

There were no people in the bay. Shalla frowned over that. Was it unguarded, with no mechanics on duty? But if the duplicitous colonel had automated instructions set up, he might require bay personnel to absent themselves when vehicles using specific passcodes arrived.

In silence, they exited the shuttle. Shalla was the first out of the bay, entering a long corridor that was eerily dim and quiet.

As she moved along the deserted corridor toward the bridge—a hike of over three kilometers—she decided that this was a ghost ship. Every other ship she'd been on had pulsed with life, a steady vibration that one could feel in the soles of her shoes and every rigid surface, a sensation so commonplace that spacegoers no longer noticed it after their first few days. This ship had no such vibration, and she imagined that if she saw someone materializing out of the gloom ahead of her, it would be a ghost.

But the first contact she had with the inhabitants of *Razor's Kiss* was not so ethereal. Barely a kilometer into her walk, a doorway to a set of private quarters hissed open beside her and a stormtrooper emerged.

He tried to bring his blaster rifle in line. "Say—"

She leaned into him, pinning the rifle to his chest, and brought her hand up, an open-palm blow that caught the trooper's helmet just at the chin. The force of the blow popped the helmet free of his head, sent it clattering into the quarters from which he'd emerged.

He backed away, trying to free his weapon, and she followed him. She crossed her arms and got both hands on the weapon, then stopped and yanked. The sudden torque ripped the blaster from his grip.

He lunged forward, grabbing, and she swung the butt up into his jaw. He fell like an anesthetized bantha.

Shalla looked around. This was a small office, perhaps a junior officer's. No one else was present. She took a look in its interior door, but it led only to an empty refresher.

Raslan was in the office when she emerged. "You could hear his helmet bouncing for fifty meters," he said, complaint in his voice, and held out his hand.

She handed him the rifle and slid past him. "You would have heard a blaster shot from three hundred."

For the next kilometer, she encountered nothing except some floor-scrubbing droids, machines so primitive that they recorded nothing but locations they had cleaned. Had she been invading *Iron Fist,* she would have been worried about their presence; a man like Zsinj would probably have adapted them to be an innocuous part of his ship security. Here, she had no such concerns.

She checked the map Bradan had transmitted to her datapad, turned left into a cross corridor . . . and bumped straight into a lean Imperial naval lieutenant standing there. The man rocked back, reached for his sidearm—and then got a good look at Shalla and relaxed. "Identify yourself," he said, his voice more curious than angry.

Shalla put her hands on her hips, a pose of naive irritation. "I'm Qatya, of course."

"Let me see your authorization."

She put a finger to her lips. "Shhh. No need to be so loud. I'm just looking for Stoghi."

"Stoghi?" He frowned. "Stoghin Learz? *Major* Learz?"

"That's him."

"Your business with Major Learz?"

She shrugged. "I missed him. It's been days since he visited."

"I see." It was clear the lieutenant didn't. "I'll check with the bridge to find out where the major is."

"I'd really appreciate that. I've been walking for kilometers and haven't found him."

"Uh-huh." The lieutenant brought up his comlink.

Shalla grabbed his hand with both of hers, twisting it and forcing his palm forward and down at a painful angle. He dropped the comlink before he understood what was happening, and as he stiffened and tried to draw away, she twisted his arm up and behind him, then shoved him forward into the bulkhead. The metal rang with the impact of his head against it. She hammered the back of his head with her forearm and the metal rang again.

The unfortunate lieutenant went limp.

Moving fast, she took his sidearm and tucked it under the waistband of her pants, beneath the hanging folds of her tunic. She bound him with his belt and stuffed his holster under his tunic. By the time her team arrived, she was merely in charge of an unconscious prisoner and there was no sign that he'd been armed.

She rose. "Was that more quiet?"

Raslan gave her an abashed look. "Yes. You're doing your job. That's what you're here for. You have my apologies."

They arrayed themselves outside the door to the security foyer leading to the bridge. Bradan took the security panel next to the door, checked it for alarm switches, and began the methodical process of opening it. The four false stormtroopers stood at the ready beside the door, as if waiting for it to open so they could relieve the previous shift on duty, and the others kept to the shadowy sides of the corridor as much as they could.

After long minutes, Bradan spoke in a whisper: "I've got it. I'm putting it on a delay. Three seconds after it opens, it closes. Don't start shooting until it closes, if you can avoid it; we don't want the sound to carry."

They formed up, stormtroopers to the fore, Shalla at the rear, and the door shot up with the customary speed of Imperial barriers.

The security foyer was beyond. Unlike the hallway, it was brightly lit, and Shalla had to blink at the sudden brilliance. But their stormtroopers, protected by the lenses of their helmets, advanced without hesitation, and Shalla heard one of them say, "Don't move and you don't die."

Shalla moved in with the others, heard the door whoosh shut behind her, heard the clattering of feet as the stormtroopers spread through the security foyer and into the bridge beyond, and her eyes cleared.

Still in the foyer was a naval officer wearing the insignia of an Imperial captain. His hands were up, his round florid face wearing an expression of extreme displeasure.

Raslan stepped up to give him a shove toward the command walkway. "Get moving." He glanced back at the sole stormtrooper remaining in the security foyer. "Guard the door. Bradan, secure the turbolift; we don't want some ambitious fool trying to get at us through the shaft. Then secure the doors out of the crew pit."

Bradan nodded and summoned the turbolift. The stormtrooper stationed himself before the doors to the main corridor. The other members of the team raced to their specific assignments, two of them heading to the weapons and defense consoles, others dropping into the crew pit to take up station at the control consoles, the other stormtroopers keeping their blaster rifles trained on the crew of four that had been occupying the bridge.

And suddenly Shalla was alone. True, she was mere meters from the stormtrooper and Bradan, but she was forgotten, her task done, her role vanished.

And the ship's main communications consoles were right here. Available to her.

But the stormtrooper and Bradan had only to turn around to see her.

Delay kills more operations than treachery, bad planning, or bad luck, her father used to say.

Moving quietly and quickly, Shalla drew a cable from her pocket. She plugged one end into her datapad. The other she fitted into the standard terminal interface on the communications console nearest her. Then she brought up Castin's program and selected the "automatic" mode that would do its best to bypass the *Razor's Kiss* security on its own, without input from Shalla, then set the datapad on the console chair and slid the chair in close, making the datapad almost impossible to see.

All the while, she overheard conversation floating up from the crew pit and out of the weapons and defense alcoves: "We have the engineering section and auxiliary bridge. Ready to send the alarm." "Wait for communications to be locked off." "That's locked off, sir." "Why didn't you say anything?" "I just finished." "All right, send the alarm. How are the gun emplacements?" "Up and ready. I've fed in the locations for the station attachments; as soon as I issue the command, they'll be metal vapor."

As a last detail, she switched off the terminal's screen so

the actions of Castin's program would not be visible, then quickly moved to the opposite console. She sat in one seat and put up her feet in another.

Bradan emerged from the turbolift and caught sight of her. "What are you doing?"

"Nothing." Shalla put her hands behind her head. "My job is done. I was going to let you professionals do the rest of the work."

Bradan's expression turned sour. "True. Well, you stay right there. Don't move."

"You can count on me. As long as you're paying, I'm inert."

Bradan turned away and headed up to the bridge and the command walkway. Shalla relaxed, but made sure her stolen blaster was close at hand. If anyone noticed the datapad in the chair, she had to make sure that he noticed nothing ever again.

General Melvar's voice was loud over the *Sungrass*'s bridge comm unit: "We have signal from the target zone. Prepare to enter hyperspace in two minutes."

Face keyed the comm. "*Sungrass,* requesting permission to launch."

"Permission granted. Have your fighters ready for instant dispersal."

"We'll be ready." He glanced at Captain Valton, but the man was already raising *Sungrass*'s repulsorlifts, drifting the cargo ship laterally to drop her from *Iron Fist*'s main hangar bay. "Good luck," Face said.

Valton nodded, and Face hurried back to *Sungrass*'s own tight-packed hangar bay.

The bridge of *Razor's Kiss* was a riot of noise.

The ship's batteries had obliterated the connections between *Razor's Kiss* and the shipbuilding station, and the Super Star Destroyer was in motion. Communications from the dying station, from Kuat, and from the main offices of the Kuat Drive Yards were demanding a response from the bridge crew. Sensors showed launches of squadrons of starfighters from

Kuat and from capital ships not far away in the system, and showed those capital ships maneuvering to intercept *Razor's Kiss* on her outbound flight. From the control console, the team's communications specialist was ordering the skeleton crew on *Razor's Kiss* to go to their stations and prepare for an Imperial assault.

Through all of it, Shalla sat comfortably in her chair, watching and listening to the others hurry about their duties.

The datapad at the communications console pinged, the audible cue that its current program had completed successfully.

Successfully. The program was in place.

The stormtrooper at the door turned toward her. "Did you hear that?"

"I did." She rose, staring intently beyond him, and came a few steps forward.

"What are you looking at?"

"The door, stupid. That's where the noise came from. The other side of the door."

"No, it was behind me. Toward you."

"Idiot, your helmet is fouling you up." She nodded significantly toward the door. "Something's on the other side."

He moved to the nearest security console, just three seats down from the seat where her datapad lay, and brought up its main screen. It was a holocam view of the hall just outside the main door. "There's nothing going on out there." He turned back to the door.

Shalla quickly picked up her datapad, yanked the cable free and pocketed it, and joined him beside the door. She took a good look at the main and secondary screens, gauging which portions of the hall outside were under direct holocam observation. "You're right. It looks clear."

"I told you."

She shook her head. "I don't trust it. They're trying something. Let me through. I'll give it a look."

The stormtrooper thought that over, then apparently activated his comlink. "Captain, we're hearing some things at the main door, but holocams show nothing. Qatya has volunteered to act as forward reconnaissance in case there actually is some activity out there."

A moment later he said, "Captain says it's a good idea."

"Can I have a sidearm?"

"You won't need one just to report activity. Do you have a comlink?"

"Yes, but I don't have your frequency."

The stormtrooper handed her a comlink. "Good luck." He keyed the main door open for her. Then she was through, the door shutting behind her. And though the air was the same here, suddenly she could breathe it more easily.

She was still under holocam observation, though. She moved forward with slow, steady confidence, as though she actually were moving in on a possible enemy emplacement, until she was beyond the range of the holocams they were monitoring.

She waited there a couple of minutes, then keyed her comlink and whispered, "Qatya here."

Bradan's voice: "Report."

"There's a security detail a few meters up the corridor. They have munitions. Looks like they're rigging a shaped charge to blow the door."

"Good work. Fall back and we'll set up to repel."

"No, wait. Their demolitions team is closest to me, and not guarded. They're not expecting an assault from this direction. I can eliminate one or two and then set off the charges they've brought. The next group they send is going to be a little put off by the mess I leave."

Moments of silence. Then: "That's authorized. The captain will put you in for a bonus if you pull this off."

"Qatya out." From the datapad she shook the four explosives Kell had rigged for her. She set two of them down on the floor against one wall. She drew the blaster she'd taken, fired three shots into the ceiling, depressed the buttons that would begin the explosives' ten-second countdowns, and began running.

Now it was time to find an escape pod and safely wait out the conclusion of this battle . . . and the one to come.

Zsinj's fleet dropped out of hyperspace well within the Kuat system, where the gravity well of Kuat herself made hyperspace progress impossible, and the sensor displays transmitted from

Sungrass's bridge showed an oncoming Super Star Destroyer and alarming numbers of starfighters from all directions.

"Launch," Face said, and roared out of the cargo bay as soon as the opening door gave minimal clearance. His temporary wingman, Kell, followed in his own interceptor and the others emerged rapidly.

Emerged into a star system very different from the one they were supposed to have expected, of course. The sun was not quite the shade of Coruscant's, and the oncoming Imperial Star Destroyers were not complemented by Mon Calamari cruisers. The comm waves suddenly became crowded with shouts and infuriated questions. In character, Face keyed his comlink. "Hawk-bat Leader to *Iron Fist*. What is this? Where's Coruscant?"

The chuckle he received in response was a familiar one; he recognized it as Melvar's. "We never said you were going to Coruscant, Hawk-bats. Welcome to Kuat. Please keep to your assigned roles. Everything will work out very profitably." There was a moment's delay, and the pitch of the general's voice lowered. "Hawk-bat Leader, I regret to inform you that the insertion team reports that they have lost Qatya."

Face's gut went cold and hard. "How?"

"She single-handedly eliminated a demolitions team and was lost in the explosion. Her action has apparently prevented any further assaults on the bridge. You have our condolences."

"Thank you." The tightening of Face's stomach eased but did not go away entirely. Melvar's story sounded like the kind of ploy Shalla might have used to get clear of the insertion team; on the other hand, the story might be entirely true. And he couldn't ask, *Did anyone* witness *her death?* It would create suspicion. He could only pray. He said, "Someone is going to die for this."

All around them, cargo ships and old cruisers were disgorging squadrons of starfighters. Some, like the Hawk-bats', were modern fighter craft in good shape. Others were older craft, kept in barely functional form by their owners. Still others were fleets of Uglies, starfighters patched together from different fighter designs when there weren't enough parts available to reconstruct a normal starfighter design.

In their groups—five here, a dozen there, a score—they turned to their assigned vectors and headed out toward the incoming strike forces.

"Hawk-bats, follow my lead." Face turned toward a distant Imperial Star Destroyer. He could not see its complement of TIE fighters, but his sensors showed them plainly, three full squadrons of them. That was only half a fully equipped Star Destroyer's complement; he wondered whether this vessel was underequipped, or whether it was holding squadrons in reserve. "Anyone recognize that?"

"Leader, Five. It's *Mauler*. Nothing special."

Nothing special. Only an average *Imperial Star Destroyer.* "That's comforting. Thanks, Five." He opened a wide transmission band. "This is Hawk-bat Leader. Who else is heading toward *Mauler*?"

The voice he got in return bore the clipped accents of an upper-class man of Coruscant. "Hawk-bat Leader, this is Vibroaxe Prime. You're the spearhead; we're the shaft."

Face's sensors did show an irregular force of between thirty and forty friendlies trailing the Hawk-bats. They were much slower and sensors couldn't lock down a consistent vehicle profile for them—probably Uglies, then. "Want to trade places, Prime?"

"Thank you, no, Hawk-bat. I'm content for you to take first blood."

"Join us when you get bored, Vibroaxe. Out."

Wedge heard the exchange between Face and Vibroaxe Prime, but kept it in the background of his conscious mind. He was still struggling with the Ewok stuffed toy that was the most visible part of his disguise.

When he sat down with the Ewok in his lap, it rode up, interfering with his vision. Now he'd managed to release the main lap strap of his pilot's harness, bring it up over the Ewok's legs, and tighten it back down again, and that seemed to have done the trick . . . but if it came loose during maneuvers, he could have more trouble with it.

A dozen seconds after the end of Face's exchange with Vibroaxe, the Hawk-bats were moments from maximum firing range of the leading edge of the *Mauler* forces. Wedge heard Face cut in again: "Break by pairs, set up for Kettch's Drill, and fire at will." Sensors showed Face swooping to port, Kell staying on his wing. Tyria and Piggy drifted to starboard. Wedge eased his yoke forward; he and Dia kept the center, losing a little altitude relative to the others.

As the range-to-target indicator dropped into numbers where a hit was an outside possibility, Wedge nudged his stick back and forth, up and down, making himself as difficult a target as possible, and opened on one of the pair of TIE fighters nearest him. Sensors showed a graze off the enemy's hull, no significant damage. The enemy TIE's green laser fire flashed over Wedge's top viewport, a near miss.

An explosion ahead and to port—Face or Kell had a kill. Wedge kept up his fire on his target, saw his own green quad-linked beams tattoo the hull again and then penetrate the forward viewport. The TIE's internal lights faded to blackness and the starfighter, now a ghost ship, began straight-line flight—still powered. Doubtless the pilot's dying convulsions had jammed the controls into full thrust.

Then they were beyond the first wave of enemies, the first half squad.

Their enemies expected them to break and dogfight with that first wave. But Wedge's tactic—Kettch's Drill—took them straight forward, at full speed, toward the second wave, a full squadron of TIEs. He saw on the sensor board the four survivors of the first wave curve around to get into position behind them, but their maneuver was a little slow, a little tentative, as they adjusted to the Hawk-bats doing something unexpected.

The second wave was in range. Wedge continued juking around, opened fire, saw lasers spraying from the solar wing arrays of Dia's interceptor to his starboard. Return fire streaked the starfield green all around him and he felt a shudder as one laser blast creased his hull. An unfamiliar sensation, and once again he wished devoutly for a return to his X-wing and its shields.

His fire and Dia's converged on a luckless TIE fighter. The

craft exploded into a ball of incandescent gas and superheated shrapnel. Their two flight paths curved around it as they plunged into the second wave and beyond.

Sensors showed the four TIEs of the first wave closing in and several starfighters of the second wave curving around to join them. He smiled. The plan was operating perfectly so far. Yes, they had a squad and a half of fighters on their tails, but the forward momentum of *Mauler*'s squadrons was slowing.

The Hawk-bats were doing their job. They were serving Zsinj well. Amused, he shook that thought away and returned his concentration to the third wave of enemies.

These they dove straight toward, each picking a target and maneuvering straight into that TIE's path, juking around enough to be a difficult target yet always homing in on the oncoming starfighter as if meaning to ram it. Wedge's continued fire hulled his target and he flew through the debris cloud, hearing clattering and banging against his hull as he did. On the sensor board, he saw Dia's target veer away from her at the last second, arcing away straight into the path of a vengeful TIE from the first wave. The sensors showed the two blips merge into one, then disappear altogether.

Ahead, the fourth wave, a half squadron. Wedge saw Face lead the abandonment of Kettch's Drill, looping up and back the way the Hawk-bats had come, the other Hawk-bats joining him in formation, three not-quite-full squadrons of TIEs following in vengeful pursuit.

In full TIE-fighter-pilot regalia, which she had found in a pilot's ready room adjacent to the secondary hangar bay, and carrying extra life-support units, Shalla lurked on the walkway above the bay's pair of TIE interceptors.

She should have been safely tucked away in an escape pod by now. But with her mission accomplished, another idea had occurred to her . . . thus the dangerous three-kilometer trek back to the bay by which she'd arrived, thus the trail of unconscious foes along the hallways and passages she'd chosen for her return trip.

Thus this skulking on the walkway. Beyond the magnetic-containment field she could see signs of distant battle: tiny flashes and slivers of light, their sources too far away to make out.

Stormtroopers, Kuat loyalists probably wondering what to do about the ship's extraordinary activities, had entered the bay mere seconds after she had and were hard at work rummaging through the intrusion team's shuttle. Others guarded the door into the bay. No matter; that wasn't the way she intended to exit. She climbed down into the left-hand interceptor, the one closest to the bulkhead and farthest from the stormtroopers. Without belting in, she began her prelaunch checklist. It was longer than usual—this interceptor, obviously a commanding officer's personal escape vehicle, had its own hyperdrive and a more elaborate navigation computer than the standard interceptor.

All systems seemed go, though she didn't power up the engines to make sure; the resulting repulsorlift rumble would be certain to alert the stormtroopers to her presence.

She stood and climbed partway out of the access hatch, hanging in place by one arm. She brought up the last of Kell's explosives, activated them, and threw them as far across the bay as she could. They clattered against the bulkhead behind the intrusion-team shuttle.

Stormtroopers perked up, swung their weapons in that direction. "What was that?" "You and you, take the far side . . ."

Shalla dropped back into the cockpit and dogged the hatch shut.

She was almost done strapping herself in when the explosions went off. She saw a ball of yellow-and-orange flame on the far side of the shuttle, saw the shuttle rock, saw stormtroopers thrown through the air like dolls. Her interceptor and the one next to it rocked as well, and a great bubble of atmosphere, shoved through the magcon field by the sudden pressure within the bay, dissipated in the vacuum beyond.

As the stormtroopers raced toward their fallen allies and shook their heads against the sudden deafening explosion, she brought her engines up and goosed them. On repulsorlifts, she squirted out through the magcon field and then took an abrupt vector toward the stern. She immediately brought her speed down to something just higher than a good running pace.

As she'd expected, the hull of the *Razor's Kiss* was littered with debris from the shipbuilding station. Long armatures hung swinging from attachment points, and other metal trash clung to or rolled about on the hull, trapped there by the ship's artificial gravity. The Super Star Destroyer was in motion, heading out-system as fast as its untried engines would take it, and distant Imperial Star Destroyers were drawing ever nearer.

She took a deep breath and tried to quiet her stomach. This improvised plan of hers was more likely to get her killed than anything else. But when she'd recognized the opportunity in front of her, she knew she had to try it.

She skimmed as close to the ship's hull as her flying skills would allow her, and occasionally rolled the interceptor to simulate the motion of debris.

She wouldn't look too odd on sensors. A direct observation or holocam view would reveal that she was a live TIE and not just debris. Then a single shot from a laser battery would turn her into debris. So, white-knuckled, she continued her absurdly slow flight and prayed that nothing noticed her.

19

The Hawk-bats roared down toward the pursuing Vibroaxes with the *Mauler*'s TIE fighters in close pursuit. The Vibro-axes, with their awkward collection of jury-rigged weaponry, opened fire at just beyond their maximum effective weapons range, and the Hawk-bats and enemy TIEs plunged into that hail of destructive energy as if bent on suicide.

Wedge's stomach felt like a refrigeration unit stuck on high. They'd been in less danger of death when flying into the teeth of their enemies than into the mass fire of these pirates, who theoretically could distinguish the Hawk-bats' sensor blips from those of the others . . . but who obviously didn't have the skills or accurate enough equipment to make the best of that distinction. Laser beams, red and green, the flashes of ion cannons, and the blue trails of proton torpedoes flashed between them, among them.

The Hawk-bats passed the leading edge of the Vibroaxe force and veered, three wing pairs turning to three different vectors. Some pursuing TIEs broke off to avoid the cloud of Uglies, others plunged into the cloud, others skirted along the leading edge of the cloud. Wedge's TIE was rocked by the detonation of a torpedo nearby; he checked his sensor and found that Dia was still on his wing, still intact.

The comm waves were suddenly full, impossible to track: "Squad Two, continue on to primary target." "Hawk-bat Five, this is Twelve, recommend you climb *now*." "I'm hit I'm hit I'm—" "Can't shake him." "I've got him, Bantha." "Archer, this is Vee Prime. Spray a pattern of torps back toward the baby, we have a whole squad cutting out to go after him." "That— Emperor's nose, that's an Ewok! They've got an Ewok pilot!"

Wedge thumbed his comlink, still set up with Castin's Ewok-voice modifications, and said, "Bleed and die, yub, yub," then rolled to starboard and relative down as he caught sight of the squadron continuing on to the new Super Star Destroyer. It had skirted the engagement zone and its ten survivors were forming up. Even before clearing the screen of friendly and enemy fighters, he opened fire, hitting one TIE fighter in the engine pod with all four beams, a beautiful shot. The fighter went off like a fireworks display, its explosive cloud enveloping its wingman, but that TIE emerged from the cloud intact.

Dia's complementary shot hit another TIE's port solar array wing, but merely punched a clean hole through it without significantly damaging the vehicle. Together, he and Dia tore out of the engagement zone and continued after the nine remaining TIEs.

Shalla saw something ahead, movement just above the hull, and brought her interceptor down against a piece of spacestation wreckage. She killed power instantly.

That dropped the new blips off her sensor screen, but she could see the source of the blips through the viewscreen. A half squadron of interceptors heading more or less in her direction, and as they came closer she could see that their solar wing arrays were decorated with the horizontal red stripes of the 181st Fighter Group—the deadly unit of Baron Soontir Fel. She stopped breathing.

The interceptors roared past her at a distance of less than a hundred meters. None varied its course to swoop closer to her; none hesitated. She relaxed. Doubtless they were doing a visual reconnaissance of the skin of *Razor's Kiss*, making sure there was no substantial damage from the Destroyer's violent departure from its berth.

She powered up again, ran through an abbreviated checklist, and brought her interceptor back into motion.

From here, she had to climb the hull to the Super Star Destroyer's command tower. It was a more difficult approach, as the ship's hull, which seemed comparatively smooth from a distance, was in the area of the command tower, a tricky terrain of graduated terraces.

Yet her terrain-following flying was fast and skilled, and within moments she settled neatly—and very delicately—into place between the deflector-shield domes atop the command tower.

She powered down all systems except her suit's life support and the starfighter's communications board. Then she changed the interceptor's comm unit to broadcast across a range of frequencies, took a deep breath, and said three words: "Parasite Two, go."

Of course, they'd probably detect that transmission. To account for it, she put as much of a masculine growl as she could manage into her voice and continued transmitting. "Kuat Central Authority, please acknowledge. This is Engineer's Mate Vula aboard *Razor's Kiss*. This vessel has been seized by Rebels or pirates. I think we're under way. I'm requesting instructions."

A hiss, then a static-blurred voice: "Vula, this is *Mauler* Control. We're aware of the situation. Where are you?"

"I can't say. This is an open transmission. They're probably listening."

"Then get to an escape pod and launch. You've done your duty."

"Acknowledged. Out." She sighed. *Get to an escape pod.* Odd to have an enemy repeat to her an order she'd already disobeyed. She hoped that the comm exchange had fooled Raslan's crew, and tried to relax.

Dia had just vaped one of the fighters, battering the top of its hull with a barrage that popped open the access hatch, filled the interior with light, and cast the remains of its pilot adrift, when Wedge heard the transmission. "Parasite Two, go."

Startled, he checked over his sensor board. That code meant that one of the Hawk-bats had successfully pretended to crash upon the hull of the second Super Star Destroyer and was in position to destroy its deflector-shield domes. But all the Hawk-bats still appeared on his screen.

The voice had been female. It had to be Shalla. Some of the chill in his stomach began to fade.

Good, that was good, and not just because it meant she'd survived her mission. Now they'd only have to try to stage the Parasite portion of their operation once. Twice, even if they could pull it off, would probably look suspicious.

Ahead, two of the TIE fighters looped around to come back at Wedge and Dia. A delaying tactic—the commander of that squadron knew his fighters couldn't outfly interceptors, so he was sacrificing two pilots to allow the others to reach their objective, the Super Star Destroyer. The sacrificial TIEs looped out at a considerable distance before coming back in, so that if the Hawk-bats continued on their course, the fighters would be able to settle in neatly behind them.

Wedge said, "Four, stay with me, then break when we're past them," and vectored toward the incoming craft. Dia tucked in neatly to his aft and port.

The incoming TIEs sprayed fire as indiscriminately as if they were watering a garden. Wedge concentrated on evasive maneuvers, returning fire when his targeting brackets suggested they were about to manage a lock, but his beams still went wide. Then the two pairs of TIEs passed one another's position and looped to come around again.

Wedge gritted his teeth and pulled the tightest, hardest loop he could manage. His gravitational compensator couldn't quite compensate, and the maneuver slammed him back in his pilot's couch, forcing blood into his head; he felt himself graying out and eased off. But his prey hadn't tried a maneuver so ambitious, and Wedge found himself, half on instinct, tucked in behind the fighter. His prey wavered and veered off to shake him, but Wedge adhered to the fighter's tail, sized up his shot, waited for the image of the target to jiggle in the targeting bracket, and fired. The fighter exploded in a rain of glowing gas and debris. Wedge twitched his yoke, a lateral drift, so he did not have to fly through the debris cloud.

He spotted Dia's sensor signal on his screen and maneuvered around to get a look. She, too, was tucked in behind her foe, firing twin-linked lasers upon it, and her fire chewed away at the enemy's twin ion engines and wing pylons. Wedge saw one pylon give way, reduced to molten slag, and one engine flame out.

That pilot shut the engine down and continued veering, trying to escape Dia.

She let him. She allowed the crippled TIE to vector off toward safety. She looped around and formed up with Wedge.

He brought them around toward their original objective and thought about that. The old Dia would have vaped that target without a second's hesitation. The new one seemed satisfied with having the objective accomplished rather than scoring the kill. He hoped the change wouldn't prove fatal to her. But all he said was, "Good flying, Four."

"Yub, yub, One."

Up ahead, toward the new Super Star Destroyer, Wedge caught flashes of light.

His sensor board showed that the six TIEs had become twelve—but the newcomers were blue dots, their transponders indicating they were friendlies from *Iron Fist*. The six red dots became five, then four, then two, then none. Wedge slowed his approach and Dia followed suit.

The newcomers continued in their direction.

Wedge opened his comlink. "Leader, what to do?"

"It's still hairy here, One. Come back in."

A new voice, clipped and martial accents: "Am I speaking to the Ewok pilot?" It was Fel's voice, and Wedge's gut chilled down to cryogenic levels again.

The sensor board showed the transmission coming from the oncoming TIE interceptors. Wedge said, "Yub, yub. Kettch here. Who talk?"

"My name Fel. Fel want to fly with Kettch." The sophisticated voice and the simplified syntax just didn't go together.

Wedge shook his head over that and brought his interceptor

back toward the engagement zone. Dia followed suit, mercifully not intruding on this conversation. "Yes," Wedge said. "Fly with. You see Kettch best pilot."

"Well, best Ewok, certainly."

"Kettch not really Ewok."

"No?" There was surprise in Fel's voice.

"Must not be. Ewoks dumb. Not under-stand astro-navigation. Not under-stand power-up check-list. Dumb."

"Sad." The six red-striped interceptors moved up alongside Wedge and Dia.

"Sad. Kettch not have mate. Ewok females too dumb."

"Even sadder."

"Fel have mate?" There it was, the question Wedge wanted to ask, had to ask. What was the fate of Fel's wife, Wedge's sister Syal?

"Oh, Fel have mate."

"Smart mate?"

"Smart mate. Actress. You understand actress?"

"Like storyteller. She good mate?"

"Good mate."

"Fly with you on big island ship?"

"No, she has her own projects. You understand projects?"

"Under-stand. Make bombs, fix star-fighters, stab humans."

"Something like that."

This brought them to the leading edge of the engagement zone. Wedge could see that the battle had not gone well for the Vibroaxes, who were down to six active combatants; they and the four Hawk-bats there were still facing fifteen TIEs.

Wedge said, "Stick with Kettch. Kettch teach good." He rolled out and dove toward the thickest patch of the fight, where three pairs of TIEs were battling Face, Kell, and the Vibroaxe command vessel, a heavily reinforced combat shuttle.

"Fel doesn't need Kettch to teach. Fel is best human pilot."

"No. Other humans say other name is best." *Provoke him; maybe he'll get angry and say something in an unguarded moment.* Wedge held off from firing. The enemy TIEs hadn't yet reacted to the new arrivals, and every second of approach improved his shot.

"Luke Skywalker, then. Rebel scum, but a good flier."

Dia finally broke in, speaking in her silky Seku voice: "Actually, we've been telling him about Wedge Antilles and Rogue Squadron."

An explosion of laughter from Fel. "Antilles? Oh, he's luck incarnate, to be certain, but he really can't fly worth a damn."

Despite himself, Wedge felt a wash of anger. At optimum range, he opened fire on the nearest TIEs, the ones pursuing Kell.

Fel opened fire at the same instant. Their sudden strafe hit both TIEs, detonating them within milliseconds of one another.

Wedge veered off to approach the rear of Face's opponent. Fel paced him. The two of them swooped in difficult circular patterns, like tiny planets orbiting an invisible sun, and fired upon Face's enemies, annihilating them with similar merciless efficiency.

Antilles and Fel, brothers-in-law, flying together again for the first time in years, since Fel's disappearance. But it wasn't a cause for joy. Fel seemed at ease in his role as Zsinj's ally, and had obviously lost all respect for Wedge in those intervening years.

They turned toward the Vibroaxe shuttle, but there were gas-and-shrapnel clouds near it, with Dia and Fel's wingman on a course to rejoin them.

The sensor board showed the remaining enemy TIEs turning back toward another Imperial Star Destroyer. Not *Mauler;* that vessel had passed the engagement zone at a considerable distance, come within range of *Iron Fist,* and traded long-range blows with the larger vessel. *Mauler* was now in a slow, uncorrected spin along her long axis, flame venting from half a dozen spots along her hull. There were no escape pods launching; the ship's commander doubtless thought he could bring the damage under control.

Mauler's absence was cause for celebration . . . but a dozen or more Imperial Star Destroyers were still coming on toward them.

"Hawk-bats, Vibroaxe, One Eighty-first." It was Melvar's voice. "Fall back, fall back. We are nearing the launch zone."

"Good flying with you, Kettch." Fel abruptly veered away toward the rest of his unit. "We'll do this again."

"Yub, yub." Wedge managed to convey more enthusiasm than he felt.

It sounded as though Fel was happy in Zsinj's service. Perhaps irredeemable. That meant the next time they flew together Wedge might have to kill him.

Iron Fist, now trailing *Razor's Kiss* by a considerable distance and acting as the center of her defensive screen, was under attack as the Hawk-bats approached *Sungrass.* The mighty Super Star Destroyer had taken some blast damage to its port side. The crippled *Mauler* and the presence, a few thousand kilometers behind *Iron Fist's* escape vector, of the burning remains of the Imperial Star Destroyer *Gilded Claw,* gave mute testimony about the source of that damage. *Iron Fist* was still suffering the strafing runs from *Gilded Claw's* TIE squadrons.

"Leader, Twelve. I don't have enough kills." Piggy, in his fighter, vectored toward *Iron Fist.*

Face took a deep breath. That was code, and Piggy was doing what the mission called for; this was the first opportunity any of them had had to get in close to *Iron Fist* without raising suspicion. Still, form dictated that he key his comlink. "Twelve, Leader. That's a negative. Return to *Sungrass.*"

"Don't hear you, Leader."

"Twelve, blast it . . . Eleven, go with him."

"Affirmative, Leader." Tyria's fighter zoomed off in Piggy's wake.

Tense, Face divided his time between docking with *Sungrass* and monitoring his sensors and comm system. The sensors showed Piggy and Tyria pursuing a lone TIE fighter up the ever-higher decks of *Iron Fist's* command tower. Their communications showed them in hot pursuit, then veering in different directions around the tower . . . and suddenly Piggy was in the lead, the fighter pursuing him, Tyria pursuing *him.* . . .

Face's stomach became a wall of knotted muscle. That was as gutsy and insane a maneuver as he'd ever seen, Piggy deliberately exposing himself to fire to account for what they needed *Iron Fist's* sensor crew to conclude. Piggy had to depend on Tyria's firing skill in those brief seconds.

Shrieks over the comlink, Tyria modulating her voice between victorious cheer and horror in a single syllable, Piggy's and the pursuing TIE's signals winking out from the sensor screen.

Finally, Tyria's voice, subdued and pained. "Leader, I have to report that Twelve is no more. Our friend Morrt is One with the universe."

Morrt. A Gamorrean parasite. That had to mean that Piggy was alive and on-station, but officially dead, and Tyria was calling him by that name to inform the others without repeating the word "parasite." Face let out a long sigh and suddenly felt ten years older and more tired. "I'm sorry, Eleven. You did the best you could. But you have less than a minute to dock before we launch. We'll raise a cup to Morrt at this evening's meal."

Piggy lay on his side, restrained from dropping to the starboard side of the cockpit only by the harness on his pilot's couch.

His crash against *Iron Fist*'s hull had only been half-simulated. His pursuer's final laser blast had hit his cockpit somewhere between and above the twin ion engines, doing damage to the fighter's electronics, and his damage diagnostics display had been lit up like a city's festival-of-lights display before he'd powered down.

Ahead, just over the artificial hill of *Iron Fist*'s command tower, he could see the top of one of the ship's shield projector domes.

But that would have to wait. For now, he began solving intricate astronautic formulae, beautiful numeric structures describing the relationship between real space and hyperspace.

The stars he could see in his disadvantaged position suddenly elongated as Zsinj's fleet entered hyperspace.

In *Iron Fist*'s main hangar bay, Face emerged from *Sungrass*'s airlock.

Quite a reception awaited him and the representatives of

the various pirate bands. Melvar was at the center of the largest open area, a phalanx of stormtroopers around him. He was shaking hands with motley-looking pilots and officers, occasionally handing out shiny new datapads to them.

As Face approached, one pirate in particular was haranguing Melvar, shaking a fist in his face, gesturing with an angry theatricality Face decided was not simulated. The man was a Devaronian, and one given much to decoration; the horns on his forehead were gilded, and his sharp teeth gleamed so brightly they had to have been augmented by some surface bonded to them. His clothes were similar to an Imperial admiral's in cut, but made of red cloth and leather, with an eye-catching red-and-gold overcloak.

As Face drew near, he could hear the Devaronian's voice; it was that of Vibroaxe Prime. ". . . malicious lies. This is not the way allies collaborate, Melvar."

Zsinj's general shrugged. "The lie was a matter of security. I did not underrepresent the forces we would be facing."

"Yes, you did! My fleet would have fared better against Y-wings and X-wings. We did simulator training against them that we could have spent against simulated TIEs. That was lost time. I've suffered eighty percent vehicle losses, nearly fifty percent pilot losses!"

Melvar's voice became soothing. "And you'll receive the bonuses we promised for those losses, in the second round of payments."

"There will be no second round! I want it all now. And not accounts—materials, precious gems, cargo. None of your datapad treachery."

Face shouldered his way to the front of the crowd and frowned. "What treachery, Melvar?"

"Ah, General Kargin." Melvar extended a hand back and one of his aides handed him a datapad. "Twenty-eight percent losses and an impressive kill rate. You're in for a bonus on that alone with the second round. For now, your initial payment, as promised." He offered the datapad.

"What's this? This isn't Imperial credits."

"It's all the information you need to access a numbered account where your payment resides. On Halmad. We thought that would be convenient for you."

"It would." He looked dubiously at the datapad. "And if, like Vibroaxe here, I want material goods?"

"You'll have them. Half the value of the payment we negotiated. If we're inconvenienced enough to have to carry hard currency and goods, we take a substantial cut. No negotiation."

Face shrugged and took the datapad. "I trust Zsinj," he announced. "Simply because it's not cost-effective for him to betray us. Word would spread to every pirate band in Imperial and Rebel space. He'd never get anything but blasters in the teeth from them afterward."

Melvar smiled. "As ever, the Hawk-bats make the intelligent choice. You have my sympathies for your losses. The woman Qatya was of special help."

"Her efforts will, I hope, be long remembered. Until the second payment, Melvar." Face brought the datapad up to his brow in a mock salute and turned back toward *Sungrass*.

Behind him, Vibroaxe Prime and others of the pirate leaders, more subdued, began accepting the datapads or negotiating for the reduced fees in material goods.

Sungrass's first hyperspace jump was straight toward Halmad, but only a light-year in length. Its second carried the cargo hauler straight to the deep-space rendezvous point where *Mon Remonda* waited.

Not just *Mon Remonda*. Other elements of General Solo's fleet were in evidence, including a *Nebulon-B*-class frigate, a Quasar *Fire*-class cruiser refitted as a light starfighter carrier, and a somewhat decrepit-looking *Marauder*-class corvette, a class of fighting ship normally found in the Corporate Sector. Wedge decided that Han Solo had to have cobbled together his force from disparate and overtaxed sources.

When Wedge reached the bridge of the Mon Calamari cruiser, General Solo was waiting with a smile and a handshake.

"Any word from the Super Star Destroyer?" Wedge asked.

"Fine, thank you," Solo said. "You?"

Wedge grinned. "Sorry. How *are* you?"

"No, no word." Han gestured at the holoprojected starfield that dominated the center of the bridge. Around it, ship's officers, chiefly Mon Calamari, ignored the humans and went about their business. "Don't be so anxious. Your pilots could use a little time to rest."

"Piggy's fighter only carries so much air, even with the extra life-support units he's carried aboard," Wedge said. "When it runs down, he has a choice to make. Try to run to freedom—which does him no good if he's in the middle of unoccupied space, since that TIE fighter won't carry him very far, assuming he can even elude *Iron Fist*'s tractors and guns. Turn himself in—which is very bad, for the usual reasons and some other ones, too. Or maybe try to sneak aboard the destroyer, very tricky. And we have no idea what Shalla Nelprin's status is. So even if our comm control program is planted correctly, the Parasite part of our plan is on a limited schedule."

"Well . . . still. Stand down for a while. *Iron Fist* and the other Destroyer may be jumping around for a while, and it could be some time before they reenter normal space and fire up their hypercomm system. Assuming, of course, that your program is planted and operational—"

The Mon Calamari captain, Onoma, swung around in his command chair and sent it gliding toward Solo and Wedge on its armature. There was excitement in his gravelly voice. "Communications reports a signal from the Donn program," he said. "We have a location on the target ship, only minutes old."

"You know, I almost never get to be right," Solo said quietly. He raised his voice: "Put that location up on the board."

A blinking yellow glow appeared in the midst of the starfield projection.

Han, Wedge, and Onoma moved next to it. Solo said, "Looks like they took a course perpendicular to a straight run back into the areas of space he controls. And that's good for us. *Mon Remonda* is the closest force to him."

Wedge asked, "Are you planning on a jump straight to the broadcast position?"

Han shook his head. "No, I want a little dispersal. See if we can have ships on all his escape vectors. He's out in deep space, away from any known gravity wells—he can jump back to hyperspace pretty quickly if we don't finish him. You have any ideas on how he'll behave in real space, before his next jump?"

"He's going to spend some time where he is, having his technicians go over the new Destroyer's hyperdrive engines." Wedge considered. "Which means stopping dead or cruising. He kept moving after he made his first jump out of Kuat system, and he was moving in the same direction as the hyperspace jump. . . . Can you indicate his course from Kuat to his current position?"

A thin white line appeared, tracing from the blinking yellow dot to a star a couple of hand spans away.

"That's my guess," Wedge said. "He'll be at cruising speed along the same course until it's time to jump again."

"Magnify it," Han said, and the holoprojected image expanded until the white line representing *Iron Fist*'s hyperspace jump dominated most of the image; only a few dozen stars remained within the magnified area.

Han pointed just ahead of the Destroyers' projected course. "All right. Calculate time to jump to this point. Compare it with *Iron Fist*'s normal cruising speed. Project its probable location based on that. That will be *Mon Remonda*'s arrival zone. Now, assuming he wants to run to his own space, we'll figure out the two most likely courses for him to take and put *Tedevium* in front of one of them and the rest of this group in front of the other one."

"*Tedevium?*" Appalled, Wedge glanced out the forward viewports to catch sight of the frigate. "That's a training vessel, not a combat-ready frigate."

Han shrugged—apparently not out of unconcern, but out of helplessness. "My fleet's in three pieces, with strength balanced as closely as I could make it between them. We use what we have. *Tedevium* has a graduating class of Y-wing pilots and a commander who's always good in a scrap."

"True. Still—trainees." Wedge suppressed a shudder.

Han put out a hand. "Good luck, Commander. Sorry you didn't get that rest I was offering."

Wedge took it. "Either way, I'm going to get it pretty soon."

20

"Accuracy was nearly ideal, sir," said Captain Raslan—or, rather, his holographic image now wavering in the security foyer of *Iron Fist*'s bridge. "Efficiency, however, is another matter. The jump here used nearly three times as much energy as it optimally should."

Zsinj kept any annoyance out of his face. This was not bad news. He'd gambled almost everything on the assumption that *Razor's Kiss* actually was as complete as its builders claimed and had made it to safety with his new prize. All other considerations were minor ones. "What about damage?"

"It appears that, contrary to safety regulations, some of the Kuat workers had jammed an airlock open where the access armature attached from the station to *Razor's Kiss*. When the ship blasted free, that section vented its atmosphere rather precipitously. We've corrected the problem. The Kuat Drive Yards workers who were on duty at that portion of the ship perished, of course. Instant corrective measures for those who disobeyed the rules."

Zsinj grinned, then suppressed it. "Very well, Captain. Carry on. Keep me updated."

"Yes, sir." The image faded.

Zsinj turned and jumped. General Melvar stood right

behind him, his makeup removed and his features returned to their usual cheerful blandness. "You did it again," Zsinj said, cross.

"Yes, sir."

"All the pirate captains happy?"

"Not one of them was happy, but none of them shot me, which I took to be a good sign. I think most of them will work with us again. Especially once those who took the credit vouchers take them to their systems of origin and determine that they're real." He gave Zsinj a curious look. "I'm surprised you're not over there now. On *Razor's Kiss,* looking at every rivet and dab of paint."

"Oh, I will be soon. Best to wait until Security has removed the last Kuat forces and possible saboteurs."

There was a sudden surge of noise from the crew pit, voices raised in fast exchanges. *Iron Fist*'s captain, Vellar, a stern-faced man just now going to fat, leaned over the command walkway to peer down into the midst of the noise, then looked back at Zsinj, unhappiness in his expression. "Several ships have just dropped from hyperspace in our vicinity. One dead ahead as we bear, the rest situated to our starboard and trailing. The one ahead is tentatively identified as a Mon Calamari cruiser."

Zsinj felt as though he'd been dropped into a polar breeze. He suppressed a shudder. "*Mon Remonda,* here?"

"That's not determined yet, sir, but—".

"Shut up. Signal *Razor's Kiss.* Coordinate a five-light-year hyperspace jump on this course and execute it."

"Sir, the cruiser is maneuvering directly into our path. We'll be on her before it's time to jump. Shall we change course to avoid?"

"No, you idiot. One Mon Calamari cruiser in the path of two Super Star Destroyers? Bring all guns of both ships to bear. Before we make the transition to lightspeed, we're going to rid the galaxy of the Rebels' most annoying cruiser . . . and of the legacy of Han Solo."

Her comlink suddenly crackled with activity on New Republic bandwidths, and Shalla jumped in surprise. Guiltily, she checked her life-support unit. She'd fallen asleep and the thing had run down almost to empty. *A really stupid way to die,* she told herself. She removed another unit from the storage compartment beneath her seat and put it on.

The comm transmissions were all encoded, but by straining her eyes she could see, in the incredible immensity of the starfield ahead of her, a distant needle of light that could not be a star. Her sensors might tell her what it was . . . then again, if activated, they might alert the *Razor's Kiss* crew to her presence.

But the domes to the right and left of her suddenly pulsed with power, bringing their mighty shields up over the Super Star Destroyer, and she decided the ship's crew had other things to worry about. She began her power-on sequence.

Wedge roared out of *Mon Remonda*'s port hangar, came around to a course matching the cruiser's, and waited as the others formed up on him.

Kell flew Piggy's X-wing, but that left the unit shy one snubfighter. Dia was in one of the TIE interceptors, hastily painted in Wraith Squadron grays to disguise its recent activities with the Hawk-bats. Wedge tried to force a nagging voice of worry from his mind. He didn't need to tell Wes to look after his underdefended wingman. He just wanted to.

The last members of his unit to launch, Face and Lara, formed up. Moments later, Rogue Squadron began emerging by twos, Tycho Celchu and Corran Horn first, and forming up by wingmates. On the opposite side of *Mon Remonda*, the A-wings of Polearm Squadron and B-wings of Nova Squadron would also be assembling.

Han's voice crackled in his ear. "They're aware of us. They're not deploying their fighter screen. That suggests they plan to blow their way through and launch back into hyperspace."

"The rest of our group?" Wedge asked.

"Coming up fast in their wake."

"Please inform them that if they're very nice, maybe we'll leave them something to shoot at."

Han Solo watched the universe tilt through the viewports as *Mon Remonda* turned on its intercept course.

He could feel Captain Onoma's eyes on him. He turned to the captain and shook his head. "Not yet," he said. "Save your fire. This is going to be a slugging match."

"You sound regretful."

"I hate slugging matches."

Piggy activated his power-on sequence.

Nothing happened. The fighter's interior remained dark and silent.

Shalla's sensors showed four squadrons of starfighters approaching.

When should she act? The later she made her assault on the shield projectors, the better it would be for her unit. But she knew her fellow pilots had to be suffering, approaching without any knowledge of whether she'd be able to accomplish her task.

She calculated their rate of approach based on sensor data. When they were thirty seconds short of firing range, she activated her repulsorlifts, bringing her interceptor up a mere meter above the deck of *Razor's Kiss* and well back from the domes. She swung toward the starboard shield projector dome and fired.

The dome blew apart in an impressive display of flaming gas and metal shards; she heard shrapnel bounce off her hull. She rotated and fired again, obliterating the second projector with similar finality.

Then she settled down again atop the rubbish-strewn tower. She'd wait a moment to launch—wait until space was crowded and confused, when she wouldn't be such an easy target.

．　　　　．　　　　．

"*Razor's Kiss* reports catastrophic failure of topside shield generators!"

Zsinj stared at the captain as though the man had suddenly grown a Devaronian's horns and teeth. "Tell me you're lying."

The captain shook his head helplessly.

Zsinj slammed his hands on the nearest bulkhead. "Change course to eight-five. Tell *Razor's Kiss* to follow closely and use us for protection from *Mon Remonda*. Calculate a new jump on that course and initiate it as soon as possible." He looked at Melvar. "Launch all fighters."

Wedge's sensor board showed the second Super Star Destroyer's topside shields evaporating. It displayed the information without emotion, without understanding of how that fact made the pilots' hearts jump.

"All squadrons, this is Wraith Leader. Prepare for strafing run on the second Destroyer. Ignore *Iron Fist* for now. X-wings, B-wings, commence with proton torpedoes. Save some for the engines." Wedge heeled over, changing course toward the second destroyer, and sent up a silent cheer for Shalla.

Iron Fist surged forward, her bow guns opening up on the oncoming starfighters, and began a slow maneuver to starboard as the second destroyer dropped back behind her. Wedge adjusted course, bringing his squadrons up over *Iron Fist*'s bow at a considerable altitude.

And then they were in the midst of it, ion cannons sending energy washes between them, laser batteries making space brilliant all around them. Wedge felt hair stand up all over his body as an ion blast came too close; his cockpit lights dimmed, but the computer and his R5 astromech did not suffer power loss. He heard one cry over the comlink—the cry of a survivor who'd just seen a wingman evaporate; Polearm Five disappeared off the sensor board.

Then they were past *Iron Fist,* the ship's horrendous field of damage tracking and following them, and the second Destroyer's guns opened up.

But now they could reply. "Fire at will," Wedge commanded, and some of the starfighters were launching proton torpedoes before he had the second word out. Faint blue trails leaped out from the starfighters, homing in on the Destroyer's bow, detonating split seconds later in huge balls of incendiary destruction.

Ahead, a tiny spark—ion-engine emissions—leaped off the command tower, then curved around in front of that projection and opened fire. Minuscule needles of green flashed between it and the destroyer's bridge . . . and Wedge watched as the bridge viewports blew in, then vented out just as suddenly in a hail of debris and atmosphere.

"New Republic forces, this is Wraith Ten. Sending transponder data. Please flag me a friendly."

"Confirm that friendly," Wedge said. "People, this is the lady who just opened the front door for us."

Cheers sounded over the comlink. Then the starfighters flashed past the command tower and its ruined summit, past the friendly interceptor that looped around and struggled to catch up. They rained their torpedoes down on the Super Star Destroyer's stern, then looped around to add the ship's engines to their list of victims.

A grating voice, Mon Calamari: "Assault force, this is *Mon Remonda*. Sensors show starfighters launching from *Iron Fist* in considerable strength."

"Understood," Wedge said. "All squadrons, stay in formation. Turn to course nine-oh but keep firing on the target destroyer until you no longer bear. Prepare for individual action."

"The *Razor's Kiss* bridge is no longer responding to communications," the captain said. His voice was dull with this recitation of what was only one new set of bad news. "Sensors show serious damage to the bridge. I think we've lost them."

Zsinj stared at the holoprojection of a live image of *Razor's Kiss*. The Super Star Destroyer, so powerful, so beautiful just minutes ago, was now awash in flame from bow to stern. Hundreds of gouts of fire had erupted from her top deck.

"What about our man on the auxiliary bridge?"

"Also not reporting. Possibly killed during the barrage."

On a fully staffed destroyer, crews would be putting out those fires. More officers would be occupying the auxiliary bridge and getting back in contact with *Iron Fist*. But this was not a fully completed Destroyer.

When Zsinj spoke, his voice was quiet, calm. "What's her course?"

"She came to eight-five as ordered. But she has not come back up to flank speed. Unless we reduce speed, we're going to leave her behind."

"Reduce—"

A voice rose from the crew pit: "Communication from *Razor's Kiss*!"

Zsinj shouted, "Well, bring it up!"

The dismal image of the crippled Destroyer was replaced by a faded holoprojection of a stormtrooper. His helmet was off, revealing a big face on a big neck, black hair just a little too shaggy to be regulation, a determined expression. "This is Trooper Second Class Gatterweld."

Zsinj frowned. He knew the names of all his agents aboard *Razor's Kiss*. This man wasn't one of them. "You're part of the ship's security detail?"

"Yes, sir."

The warlord smiled. A social call from an enemy who wasn't even an officer. The ridiculousness of it pleased him. "And what can I do for you this fine day, Trooper Gatterweld?"

"Sir, I'd just taken the auxiliary bridge to gain control of this ship when the attack came. But I'd prefer to see this fine lady intact in *your* hands rather than destroyed at the hands of the Rebels."

Zsinj's knees went weak. "I'm going to put a communications officer on. He's going to talk you through the process of slaving *Razor's Edge* to our bridge. Then we'll save her."

"Yes, sir."

"Gatterweld, I'm going to make you a very rich man."

"I don't care about that, sir. I'm just doing my duty."

Zsinj tottered away to let Melvar take over. Suddenly exhausted, he sank into a chair at the communications console.

Events like this reminded him, from time to time, that there *was* good in the universe, that with enough faith and determination he *could* win. He could win everything.

Piggy was up to his armpits in wiring when he found the problem. His port-side ion engine was completely out of commission, its connections severed, with trailing cables from the power generator having fallen into other wiring, destroying he knew not how much additional equipment.

He'd have to cut the destroyed engine out of the loop, patch everything else back together as best he could, and then see if the thing would start. He devoutly wished Kell, with his mechanic's skills, were here.

On the other hand, he wouldn't wish "here" on anyone he actually liked.

He got to work.

They boiled out of *Iron Fist*'s sides like angry stinging insects emerging from a shaken hive, squadron after squadron of TIEs—fighters, interceptors, even bombers. They curved in their streams back toward the New Alliance squadrons.

Face heard Wedge issue orders, perhaps the last set of group orders they'd receive before this fight was done: "Break by pairs. Take shots at *Iron Fist* when you can, but your main objective is to protect yourselves and hold the starfighters. Polearm, you're our spearhead—break up their formation, deny them their united inertia before they get to us. Rogues next. Wraiths, hang back, every pair protect a pair of B-wings. That's all."

"Polearm Leader acknowledging."

"This is Rogue Leader, we're on it."

"This is Nova Leader, thanks."

From the Wraiths there were only a few scattered groans. Face felt like complaining himself. To be relegated to baby-sitting duty while the Polearms and Rogues were up front—but Face knew, deep down, the reason for it. More than half the

Wraiths were just back from an earlier action. They were tired, even if they didn't realize it yet.

Ahead, the A-wings of Polearm Squadron roared toward the massed TIEs with speed no X-wing could match. Face could see the deadly formation of starfighters stream straight into the squadrons of TIEs, their laser fire reaping heavy casualties in the target-heavy environment. The enemy forces seemed even more to be a swarm of stinging insects as their formation lost coherence, groups of two and four and six TIEs going after each A-wing.

Then the Rogues were among them. Face watched the unit expertly break up into pairs, each pair moving as one, each pilot firing with the skill of years of experience. Face felt something like a shudder of dread, a feeling nearly of sympathy for the TIE fighters facing those formidable pilots, and suddenly he felt inadequate. He knew he wasn't up to their standard of performance.

"Orders?" That was Lara's voice in his ear, calling him back to the present situation.

"Right. Follow me." He dove relative to the formation and brought himself and his wingman up before a pair of B-wings. He dropped transmission power. "This is Wraith Eight and Wraith Thirteen. We're your escorts for this evening. What's your pleasure?"

"You have Nova Three and Nova Four. We can play with the TIEs, but we're much better suited to unloading on that ugly hunk of metal the warlord is driving."

"Tuck in tight, we'll get you close." Face goosed his thrusters and the foursome of starfighters veered off, away from the center of the dogfight, toward *Iron Fist*.

Ahead, a group of fighters—nine, nearly an entire squadron—broke from the main engagement zone and moved out to intercept them. Face switched to dual fire and opened up with his lasers at maximum range.

The backstop for his fire was *Iron Fist*. No expended fire would be wasted.

The TIEs came on, twisting, bobbing, weaving, difficult targets. Face wished he hadn't expended all his proton torpedoes on the other Destroyer. On the other hand, it burned nicely, and he had no time for regrets.

One of the oncoming TIEs exploded under Lara's sustained fire and he heard a hissed "Yesss" from her. Why? Oh, yes, she entered this fight with four silhouettes on her canopy. She'd just made ace.

Another TIE drifted right through the ion-cannon wash from one of the B-wings and went ballistic, helplessly rolling in uncontrolled straight-line flight. Face saw one of the oncoming TIEs was making unpredictable moves at predictable intervals; he waited for the next interval, guessed at the pilot's next move, fired in that direction, and was rewarded when the fighter drifted right into his fire. It detonated and its wingman flew right through the debris, emerging intact.

Face felt a blow as his forward shields were hit and some of the laser energy penetrated to score his hull. Then they were past, nothing between them and *Iron Fist*.

"Thirteen, drop back, shore up your rear shields," he said. "Let's give the Novas all the protection we can." *In other words, let's be targets for a while. The way the raiders on the first Death Star trenches were before they died.*

"Understood."

Wedge, unencumbered by a wingman, switched his encryption code so only the Rogues would hear him. "This is Wraith Leader. Any sign of the One Eighty-first?"

Tycho Celchu's voice, strained: "We're in the thick of them. You offering help?"

Wedge sighed. He'd like nothing better than to demonstrate to Baron Fel the error of his evaluation of Wedge's flying skills. Then he glanced back at the pair of B-wings following in his wake. "I'd love to. But can't. They'll be here soon enough."

"Understood."

Then they were before him, a half squad of TIEs, four fighters and two bombers. He saw one veer to starboard, picked out that one's wingman, fired ahead of its course if it turned the same way, and it did, erupting into a glowing shrapnel cloud—one kill, one second into the dogfight.

. . .

"Now reaching *Iron Fist*'s escape vector."

"All stop." Han felt fluttering in his stomach as though it were occupied by alien invaders, but he tried to keep his discomfort from his face. "All starboard batteries to begin fire on my command. Prepare for axial roll. Captain, maintain our position directly ahead of *Iron Fist*. Continue correcting as it's recalculated. And when any bank of batteries falls below eighty percent, perform enough roll to bring new guns to bear, and increase shield strength on the firing side as you do so."

"Yes, sir."

Iron Fist opened up, her laser batteries streaking by in such profusion that they looked like the star elongation that was the first visual manifestation of a hyperspace jump. Han tensed against the blows he knew were to come. "Open fire."

Piggy flipped the power-up switch and was rewarded with an erratic whine from the engines and the sudden lighting of his weapons and flight boards.

His diagnostics board said that all systems were down.

He grunted. *No use listening to people—or systems—who are inclined to tell you that you can't do something.* Not yet daring to commence powered flight, he brought his targeting system up and tried to bracket the distant shield projector dome.

One small piece of the dome fell within his targeting bracket, and jittered there, showing a clean lock, only moments at a time.

Wedge blinked away at the stinging of his eyes. The third TIE fighter had nailed him with a good fuselage shot just before Wedge had vaped him, and his cockpit was now filling with smoke.

Sensors showed that of the flight of nine that had moved against him, four were down—one having fallen prey to one of the B-wings. One of his B-wings remained, battered, char marks on its hull from insistent laser fire; the other was a rapidly dissipating cloud a dozen kilometers back.

He brought his targeting brackets over another TIE. They overshot as the starfighter sideslipped. Then the vehicle exploded, hit by lateral fire.

Incoming vehicles on the sensors, from the direction of the second destroyer—an A-wing leading a flying wedge of unscathed Y-wings. They continued firing and the TIEs bedeviling Wedge evaporated under their massed lasers.

"Wraith Leader to newcomers. Who am I talking to?"

The voice that came back was hard and military, but he heard an amused tone within it. "Why, Commander. You forget old friends so soon."

"General Crespin!" This was the frigate's starfighter force, then, finally catching up from the rear.

"And the Screaming Wookiee Training Squadron."

"Can you escort Nova Three?"

"Hand over all the B-wings, sonny, and I'll show you some old-fashioned mass-fire tactics."

"Nova Squadron, this is Wraith Leader. Form up with the Screaming Wookiee." Wedge coughed against the smoke. "I'm outbound, General, have to visit some old friends."

"Good luck."

"Wraiths, see your charges back to the general, then join the Rogues." Wedge heeled over and headed into the thickest part of the engagement zone.

Far ahead, past *Iron Fist*'s bow, the tiny needle that was *Mon Remonda* opened up with laser barrages. They flared and were expended uselessly against *Iron Fist*'s shields.

"Do you think he plans to sacrifice *Mon Remonda* to stop us?" Zsinj, chin in hand, steadily regarded the tiny but growing cruiser ahead.

"He continues correcting his position to be more and more precisely in our path," said Melvar. "We can't be sure of his intent until we're past the point of no return. Then, either he moves out of our path and we can get through and go to hyperspace . . . or we hit *Mon Remonda* and both vessels probably perish."

"He actually has more firepower to unload than we do at the moment. He can bring almost half his guns to bear at any time. We're limited to the forward guns that can depress far enough to target him." Zsinj shook his head. "All right. Bring all our guns to bear on her engines. Stop her dead in space. The sooner you do it, the greater margin we'll have to squeak past him."

Zsinj's stomach began churning. This was still winnable. But the New Republic assault, the way they'd accurately calculated his position, the way they relied on his protectiveness of *Razor's Kiss* to slow him, was upsetting.

It was a TIE interceptor, but it moved more sluggishly than the standard interceptor. A few kilometers from *Iron Fist*'s bridge, it had one TIE fighter under its guns and was stitching it with dual-linked fire while another fighter maneuvered behind it.

Wedge targeted the second fighter, bracketed it with his targeting computer before it was aware of his proximity, and shredded it with quad-linked lasers even as the interceptor vaped the first fighter. "Ten, is that you?"

"Good to hear from you, Leader. I hate this thing. It's as fragile as an interceptor and as slow as an X-wing."

"Well, stop playing by yourself, then. You're my wing."

"Yes, sir."

In spite of the smoke blurring his vision, Wedge saw the tiny green needle on *Iron Fist*'s hull below him—a long, tentative streak that hit the port-side shield projector dome, hit it twice, hit it a third time—and then the dome exploded.

The source of the laser fire, a TIE fighter, leaped up from *Iron Fist*'s hull. It shot up through her defensive shields as if the maneuver were an accident, then looped around as if flown by a drunken skimmer pilot, apparently setting up for a descent and run on the second dome projector, but an ion-cannon beam swept across it. The fighter continued off on a straight-line course toward the stars.

．　　　．　　　．

The captain's shout was jubilant: "*Mon Remonda* no longer maneuvering. We have their engines, Warlord!"

"Excel—"

The bridge rocked, its lights dimming, fragments of ceiling descending into the crew pit. Zsinj tottered and fell. He looked up; Melvar was looking away, not extending a hand. That was correct, that was proper. No one was supposed to see the warlord discommoded.

Zsinj clambered to his feet. "What happened?"

The captain had gone from cheer to despair in just a second. "We've lost the port-side shield projector. We're down to half shield strength above the midline."

Zsinj felt as though he, too, were suddenly at half strength. He calculated the numbers. "Is that frigate still on our tail?"

"Still catching up. It will be within firing range in two minutes at this rate."

Zsinj closed his eyes. "Recall the fighters. Bring *Iron Fist* up to flank speed. Communicate with *Razor's Kiss,* issue the command 'abandon ship.' " He didn't have to add, *We've lost this battle.*

Face caught sight of the interceptors emerging from the flurry of fighters, headed their way. "Thirteen, incoming!" He turned into the path of the incoming TIEs, threw all discretionary power onto forward shields—

Too late. Laser fire from the lead interceptor punched through his unboosted shield and then through his cockpit. He felt a sudden blast of agonizing heat to his left side, then cold just as intense. He watched in idle curiosity as his vision changed—first as the atmosphere of his cockpit was vented, then as the emergency magcon field on his suit came up and tried to cope with the sudden vacuum. He caught a glimpse of the red stripe on his attacker's solar wing arrays as it sped past.

"Eight, can you hear me?"

There was no response, and Face felt a distant sadness. Eight, whoever he was, must have been vaped.

"Eight, this is Thirteen, can you hear me?"

There was an additional squeal from Vape, Face's R2 unit, and Face wished the whole universe would just shut up for a while.

"Squad, this is Thirteen. We need help here. I can't handle these two—"

"Wraith Three here. Four and I are coming in. Hold on."

"Five here, I'm almost there."

It took Face another long moment to understand. He was hit, he was done. He couldn't move for the pain. *Iron Fist* loomed in the near distance ahead. He was going to crash and his debt would be paid.

He should have felt at peace with that. Peace was what he'd expected all this time. But it eluded him. Was something left undone?

Well, there was that second shield projector dome. If he could make his hand move, he might be able to steer straight into it. If the Destroyer's guns didn't get him, if its shields didn't destroy him, he might, just might be able to angle into that dome and destroy it, too.

The odds one in a million. Less, really. But it seemed like a good way to go out. He brought his cold, cold hand up to the pilot's yoke and gripped it. He couldn't feel his fingers close on it, but could see them.

"Got him, got him—dammit, he's slipped by."

"This is Five, I'm on the second one."

"Hold him, hold him—"

"He's not shaking me, Three. You see after Eight."

Oh, yes, *he* was Eight. Why were they worried about him? Didn't they realize he was already dead?

No, they didn't. Bless their optimistic little hearts, they actually thought he was going to make it. Now he knew how Phanan had felt with Face fussing over him. The Wraiths didn't realize it was his time, time to balance the account.

The account doesn't need balancing. Ton Phanan's voice

from some forgotten conversation. *You can't reduce sapient lives to numbers and exchange them like credits.*

The snubfighter shuddered again as more laser fire hit him. It must have hit the X-wing's rear; at least he wasn't feeling any more pain. *Iron Fist* was getting bigger.

And Ton was right. Ton, who had suffered from the Empire's success as much as anyone he'd ever met, should know. He didn't have to close out his account now.

An X-wing blasted past him to port, juking and jinking. He thought he recognized it as Wraith Eleven. Tyria.

If she was doing that, she was being pursued. With his numbed fingers, he brought up his targeting system and swung it just to port of his flight path.

An interceptor flashed into his brackets and he fired. With detached interest, he watched the laser blast shear through its starboard wing and pylon, straight through the canopy. The interceptor exploded and bits of it glowed as they bounced off his forward shields.

Donos's voice: "Nice shot, Eight! Are you back with us?"

" 'M here."

"Eight, this is Thirteen. I'm coming up beside you." Lara slid in place to his starboard, then ahead. "I'm going to lead you back to *Tedevium*. Will you follow me?"

"Sure."

"Can you make it?"

"Sure. Wake me up if I fall asleep."

"Will do."

Another TIE fighter went to pieces under Wedge's lasers and he had a clear path to the center of the engagement, where members of the 181st—where Baron Fel—awaited him.

But those fighters veered off toward *Iron Fist*.

All the TIEs began veering off toward *Iron Fist*, even if it meant exposing their backs to New Republic guns.

And *Iron Fist* was picking up speed.

"Oh, no, you don't." Wedge kicked his thrusters as high as they'd go and added some discretionary power to them. But the faster TIEs leaped out ahead, arcing down beneath the Super Star Destroyer and toward her landing bay. Wraiths, Rogues, Polearms, and Novas took parting shots, achieving more kills in those few seconds than in the entire dogfight, but still the TIEs ran.

Iron Fist cruised past *Mon Remonda,* lying at a dead stop, her engines flaming, mere kilometers away. The two capital ships exchanged barrage after barrage. Wedge, looping well around the corridor of fire between them, saw laser batteries take out chunks from the hulls of both vessels. Nova Squadron's B-wings continued pouring heavy fire into *Iron Fist's* stern from as close a distance as they could afford, but the Destroyer's shields held.

Then the Destroyer leaped forward and was gone, lost into hyperspace.

Far behind, the other Destroyer began firing off escape pods like mold spores as more and more flames gouted up from beneath her surface. Then the brightest flame of all rose out of her midsection, a globe-shaped inferno, and began eating away at the vessel in all directions. The few starfighters remaining in its vicinity raced away at full speed.

One last flash, bright as a nova, and the Destroyer hurled asteroid-sized pieces of itself in all directions.

21

Hours later, Wedge—freshly scrubbed and uniformed, a little bacta treatment having rid his lungs of the smoky crud that had coated them but also having left a nasty taste in his mouth—marched into *Mon Remonda*'s bridge.

It wasn't quite the same bridge. The armature of the captain's chair had broken and Onoma was standing over his control board. Portions of the deck were crumpled and an entire control board was still black from burn. A new shift of officers was at work. Han Solo had his back to the bridge; he was lost in thought, staring into the depths of hyperspace.

Wedge approached to stand beside him. "Commander Antilles reporting."

Solo didn't answer for long moments. He looked tired, the lines in his craggy face deeper than Wedge had ever seen them. He took a deep breath. "We lost him."

"We hurt him. We eliminated the other Destroyer. *Razor's Kiss*."

"But Zsinj is still at large."

"We'll get him next time."

"I am so sick of next time." Finally, Han grinned, looking briefly like his old self. "I'll bet you're just as sick of the gloomy Han Solo."

"We'll vape Zsinj together and you can go back to a life of irresponsible good cheer."

"I'll drink to that. How are your people?"

"Good. Lieutenant Loran will make it. We almost lost Piggy saBinring—he was floating off to oblivion with no thrusters, no lasers, no comlink—but Shalla Nelprin calculated his last known course and *Sungrass* retrieved him. We even picked up a hyperdrive-equipped interceptor out of the deal."

"If they ever make you a general, demand to be head of the quartermasters. You're really learning to turn a profit."

Wedge watched him return to his distracted, distant staring. "Han, what's it like? Actually being someone's personal enemy?"

"I hate it. But I can't just hand the job off. Not until someone feels about him the way I do."

"Still up for that drink?"

Han snorted. "What do *you* think?"

Melvar appeared with his customary stealthiness beside Zsinj's desk in his private office. He put a datacard before the warlord. "The final tally of losses."

Zsinj barely stirred. He seemed drained of energy, so drained that even his fat sagged. "I'll look at it later."

"How do you think they did it?"

"One of the pirates," Zsinj said. "He must have planted a transmitter on *Iron Fist* while collecting his pay, in spite of our sweeps, in spite of our sensors. I don't know how. We'll find out."

"Your orders?"

Zsinj nodded listlessly. "Get all available cargo ships and tugs back to the last engagement zone. I want them to collect every piece they can find, no matter how large or small, of *Razor's Kiss* for transportation back to Rancor Base."

"Yes, sir." Melvar waited a polite few seconds. "May I ask why?"

"Ask tomorrow. No more talk today."

Melvar saluted—one of his few genuine salutes—and took his leave.

. . . .

Face jumped as Kell came barging through the door, potted flowers in his hands. The big man took a look around, ignoring Face, and set the wavy mass of violet-colored vegetation down on a meal table. Then Kell caught sight of Dia, seated next to Face's bed; she had an arm around his neck, her other hand stroking his brow, in what had been a most comfortable pose until Kell's sudden arrival. "Oh, I see," Kell said. "Celebration's already started."

Face glared. "What celebration?"

"Ask the commander."

Behind Kell came Piggy, Janson, all the other Wraiths. Tyria was holding some sort of figurine, a gray human figure half the length of a forearm; it gripped something in its upraised hand. Wedge came in last.

"All present?" Wedge asked.

"And no accounting for," Janson said.

Wedge turned toward Face, his expression stern. "Lieutenant Loran. You returned your X-wing to the training frigate *Tedevium* in the worst shape her mechanics had ever seen a flying snubfighter. You arrived in similar shape for an organism. As I understand it, parts of you and your X-wing were intermingled."

"He had to be cut out of the cockpit," Lara confirmed. "Kept wanting to talk to the medics about surgery."

"Well, I've been meaning to tell you about that . . ." Face said.

"For this," Wedge continued, "we present to you the Award of the Mechanic's Nightmare."

Tyria held out the statuette, which was of a New Republic mechanic with wrench upraised as a weapon. The mechanic's expression was of pure, if silly, rage.

Face took the thing. "Looks like one of Cubber's children." He looked around the room. "I want to thank everyone who retrieved pieces of me, everyone who retrieved pieces of my X-wing, and especially those who sorted them out correctly."

"On a more serious note," Wedge said. "Attention."